In
This
Moment

Books by Gabrielle Meyer

In This Moment

GABRIELLE MEYER

BETHANYHOUSE

a division of Baker Publishing Group
Minneapolis, Minnesota

Published by Bethany House Publishers
Minneapolis, Minnesota
www.bethanyhouse.com

Bethany House Publishers is a division of
Baker Publishing Group, Grand Rapids, Michigan

Printed in the United States of America

Library of Congress Cataloging-in-Publication Data
Names: Meyer, Gabrielle, author.
Title: In this moment / Gabrielle Meyer.
Description: Minneapolis, Minnesota : Bethany House Publishers, a division
   of Baker Publishing Group, [2023] | Series: Timeless ; 2
Identifiers: LCCN 2022053718 | ISBN 9780764239755 (trade paper) | ISBN
   9780764241796 (casebound) | ISBN 9781493442102 (ebook)
Classification: LCC PS3613.E956 I68 2023 | DDC 813/.6--dc23
LC record available at https://lccn.loc.gov/2022053718

Scripture quotations are from the New American Standard Bible® (NASB), copyright © 1960, 1962, 1963, 1968, 1971, 1972, 1973, 1975, 1977, 1995 by The Lockman Foundation. Used by permission. www.Lockman.org

This is a work of historical reconstruction; the appearances of certain historical figures are therefore inevitable. All other characters, however, are products of the author's imagination, and any resemblance to actual persons, living or dead, is coincidental.

Cover design by Jennifer Parker

Front cover images of women by Richard Jenkins, London, England

Published in association with Books & Such Literary Management, www.booksandsuch.com

Baker Publishing Group publications use paper produced from sustainable forestry practices and post-consumer waste whenever possible.

23 24 25 26 27 28 29   7 6 5 4 3 2 1

To my parents,
George and Cathy VanRisseghem.
Your faith in Christ and your belief in me
are two of the greatest gifts I've ever been given.
Thank you for everything.
I love you.

But do not let this one fact escape your notice, beloved, that with the Lord one day is like a thousand years, and a thousand years like one day.

—2 Peter 3:8

1

APRIL 18, 1861
WASHINGTON, DC

Most days, I could pretend that my life was normal. I was a twenty-year-old woman searching for my place in the world, trying to decide my future. The only difference was that I had *three* normal lives, and on my twenty-first birthday, just eight and a half months from now, I would have to choose which one to keep and which to forfeit. Forever.

As I stood in my home on Lafayette Square, pulling long satin gloves onto my hands, it was easier not to think about the daunting choices set before me, or the other paths I occupied. I had become adept at living in the moment—a skill many people wished they could master, though it had come at a great cost to me.

Here, I was the daughter of an important US Senator and had served as his official hostess since my mother died. We were also on the cusp of the American Civil War.

But at the moment, we were late to the White House.

"Papa," I called from the foyer as Saphira, my maid, handed

me the second glove. "Mrs. Lincoln does not like when we're late."

Papa finally left his office and joined me, pulling on his own gloves. "I'm surprised she didn't cancel," he said, his usual good mood snuffed out by the stress of the week.

"She's waited her entire life to be in the White House." I reminded him, knowing how much Mary Todd Lincoln reveled in being the First Lady. "She'd hardly let a little thing like a war dampen her plans."

Papa smiled for the first time in days. "I'm sorry to be late, Margaret. I was distracted." He accepted his cape from Joseph, our butler and man-of-all-work. There was agitation and worry in the tilt of Papa's distinguished eyebrows, and I suspected it was more than distraction that had made him late.

"Is something wrong?" I asked.

Papa tried to wipe the worry from his face. "Nothing to concern you with, my dear. Just work."

"When you are one of President Lincoln's advisers, work is not just work."

Saphira lifted my blue velvet cape over my shoulders, but I didn't take my eyes off Papa. He was never difficult to read. He'd been a minister and a military man, once upon a time, and held himself with confidence and purpose. Now he was a senator and close confidante of the president. But I'd never seen his shoulders stoop so low or his face fill with such grief.

"I do not wish to ruin your evening." He put his hand at the small of my back and guided me toward the front door. "The carriage is waiting, and this is supposed to be an enjoyable dinner party."

He nodded for Joseph to open the front door, allowing me to glimpse the gloomy evening. The day had been cold and dreary, with constant raindrops falling upon the roof of our townhouse and turning the streets to mud.

"You do not need to shelter me from the truth," I said as I

set the hood of my cape over my dark brown curls, intricately woven together by Saphira's talented hands.

"You are right," he agreed, offering a placating smile. "But this is my problem, not yours."

Wet mist hit my face, though Joseph lifted an umbrella over my head. He and Saphira were two of the three servants we had employed since arriving in the capital. We'd only been in Washington for five months, but I had quickly acclimated, since I also lived there in 2001. Much had changed, but many things were still the same. And it was much better than living in the wilds of Salem, Oregon, where Papa had moved us last year to run for the Senate.

The rain splattered mud everywhere and caused the white stucco of nearby St. John's Church to look like it was weeping. I hiked up my silk skirts, hoping to avoid the mud as Papa held my elbow and helped me to the carriage.

The driver jumped off the top of the vehicle and opened the side door. I accepted his help as I stepped into the carriage and arranged my voluminous skirts around me. The width of fashionable hoopskirts, especially here in Washington, had become extravagant—as had most things among the upper echelon of Washington society. I couldn't imagine what my fellow medical students at Georgetown University Hospital in 2001 would think of the clothing I wore in 1861. I shuddered to think of walking into the ER in my hoopskirts and silk gown.

Papa took the seat across from me as Joseph closed the door and the carriage began to move toward the White House. If it hadn't been raining, we would have walked, but the mud was so thick, our shoes and clothing would be ruined by the time we got there.

"This rain is such a nuisance," Papa said, trying to change the subject, but I could still see the concern in his eyes.

I leaned forward and put my hand on his knee. "You can trust me, Papa. What is troubling you?"

There was nothing he could tell me that would shock or surprise me. I knew more than he did about the coming war—things he could never imagine—because I also lived in 1941 and 2001. When I went to sleep here, I woke up in 1941, and then I woke up in 2001 the day after that, with no time passing here while I was away. I knew how the future would play out for America.

I just wish I knew how it would play out for me.

I wanted to tell Papa that our nation would survive, though the cost would be devastating and we would lose our beloved president and friend. But he didn't know I was a time-crosser and would not understand. Besides, I didn't want to risk changing history by telling him the truth.

He must have seen the determination in my face, because he said, "It's becoming increasingly obvious that there are spies in Washington sending information to Jefferson Davis in Richmond, and we have no idea who they are or how to find them. It's almost impossible to strategize when we don't know who is carrying our plans to the south. Now that Virginia has seceded from the Union, the risk is even greater."

Everyone had been preoccupied with war for months, but this week was different. It had been six days since Confederate soldiers in South Carolina fired upon Fort Sumter, three days since President Lincoln called for seventy-five thousand volunteers to defend the Union, and one day since Virginia joined the Southern cause. We'd known it was coming, yet it felt like the final blow. Virginia lay just across the Potomac River from Washington, and at any moment the Virginians could cross the river and overtake our defenseless capital. With only a handful of soldiers to protect the president, they could easily win this war before it even started.

Papa placed his hand over mine and gave it a light squeeze. "I can see the news distresses you. Put it from your mind, Margaret. It is not your burden to carry."

"It is no more distressing than the other news we've had this week." Just beyond the windows of the carriage, the White House came into view, shining like a beacon of hope amid the storm clouds. If I was going to learn anything more from Papa, I needed to hurry. "Do we know where the spies are getting their information? Are they in the White House? Congress? Could one of them be at the gathering tonight?"

"I'm afraid it is entirely possible, but I don't want you to worry."

"How could I not worry? What if I inadvertently give information to the wrong person?"

"You don't know anything you shouldn't. Besides, as I've said, this is my problem, not yours." He stared at me for several moments, dropping his chin to really look at me. "You're not going to let this go, are you?"

I leaned forward, a smile tilting my lips. I knew my dimples undid his resolve. "I can help. I have connections, Pa—"

"No."

"If the spies move within our social circles, I can find them."

"It is far too dangerous. These spies are risking their lives, and they would not hesitate to take yours. You know nothing about espionage."

"Most of the people spying for the war effort know nothing about espionage." I leaned a little closer, my corset tightening. "Where do you suspect the Southern spies are getting their information?"

He sighed. He'd battled my strong will before and knew I wouldn't give up. "We don't know if they are getting information through their work or if it's coming through social connections. What we do know is that they are passing along vital information that only the people closest to the president know—so they are working at the very top."

The carriage rolled to a stop at the front door of the White House and jolted as the driver climbed down. My mind spun with the possibilities of who might be spying on the president and his cabinet. Did I know them? Was it someone I was close to? Would they be sitting next to me at dinner tonight?

The driver opened the door, and Papa stepped out, looking relieved to end the conversation. He extended his hand to me, and I allowed him to help me alight from the carriage under the large portico of the White House.

When my skirts were settled about me, Papa tucked my hand into the crook of his elbow. "Forget I mentioned any of it, Margaret."

I could not forget what he'd said. If spies were working in the social circles I moved in, I needed to be careful.

"Don't look so serious." Papa lifted my chin with his gloved hand. "If we're fortunate and God Almighty shines His favor upon our cause, the war will be over before it starts. Everyone knows the South is bluffing, and when the fighting gets underway, they'll soon realize we are serious. They'll come to their senses, and we'll have a resolution we can all live with."

Even as he said the words, a cold wind sliced through the White House portico, portending a future I knew to be far different.

A doorman opened the front door and allowed Papa and me to enter without asking for our names or invitations or searching us to see if we had weapons. Papa had told me the doormen kept concealed pistols on their person, but they allowed anyone and everyone to enter the White House. At any given moment, there could be a hundred or more strangers waiting in the halls for an audience with Mr. Lincoln, sometimes for days on end. It was also common to see Tad and Willie Lincoln, the president's young sons, running wild and unchaperoned through the large house, upon the roof, or in the yard and nearby neighborhood.

How different the security of the White House was in 1861, as opposed to 1941 or 2001.

We were directed through the entrance hall to the Red Room at the back of the house, but before we reached it, a set of doors opened down the hallway, and the Lincolns appeared. A gentleman was at the president's side, speaking quickly. Abraham Lincoln bent to hear, his face solemn and serious as he nodded.

President Lincoln was not a handsome man, but he was kind and wise. I'd known him most of my life, since he and Papa had been close friends from their days serving in the Illinois House of Representatives. But no matter how many times I was in his company, I never tired of the awe I felt, though it was always followed by dread. To know he would die in less than four years—and I could do nothing to stop it—tore my heart in two. It was one of the things my time-crossing parents in 1941 had taught me from an early age. I could not knowingly change history. If I did, I would forfeit my life in that path.

The president noticed us standing there and lifted his head, causing the man beside him to stop talking and look our way. My gaze caught with the stranger's. I had never seen him before. He was new to the White House—or at least, he was new to me.

The Lincolns greeted my father, and then the president turned his tired smile upon me. "It's nice to see you again, Miss Wakefield," he said, taking my gloved hand in his.

I curtsied with deference. "And you, Mr. President." Then I turned to Mrs. Lincoln and offered her a curtsy as well.

"May I present Mr. Graydon Cooper?" the president asked.

I was deeply conscious of Mr. Cooper, though I'd focused on the Lincolns. When our gazes collided again, this time much closer, I couldn't help but admire him. He was dressed in a fine black tailcoat with a white vest and black trousers. In his late twenties, he already possessed an air of sophistication and charm many of the stodgy politicians in Washington lacked. His dark brown hair was thick and wavy, short on the sides and a bit longer on the top. But it was his eyes, which were a deep, velvet brown, that arrested my attention.

"Mr. Graydon Cooper," President Lincoln continued, "may I present to you Senator Edward Wakefield and his daughter, Miss Margaret Wakefield?"

"How do you do?" Mr. Cooper shook Papa's hand and then bowed over mine. Though he had recently been in a deep and serious conversation with the president of the United States, his eyes were smiling now, as if he knew something I didn't. His voice held a cultured British accent, and his grip was surprisingly strong.

"How do you do?" I responded as I curtsied, mindful of his warm touch through the layers of our gloves. He was a splendidly handsome man, though from the confidence he exuded, I suspected he knew it.

"Mr. Cooper was just appointed to a position within the War Department," the president explained, obviously happy at the announcement. "He'll be one of Mr. Cameron's aides."

"We're quite pleased with him," Mrs. Lincoln added in her Kentucky drawl. She was festooned in a beautiful rose-colored silk gown and elaborate headdress. "Mr. Cooper is new to Washington, so I hoped you young people might get acquainted this evening." She looked between Mr. Cooper and me with a self-satisfied smile. "I've put you together at supper. I hope you don't mind."

I had never known her to be a matchmaker, but she had a sparkle in her eyes. She was not popular in Washington, but I liked her.

"I don't mind," Mr. Cooper said, meeting my gaze again.

"Speaking of supper." Mrs. Lincoln moved toward the doors to the Red Room. "It's time we greet our guests and lead them into the dining room. Mr. Lincoln and I were late, and we've held up the meal. Shall we?"

"*I* was late?" Mr. Lincoln asked with a chuckle. He touched the lace at his wife's sleeve with his gloved hand. "Perhaps you and Mrs. Keckley should start your work earlier in the day."

She ignored his comment about her dressmaker and pushed her way into the Red Room. There, in her abrupt fashion, she announced that everyone must follow her into dinner.

Mr. Cooper offered his arm to me, his eyes still smiling. "It appears we've been paired, Miss Wakefield. If we're to sit together, may I escort you into dinner?"

Why did his question feel more like a challenge? One I wanted to accept? "You may."

I slipped my hand into the crook of his arm, and we walked into the State Dining Room. A large, gaudy chandelier hung from the center of the ceiling, and a white tablecloth lined the table, which was laden with fine china and crystal goblets. Yellow flowers graced the center of the table, matching the yellowed wallpaper and discolored rug. This room, like almost all the others in the White House, was drafty and rundown. Mold grew in the corners, and the furniture was in a sorry state of disrepair. Mrs. Lincoln lamented the condition of the home and often discussed her plans to make it the showpiece it was meant to be, but many naysayers thought it a frivolous expense, given the oncoming war. It was one of the many things that made her unpopular, even with men and women in her own political party.

Mr. Cooper held out my chair, and I thanked him. He seemed to be studying me. For some reason, it put me on edge, though I had nothing to hide—not really. He smelled of a heady cologne I didn't recognize, and when he drew close to take his seat, I had to force myself to think about something other than his nearness. There were spies to uncover, and a handsome stranger was a terrible distraction.

Mrs. Lincoln presided over the dinner table. "Let us not speak a word of war this evening." She looked at her husband pointedly. "Tonight," she continued, "we will strive to forget about the rebels in the South, and those still among us in this godforsaken city, and enjoy ourselves like civilized folks."

"Hear, hear," several men said as they raised their crystal goblets.

I studied the men and women around the table. There were twenty of us, all important in Mr. Lincoln's world. Could one of them be a spy? It was impossible to know without listening to conversations, taking note of strange behaviors, and watching for unlikely alliances.

No one held my attention as much as the man beside me, though. He did not raise his goblet to toast like the others, nor smile in agreement, and it made me pause. If he was loyal to the Lincolns, serving in the War Department, shouldn't he have shown the same enthusiasm as everyone else? Instead, his face remained neutral, almost calculating.

Who was this man? Where had he come from? Almost everyone in President Lincoln's close circle was a person I had known or known of for most of my life. Mr. Cooper was completely new to me. Not to mention, he was a foreigner.

A bowl of steaming tomato soup was set before me, redolent with the scent of basil, yet I suddenly had no appetite. Nerves bound up my stomach as I wondered about Mr. Cooper's allegiance to the Union. Was he a risk to the country and the president I loved?

"Do you enjoy these sorts of affairs, Miss Wakefield?" Mr. Cooper asked, interrupting my thoughts.

"I don't mind them. Do you?" I asked in return.

That same smile tilted his eyes—the one that suggested he knew a joke I didn't. "I think this one might turn out to be quite enjoyable."

"I have a feeling you might be right."

"I'm rarely wrong."

I laughed at that—I couldn't help it. He seemed completely sure of himself, though I could tell he was teasing.

He smiled with me. "I believe you enjoy these social responsibilities, but I'd wager you would much prefer to do something with more substance or purpose. Perhaps you have a cause you like to champion, one that might not be socially acceptable."

His comment took me off guard, though I tried hard not to show it. I would prefer to be studying medicine or treating the sick and injured—but those were jobs I did in 1941 and 2001. Here, in 1861, I was not free to follow my passion. Not yet.

I could not let him know he was right. It would be easier to tease him back and ask a leading question of my own. "Are you a mind reader, Mr. Cooper? Perhaps part of a circus act before you joined us in Washington?"

He picked up his silver spoon and dipped it into his soup, the smile still in his eyes. "A circus act? No. A mind reader? Perhaps."

"Then I will strive to think of nothing when I'm in your presence."

"That would be a shame." He had a way of making me feel like I was the only other person in the room with him. "I see great intelligence in your eyes. You are an old soul, Miss Wakefield. Wise beyond your years. I would hate for you to hide that from me."

My mood grew serious as we studied one another. Could he see the truth behind my eyes? I *was* an old soul. I'd lived for over sixty years, in three different paths, gaining wisdom and knowledge. I had three different bodies but one conscious mind. I looked identical in each time—twenty years old—but what happened to me in one path didn't affect my physical bodies in the others. If I was sick with measles in one, I was healthy in the other. If I fractured a bone in one, my bones in the other were completely intact. The only thing that remained the same was my mind, gathering memories, information, and knowledge from each path.

Could Mr. Cooper truly see all that just by looking into my eyes?

It wasn't possible, yet the way he watched me now, as if he could see deep inside my soul, made my stomach turn with butterflies and my cheeks fill with heat.

"Have I made you nervous?" he asked as he lowered his soup spoon into his bowl, still watching, evaluating.

I put on a practiced smile, one I'd mastered on the campaign trail with my father to hide my true feelings. "I am quite relaxed."

"You are lying." He smiled and took a sip of his soup before dipping the spoon back into his bowl. "But it doesn't matter. I shall discover your secrets either way."

"And I shall discover yours."

"What makes you think I have secrets?"

"Everyone has secrets, Mr. Cooper."

He nodded and lifted his goblet in a mock salute. "Then we shall see who uncovers the other's secrets first. May the best man—or woman—win."

I lifted my own goblet and nodded, feeling a surge of excitement and energy.

This would be fun, though it could also be very dangerous.

2

APRIL 18, 1941
WILLIAMSBURG, VIRGINIA

I should have been focused on packing as I stood in my cozy bedroom in Williamsburg in 1941. But memories of being in the White House the night before, with the charming Mr. Cooper at my side, distracted me. I couldn't stop smiling or thinking over our conversation. We'd bantered all evening, yet it was silly to be so preoccupied with a gentleman I had just met when I knew so little about him—especially because I never let men distract me.

"Maggie?" Mama bustled into my room with a handful of my undergarments, freshly pressed, and interrupted my wool-gathering. She didn't usually look frazzled, but today was unique. "Have you seen Anna's black heels? I can't find them anywhere. She'll need them if you can get her out dancing."

I retrieved my sister's shoes from my closet. "I borrowed them from her months ago."

Mama took the shoes and sighed. "I wish she would show some excitement about going to Washington. You've both worked so hard for this. I've practically packed her entire bag. All she's managed to do is pack Richard's picture."

Straightening my shoulders, I offered Mama a confident smile. "This move will be good for her. I'll make sure of it."

At forty-six, Libby Hollingsworth, my time-crossing mama, was just as beautiful as she'd been when I was a child. She wore a pretty green skirt with a green-and-black-checkered jacket, which complemented her green eyes. I had inherited her dark brown curls and the sunburst birthmark over my heart that marked me as a time-crosser, but everything else I inherited from my father, Henry. From him, I'd received the time-crossing birthmark at the base of my skull, which was hidden underneath my hair, and his brilliant blue eyes. One of my features that neither possessed were the deep dimples in my cheeks, which were identical to my 2001 mother's dimples.

Mama paused as she scanned my room, her gaze landing on me. "What?" she asked, a gentle smile easing the stress that had been her constant companion these past few days as she'd helped Anna and me prepare to work at the Naval Medical Center in Washington, DC. We were both nurses, recently graduated and ready to start our new jobs.

Tears stung the backs of my eyes, though I tried to smile. "I'm going to miss you."

Without hesitation, she wrapped me in a tight hug. "I'm going to miss you too," she whispered.

This was not the first time I'd left home, though this time I wasn't sure if I'd ever see her again, since my twenty-first birthday was in less than nine months. If I didn't choose 1941, my physical body would die in this path, and my loved ones would be left to grieve.

I tightened my hold, unable to accept such a fate. I did not want to lose my marked mother or father.

"You've been away before," she reassured me as she pulled back and wiped my tears with a handkerchief that had been in her hand all day for that very purpose.

"But this time—" I paused and pressed my lips together.

She nodded, understanding better than anyone. "No matter what happens, Maggie, God will guide you, just as He guided your father and me. From the day you were born and we saw both your marks, we knew you were in His hands and your future was laid out for you. I trust Him fully, and you should too."

I wished I shared her assurance. She believed God had a perfect plan for me, but He had not yet revealed it, and I was afraid He wouldn't. I loved each of my lives equally. What would I do if I came to January 1 and still had no idea what He wanted me to choose?

"What if this is good-bye forever?" I asked.

She tucked one of my curls behind my ear, trying to control her emotions. "None of us is guaranteed tomorrow. I pray that you choose 1941 with all of my heart. But if you don't, I know that wherever you go, you will love us for the rest of your life. And we will love you."

Her words should have made me feel better, but they made me melancholy instead. The rest of my life without her seemed like a long, long time.

"Don't think about January," she said, putting her hands on my arms and looking me over. I wore a traveling suit of light blue with a matching hat. Seamed nylons and black heels completed my outfit. "Focus on today."

I nodded, accepting her instructions, and closed my suitcase. Just like in 1861, it was easier to distract my mind and stay busy. Then I wouldn't think about the decision or the fact that God seemed silent on the matter. If I was lucky, something would happen, and I would have no doubt in my mind which path to choose. That had happened to Mama, though a lot of heartache had preceded her choice.

"Are you coming, Anna?" I called to my sister in the next room.

A horn at the front of the house sounded, and I looked out my window to see Daddy getting out of our maroon Studebaker to grab Anna's suitcase, which Mama had already placed on the front stoop. He looked up at my window and pointed at his wristwatch.

I nodded and called out to my sister, "We don't want to miss the train."

Grabbing my handbag and gloves from the nightstand, I followed Mama down the hall to Anna's room. She was sitting on her bed, staring out the window.

She'd lost so much weight these past three years, and her face was pale. The anniversary of Richard's death was next week, which had brought about another wave of melancholy. If we had not been committed to going to Washington, I was certain she would insist on staying home. It was my hope that I could distract her and give her a purpose in her work so she wouldn't focus on her loss. I had wanted to go to medical school to become a doctor, but when Anna said she wanted to be a nurse and wouldn't go to nursing school without me, I changed course.

"Anna," I said gently, "Daddy's waiting. We need to leave."

She slowly rose, clutching her pink hat. There were tearstains trailing down her cheeks. Her green eyes, so much like Mama's, were dull with grief. She had been born three years before me, though I felt like the older sister in almost every way.

Mama went to her and embraced her, just like she had hugged me, then took Anna's hand to lead her down to the waiting Studebaker. Daddy's concerned gaze mingled with Mama's. She smiled at him, and he returned the sad smile.

When he looked at me, I saw pride in his blue eyes—though there was also apprehension. Just last night, he'd warned me not to press Anna too fast. Not to ask too much of her. He knew my propensity to take control and fix things. It served me well in a hospital but didn't always translate to other areas of my life.

We all got into the Studebaker, and Daddy pulled away from the house. It was clear that he and Mama were worried for us. They knew another war was imminent, but they didn't know the details. I had no heart to tell them, nor did I want to risk changing history. Anna was aware that Daddy, Mama, and I were time-crossers, but she was not. I was able to speak to her about my other paths, but she struggled to understand. It was Mama and Daddy, and my grandfather Hollingsworth, who understood more than anyone else.

No one spoke as we drove to the depot. The day was overcast and threatened rain, matching the mood in the car. I tried to think of something to say—anything. This could be the last time I saw my parents, yet my mind was blank. How did one have such a conversation? Especially when Anna was struggling beside me with her own grief?

"You're both making us proud," Daddy finally said when we pulled up to the depot.

"We'll pray for you every single day." Mama reached into the backseat and took each of our hands in hers. "I cannot wait to see what God does with your lives."

Daddy jumped out of the car and grabbed our suitcases. We followed him into the depot, where he purchased our tickets. Mama wrapped one arm through Anna's elbow and one through mine as we walked to the platform, watching the train pull into the station. She hugged Anna and then me before Daddy took us into his arms.

"Take care of each other," he said to us, kissing our foreheads. "And write often."

"Be careful," Mama added. "If you can come home and visit, please do. I know you'll be having fun with all those naval officers, but don't forget about us."

Her teasing brought a small smile to Anna's lips, and it bolstered my hope. This move was going to do wonders for her. It had to.

"All aboard!" the stationmaster called. A dozen other passengers prepared to board the train as we gave our parents one more hug.

"Don't forget to say hello to your grandfather for us," Mama said, blowing kisses. "Good-bye! I love you."

"I love you, too," I called to her and Daddy as I stepped onto the stairs and boarded the train, Anna right ahead of me.

Waving one last time, I entered the warm train car, my suitcase in hand.

A porter took our luggage, and we found seats facing the depot. Daddy stood with his arm around Mama as they gazed up at the train, searching the windows for one last glimpse of us.

"Not everyone is as lucky as us, are they?" Anna asked, her voice melancholy.

I shook my head and wrapped my arm through hers. "No." Not everyone was as lucky as us.

And I had been blessed with three sets of loving parents—three equally amazing lives—making it even harder to know which path was the one I should choose.

The newly built Naval Medical Center stood in Bethesda, Maryland, less than ten miles north of Washington, DC. The tall, white, gleaming building was an impressive structure that would serve countless military personnel, as well as every US president in the future, though it would be called the Walter Reed National Military Medical Center in my 2001 path. For now, it was fresh and new, having just opened the previous fall.

I stood in the small dorm room Anna and I had been assigned as the newest nurse recruits for the United States Navy. We had entered service with relative rank as lieutenants. Though we did not have official military status, we would be treated like officers.

But military status wasn't on my mind. All I could think about was finally starting our duties tomorrow—and taking a nap after unpacking. As long as I woke up before midnight, I would remain in this same time and place. If midnight came and went while I slept, I would wake up in 2001. If I stayed awake past midnight, as was common while on duty in 1941 or 2001 or at a social function in 1861, I would not cross over until I went to sleep.

On my twenty-first birthday, January 1, I would choose the time I wanted to keep forever by staying awake past midnight in that path, and I would never wake up in the other two again.

A shiver ran up my spine as I tried not to think about that day. I hoped and prayed Mama was right and God would make my choice clear by then.

I unlatched my suitcase and popped the lid open. Everything smelled fresh and new. The dorm walls were painted white, the bed linens were crisp, and the floors were a shiny gray linoleum. The only bit of color in the room was the two red chairs pushed against brown desks on opposite walls. A window faced the rolling grounds of the hospital, with small saplings planted in neat rows along the drive. Tiny blades of grass peeked through the dirt, promising a lush carpet in the weeks and months ahead.

Anna set her suitcase on one of the beds. "I hope they have enough work for us so we don't have to spend much time in our room."

"A few well-placed pictures of Clark Gable and Gary Cooper would brighten this place up," I teased her, since she was crazy about movie stars. It was one thing that made her smile.

"Luckily," she said with an uncharacteristic lightheartedness, "I might have one or two."

A knock at the door made me stop laughing. I found a young private at our door, wearing a blue navy uniform with a flat hat. He saluted me.

"Lieutenant Margaret Hollingsworth?"

"Yes."

"Nurse Daly would like to see you in her office, ma'am."

I looked at Anna, surprised to be called to the Chief Nurse's office so soon after arriving. I had not yet taken off my gloves or my hat, so I nodded at the private. "Can you tell me where to find her office?"

"This way." He took a step back and motioned down the long hallway.

"Here only five minutes and already in trouble," Anna said with a glint of humor. I made a face at her and closed the door to follow the private.

A few other dorm rooms were open, allowing me to glimpse the nurses inside. Some smiled, while others appeared not to notice me as I passed. An occasional laugh filtered into the hall, and someone was listening to a Bing Crosby record. I took a left and then a right before coming to a door with a glass window and the name *Lieutenant Helen Daly* painted on it. The private stopped and saluted me again before turning away.

I tapped on the door and waited for Nurse Daly to welcome me in.

She rose at my entrance, wearing a navy-blue skirt and matching jacket with brass buttons down the front. Under her jacket was a white blouse with brass pins at the collar.

"Nurse Hollingsworth?" she asked.

"Yes, ma'am." I closed the door behind me and then went to her desk, where I shook her hand. "It's a pleasure to meet you."

Helen Daly was a pleasant-looking woman, not beautiful but not plain either. She wore her brown hair in rolls along the side of her head to a bun in back and had on a pair of spectacles. I would have placed her in her early thirties, energetic and healthy. As the Chief Nurse, she was our superior and boss.

"Won't you have a seat?" she asked.

The setting sun created a cascade of colors outside the office window. I took the seat across from her organized desk, trying not to fidget. I could think of no reason she would want to see me alone.

She opened a folder and pulled out a piece of paper with an official-looking seal. Meticulously, taking her time, she closed the folder and laid the letter on top before clasping her hands together and smiling at me.

I returned the smile, waiting for her to start the conversation.

"I am very pleased to have you here with us," she began. "I spoke to several of your instructors at the Virginia Commonwealth University School of Nursing. They said you are intelligent, quick to take instruction, and could have easily completed your training in half the time it takes others."

If they knew the reason was because of my advanced studies in 2001, they might not be so impressed.

"However," Nurse Daly continued as she looked back at the letter, "our policy states that a nurse must be at least twenty-one before she is accepted to serve in the United States Navy."

"I am aware," I said, hoping this would not be a problem. "I believe my grandfather sent you a—"

"Yes." She picked up the paper. "Not only did I receive a copy of the letter Congressman Hollingsworth sent to Rear Admiral Stark, I also received a phone call from the Rear Admiral's office, instructing us to allow you to enter service here." She lifted an eyebrow. "Should I be impressed or intimidated, Nurse Hollingsworth?"

Heat warmed my cheeks at the fuss this had caused. "I will be twenty-one in less than nine months," I was quick to assure her.

"Then why not wait nine months?" Her voice was pleasant and entreating. "What is the hurry?"

I thought of Anna, of her need to start living her life again and doing it as soon as possible. I didn't want to make her wait until January—especially when I didn't know if I would still be here after my birthday. If I hadn't come with her, I was certain she wouldn't have come on her own.

But would Anna want me to share such an intimate part of her life with our superior, even if it did answer her question?

"As you said," I began, trying to make my voice sound neutral, "I could have easily finished my training in half the time it took. Nursing is second nature to me. I didn't want to wait nine more months, not when I was ready to start making a difference now."

"A noble calling, indeed." Nurse Daly tucked Grandfather Hollingsworth's letter back into the file. She clasped her hands again, setting them on the desk. "My best advice is to keep your age to yourself—as well as your connection to Rear Admiral Stark. There are a lot of nurses here who don't have a powerful grandfather to get them in the door. They had to wait for the honor of serving in the United States Navy, and they will not take kindly to someone who didn't jump through the same hoops. It could cause a lot of resentment, and I'd hate to see that."

I nodded, not wishing to make any waves.

"Now." She stood. "I imagine you are tired and would like to unpack."

A knock at the door made both of us turn. A tall officer stood on the other side of the glass.

"Yes?" Nurse Daly called.

The door opened, and a captain walked in, wearing a navy-blue dress uniform. He bore the insignia of the medical corps, indicating he was not only an officer but a doctor as well. His bearing suggested years in military service, with perfect posture, broad shoulders, and arrogance to spare.

"Dr. Philips," Nurse Daly said with a smile, motioning to me. "May I introduce you to Nurse Margaret Hollingsworth? She specializes in surgical nursing and will be helping you in the operating room."

His brooding eyes turned to me. Dr. Philips was easily in his early thirties, if not a bit older. His blue eyes and dark hair complemented his tanned skin, though it appeared a bit sallow at the moment. He had the look of the sea about him, creasing the skin at his eyes, as if he'd spent years squinting under the sun.

I stood at the introduction.

"How do you do?" he asked curtly, standing at attention. He did not smile or offer a welcoming gaze. If anything, he appeared to want to be done with me and finish the errand that had brought him to Nurse Daly's office.

"How do you do?" I replied.

"This is the nurse I spoke to you about," Nurse Daly said as if choosing her words carefully. "The one who came so highly recommended by Rear Admiral Stark."

Dr. Philips snapped his attention back to me. "You must be a remarkable nurse to have caught the attention of the Chief of Naval Operations."

"He's a friend of my grandfather's."

No sign of emotion emanated from his gaze. "I suppose we'll have to treat you with kid gloves so we don't make the boss mad."

Nurse Daly made the slightest noise, indicating her displeasure at his words, but he didn't seem to notice or care.

My back stiffened. I did not personally know Rear Admiral Stark, but I would not admit that to this man. "I do not wish for special treatment."

"What you wish for and what you receive are rarely the same thing, Nurse Hollingsworth. You cannot come here under special instructions from the Chief of Naval Operations and pretend to be like the rest of us."

"Did you need something from me, Captain?" Nurse Daly interrupted.

His irritated gaze finally turned away from me as he opened the door and muttered, "I've forgotten."

As soon as the door closed, Nurse Daly sighed. "I'm afraid I should apologize for him, but if I start now, I would never stop. Dr. Zechariah Philips tends to say whatever is on his mind.

You'll realize soon enough that he has a loud bark, though he rarely bites. Learning how to work with him will probably be your biggest challenge in the navy."

I wished she was correct, but with WWII looming in this path and Anna's mental health on tenterhooks, a cranky doctor was the least of my worries.

3

APRIL 18, 2001
WASHINGTON, DC

The next day, the locker room was quiet as I changed into my street clothes at Georgetown University Hospital following my afternoon shift. I was in my fourth year of medical school and was doing a four-week emergency medicine rotation. The day had been busy. Two heart attacks, a car accident, and a burn victim had kept me running, but I wouldn't have it any other way. My days were filled with purpose—and kept me distracted.

"Meg?" A nurse found me in the locker room. "Dr. Erdman would like to see you before you go home."

In 2001, I was Margaret Clarke. Miraculously, I bore the same first name in each of my paths, though Mama and Daddy said it wasn't that much of a miracle. They had both had similar names in their two paths. Perhaps it was the name God had inspired each set of parents to give me. But my last names were different, and each family called me something unique. In 1861, Papa called me Margaret. In 1941, I had been Maggie from birth. And in 2001, my parents and friends called me Meg. It reminded me that though I was the same person, I had three distinct lives.

"Thanks," I called out to the nurse as I shoved my scrubs into the laundry bin and grabbed my backpack out of my locker. A quick look at my watch told me I was already running late, but I couldn't ignore my professor.

It seemed like I was always running late to something since starting med school. If I had the choice in 2001, I would spend every waking moment at the hospital or studying at the library. The knowledge I gained in this path would never be equaled in 1941 or 1861, and I wanted to know as much as possible.

It was like a fever, this burning desire to learn everything I could. If I didn't stay in 2001, all of this medical advancement would be lost to me. Though I couldn't use any of it in my other paths, for fear I would change history, I still wanted to know what made the human body work. And if I stayed here, I wanted to be prepared to be of use to the most people.

I walked down the hall to Dr. Erdman's office and tapped on his door. Though the circumstances were different, it reminded me of visiting Nurse Daly's office the day before in 1941. I could still see the disdain in Dr. Zechariah Philips's gaze as he regarded me. Perhaps I wasn't yet twenty-one, but I had more experience and knowledge than most of the nurses in that hospital. It was the reason I didn't feel guilty about my grandfather pulling strings for me and why I wouldn't let Dr. Philips intimidate me. I had much more important things to worry about.

"Come in," Dr. Erdman called.

I stepped into his disorganized office, noting the sun through his window as it sank in the western sky. My mom would be irritated that I was late, though she'd come to expect it.

"Ah, Meg. Thank you for coming. Please, have a seat."

I sat on the hard leather chair, hoping he had good news.

"I will get right to the point, since I know you're probably eager to go home." He leaned forward, his gray hair falling over his eye before he pushed it back. "You are a remarkable young woman, one we have been honored to work with these past three years. It's very rare when a seventeen-year-old enters this program and thrives."

"Thank you." I accepted the compliment with grace, having received a great deal of attention since I graduated from high school at the age of fourteen and then completed my pre-med degree by the age of seventeen. In actuality, I had been living for forty-two years by the time I graduated from high school in this path, which made it much easier than anyone realized.

"As you know," he continued, "you will soon need to declare which field you will apply to for residency."

I nodded.

"It is my hope that you will choose general surgery as your field, and that you will choose to stay here at Georgetown University Hospital."

I smiled, thankful for his vote of confidence. Surgery was the most fascinating field of study to me, and I hoped to become a general surgeon one day.

"What you don't know," Dr. Erdman continued, "is that two other students have expressed interest in a residency position in the surgery department here, but there is only one position available. It's my job to find out if you're interested in the position as well."

"I am. Very much." I would love to stay in the DC area. It was close to my parents, who lived in Georgetown, less than a mile from my apartment.

"Good. But let me warn you, your competition is fierce. We will take several things into consideration while making our decision, which should come in October. So be sure to give every last bit of energy to your final months here. We are looking for someone who is dedicated."

"Thank you for letting me know." I was ready and willing

to meet that call. After all, I had been putting my education first above all else my entire life. Nothing would change now.

"You may go," Dr. Erdman said. "Get a good night's sleep, and I'll see you bright and early tomorrow morning."

I stood, smiling as I shook his hand. "Thank you for considering me for the position. I won't let you down."

It was already six o'clock, and my mother was expecting me in half an hour, though there was no way I was going to make it in time. I rushed out of the hospital complex and found my car. In less than ten minutes, I was on P Street, where I lived with my roommate in a beautiful red-brick row house.

The old trolley tracks ran up the cobble road of P Street, and black wrought-iron fences encircled the small front yards. It took forever to find a place to park, and then I jogged toward our apartment. We had lived on the third floor of the old town-home for the past two years. It was about a six-minute drive to the hospital and less than a seven-minute walk to the Department of Art and Art History at Georgetown University for my roommate, Delilah. She was a junior studying art history, though she didn't know what she hoped to do with the degree. It was more of a requirement from her parents, who insisted she attend college and paid generously for her to room with me.

I took the stairs two at a time to our apartment and was fumbling with my key when the door popped open. Delilah stood on the other side.

"You're late," she said.

"I know." I tossed my backpack onto the hook near the door and started taking off my sneakers as I ran down the hall to my room. "My mother should be used to it by now."

Delilah held a bowl of cookie dough as she followed me, dipping her spoon into the gooey batter before licking it. She was wearing her painting apron, which was splattered with a hundred different colors, and had her short blue hair in pigtails. We'd met at church as kids, and when I was looking to move out of my parents' house two years ago, she came with me. Where I was neat and tidy, she was messy and generally disheveled. I tried to eat a healthy, well-rounded diet, but she loved cookie dough and Mountain Dew. We couldn't be more different—or more compatible.

The most remarkable thing? She knew about my time-crossing and didn't doubt me for a second. The truth had come out when we were ten years old and I was spouting off information about the California gold rush, since I lived in San Francisco in 1851 in my other path. She'd asked me how I knew so much, and I had told her. Just like that. I trusted Delilah completely, and she trusted me. Ever since then, I'd been open with her, just as I was with Anna and my parents in 1941. We often talked about my final decision, though Delilah was certain I would choose 2001. She wouldn't accept any other possibility.

"What will you wear?" Delilah asked, flopping down on my bed with her cookie dough.

"You shouldn't be eating that," I told her, trying in vain to get her to eat healthier.

She made a face at me and kept eating it.

"I was thinking about wearing my long black evening gown." I opened my closet, and since it was color-coded, I knew exactly where to find it.

"You're so boring."

I smiled. "What would you wear to a reception at the White House?"

"If my mom was the social secretary for the president and I'd been invited to a congressional reception in the East Room?" She lifted a perfectly sculpted eyebrow, her voice monotone with sarcasm. "I can't even imagine."

I had showered in the locker room at work, and my hair was still damp. It curled around my shoulders, since I kept it shorter in 2001 than I did in my other paths. A simple clip would have to do. Taking the dress and hair clip into the bathroom, I changed quickly, leaving my street clothes on the floor—something I would never do if I had time to spare—and secured one side of my curls up off my face.

"Don't forget to put on a little mascara," Delilah said. "Who knows who you might meet tonight."

It took a few minutes to put on some makeup, and then I had to find my black heels.

"I think I'm ready," I said as I grabbed a small black purse and put my lipstick, cell phone, and a few dollars inside.

Delilah followed me back to the front door, a forlorn look on her face. "I wish my mom invited me to the White House as often as yours does."

"Has your mom *ever* invited you to the White House?"

"You know what I mean."

I opened the door and stepped out into the hall, closing my purse. "Hey, I have a lot to tell you when I get home, so wait up for me, will you?"

"Is it about one of your other paths?" Delilah leaned forward, her brown eyes filled with curiosity.

"Both of them. There's so much going on." Mr. Cooper and Dr. Philips came to mind, but I didn't plan to tell her about the two men I had met. I could talk to Anna, but she'd been so preoccupied with her grief these past three years that I didn't want to trouble her. Delilah was easier to talk to.

She laughed and shook her head. "What a strange existence you live, Meg."

"I also found out that I am being considered for the residency position in the surgery department at GUH."

"Yay!" Delilah grinned. "Another reason you should stay in 2001."

I playfully rolled my eyes and smiled. "See you later."

"Have fun!"

I closed the door and rushed down the steps to my car. My

life in 2001 was busy and stressful, but at least there wasn't a
war looming.

It was almost eight o'clock by the time I made it to the White
House. Traffic had been a bear, and it was impossible to find
a place to park near 1600 Pennsylvania Avenue. I had to walk
several blocks from my parking spot to the Executive Mansion
as the sun slowly sank behind the horizon.

I passed St. John's Church, still boasting its yellow stucco
and white columns, and paused as I took in Lafayette Square.
The home I occupied in 1861 stood on the corner of H Street
and Vermont Avenue. It looked much the same in 2001, but
there had been some changes over the years. The three-story
house was now yellow with green shutters and white trim. A
black, wrought-iron porch faced the square on the main level.
Just seeing it made me miss Papa—though I'd see him when I
woke up tomorrow. I could envision him sitting on that porch,
waiting for me to come home.

Shaking off the thought, and thankful that the roads were
now paved and there was no mud, I hastened across the square
to the White House. Mom had placed me on the guest list, as
she so often did since she'd been appointed Social Secretary by
George W. Bush when he'd taken office in January. Mom was
at the height of her career as a caterer and events planner and
took her job very seriously. She was responsible for planning,
coordinating, and executing the official social events held in
the White House. It was a big job, and she worked closely with
the White House Chief Usher and the domestic staff to make
sure they came off without a hitch. I rarely saw her since she'd
taken on the role, so nights like tonight, when she invited me
to attend, were meaningful.

I just wished I wasn't so late.

Having been through security at the White House before, I knew what to expect as I stepped through the southeast entrance off Executive Avenue. The thought of simply walking in the front door, like I had done in 1861, was laughable in the twenty-first century.

There were other guests still arriving, though the crush of people had probably arrived an hour ago. Thankfully, the guards allowed me to pass without trouble. I walked along the East Colonnade and then through the East Garden Room, my heels clicking across the checkered tiles. A long red carpet stretched down the Center Hall, and I took a right and climbed the stairs to the large East Room, where the congressional reception was being held. The State Dining Room, where I had dined with Mr. Cooper and the Lincolns, was on the opposite side of the White House on this same floor.

It was a marvel that I had been in this same building one hundred and forty years ago, though to me it had only been two days. So much had changed in the building—and in the country.

The East Room was filled to capacity with congressmen and women, aides, and their guests. Fresh flower bouquets sat atop a handful of high tables. Gold drapes hung from the large windows, and the cream-colored walls boasted beautiful trim work. A massive buffet table had been set out with appetizers, and a bar was situated in one corner. Live music came from a trio of musicians in the opposite corner. Everyone looked like they were having a good time and it was due, for the most part, to my mom. Pride filled my chest at the thought.

"There you are." Mom came up beside me, her pretty face wearing a bright smile, revealing the dimples I had inherited. She seemed to be everywhere, all at once.

"How did you find me so quickly?" I gave her a hug.

"I was watching for you." She moved my hair off my shoulder. "You're late."

Putting my hair back, I smiled. "I have wonderful news. Dr. Erdman is considering me for a residency position at GUH."

Her blue eyes shone. "That's wonderful!" She had always been proud of me, though she'd spent most of my life pursuing her own career and dreams. She wasn't absent from my life, just busy. It had been easy to throw myself into my studies since she had no expectations of me being like other children and teenagers. I was never involved in sports or extracurricular activities. Just school, school, and more school.

"Your father is here somewhere," she said, looking around the room. "You just missed the Bushes. They were here for about thirty minutes."

"I'm sorry I missed them."

"You should be," she teased. "It isn't every day that you're invited to the White House."

I laughed and shook my head, having lost track of how many times I'd been in the White House in 1861. "You're right."

She gave me a more serious look. "You need to take some time off before you get burnt out. Have a little fun now and again, Meg."

"This coming from you," I teased back. "One of the hardest-working women I've ever met."

"I blame myself for your lack of a social life. And me, the Social Secretary of the President!"

I squeezed her arm and shook my head. "We both like our careers. There's nothing wrong with that."

"Oh! I see your father, and he's speaking to someone I want you to meet." Mom led the way across the room, greeting a few representatives and senators and directing a staff member to refresh the shrimp platter.

Near the large portrait of George Washington hanging proudly on the east wall, we found my father. To the outside world, he was retired General Jonathan Clarke, current Assistant Secretary of the Navy for energy, installation, and environment.

To me, he was Dad. He stood erect and proud, wearing a black tuxedo, speaking to a young man also wearing a tuxedo.

When we approached, they both looked our way.

"Meg!" Dad kissed my cheek as I reached up and took his arm. His head was balding, but he still looked dignified to me. "I was hoping you could make it."

"Sorry I'm late."

"No trouble." He turned his attention back to the young man he was speaking to. "You're just in time to meet Congressman Wallace."

"Congressman?" I studied the young man a little closer, surprised that he didn't look much older than me.

Mr. Wallace extended his hand. "It's a pleasure to meet you, Miss Clarke," he said. "My name is Seth."

"Please," I told him, returning his firm grasp, "call me Meg. You're a congressman?"

"The youngest by three days," he said with a disarming smile. "Well, unless you count William Claiborne, who started his service in 1797 and was possibly three years younger than me." He shrugged, a teasing gleam in his eyes. "But there's no solid proof."

"Meg can relate to being the youngest at her profession, as well," Mom said with pride. "She is set to graduate medical school at the age of twenty-one."

Seth looked duly impressed. "Then we have a lot in common." He was physically fit and handsome in his tuxedo, and his blond hair, blue eyes, and tan made me think of a Ken doll and not a stuffy congressman.

"I hate to run," Mom said, "but I need to make sure that shrimp is being taken care of. We don't want anyone getting sick."

"And I see a senator I need to speak to," Dad said. "Don't forget to visit the Pentagon when you get a chance," he told Seth. "The renovations in Wedge One are underway, and as a member of the Committee of Military Construction, you'll want to familiarize yourself with the project."

"I'll definitely come by soon." Seth became all business. "I'll have my aide call your office and set up an appointment."

"Great. It was nice to see you again." Dad touched my shoulder as he walked away, leaving me to speak to Seth.

One glance in my mother's direction told me she was watching Seth and me closely, and I had the distinct feeling she had set up this little meeting. She'd been trying to set me up on dates for the past year, but she had no idea why I was being stubborn. I wasn't going to let my heart get entangled in romance before my final decision. It would only make things more complicated—and they were already complicated enough.

"What state do you represent, Congressman?" I asked Seth, turning my attention away from my mother and her matchmaking ways.

"Call me Seth," he said, his congenial personality replacing his brusque business persona. "And I'm from South Carolina."

"Ah." Why hadn't I recognized the accent? "South Carolina, the state that finally drew us into the Civil War."

A slight frown tilted his brow. "I suppose, though that's not usually people's first response when I tell them where I'm from."

"Sorry." I tried to hide the embarrassment creeping up my neck. Mama often told me not to let one path affect the other, but sometimes it was difficult to separate them. In 1861, all we'd been talking about for days was South Carolina. "I'm sure South Carolina has many fine qualities."

"Have you been there?"

"I'm afraid not. I've spent most of my life in the DC area."

"Then you're familiar with the town?"

"Yes." I smiled. "I know it very well."

"Would you be willing to give me a personal tour?" He offered me a brilliant smile. "I've only been here since January, and I've been so busy, I haven't had the opportunity to sightsee.

I know you must be extremely busy, and I hate to ask, but I'm embarrassed to admit that I still need a map to get from the Capitol to the White House."

I laughed, knowing he was teasing. It would have been almost impossible to get lost since both buildings sat on Pennsylvania Avenue.

"Whenever I admit my inability to someone else, I get treated like a child." He shook his head, a bit of his humor fading. "I'm already singled out for my lack of experience. I'd hate to ask one of the *adults* in the room to give me a tour."

My laughter continued, though it slowly faded. I couldn't count how many times I had been treated like a child in my profession. It was a frustrating feeling.

"How about this Saturday?" he asked, his blue eyes alight with hope.

Without realizing it, I let out a heavy breath. My schedule had been so hectic lately that I'd hardly had time to sleep, let alone sightsee. Yet I didn't have any plans for Saturday, for the first time in months. Perhaps playing tourist would be as close to a vacation as I'd get before the end of the year.

He watched me, waiting. How could I say no to the youngest member of Congress, recently arrived in Washington?

"I would love to show you around the city," I said.

"Wonderful!" He grinned and then nodded toward the buffet table. "Now, how about we take our chances with that shrimp?"

I laughed, already enjoying his easygoing personality. No wonder he was elected to Congress at a young age.

It was hard not to like Seth Wallace.

4

APRIL 19, 1861
WASHINGTON, DC

The rain had not let up by Friday afternoon, keeping everyone indoors and canceling a garden party I had planned to attend. Instead, I sat in the front parlor of our home on Lafayette Square, trying to stay busy by knitting a pair of socks I would one day give to a soldier. The need for medical and food supplies was going to be great, but I could not begin to act until others were acting, for fear I would change the course of events. Even one little change could have catastrophic ramifications for America.

Joseph entered the parlor with a load of firewood stacked in his arms and fed the fire crackling in the hearth. I set aside my knitting to stretch and extend my cold fingers to the heat.

Papa had walked to the White House earlier, tight-lipped about what was happening with the war effort. He did not speak to me about the spies again, but that didn't mean I could forget. Everywhere I went, I was aware of the threat. I guarded what I said and who I spoke to with great care, always on the lookout for possible enemies.

"Any news today?" I asked Joseph, who had been running errands for Papa.

Joseph stood and brushed his hands off over the fire to remove the debris that clung to his skin. "Word finally arrived about those soldiers coming through Baltimore."

For days, we'd been waiting for help from the north, fearing that our enemies might attack at any moment. But the only way into Washington from the north was through Baltimore, which was a Southern-sympathizing city.

"Are they here?"

He shook his head. "Not yet. They were due to arrive this afternoon, but they met with trouble switching trains."

There were two stations in Baltimore, about ten blocks apart. To switch from one station to the next, either a carriage was taken or the train cars were pulled by horse along a set of tracks. It was one of the reasons Pinkerton's men had been concerned about Lincoln going through Baltimore on his way into Washington before his inauguration. So much could happen in those ten blocks, and it appeared the soldiers had experienced it firsthand.

"Was anyone hurt?"

"Reports are saying over nine hundred soldiers were involved and at least thirty of them were injured. Four died."

I looked out the window, thinking of all those men traveling to the city in need of help. The only hospital in town, the City Infirmary, would not be able to meet the need, especially if there were serious cases. "When is the train expected?"

"In a couple of hours."

I stood and paced to the window, wondering when the rain would let up. There would be others helping at the train station, so why couldn't I?

Then Clara Barton came to mind. I had learned about her in a medical history class. She had been living in Washington, working in the US Patent Office. When she heard about the men coming in from Baltimore, she had leapt into action. Many of the men were from Massachusetts, her home state, and she would know them. She would realize the great need in the city and launch a campaign to gather supplies for the soldiers. It would eventually lead her to start the American Red Cross in the 1880s, ultimately saving countless lives.

At this very moment, Clara was probably on her way to the train station, which was north of the Capitol Building.

"Joseph?" I turned back to him as he was about to leave the room. "Will you hitch up the carriage?"

He glanced toward the rain-covered window. "Miss?"

"I'd like to go to the train station to see if I can help those injured soldiers."

"Your father won't be happy."

He was right. If anyone in society knew I had gone to help the injured soldiers, there would be talk. And talk was never good for a politician or his family. Yet I couldn't sit back and do nothing.

"I appreciate your attempt to protect me, but if he can do his part for the cause, then I can too."

Joseph didn't look convinced, but he nodded. "I'll be ready to go in thirty minutes."

I tried to push aside the misgivings I felt. I didn't want to hurt Papa's political career, but I also couldn't deny my own need to help.

"Saphira," I called as I walked through the parlor, across the elegant dining room, and into the back kitchen.

Saphira was sitting at the table with our cook, Goldie, peeling potatoes. Both women looked up, surprised to find me in their domain, and stood at my entrance.

"We're going to need a few supplies," I told the ladies. "Bandages, whiskey, a needle and thread, and any morphine that we might have in the house."

Saphira and Goldie stared at me, their potatoes and peeling knives forgotten in their hands.

"We'll also need any food we can spare that will travel well. Biscuits, fruit, bread."

Neither one moved, looking at me as if I had just lost my head, and I realized I hadn't told them what I planned to do.

"I'm going to the station to meet the soldiers coming in from Baltimore. There will be injuries, and they will be hungry."

"What will you do with the needle and thread?" Saphira asked.

"I intend to sew up wounds, if there are any."

Saphira's face blanched. "S-sew? Skin?"

"I have no time to explain," I told her. "I must go change and meet Joseph outside in thirty minutes. Will you please place everything into baskets? And if we can spare a blanket or two, please add those as well. I'm sure we'll need them."

Saphira looked to Goldie, who hadn't said a word, and then nodded at me. "Yes, Miss Margaret."

I went upstairs to change into an old gown, slipping off several cumbersome petticoats, as they'd only be in my way. I put on comfortable shoes and was thankful my hair was in a snood so I would not need to deal with misplaced pins or wayward hair.

Thirty minutes later, I was tucking the blankets around the supplies Saphira and Goldie had gathered in the kitchen. Joseph entered, his overcoat wet from the rain, and silently took the baskets and walked back outside.

"What will we say to your father when he gets home?" Goldie finally asked as I was about to leave through the back door.

I paused, knowing I'd have to deal with it sooner or later. After today, Papa might ban me from ever doing something like this again, but I had to try.

"Tell him I'm doing charity work. I'll be home as soon as I can."

With that, I stepped out into the rain and walked across the wet ground to the waiting carriage.

It took an eternity to arrive at the station. The mud and rain had made the roads a mess. If I wasn't so excited and anxious, I would have been shivering in the cold carriage. As it was, I sat on the edge of my seat as we arrived, surprised to see such a large crowd gathered to meet the train. Would anyone recognize me?

More importantly, where was Clara Barton? No matter what happened today, I was determined to befriend her. She would do some of the best work in Washington in the coming years, and I planned to be at her side—quietly, of course.

As Joseph waited in line to drop me off, I looked at the medical supplies inside the basket closest to me. Though it wasn't yet common practice to disinfect wounds—it would be several years before Joseph Lister made carbolic acid a common antiseptic—even ancient civilizations used alcohol in wound care, so I wasn't using modern techniques.

When Joseph came to the door to help me carry my supplies, I had a moment of hesitation. It was one thing to help like the others would help, but what if I saved a life that wasn't supposed to be saved? Or what if someone recognized me stitching up a wound? It wasn't seemly for a woman to do doctor's work—not yet. By the time the war was over, it would be common for women to administer medical aid. But now? What if these men didn't even want a woman ministering to them?

"Miss Margaret?" Joseph asked, a frown tilting his brow.

I looked past him to the throng of waiting people, saw that no one was carrying any sort of supplies, and made a decision that I prayed I wouldn't regret. I couldn't sit back and let Clara Barton work alone.

Handing Joseph the basket of medical supplies and taking the hand he offered, I alighted into the elements. He had found a spot close to the depot, so it didn't take long to reach shelter. Joseph carried both baskets and followed me as I looked through the crowd for a young woman who could be Clara. I had never met her and didn't remember what her picture looked like in my medical history textbook, so I had to guess.

Finally, I found a young woman who could be her. She was of medium height, with brown hair and a plain face, though the kindness in her eyes made them remarkable. Her dark hair was parted down the middle and held back in a snood, just like mine. The dress she wore was dark and plain, and the only jewelry adorning her outfit was a beautiful brooch at her throat.

People milled about. Thankfully, I didn't recognize anyone. Most people spoke in excited tones as they waited, but not Clara. She stood alone near the tracks, watching silently for the train to arrive.

I walked up to her and stood a few feet away. In 1861, it wasn't considered proper to introduce myself to a stranger. As I stood there, trying to catch her eye, not even knowing if this *was* Clara Barton, I suddenly felt like a time-crossing stalker. Despite the seriousness of the moment, I had to stifle a giggle.

She glanced at me then and looked behind me at Joseph, who still held my baskets. Her gaze returned to me, and I smiled.

"How smart," she said, "to bring supplies. I didn't think to grab anything as I ran out of work to come here."

"I heard the soldiers met with trouble in Baltimore, so I brought some food and a few medical supplies in case there are injuries." I motioned to the baskets. "You are free to help me distribute them. I'm sure we will need all the help we can get."

"That's very kind and thoughtful." She took a step toward me and extended her gloved hand. "I'm Miss Clara Barton."

I was awestruck for a moment, aware of the great things this woman would do with her life, and I felt small compared to her. But I rallied in a heartbeat and accepted her hand. "I'm Miss Margaret Wakefield. How do you do?"

"It's a pleasure to meet you." She let go of my hand. "Any relation to Senator Wakefield?"

I hesitated, not wanting to make the connection for fear she would repeat my name to someone who would tell him, or someone who would spread gossip. But this was Clara Barton; how could I not tell her the truth? "He is my father."

She studied me with a critical eye, probably wondering why I was risking my and my father's reputations, but she said nothing.

A train whistle sounded in the distance, and all of us looked toward the tracks again.

Several hundred people began to cheer, though none of us knew what we would encounter when the train unloaded. It might be full of injured soldiers—or no soldiers at all. It could be a false alarm.

When the train came to a stop and the soldiers started to stream out of the cars, the crowd erupted in more cheers. But it didn't take long to see that several of them were wounded, some of them so much so that they would need more than a few stitches and a bandage to make them well.

"I know many of these men. Come," Clara said. She took my hand and pulled me through the crowd toward them. "I'll introduce you, and we'll see what we can do to help."

I nodded once, having been ready for this moment my entire life.

It was late by the time the carriage arrived back at our home. The sun had already set, and I knew my father would not only be worried, he'd be angry.

Especially when he realized I had brought two soldiers home to recuperate.

"It's mighty kind of you to take us in," Private Bartholomew Anderson said as he sat with his brother's head on his lap. Both men were young—only seventeen and nineteen years old. They were not hardened soldiers but simple farmers who had answered Lincoln's call to maintain the Union. Farnum Anderson had suffered a bullet wound, which passed through his arm. I had done my best to clean out the debris and stitch up the entrance and exit wounds. He'd also been trampled when he fell to the ground and had been unconscious for most of the train ride into Washington. Thankfully, he'd regained consciousness by the time I encountered them, but he had signs of concussion and needed rest.

"It's my pleasure," I said a moment before Joseph opened the carriage door. Several of the lights were lit within the house. "Will you please assist Farnum?" I asked Joseph.

Bartholomew had also sustained several injuries, including a brick to the head, so he wouldn't be able to help his brother. Thankfully, he had no signs of concussion, but he had a laceration and a large hematoma on his forehead. His shoulder had been dislocated, and he'd been in extreme pain when I approached him at the station. I had been able to put the joint back into place with Joseph's help, but it was sore and would need a couple of weeks to heal.

"Yes, Miss Margaret." Joseph helped me out of the carriage and then assisted Bartholomew and, finally, Farnum.

Joseph had watched in awe while I worked at the station. I knew he had a hundred questions, but I was trying to ignore his probing gaze. I could never explain to him how I knew what to do with a dislocated shoulder or why I had asked Farnum dozens of questions and performed a neurological examination to ascertain the severity of his concussion.

The rain had started to let up, but a gentle mist still lingered in the air as we walked to the back door and entered the kitchen. Roast beef and vegetables were warming at the back of the stove, sending off a profusion of delicious scents. I was surprised Papa had waited supper for me, but I was also thankful because I was famished. Once I had Bartholomew and Farnum situated upstairs, I would join him.

And face his ire. I knew it was inevitable once I decided to take the Anderson brothers into our home, but I had little choice.

Goldie turned from the stove, a fork in hand that she'd been using to stir the gravy. "Your papa's been waiting in the parlor with some guests." She looked me over and shook her head. "Best you clean up first before you join them."

For the first time, I looked down at my gown. Mud lined the hem, and bloodstains were smeared along the front. I put my hand to my hair and realized it was also disheveled and probably looked a fright.

"Can you please prepare two extra plates for our guests?" I asked Goldie. "They'll stay in the spare room at the top of the back stairs."

"Margaret?" Papa pushed through the kitchen door. Worry lines had deepened around his eyes and mouth but were soon replaced with surprise—and then anger. "What is the meaning of this?"

Joseph was holding up Farnum, and Bartholomew was just behind them. He stood at attention when Papa entered the room.

I had a lot of talking to do, and it needed to be done fast. "I went to the station to meet the soldiers who arrived from Baltimore. I'm sure you've heard there was a mob and the soldiers were ambushed. I was able to bring food and medical supplies, and I met a young woman named Miss Clara Barton who knew many of these men, including Bartholomew and Farnum Anderson. There's nowhere for the soldiers to stay, so they're being taken to the Capitol Building—"

"I'm quite aware of where they're going," Papa interrupted. "They're bivouacking in the Senate and House chambers. But that does not explain why you've brought two complete strangers into our house—or why you went there to help in the first place."

"Miss Barton offered to take home a few of her friends who were injured and could not recover properly at the Capitol. So I agreed to do the same. These men have sustained serious injuries, and they need to rest in comfort for a few days before they can return to their regiment. I couldn't leave them to suffer at the Capitol when they've risked their lives for us."

He stared at me for several long, uncomfortable moments while no one else spoke. I hated upsetting or disappointing him, but I could endure it more than the thought of these men on the cold, hard floor of the Senate chambers.

"I suppose we cannot turn them out now." Papa looked to Goldie. "See that they're fed. And Joseph"—he turned to our man-of-all-work—"I want you to take care of them while they're in this house." He walked across the room and shook Bartholomew's hand and then Farnum's uninjured one. "I'm honored to have you as guests, and I thank you for your courage and valor today. My argument is not with you but with my impetuous daughter."

The soldiers nodded and dipped their heads in deference to my father, who indicated they were free to leave the kitchen.

When they were gone, Papa turned to me, his emotions hard to read. "Mr. Cameron and Mr. Cooper are in the parlor, waiting patiently for their supper. I've tried to explain your absence as best I could, but I had no idea where you had gone. I want you to change as quickly as possible and return downstairs."

"Of course."

"And when everyone is gone, you and I will talk."

I nodded, expecting no less.

Twenty minutes later, I walked down the front stairs in a fresh gown, with clean hands and my hair properly restored. Ever since Papa had said Mr. Cooper was in the house, my senses had been heightened, and I was thankful he had not witnessed my state of upheaval.

When I entered the front parlor, Mr. Cameron and Mr. Cooper rose from their chairs to greet me.

Though it had only been a day in this path since I'd seen Mr. Cooper, to me it had been three days. He looked just as dashing tonight as he had at the White House, and those intense brown eyes of his instantly made me conscious of everything about myself. I didn't usually care too much about my appearance, but Mr. Cooper's opinion of me suddenly mattered a great deal.

He took me in with an admiring smile and a slight bow.

"I'm sorry to have kept all of you waiting," I said. "I didn't intend to be gone for so long. Had I known we were expecting company, I would have been home much sooner."

"Please don't concern yourself over us," Mr. Cameron said. "We've had plenty to talk about as we waited."

"Shall we go in to supper?" Papa asked, indicating that everyone move into the dining room.

Mr. Cameron followed Papa, putting his hand on Papa's shoulder as he spoke to him in quiet tones.

Mr. Cooper met me near the door and said, "You look lovely this evening, Miss Wakefield. Well worth the wait." He halted, and I followed suit as he tilted his head and looked closely at my neck.

I froze, surprised at his scrutiny.

"I apologize," he said, "but I believe you have . . . mud behind your ear."

My hand went to my neck, and I felt a clump of dried mud. Heat rose from my chest up my throat as I pulled it away.

"Do you enjoy rolling in the mud, Miss Wakefield?" he asked with a twinkle in his eye.

"It is my favorite pastime," I said with a smile.

"One wonders what kept you so long on such a dreary night as this." He tilted an eyebrow. "That involves mud. Perhaps it's one of your many secrets?"

Papa and Mr. Cameron had entered the dining room and

were now out of sight. I was certain Papa would not want me discussing what had kept me, but I couldn't explain the mud in any other way without raising more questions.

"It's not a secret. I met the train of soldiers who came in from Baltimore and brought them food and medical supplies." I wouldn't tell him I had provided medical assistance—*that* would need to remain a secret. Or that I had brought two of them home with me.

The teasing gleam disappeared from his gaze, replaced with a combination of surprise and admiration. "Truly?"

For some reason, this new look warmed me far more than his teasing one. "We will all be called to sacrifice in the weeks and months ahead. I am simply doing what I can."

"An admirable attitude, Miss Wakefield." He glanced toward the dining room and then back at me, lowering his voice. "Perhaps if we all focused on what was best for this country and not on our own careers or reputations, we'd be a lot more prepared for the battle ahead."

What *did* he think was best for the country? Was he in favor of the Union or the Confederacy?

"Margaret?" Papa appeared at the door, a question in his voice.

"Coming," I said to him as Mr. Cooper offered his arm to escort me.

"Your actions tonight speak volumes about your character," Mr. Cooper said with a smile. "You're not afraid to flout convention or put your reputation in danger for a cause you are passionate about."

I dipped my head, acknowledging his assessment.

"Which suggests," he said, leaning a little closer to me as we entered the dining room, making my pulse pick up speed, "that perhaps you're hiding more secrets than I first suspected."

It had been a long day, and my inhibitions had been set aside, so I gave him an answer I might one day regret.

"Perhaps I am." I decided not to leave it there. "But your suggestion begs a few questions of my own. What brings a man from Great Britain all the way across the sea to work in the White House? And how does he achieve such a lofty position in such a short amount of time? Perhaps you're hiding more secrets than I first suspected."

It was hard to read his expression as he dipped his head and said, "Perhaps I am."

5

APRIL 19, 1941
BETHESDA, MARYLAND

"You'll be working in surgery today with Dr. Philips," Nurse Daly told me as I reported for duty on my first full day at the naval hospital.

"Dr. Zechariah Philips?"

"Yes. He'll be using operating room three. Your first surgery is scheduled in thirty minutes, so you'll need to hurry."

I had already left Anna, who was working in the pediatric ward. She seemed a little happier that morning, knowing she would be treating children. I had been eager to get started as well—until I learned who I would work with that day.

It didn't take long to find the right operating room. There were two other nurses already on duty, preparing the room for surgery. After scrubbing my hands and arms, I joined them. Thankfully, sanitary practices in the operating room had become widely accepted by 1941, though they were not up to 2001 standards. The nurses were allowed to wear their uniforms in and out of the operating room and were only instructed to change if they were visibly soiled.

"We have an appendectomy today," the first nurse said to me. "Have you assisted with appendectomies in the past?"

I had assisted with many of them during my medical school rotations in 2001, not to mention my nurse's surgical training in 1941. "Yes," I said simply.

"Good. I'll be going off duty soon, and Dr. Philips cannot abide incompetence."

Despite my confidence and experience, I still felt a twinge of nerves at the thought of working with him. Part of me wanted to prove something—to him and to me. I didn't even know him, but from the few conversations I'd had with nurses who did, I'd learned he was exacting, tactless, and brilliant. In 2001 I had already proven myself, though people constantly challenged me. For reasons I couldn't identify, I wanted Dr. Philips to know I was capable too.

The time passed quickly as I prepared the room and gathered the surgical instruments Dr. Philips would need. I was often teased for my love of order and precision outside the hospital, but in the operating room, it was an essential skill.

At the appointed time, the operating room door opened, and Dr. Philips entered. I wore my white face mask and my standard-issue nursing uniform. I also had a white cap covering my hair. But the moment he entered the room, he stopped and stared at me.

I hadn't expected him to recognize me, covered as I was and having only briefly met, but he did.

"Nurse Hollingsworth," he said. "I didn't expect to see you here."

Without responding, I moved away from the surgical instruments and went to the white gowns hanging on a nearby hook. I took one and turned to Dr. Philips, ready to help him into the gown so we could begin the surgery.

He slipped his arms through the gown and turned so I could tie it in the back. He was also wearing a white mask and cap, but his blue eyes were unmistakable. "I specifically requested not to work with you."

His words struck like a serpent. "Do you have an objection to me, Doctor?"

"Several, in fact."

"You hardly know me."

"Yet what I know indicates that you are the last nurse who should be assisting me in the operating room."

I glanced at the other nurse, but she had her back to us against the far wall and didn't seem to notice—or care—about our conversation.

My cheeks were warm with embarrassment, but I lifted my chin and met Dr. Philips's stare. "I'm not certain what you've heard, but I can assure you it's not true."

"It's not true that you were allowed into the navy a year early because you have a connection to Rear Admiral Stark?"

"How does that make me incompetent?" I asked quietly, hoping the other nurse wouldn't hear. "It's a silly policy. If someone has passed their studies and has a full understanding of their duties, what does age matter?"

"Bending rules and doing things out of order are dangerous in an operating room. Behavior is the best indicator of character, and I've found yours lacking."

My mouth slipped open at his comment, and all I could do was stare. Just the day before, Mr. Cooper had commended my character. If Dr. Philips only knew my reason for bending this particular rule, perhaps he'd realize I had an honorable motive for my behavior.

He turned away from me and approached the instrument table. He stood for a moment looking it over and then glanced up. "Who set out these instruments?"

I lifted my chin. "I did."

He didn't respond but silently moved a few tools around to suit his taste.

When the patient was finally rolled into the room, I was ready and waiting near the instruments to hand them to Dr. Philips as he needed them. The anesthesiologist was there, as were two other nurses who had joined us. Soon they had the patient under anesthesia, and it was time to perform the surgery.

For several minutes, I watched Dr. Philips, impressed with his skill. He worked with sure, steady hands and a furrowed, concerned brow. From time to time, he asked for different surgical instruments, which I handed to him without hesitation.

After he opened the patient's abdomen and made an examination, he paused. "It looks like peritonitis," he said to the room at large, disappointment in his voice. For all his gruffness, his entire demeanor softened when he spoke of the diagnosis. "The appendix has ruptured, and the infection has spread throughout the abdomen. We didn't get here in time."

There was a quiet hush in the room, and I knew what each of them was thinking. The patient was going to die. Once the appendix ruptured and the infection spread, it had become a life-threatening illness.

But I knew something from my medical history class they didn't, something that was not yet widely known.

"Doctors in Europe are having success treating peritonitis with antibiotics. Perhaps it would help Private Edmund to administer sulfonamide after you remove the appendix."

Four sets of eyes turned to me, but it was Dr. Philips's that seemed to bore a hole into my soul. Did anyone else ever question or challenge him?

"Sulfonamide?" he repeated.

I nodded. The life-saving medicine was being used in England to great success, especially with peritonitis. In the coming year, penicillin would be brought to America and mass-produced, further revolutionizing the medical world.

But for now, sulfonamide wasn't as widely known, even in medical circles.

No one spoke as they waited for Dr. Philips to address my suggestion. I watched him, wondering if he'd tell me I was a fool or simply ignore me.

In the end, he ignored me and continued with the surgery. With deft, able hands, he removed the appendix and cleaned out the infection as best as he could.

When he was finished, and after he had stitched up the surgical wound, he took off his rubber surgical gloves and tossed them into the garbage.

"Nurse Hollingsworth, see that Private Edmund receives the sulfonamide. If you cannot locate it, let me know immediately. I want him to start the treatment as soon as possible."

I stared at him, shocked he had taken my suggestion. "Thank you."

"I'm not doing it for you. I'm doing it for him." His gruffness had returned. "If I do nothing, the private dies. I'm willing to try whatever it takes to save his life."

He absent-mindedly scratched at his hand, which was covered in dermatitis. Was it from the rubber gloves he was wearing or something else?

He noticed my gaze and put his hands behind his back. "The next surgery is in an hour. See that the operating room is ready." With that, he left.

As the patient was rolled out to recovery, I was thankful I still wore my mask so my grin was concealed. Private Edmund would live, and perhaps Dr. Philips would know that I was just as competent as he was.

The sun had already set by the time Anna and I arrived at the White House that evening to attend a dinner with my grandfather. We wore cocktail-length gowns and jackets with stiff shoulder pads, but it was chilly, and I was eager to get inside.

Lights illuminated the White House as we greeted Grandfather, who was waiting for us outside the East Entrance. He had been a permanent fixture in Washington, DC, since he was elected to the US House of Representatives from Virginia in 1910 and had befriended Franklin Delano Roosevelt when FDR served in the Senate.

What Dr. Philips didn't realize was that if Rear Admiral Stark hadn't recommended me for the navy, President Roosevelt would have—though I would never admit that to the doctor.

"Anna," Grandfather said, folding her into his arms for a hug. He briefly closed his eyes, and I suspected he was praying for her, as all of us had been doing these past few years. "How are you, my girl?"

Anna attempted a smile and said, "I think the move will be good for me."

My heart soared at her declaration, and I prayed it was true. Grandfather put his hand on her cheek and smiled.

He turned to me, then, opening his arms. I accepted his hug, reveling in the smell of pipe tobacco emanating from his suit. He was a time-crosser and had lived in the 1500s but had ultimately chosen this path. I had loved hearing stories about his life while growing up. It made me feel less lonely, knowing my parents and grandfather had gone before me, but they had all made their choices and mine was yet to come. They had each other. If I chose a different path, I would have none of them.

"Maggie, my love," he said. "Have you made your choice yet?"

It was as if he had read my thoughts. I shook my head. "How did you choose?"

Anna looked away, as she often did when we spoke of such things. It had been hard for her growing up without the mark that set the rest of us apart. She'd had our older brother, Teddy, who wasn't marked, but they'd never been close. I didn't want to leave her out, but I had such a big decision to make, and any wisdom or advice my grandfather could give me was priceless.

"I didn't choose," he said with a smile. "God chose my path for me. You'll know when you need to."

Anxiety filled me at his words. I wasn't the type of person who liked to sit around and let things happen *to* me. I wanted to know what my future would hold or, at the very least, how I should choose. I couldn't decide based on my loved ones, because each of them was equally important to me. I couldn't choose based on my career, because I loved what I was doing in each path. I was confident and sure of myself in each life I lived, yet I was a ball of uncertainty when it came to this decision.

"Now," he said, rubbing his hands together and pushing the conversation aside as if it bore no consequence on this evening. "Are you ready to meet the President of the United States? He's been looking forward to meeting both of you."

I knew this evening was important to him, so I turned my thoughts away from me and teased him. "I dined here with the Lincolns four days ago and was here for a congressional party in the East Room just yesterday."

Grandfather chuckled and shook his head. "And here I thought this was a special treat for you."

"Seeing you is always a special treat." I took one of his arms, and Anna took the other as we walked into the East Entrance.

Anna had never been to the White House, and if 1941 were my only path, this would be my first time as well.

The security guards let us through with little trouble, since they were expecting us and they knew Grandfather. Everything looked very much the same as it had when I was there for Mom's congressional party, though the carpet was different and some of the light fixtures had been changed.

As we passed the China Room, Anna asked if she could look inside.

"Of course," Grandfather said. "I need to speak to Maggie for a moment. Will you excuse us?"

Anna nodded and left us to look at the presidential china on display.

I waited for Grandfather to turn to me. Concern lined his blue eyes, which were so much like my own. His hair was white now, and he wore a mustache. He'd always been a gregarious sort of fellow with a big laugh and a heart of gold.

Now, as he studied me, he looked old and tired.

My concern mounted, and I took a step closer to him, putting my hand on his arm. "What's wrong?"

"I'm not sure. I've been so tired lately, and I easily lose my breath while walking up stairs or being active."

"Are you having chest pains or back pains?"

He shook his head. "But my indigestion has been terrible lately, and my feet and ankles are swelling."

All my medical knowledge rushed in, fighting to be heard. But even as I listened to his symptoms, I knew there was little I could offer him for treatment. If it were 2001, I would check his blood pressure, cholesterol, and run an echocardiogram because I suspected heart disease. But there was no medication available for hypertension or hypercholesterolemia in 1941. The best I, or anyone else, could suggest was a healthier lifestyle, but that only went so far if he had a genetic predisposition for high cholesterol. The most common suggestion for dealing with hypertension in 1941 was eating a rice-based diet. My 2001 knowledge knew that wasn't necessary, that he needed to follow a heart-healthy diet of fresh fruits and vegetables, high fiber, little to no sugar or salt, and to eliminate alcohol. He should also stop smoking his pipe.

"What is it?" he asked me, and I realized I was doing a poor job of keeping the concern from my face. "You know what it is, don't you?"

"I have a suspicion, but, Grandfather—" I swallowed, trying

not to let my alarm color my voice. Knowing what he needed to do but not being able to tell him because it wasn't yet common knowledge was heart-wrenching. How could that be right? "I believe you have hypertension, but no one in 1941 will be able to help you with medicine—and I cannot give you information that is not available to anyone else right now." I hated that my hands were tied. "There are people researching it, and they are making great improvements, but there won't be medication to treat it for almost a decade."

He studied me for a moment but then slowly nodded his head. "I should have known not to ask you. It's wrong of me to make you feel torn. I, of all people, should know not to tempt fate by changing history."

"There have been some advancements regarding diet changes." I told him about the rice diet and reducing the fatty food he liked so much, which would help him lose weight. It would be better than doing nothing at all.

Grandfather listened intently, nodding.

"I want you to go see your regular physician," I told him. "He will be able to give you more information. And perhaps I'm wrong."

"You're brilliant, Maggie. I'm sure you're right."

"I hope I'm not." But everything I knew about hypertension told me I was.

"Anna?" Grandfather called. "Are you ready to meet the President?"

Anna came out of the China Room, and when I saw the look on her face, I knew she had been eavesdropping on our conversation. She had the acute grief in her eyes that had plagued her after Richard died. If she lost Grandfather right now, I wasn't sure how she would survive.

What would happen if I chose not to stay in 1941? She was still fragile in so many ways. The thought of forcing her to grieve my loss scared me more than almost anything else.

Wrapping my arm around Anna's elbow, I followed Grandfather up to the State Floor and into the Yellow Oval Room to meet the President. Concerns for Grandfather's physical health and Anna's mental health lingered long into the evening.

6

I lay in bed for a long time on Saturday morning, staring out my window at the trees along P Street. Birds sang their sweet trills, and the bright blue sky promised a warm and pleasant afternoon of sightseeing with Seth.

It had been several days since I'd been at the White House with Grandfather and Anna. Though I had three days to everyone else's one, it still passed by far too fast, especially here in 2001. I often woke up to an alarm clock before the sun rose and ran from one thing to the next until I crashed into bed at night. I rarely took the time to wake up at my leisure and just lie in bed and think.

I turned on my side and pulled the thick comforter up to my ear as I let out a long sigh.

"Knock, knock," Delilah said a moment before she opened my bedroom door, two cups of coffee in her hands. "It's so unlike you to wake up after me that I had to come see if you were still alive."

I made a face at her and sat up to stretch, happily accepting the cup of coffee she handed me. It was warm in my hands and smelled like energy. Thankfully, no matter what path I inhabited, coffee was a constant source of joy.

Delilah wore a pair of checkered pajama pants and a faded Prince t-shirt. She sat on the padded window seat and tucked her bare feet up under her. "So," she said with a wiggle of her eyebrows, "are you nervous?"

"Nervous?" I took a sip of the hot coffee, savoring the bitter flavor as it went down my parched throat. "For what?"

"You've never been on a date before, have you?"

"Who has time? Besides, this isn't a date."

"Uh." Delilah pressed her lips together and frowned. "A handsome, *very* eligible—if the internet can be trusted—successful congressman asked you to show him around town. That sounds like a date to me."

"It can't be a date." I held the mug in both hands, wondering when Delilah had changed her hair from blue to pink, and tried to remember her natural color. It had been at least a year since I saw it last, though her brown eyebrows were a strong indication.

"Why not?" She continued to frown. "I go on dates all the time. It doesn't have to mean anything."

"To me it does." I moved my toes under the comforter, trying not to meet her gaze, knowing I would see censure there. "I have big decisions to make by January, and I already have a lot of reasons to stay in each path. I don't need a romantic entanglement to make matters worse."

"There is a way for you to know for sure where you belong." Delilah moved off the window seat and sat on the edge of my bed.

"How?" I'd been looking for the answer for years, but every time I asked my marked parents or grandfather for advice, they always said the same thing. *I'd know when the time was right*, or *God had a plan and I just needed to trust Him*. While

I didn't disagree, it still left me at a loss. The clock was ticking, and He hadn't shown me yet.

Delilah's brown eyes filled with compassion, and she smiled. "Which path is *you*, Meg? At your very core, are you Margaret Wakefield, Maggie Hollingsworth, or Meg Clarke? Who are you?"

I stared at her for a long time as I pondered her question. Who *was* I? "No one has ever boiled it down to such a basic question for me."

"I know I can't possibly understand your struggle," Delilah continued, "but I can relate. I always ask myself that question. What Delilah is the real me? Am I the real me eating dinner with my parents and trying to live up to their expectations? Am I the real me when I'm hanging out with my friends, discussing life's biggest questions? Or am I the real me when I'm in an art class, lost in a creation I've made? I don't think it'll end, either. Someday I might wonder if I'm the truest version of myself as a wife, a mom, a professional. We each have to make those kinds of decisions every day—yours just has more finality than most."

I found myself slowly nodding. "I am three very different people in each path. I wish you could know me in 1861 and 1941. I'd love to introduce you to Anna and my marked parents, and Papa."

"I know them," she said with a smile. "Better than you might realize."

I returned her smile. "You've given me a lot to think about."

She lifted a shoulder. "What are best friends for, if not to help you navigate your three lives?"

Laughter flowed from us, and I shook my head. "I'm so happy you know the truth. It's hard not to share this part of myself with others, especially in 1861. No one knows who I really am there."

"Maybe that's the first life you can cross off your list."

My stomach clenched at her words, turning the coffee sour.

I didn't want to give up Papa or the Lincolns or the oncoming war. We were in for heartache and trials, but I wanted to help the nation and my friends. I had so much to offer them, if Papa would let me. He and I had spoken after supper the night I brought the soldiers to our home—or rather, he had lectured me about propriety and social expectations. He had been very angry, and rightfully so. He'd asked if anyone had seen me or if I had done anything that might bring criticism upon us. He cautioned me that I did not represent merely myself or him, but also the Lincolns and the very cause of freedom. I had to live above reproach.

I wasn't allowed to nurse the Anderson brothers, so I had to give Joseph instructions for their care. Worse, Papa forbade me from doing something like it again.

As much as I loved him and tried to accept his nineteenth-century views, I struggled to honor him in this regard. I knew what was coming and how much help would be needed. Eventually, he wouldn't be able to stop me.

But that was a debate and argument for another day.

"I should probably get ready," I told Delilah. "Seth will be here in about an hour."

"Where will you take him?"

Shrugging, I pushed the covers aside to get out of bed. "I was thinking about taking him on a monuments tour first, and then we can visit some of the Smithsonian Museums. If we have time, maybe we'll go to the National Archives Building and see the Declaration of Independence."

"You might be out all day with him."

"Maybe—but I do need to read an article and write a quick paper about it tonight."

"A quick paper." Delilah rose from my bed, shaking her head in mock disgust. "It would take me days to write a 'quick paper.'"

I smiled and walked over to my closet to decide what to wear.

I would need to shove aside our conversation, because I was not ready or willing to write off 1861.

An hour later, I was dressed in a pair of jeans and a plaid shirt, buttoned down the front. I had gone for casual since we'd be walking most of the day. On my feet were a simple pair of sandals, and I threw my dark hair up into a ponytail. I didn't want to dress up or look like I had taken a great deal of time with my appearance. This wasn't a date. It was a casual outing with a new friend.

A new, handsome friend.

Delilah came out of the kitchen eating a donut and met me by the front door as I tucked a few things into my oversized bag. I made a point to look at her donut with disapproval, but she took a big bite and grinned.

"Well," she said as she sized me up. "Nothing fancy, but you look nice and relaxed. It's good to see you taking a little time off for some fun."

"But it's not a date," I reminded her. "We're just hanging out."

The front buzzer sounded, and I pressed the speaker. "Hello?"

"It's Seth. Can I come up?"

Delilah nodded emphatically. If I didn't let her meet Seth, I wouldn't hear the end of it.

"Sure. We're up on the top floor."

"Great. See you in a minute."

Delilah ran to the kitchen and set down her donut before coming back, licking the frosting off one finger. She looked more excited than I felt—though I was nervous, despite what I'd told her earlier. Even if this wasn't a date, I rarely hung out with a man alone in any of my paths. In 1861, it was socially unacceptable. In 1941 and 2001, it was out of the fear of falling in love and complicating my choices.

What if Seth and I had nothing to talk about?

Worse—what if we had everything to talk about and I really liked him?

I glanced into the mirror hanging on the wall and took a deep, steadying breath. I could do this. I'd done a lot harder things.

Even though I knew it was coming, the knock startled me, and Delilah stifled a giggle at my reaction. I sent her a warning glare, and she pressed her lips together, her eyes dancing with mirth.

Opening the door, I wasn't prepared for the man who stood in front of me. Today, he looked casual and alarmingly attractive. He'd been striking in his tuxedo, but the room had been dim, and there had been a lot of people to distract me.

Now Seth stood before me in a pair of blue jeans and a long-sleeved knit shirt with a couple of buttons at his throat, which were undone. He had pushed up his sleeves, revealing muscular arms, and tucked the shirt into his trim waist. His blond hair had a bit of a windblown look, and his smile was brilliant and blinding.

"Hi," he said, taking me in with a quick, appreciative glance. "You look great."

"So do you." I tried to smile, but my insides were all mushy, and I couldn't seem to conjure a logical thought or reaction. Delilah cleared her throat, and I startled again. "This is my roommate, Delilah LeBlanc."

"Roommate and best friend," Delilah amended as she reached for Seth's hand. "Meg told me you're one of the newest congressmen in town. Congrats."

"Thanks." He tilted his head toward the stairs, glancing in my direction. "I kind of double-parked."

"Got it." I grabbed my bag. "I'll see you later, Delilah."

"Have fun," she said in a knowing, teasing voice.

I rolled my eyes at her while Seth's back was turned, and she laughed.

Thirty minutes later, we were at the Ronald Reagan Building and International Trade Center. A convenient public parking garage would give us good access to the National Museum of American History, the National Museum of Natural History, and the National Mall.

It didn't take long to park and find our way out into the gorgeous day. The Capitol Building stood at one end of the Mall, the Washington Monument stood in the middle, and the Lincoln Memorial flanked the other end. Scattered in between, along both sides of the Mall, were the Smithsonian buildings, the red-brick Smithsonian Castle being one of the more recognizable.

It was already hot as we stood on the crushed gravel path, looking toward the Washington Monument obelisk.

"Can you see where the stone changes color, about a third of the way up?" I asked.

Seth nodded, shading his eyes from the sun.

"They had only gotten that far by the Civil War and didn't finish it for over twenty years. It was the tallest structure in the world until the Eiffel Tower was built in France."

"Wow," Seth said, clearly impressed with the history. "It would have been amazing to live in Washington during the Civil War."

I smiled to myself, wondering if he would have really enjoyed it. "The city was nothing then like it is today. The streets were muddy, and the federal buildings were so far apart, it was hard to get from one place to the next. But the worst part was probably the dirty canal. It ran through the city, directly between the White House and Washington's unfinished monument, carrying disease and filth. Some people believe Willie Lincoln contracted typhoid fever from the canal." I hated thinking about poor little Willie and what his death would do to his parents. "If that wasn't bad enough, there were constant threats to the residents. You never knew, from one day to the next, if the Confederates were going to over-take the capital."

Seth stared at me, his eyes shining with admiration and awe. "How do you know so much about the city at that time?"

If he only knew the truth—but he'd never believe me, and I'd never tell him. "I love history," I said with a smile. "Now, what would you like to do? The city is yours."

"I'll go anywhere and do anything you want today. The city might be mine, but today, I'm all yours."

His words brought heat to my cheeks, though I saw the teas-ing gleam in his eyes.

"How about we walk to the Lincoln Memorial and then check out the Vietnam Memorial and the Korean War Memorial before we find somewhere to eat lunch? I know this amazing restaurant in Chinatown, if you like Chinese food."

"I love it. And if you recommend it, I'm sure it'll be perfect."

"You're quite the charmer, aren't you?" We started walking west toward the Lincoln Memorial and the Reflecting Pool.

"I guess it takes a bit of charm to be elected to the US House of Representatives at the age of twenty-five." He grinned at me. "What about you? You're over here being brilliant, spouting off facts as if you lived through the history personally, and doing it as a fourth-year med student—at the age of twenty. I'm going to be honest, it's a little intimidating being around you. I feel like I'm going to say something and give away the fact that I'm actually an idiot."

I laughed and shook my head. "Believe me, I'm not that brilliant. I just work *a lot* and have no life. Most people could do what I've done if they did nothing but study."

"I hardly believe that, and now I'm adding humility to your growing list of attributes." He brushed his hand against mine and said, "Not to mention that you're beautiful. I've never met anyone like you, Meg. I really do feel honored to spend the day with you."

His words sounded genuine, though I didn't deserve such praise. I knew my faults and limitations, but my heart did a little flip anyway. "Thank you. I feel the same way about you."

"Mutual admiration is a great way to start a friendship." He grinned. Then slowly, as if weighing his words carefully, he said, "I was going to wait until the end of the day to ask you this—after I knew whether or not you liked me—but I have tickets for the National Symphony Orchestra's spring concert at the Kennedy Center next weekend, and I was wondering if you'd like to come with me."

I focused my attention on the Washington Monument as we passed by. It was easy to like Seth Wallace—too easy. If I didn't have 1861 and 1941, I could see myself saying yes to his invitation. Being with him felt effortless and a little thrilling. Having him look at me the way he did, with those charming blue eyes, made my stomach fill with butterflies. Yet I had made a promise to myself, and I would stick to that promise. I couldn't allow myself to fall for anyone, at any time, until I'd made my final decision.

"I'm sorry, Seth." I swallowed my disappointment. "I do enjoy your company very much, but I have less than nine months left—of med school. I really have to focus all of my attention on my work right now if I want to get a residency position at GUH. If things were different, I would say yes without a doubt."

"I suppose there has to be some sacrifice, if you're going to be brilliant."

I smiled, appreciating his willingness to accept my decision without making me feel uncomfortable. So many others made me feel guilty for putting my work above everything else. "A lot of sacrifice, especially for the next nine months."

"So," he said gently, slowly, "you're saying that I have a chance in January?"

Warmth filled my cheeks again, and I dipped my head. "Maybe."

"Then that's all I need to know." He motioned toward the Reflecting Pool. "Let's go have some fun and not talk about it anymore."

"I like the sound of that."

"But I can't promise I won't be secretly looking forward to January."

For the first time in my life, I could say the same thing . . . almost.

7

APRIL 25, 1861
WASHINGTON, DC

Spring had finally returned to the city, bringing with it warmth and sunshine, drying some of the mud, and coaxing tiny flowers from the earth. Leaves unfurled on the trees, and birds twittered in the branches, unaware of the growing threats on every side of the city.

It had already been a week since nine hundred soldiers arrived from Baltimore, but along with them, word had come that twenty miles of train tracks had been destroyed between Baltimore and Washington, cutting us off from the rest of the nation and preventing more soldiers from arriving. Telegraph wires had also been cut, our mail and newspapers were being withheld, and Virginia farmers refused to cross the Potomac to bring food into the nation's capital.

Though the president had called for seventy-five thousand soldiers ten days ago, less than two thousand had arrived. Threats of a Confederate invasion pulsated through the city, and everyone believed an attack was imminent. The local militia, which should have amounted to seven thousand men, was drastically reduced as Southern sympathizers refused to swear an oath to the Constitution, and many of them left to join the regiments assembling in Virginia.

The fear was palpable as I walked into the US Capitol Building that morning. My own trepidation at disobeying Papa made my heart pound fast. What if he learned that I had come to nurse the injured soldiers? I had never willfully disobeyed him in the past. To do so now, on top of all his other worries and concerns, would devastate him. Yet I could not sit back and do nothing while others were suffering.

The Capitol was Papa's usual domain, but now that the Senate was in recess, the risk of being seen by someone who might know him—or me—was not as great. Though there was still a risk. I scanned the rotunda for acquaintances as I made my way down the long hall to the Senate chambers, trying to hide my face as best as I could.

When I entered the Senate chambers, I immediately found Clara Barton serving soup from a big tureen. Massachusetts soldiers made a winding line through the room. Several of the men smiled at me when they recognized me from the train station.

"Good afternoon, Miss Barton," I said. I had not seen her since the Baltimore soldiers had arrived—or since Papa had forbidden me from helping them. There was only one way I could continue to do so. "May I speak to you?"

"Yes, of course." She wiped her hands on her apron and handed the soup ladle to a capable-looking soldier. "What can I help you with?"

It was embarrassing to admit the truth, but there was nothing I could do about it. "My father was angry when he learned I assisted at the train station last week."

She pressed her lips together and nodded. "I'm not surprised. He has a reputation to uphold."

"He doesn't want me to help any further, but if I can alleviate the suffering of just one person, I must."

"I know how you feel."

I thought she might. "I must ask that you call me by a different name when I am in public and that you do not tell anyone else about my involvement. I cannot risk him knowing."

She didn't hesitate. "What shall I call you?"

"Maggie Hollingsworth."

"Agreed, Miss Hollingsworth." She smiled. "I saw that the Anderson brothers returned to their regiment yesterday."

"Bartholomew is completely recovered," I assured her. "I'm here to check on Farnum."

"He seems to be resting comfortably." Clara indicated where Farnum was lying on the Senate Chamber floor near a large marble column. "But I'm sure he'll be happy to see you. I think you've gained an admirer."

Noise echoed in the room as the men laughed and joked, waiting for instructions from their superiors. Daily drills were taking place on the Capitol lawn, and everyone was on high alert, should they be called up to defend the city.

"I'm happy you've come," Clara said with deep concern in her eyes. "I've been doing all I can to gather supplies for these men, but I've exhausted many of my resources. I've tried to gain an audience with Mr. Lincoln, but he's been preoccupied, as you can imagine."

"What can I do to help?"

"I don't move within the same circles as you, and there is a great untapped potential with those who have the means to procure the supplies we need."

She meant that my friends could afford more than most.

"Will you campaign for help?" Clara asked. "With more soldiers expected, I believe the need will only increase."

Her request would be easy to fulfill. Tonight, I would attend a ball at the home of Salmon Chase, the Secretary of the Treasury. His daughter, Kate, was the belle of Washington, and her parties were often attended by elite members of society. Some of her guests were key strategists in the war, and others might be part of the Southern spy ring that was sneaking information out of Washington. But no one could be certain.

I planned to keep my eyes and ears open.

"I will gladly put out the call for supplies," I assured Clara. "And I will start this very night."

"You are a godsend." She placed her gentle hand on my arm. "I don't know what we would have done without you at the train station." She had not asked me where I learned my medical skills, and I hoped she never would. I didn't want to lie, but I could hardly tell her the truth.

A few moments later, I approached Farnum to check his wound. "Good afternoon, Mr. Anderson," I said as I knelt beside his makeshift pallet. It was a far cry from the guest bed at our home, but Papa had given us no choice but to return the Anderson brothers to their regiment.

Today I wore a simple dress, appropriate for work, though it still ballooned around me with petticoats, and I had to push it back to get close to him. How I missed my scrubs.

He opened his eyes and offered me a surprised smile while trying to sit up.

"Please don't." I laid my hand on his arm. "I'm just here to look at your wound and see if it's healing properly."

"It still hurts a mite," he said, "but it don't feel infected."

"I'm happy to hear that. May I look?"

He nodded and laid his arm across his stomach while I slowly removed the bandages. To my relief, I found it healing well and the stitches still holding secure. "I'll remove the stitching in a day or two," I told him. "Everything looks good."

"You're coming back?" he asked, hopeful.

Smiling, I applied fresh bandages and nodded.

As I worked, I looked up and noticed a gentleman speaking to a soldier behind one of the large columns. The gentleman had his back toward me, but he looked like Mr. Cooper. The two spoke in hushed tones, and the soldier glanced over his shoulder from time to time, as if he was afraid he'd be caught.

When the gentleman turned to look out at the room, I saw his side profile and realized it *was* Mr. Cooper. He, too, looked to see if anyone was listening to their conversation.

I lowered my face quickly, hoping he wouldn't see me, confused by what I saw. Why would Graydon Cooper be in the Senate Chambers speaking to a soldier? And why did it look so secretive? Did these men know each other?

"Farnum," I said as I finished bandaging his arm, "do you know that solider near the column?" I motioned to him with my head since my hands were occupied.

Farnum glanced over and squinted, then said with a scowl, "His name's John Severs, and he's from Kentucky. Joined up with our troops just before we got to Baltimore, claiming he wanted to support the Union. He keeps to himself, but everyone thinks he's a Southern sympathizer. No one talks to him for fear he's working for the enemy. I don't know the other fellow."

What in the world was Mr. Cooper talking to a Kentuckian about?

As I watched, the conversation came to an end, and Mr. Cooper turned to leave. My heart pounded in my ears as I faced away from him again, not wanting him to see me.

When I finally chanced a look back, he was gone.

I could hardly think of anything other than Mr. Cooper as I traveled in the carriage to the Chases' mansion on E Street that evening with Papa. The Chases lived in a beautiful house nine blocks east of the White House. Kate, like myself, played official hostess for her father, a widower. He had tried to get the Republican nomination for president the year before, but it had gone to Abraham Lincoln and, in the process, Kate had snubbed Mary Lincoln. Their public rivalry continued when President Lincoln asked Mr. Chase to be the Secretary of the Treasury and Kate had moved to Washington with her father. She snubbed Mrs. Lincoln every chance she could get, and since most people did not care for Mrs. Lincoln, Kate had become Washington's sweetheart.

But none of that mattered to me. I played my part for Papa's sake, but that was all. Soon our lives would change drastically, and none of this social climbing would matter.

The Chase mansion was lit from top to bottom, and carriages dropped off their occupants at the front door. Papa had almost canceled, since the 7th New York Regiment had finally arrived that day, to the great relief of the city. Telegraph lines and train tracks had been restored, and he had been at the White House with the president for hours as they reestablished communication with the north.

He was in a good mood as we waited patiently for our turn to disembark. I was trying not to get nervous about seeing Mr. Cooper, but my hands were shaking, and my heart was beating an irregular rhythm. Papa looked at me closely as he stepped out of the carriage and offered me his hand.

My gown was made of layers and layers of petticoats over a wide hoop skirt. The robin's-egg blue silk taffeta was lavishly trimmed with white satin, tulle, and lace. It was gathered at the bodice, while the skirt was pleated with a fashionable train. The color of the gown complemented my eyes perfectly, as did the blue sapphires dangling from my earlobes. My dark curls were set in a low chignon with a matching blue comb in back. I felt beautiful, and I was planning to use my feminine wiles to discover why Mr. Cooper had been at the Capitol, if necessary.

"It's a pleasure to see you again, Senator Wakefield," a familiar British voice said, causing me to look up as I maneuvered down the carriage step, holding my voluminous skirts in one hand. Despite Papa's hold on me, I tripped—landing squarely into Mr. Cooper's chest.

So much for my feminine wiles.

"Good evening," Mr. Cooper said in a quiet, pleased tone.

Mortified, I righted myself and pushed away from his chest, my cheeks burning. "Pardon me."

Both men looked surprised—though Mr. Cooper also looked amused. He was magnificent in a black tailcoat with matching waistcoat and trousers. He wore the clothing well, indicating his supreme confidence in every cut and line of his movement.

I closed my eyes briefly, wishing it had been anyone but him. But I couldn't ignore him, so I lifted my chin and offered a smile. "Good evening, Mr. Cooper."

His grin was mischievous, as if he'd planned the whole thing. And perhaps he had.

"Shall we go inside?" Papa asked, masking his humor.

I took his arm, grateful for his presence as I regained my composure. Mr. Cooper walked behind us, and I was sure he was chuckling to himself, though I couldn't hear it. When I looked back at him, he grinned at me.

I faced forward again, trying to figure out what he'd been doing at the Capitol. Was he gathering information from other Southern sympathizers? Soldiers who had an inside look at what was happening in Washington?

More importantly, I wanted to know if he saw me at the Capitol today, and if he would tell Papa.

"Welcome, Margaret," Kate Chase said as she greeted me in the foyer. She was elegance personified, with not a hair out of place. She kissed each of my cheeks, behaving as if we were long-lost friends and not merely acquaintances who moved in the same circle.

Her father stood at her side and greeted us, then said, "Kate, may I present Mr. Graydon Cooper of the War Department? Mr. Cooper, this is my daughter, Miss Kate Chase."

"How do you do, Miss Chase?" Mr. Cooper took her hand and bowed over it.

I saw the interest in Kate's gaze. "Welcome to our home, Mr. Cooper. We hope you'll make yourself comfortable."

Mr. Cooper offered her one of his charming smiles. "Thank you. I hope I'll have a chance to dance with you this evening."

"Of course," she said. "I look forward to it."

Mr. Chase addressed Mr. Cooper. "How have you found Washington?"

Mr. Cooper glanced at me. "I have found it to be surprising."

"How mysterious," Kate said with a silvery laugh. "You must sit beside me at supper tonight, Mr. Cooper. I shall have so much fun talking with you."

Another couple entered the foyer behind us, forcing Papa, Mr. Cooper, and me to move into the large front parlor, where the dancing was already in progress. The furniture had been removed from the room, allowing ample space for the twirling couples.

There were at least three dozen people here, and I knew many of them. Two who immediately caught my eye were Mrs. Rose Greenhow and Senator Henry Wilson of Massachusetts. Rose was a widow from Maryland who had become a socialite in the city, moving between northerners and southerners alike. She lived on Lafayette Square, not far from our home. She was a notorious flirt, and she was standing awfully close to Senator Wilson even now, though the senator was married.

Papa excused himself and went to Mrs. Greenhow's side to greet her.

Leaving Mr. Cooper and me alone.

"You didn't need to throw yourself at me, Miss Wakefield," Mr. Cooper said for my ears alone. "I would have happily asked you to dance with me, if you had given me a few more minutes."

"You're insufferable," I said, allowing myself to smile at his teasing. "And for that, I will insist you dance with me now."

"It would be my pleasure." He offered me his hand, and I took it, trying not to notice the awareness that always seemed to hum between us.

The orchestra began a new waltz, "Tales of the Ball" by Johann Strauss. It was a lively song, full of energy, teasing the listener and drawing them into the tune.

We faced each other, and my full skirts pressed against his legs. He looked down at me, his brown eyes taking in my gown, my hair, my face. And for the first time, his gaze wasn't teasing.

My breath stilled. I loved the way he looked at me. There were several other women in the room who might have caught his eye, but I had his full attention. It was a powerful feeling.

We began to dance, spinning around the room in time to the music. He was a magnificent dancer. Strong, confident, and sure of himself. He didn't speak as he studied me, and I couldn't help but wonder if he'd seen me at the Capitol. Apprehension stirred in my chest—until I realized that I had also seen him. If he admitted that he'd seen me, then he'd be admitting that he was also there.

A slow smile tilted his lips. I matched it with one of my own.

"How goes your work with Clara Barton?" he asked, his voice low, questioning and challenging. Was he trying to get me to admit I had been at the Capitol with her?

"Are you a friend of Miss Barton?" I asked, playing his game.

"We are acquainted. She's been to the War Department, petitioning for help."

"Why do you assume I work with her?"

He was quiet for a moment, and I could see he was weighing his words. "You were at the train station helping the men from the Baltimore riot. Since she was there that day, doing the same, I assumed you were working together. Perhaps it's not a fair assumption?"

"I am acquainted with Miss Barton," I told him. "And I hope

to do all I can to help her cause. What about you? Is the War Department sending you all over Washington?"

I wanted him to know that I saw him at the Capitol—and that I was watching his movements. If he was a Southern sympathizer, I would find out.

"I do see a great deal of Washington," he said with a lazy smile. "For instance, I was at the White House today, and then I went to the Capitol, checking on the status of the soldiers bivouacked there."

He was admitting he was there, but was it as simple as that? Was he just doing his job?

"I was not aware that Mr. Cameron's aide was in charge of checking on the status of common soldiers. One would think you had more important matters to attend to."

"And one would think the daughter of a senator would be planning and hosting lavish parties instead of tending to the wounds of a young soldier. I'm surprised your father would allow you to be at the Capitol with all those men. Unless he doesn't know . . . Maggie Hollingsworth."

My pulse thumped. How did he know my name from 1941? "Where did you hear that name?"

He frowned, probably at my reaction, which I couldn't hide. I needed to calm down. He couldn't possibly know about my time-crossing.

"I asked Miss Barton if she knew you," he explained. "She told me your name was Maggie Hollingsworth. Of course, it made me curious. Why would you give her an alias, unless you didn't want your father to know?"

The adrenaline stopped pumping, and I was able to breathe again—until he mentioned Papa. I couldn't help but glance in Papa's direction, but too late I realized it made me look guilty.

"Your father doesn't know, does he?"

I lifted my chin. "Will you try to blackmail me?"

He had grown very serious. "I would never stop you from helping, even if it means disobeying your father's wishes."

We stared at one another for several heartbeats, and I finally asked him the question that had been burning foremost in my mind. "How did you end up here, Mr. Cooper? In America, working in the White House?"

"There's not much to tell, I'm afraid."

"I doubt that very much."

"Do you really want to know the boring story?"

"I really do."

We continued to spin around the dance floor with the other couples, but it felt as if we were alone.

"The truth is that my father was the third-born son of a poor baron," he finally said, "and my mother was the daughter of an earl. She married beneath herself, or so I was told constantly growing up, and I found that I had very few prospects in England."

I could see by the vulnerability in his gaze that it was the truth, though it didn't answer my question. "How did you end up at the White House?"

"My father died shortly after I was born," he continued, "so my mother and I moved in with my uncle, the earl. I was raised at the ancestral home with his four daughters and was the next in line to inherit. When I was fifteen, my aunt produced a son, to my uncle's great delight, and I was without a future." He shrugged. "I'd been educated and prepared to be an earl, but my plans changed. When I turned sixteen, I left England and decided to pursue a future in America instead. I worked my way across the country and ended up in Illinois, where I met the president-elect at the time. He liked me and recommended me for the position. And that, Miss Wakefield, is why I am standing here today."

He had given me an explanation, but there were pieces missing. If I was going to uncover his true allegiance, I would have to dig deeper.

"As you worked your way across the country, did you ever live in the South?" I asked, keeping my voice level.

He studied me, and I could tell he knew what I was suggesting. "For a time. What about you? Did you live in the South?"

"No."

"But you lived in California?"

I frowned. Had Papa told him we lived there? "Yes. For almost a decade."

"There are Southern sympathizers in California, are there not?"

"There are Southern sympathizers in this very city," I shot back at him.

He nodded, conceding the point.

We were both silent for a moment as we danced. I enjoyed how effortlessly we moved together, even if I felt tense.

"Are we to be friends, Miss Wakefield?" he finally asked. "Or enemies?"

"Do you have a preference, Mr. Cooper?"

He studied me, his voice low. "Indeed, I do."

A shiver of excitement ran up my spine. I could get lost in the depths of his brown eyes.

But could we be friends? If we were, then perhaps I could keep a better watch on his activities. "I suppose we will be friends."

He smiled and truly looked pleased. "Then you must call me Gray."

"If we are to be friends," I replied, a bit tired of the formality my 1861 path demanded, "then you must call me Maggie."

"Then Maggie is not an alias after all."

"Not entirely, no."

He continued to study me, as if he couldn't quite unravel a mystery burning within him.

I recognized the look, because I had one burning within me as well.

8

MAY 3, 1941
BETHESDA, MARYLAND

The evening festivities beckoned to me as I finished my rounds. We had been invited to a dance at the Army and Navy Club, and I had been looking forward to it for days.

Anna had not wanted to go at first, but I convinced her it would be good for her. She had been smiling a little more lately, though I still heard her crying into her pillow from time to time. It took several days of cajoling, but she'd finally agreed to go.

She'd been off duty for over an hour and would be waiting for me in our dorm, no doubt catching up on all the Hollywood drama in *Photoplay* or reading about the latest fashion trends in *Cosmopolitan*. She devoured popular culture in ways I would never understand, though it made her well-liked among the other nurses since most of them loved to gossip about the celebrities they'd never meet. And it seemed to be one of the only things that brought her joy.

The hospital was quiet as I stood at the sink and washed my hands outside the recovery room. I had assisted in five operations that day, and though I would have loved to be the surgeon, helping Dr. Philips had been just as rewarding. After two weeks, he still treated me as if he didn't want me there, but he never mocked or derided me when I made suggestions.

Thankfully, Private Edmund had made a full recovery after his appendectomy, though Dr. Philips never spoke to me about it—or any of the other successes we'd had. It didn't matter. I knew that *he* knew, and it was enough.

I had to pass Dr. Philips's office on my way back to my dorm. Usually the door was closed, and I could slip by without notice. But today the door was open, and I saw him sitting at his desk with a large book open before him. He was reading from it, his right hand sitting on the desk with a pencil poised over a piece of paper.

I had noticed his dermatitis several times and observed the sallowness of his skin. He also looked like he'd lost weight since I'd arrived, making me wonder if he was suffering from an illness. Stress could easily cause all of those symptoms, but perhaps it was something more. Something Dr. Philips didn't even understand.

Suddenly I realized why he was so crabby. He was suffering. I'd seen it hundreds of times with patients. Illness had a way of bringing out the worst in some people, and I had definitely seen the worst in Dr. Philips.

I paused outside his office door, thankful for the shadows of the hallway that would keep me out of his peripheral vision.

Slowly, he closed the book and began to write on the paper. It gave me the opportunity to see its title: *American Journal of Digestive Diseases*. Near the book was a glass of water with the telltale signs of fizzing from an Alka-Seltzer tablet.

Was Dr. Philips suffering from a digestive disorder? Did that account for his sallowness, weight loss, and dermatitis? If so, it appeared to be a puzzle to him, if he was doing research. Did he know what ailed him, or was he stumped?

I wanted to ask him about his medical history and his current symptoms. There was still so much we didn't know in 2001, but there was so much we *did* know. And the chasm between medical knowledge in 1941 and 2001 was immense.

Deciding I would never know if I didn't ask, I tapped lightly on the doorframe of his office.

He looked up, startled, and frowned at me. "What do you want?"

"I'm going off duty," I said, trying to smile at a man who had never once smiled at me.

"Why does that concern me?" His usually meticulous hair was disheveled, as if he'd run his hand through it several times. He looked back at his paper and continued to write.

"A fascinating topic," I said, gingerly entering his office. It wasn't very large, but it was clean and orderly, just as I would keep it if it were mine. Outside, the sun was setting, painting a multicolored canvas of light across the heavens.

"You are familiar with digestive diseases?" His question seemed more like mockery, as if I could not possibly know anything about the subject.

He galled me, so I said, "More than you might realize."

With a grunt, he pushed his paper under the book and turned to me. "What do you want, Nurse Hollingsworth?"

What *did* I want? Truly? "For us to be friends."

I think my answer surprised him as much as it did me. Until then, I hadn't realized how much I wanted to be friends with Dr. Philips. I was a generally likable person, though sometimes I exasperated people with my tendency to overhelp. But I hated that Dr. Philips disliked me—and I was determined to fix it.

"Why?" He frowned, a bit of his facade slipping.

"You're brilliant," I said, much to my own chagrin. "And medicine fascinates me. I would love to know what you know, and I believe you might enjoy learning from me, too."

We sat in silence for a moment as we regarded one another. In the operating room, he was the master of his domain, commanding everyone's obedience. But he wasn't as intimidating sitting at his desk in his small office. Here, he was just a person with a quest for answers. The same as me.

"I will admit I've been impressed with your knowledge," he said as if the words felt like gravel on his teeth.

I tried not to look pleased at his statement, knowing it was difficult for him to say. Instead, I looked down at my hands, clasped before my white nurse's uniform.

"Your recommendation for Private Edmund probably saved his life, and it's prompted me to do more research on the topic." He crossed his arms as he studied me, much like Gray did, as if I was a puzzle to him. "Where did you learn of sulfonamide treatment?"

I couldn't admit the truth, but I didn't want to lie, so I simply said, "I read about it."

"Do you enjoy reading about diseases?"

"I've spent much of my life fascinated with medicine and have studied it for years."

For the first time since I met him, he didn't scowl at me. But neither did he soften and smile.

"Are you researching digestive diseases for a patient . . . or yourself?"

It took him a long time to answer. Dr. Zechariah Philips was always in control—always. To have a disease he didn't understand or couldn't master was probably eating him alive.

Would he admit his weakness to me? Someone he had determined to dislike from the start?

"Perhaps I have read something about the disease that would be helpful," I offered gently.

"The patient is complaining of digestive issues," he began, not admitting it was himself—but at least he would discuss it with me. "Pain, nausea, bloating, bowel disturbances, and vomiting on occasion."

I nodded, thinking of a dozen possibilities, some recognized in 1941 and some yet to be discovered.

"Along with digestive complaints, the patient is also easily fatigued, has mouth ulcers, dermatitis, anemia, and complains of tingling in the hands and feet." He stared at me, as if he had given me an unanswerable riddle.

A professor had once told me that if he couldn't diagnose a disease within five minutes of examining a patient, he probably never would. I kept that in mind as one of the first possibilities presented itself to me. Celiac disease. It was an autoimmune disorder that developed when a patient ate the protein gluten, found in wheat, rye, and barley. But it would be impossible to diagnose for certain without blood tests and a biopsy of his colon that would look for things not yet discovered.

It was one possibility, though he might be suffering from something else entirely.

"If it is a complaint mostly of the digestive tract," I said, finding the confident yet gentle tone I used to speak to patients in 2001, "my recommendation would be to do an elimination diet to see if a type of food is the culprit."

"An elimination diet?" He scoffed. "How would food be affecting the neurological system or creating anemia?"

I hated his condescending tone and met it with a bit of my own attitude. "There are things science has yet to explain, but you might be surprised. Our organs and systems do not work independently of each other. The heart and brain are perfect examples. They need each other to function properly. The stomach and the neurological system work hand-in-hand as well. Nothing stands on its own."

It was a discovery that some doctors were still struggling to accept in 2001, so I wasn't certain Dr. Philips would accept it, either.

Instead of scoffing again, he just looked at me, though I could tell he was mulling over what I had just told him.

"Are you going to the dance at the Army and Navy Club?" I

needed to change the subject so I didn't inadvertently tell him something I shouldn't. Already I had said more than I intended.

"A dance?" There was that sneer I was coming to expect. "Who has time for frivolity when there is so much work to be done?"

A sentiment I'd uttered many times myself.

"Too much work and not enough play and relaxation is not good for us," I told him. "Believe me, I know it all too well."

"Go. Dance with the officers and beguile them with your brilliance. I have real work to do."

Beguile them with my brilliance? Had I beguiled Dr. Philips?

His behavior was not an indication of beguilement—or was it?

The Army and Navy Club was housed in an elegant building on Farragut Square, just two blocks from the White House. It stood tall and proud, with a long and prestigious history dating back to 1885, or so the plaque near the front door said. Anna and I arrived with six other nurses who had the night off and were ready to enjoy a little fun. Even Helen Daly had joined us, surprising most of the nurses, who saw our superior as unapproachable.

I saw a woman in her early thirties who craved friendship as much as the rest of us.

The night was cool, but I felt warm in my long, pink evening gown with stiff shoulder pads and a V neck, the same one I'd worn to the White House a few weeks ago. Though I hadn't had a lot of time to prepare, Anna was a whiz with my hair and had twisted back the sides and secured it all in a stylish snood, similar to the one I wore in 1861.

As I entered the large officer's club, I felt attractive, especially with all the other pretty nurses at my side, laughing and chatting. We checked our coats and then caused quite a stir walking into the dark-paneled ballroom. Wall sconces offered dim light, and a beautiful mural of water nymphs near the ceiling gave a whimsical charm to the room.

A big band was playing Glenn Miller's "Blueberry Hill," and there were already couples dancing. At least two hundred people, mostly officers, were milling about, enjoying the revelry. Talk of war in Europe was always close at hand, and everyone weighed in on whether or not we should join the fray. The America First Committee, led by famed aviator Charles A. Lindbergh and actress Lillian Gish, advocated for staying out of the war, while President Roosevelt, trying to rebuild America's economy and provide jobs to those who were still clawing out of the Great Depression, was eager to get involved. It was a debate that plagued America and had for nearly two years since Hitler invaded Poland.

I knew what was coming, though as I stood in the Army and Navy Club, no one else knew, and I needed—*wanted*—to pretend it wasn't just a few months off.

"Let's find a table," Helen said to the rest of us. "That is, if we can get to one before everyone is whisked off to dance."

Already, several officers were on their way over to us. Anna was one of the first to be asked to dance. She shied away, but I nudged her forward.

"Go," I whispered in her ear. "Allow yourself to have a little fun."

She went, but she cast a desperate look over her shoulder at me.

"May I have this dance?" a lieutenant asked me, giving a slight bow at the waist.

I didn't want to dance—not yet. I wanted to ask Helen about Dr. Philips. But I didn't want to be rude either. There would be time enough for talking later.

"Alright," I said with a smile.

Soon, all of us, even Helen, were dancing. The lieutenant was a fine dancer, spinning me around the parquet floor with a grin. He didn't talk much, but he didn't need to. I smiled as I kicked up my heels. Dancing was one of my favorite activities. Whether I was dancing a waltz in 1861 or swing dancing in 1941, I could forget about almost everything else.

After "Blueberry Hill," the band played a new song, "Boogie Woogie Bugle Boy." Everyone cheered, and dance partners were shuffled around as the up-tempo song played.

I was winded and exhausted and happy when I finally returned to our table to rest my feet. It had been a long day at the hospital, and I was drained. Helen was sitting down, enjoying a soft drink, and she smiled at me.

"Tired?" she asked.

I took the seat next to her and nodded. "I wish I wasn't. I'd love to dance all night."

"I'm sure there will be many more dances in your future."

A waiter appeared at our table and offered me a soft drink. "Compliments of the lieutenant."

Looking around the room, I finally saw the first gentleman I had danced with, and he saluted me. I raised my glass and nodded my thanks in his direction.

"It seems you gather admirers wherever you go," Helen said.

"Not everywhere." I chuckled, thinking of Dr. Philips. "Surely not in the operating room."

"On the contrary," Helen replied. "I've worked with Dr. Philips for years, first on the hospital ship the USS *Relief* and then at the Naval Medical Center. And I've never known him to speak so highly of a nurse before."

I turned incredulously to her. "Speak so high—? Dr. Philips? He barely tolerates me."

She offered a soft smile, playing with her straw. "Dr. Philips is the best surgeon I've ever known, and he expects excellence from anyone who helps him. He does so with a gruff exterior, but it seems to work. It's a trial by fire. Either the nurses are fueled by his behavior and strive for perfection, or they are weeded out and move on to a different ward. You seem fueled by his personality, and though he would hate that I was telling you this, he has spoken very highly of you behind closed doors, Maggie."

"I can hardly believe it."

"Don't tell him I told you." She grinned. "Zechariah and I have worked together for seven years, and we have great respect for one another. I've watched nurses come and go, but none have impressed him as much as you."

Shaking my head, I still couldn't believe what she'd said. Was there a gentler, kinder side to Dr. Philips? One he only revealed to those he trusted, like Helen? Would he ever trust me enough to show me?

But to what end?

I had no desire to get close to Dr. Philips. My growing interest in Gray and Seth was troubling enough. Though I wasn't sure of Gray's loyalty to the Union, I could not discredit the attraction that crackled between us.

And then there was Seth. He hadn't pressured me or made me feel guilty about my chosen profession. He had charmed me and made me feel brilliant and desirable.

Dr. Philips didn't make me feel desirable. He didn't even make me feel brilliant, as I fought to prove myself to him. But he had said I was beguiling—kind of—and I did love how we challenged each other.

Each man was so different, shining light on different facets of myself.

It drew Delilah's question out of the recesses of my mind. Did any of these men bring out the true me? Or was I simply a different version of myself with each of them? And, in the end, would it matter? Was it necessary for me to analyze my paths if God would eventually show me which one I should choose anyway? My parents and grandfather assured me it would work that way, but God had given me a mind, and I couldn't imagine Him asking me not to use it when it came to something this important.

The band continued to play, and Helen and I listened, each lost in our own thoughts. Finally I asked her, "If you've known Dr. Philips for so long, do you know anything about his past?"

"Not as much as you'd think. He doesn't open up easily, and when he does, he's careful about what he shares." She sighed. "The only thing I really know is that his parents were missionaries to China when he was a child. Both his mother and father were doctors."

"Really?" I gave her more of my attention. "His mother was a doctor?"

"Remarkable, I know. From what I've gathered, Zechariah went to China with them in 1912 when he was about five years old. His father died when he was young, but instead of returning to the States, his mother continued their ministry, and Zechariah was raised in boarding schools."

"How long has he been in the military?"

"I'm not sure. I met him in 1933 on the USS *Relief*. We were both sent to the Naval Medical Center last fall to get it off the ground, but I don't know how long we'll stay—or if we'll be given orders to go together to our next assignment." She toyed with her straw again, not meeting my gaze. "We work well together."

She said it quietly, as if it was of little consequence, but I wondered if she had feelings for him. Perhaps she knew about his disease.

"When I left tonight, he was reading a book on digestive diseases, and since arriving, I've noticed he's lost weight and is pale. Do you know what he's suffering from?"

Helen frowned. "He never complains. I thought perhaps he was overworking himself."

"I don't think it's work that's ailing him." If it was celiac disease, the only cure would be to eliminate gluten from his diet, but how much advice could I give? Celiac disease wouldn't be recognized for another decade. I had already suggested he go on an elimination diet, but would that be enough for him to find the cause?

"I'll keep my eye on him," Helen promised, "and see if I can help. If you have any suggestions, I know he'll listen to you, even if he pretends otherwise." She regarded me for a moment. "If anyone can break down that tough exterior of his, I believe it might be you. His admiration and respect for you could be the gateway we've all been looking for."

I couldn't tell if she was happy about that or jealous. Nothing about Helen Daly suggested how she truly felt.

Either way, I wasn't sure I wanted to break down his defenses—because then I might have to break down some of my own.

9

The day after I attended the dance at the Army and Navy Club in 1941, I found myself walking to my parents' house on O Street, Delilah beside me. Mom had invited me to a small dinner party she was hosting at her house that evening, and I had been happy to accept. She'd extended the invitation to Delilah as well.

"Is Papa still forbidding you from helping with the soldiers?" Delilah asked as we walked under the green leaves and setting sun along O Street. Beautiful homes graced this road, but my parents' house was one of the showpieces. "Does he know you've been doing it anyway?"

I loved how Delilah called him Papa, as if she knew him personally. "Yes, he's still forbidding me, and no, he doesn't know I've been helping at the Capitol." Unless Gray had told him, but I didn't think he would.

"Papa was in the military, wasn't he?"

I frowned at Delilah's question. "Years ago, before I was born. Why?"

"I'm wondering if he'll plan to fight in the war."

Her question bothered me. I had worried about the same thing, though I hadn't voiced my concern to anyone else. "Why would he? He's a senator now."

"I just wondered. If something happened to him, would you still want to stay in 1861?"

"He's not going to die," I told her, my voice raised with fear masquerading as irritation. I forced myself to lower it. "Besides, there are other reasons to stay in 1861. I could do a lot of good during the war years, and when it's over, there will be reconstruction."

She was quiet for a moment, and then she said, in a gentle voice, "Do you ever get scared?"

"Of what?"

"Saying good-bye . . . forever?"

Her question pulled the top off the well of emotions and fear I tried to keep closed. Something akin to panic clawed at my throat, but then I was reminded of Mama and Daddy in 1941, and the feeling eased. They had taught me that I could trust God's plan for my life, even if it didn't feel like things were under control. "Every day of my life, but I take consolation in the fact that my marked parents walked a similar path and they're happy. Mama said she grieved for her loved ones in 1775 for a long time, but over the years, the grieving eased, and she can think fondly of those she lost without the bitter sadness. I hope it will be the same for me, though I dread the grief."

Delilah put her arm through mine and smiled. "You don't have to worry about losing me, since you're staying in 2001."

I smiled, though it was a sad smile. "What if I don't, Delilah? Will you be angry with me for the rest of your life?"

She shook her head, her own sadness pulling down her lips. "No. I know you have a lot to live for in your other paths. People you love and things you care about. But I can't imagine life without my best friend."

My parents' house was up ahead, and I took a deep breath to pull myself out of the melancholy that had dragged me down. Mom and Dad had no idea what I was facing, and I wasn't going to tell them. Either I'd stay in 2001 and they'd never know I was contemplating different paths, or my body would die here, and they would have no idea I'd chosen a different life than this one. It was a strange reality, but I had been trying to prepare myself for sixty years—a lifetime for some people.

In moments like this, I had to turn my prayers heavenward, hoping God was listening as I asked Him to guide my steps when I wasn't sure which way to go. When the mind He gave me couldn't comprehend the choices He set before me.

We walked up the brick steps from the public sidewalk and followed the path to the front door. My parents' house was enormous, and my mother had made many updates and alterations over the years. It was a gray-painted brick with a bright-red front door and white trim. Lush landscaping encircled the home and courtyard in back, making it almost impossible to see from the street. Inside, almost all the fabric and built-ins were a shade of white, with white walls and white trim. Dark wood tables and accents added relief to the white. It was a very elegant and impressive home, if a bit uncomfortable. Mom often met with clients at the house, and she needed it to be a showpiece.

"I used to be scared to come to your house when I was a kid," Delilah said. "I was always afraid I'd wreck something." She frowned. "Come to think of it, I'm still afraid I'm going to break something. But don't tell your mom."

I laughed as I opened the front door and entered the cool hall, greeting the housekeeper who was stationed at the door.

There were already voices filtering out from the back of the house where the kitchen, dining room, and family rooms were located.

"How many people are going to be here?" Delilah asked as we handed our jackets to the housekeeper. Delilah wore a skirt and shirt she'd made herself with a lawn of black-and-white polka dots and small orange and purple flowers scattered throughout.

"I have no idea. But my mom never disappoints." She had a vast array of friends from all walks of life and liked to intermingle them whenever possible. I had been at dinner parties that included dignitaries from around the world—as well as the little old lady who lived next door.

My heels tapped against the dark wood floor as we walked down the hallway. A delicious aroma wafted out of the kitchen, and the sound of tinkling laughter floated on the air.

At least a dozen people were mingling in the family room. Dad stood near the gas fireplace, which was lit, speaking to two men with turbans. Mom was near the French doors, which led out into the beautiful courtyard, speaking to a man and woman I'd never met before.

But it was Seth Wallace, sitting on the sofa with a woman from church, who caught my attention and made me pause.

"What is it?" Delilah whispered next to me.

"Seth."

"Where?" Her voice held an excitement I hadn't yet mustered. "Oh, there. What's wrong?"

"He asked me out again, but I told him I wasn't ready to get involved right now—at least, not until January."

"So? Having dinner at your parents' house isn't 'getting involved.'" She made air quotes with her fingers. "It's a nice surprise, if you ask me."

"I wonder if it was my mom or dad's idea. Mom's been trying to hook me up with someone for months now."

"They just want you to be happy."

"I am happy."

"You know what I mean."

Mom noticed us, and her face lit up. She excused herself from the couple she was speaking to and made her way over.

She was as elegant and well-presented as her home. Her short brown hair was perfectly styled, her slacks had a defined crease, and her blouse was flowing and simple.

"There you two are." She hugged Delilah and then gave me a kiss on the cheek. "I made your favorite pasta dish tonight."

"Baked manicotti?" My mouth started to water.

"Turns out it's Seth's favorite, too. Can you imagine that? You two have so much in common."

"Mom." I gave her a warning glance. "I already told him I'm not interested in dating right now."

"Oh, pishposh. There's never a right time for anything in your life. You're going to have to learn that life keeps moving, whether you're ready for it or not."

A sentiment that rang all too clear.

"Are you trying to set us up?" I asked quietly, hoping she wasn't.

"Your dad put him on the list." She shrugged one shoulder. "Apparently, there's been a bit of trouble between the Navy Department and the congressional Committee of Military Construction. Since Seth's the newest member and young and impressionable, Dad thought it would be smart to befriend him. Just a little politics."

"I hope that's all it is."

She laughed, revealing her dimples, and gently pushed me toward the family room. "Come say hi. He won't bite."

"If you won't say hi," Delilah said to me, "I will."

"You can come with me." Mom linked arms with Delilah, steering her away from Seth. "I want to show you the cool gift the Ambassador of Bulgaria gave me last week."

Seth glanced up as Mom and Delilah passed him, and he must have remembered who Delilah was because he instantly looked toward the door to see if I had arrived, too. When he saw me, he quickly excused himself from the lady sitting with him and approached me with his blinding smile.

Oy, he was cute.

"Hello, Meg," he said.

"Hi." I was thankful Delilah had talked me into wearing my yellow dress with the black bow-tie belt and not the slacks and blouse I'd been wearing at the hospital that day. I felt a bit more like a twenty-year-old college student than a tired, overworked med student.

"You look beautiful," he said, his eyes sparkling with appreciation.

"Thanks." He looked good, too, wearing a blue pinstripe suit and tie.

"How have you been?"

"Good. Busy." I didn't want this to be awkward, especially because our day together had been so effortless. "I'm surprised to see you here."

"I couldn't pass up this invitation if it meant there was a chance I might see you again."

My neck warmed at his comment. "I forgot how charming you are."

He shrugged. "It's easy when it comes to you."

"Ha." I shook my head. "I think it comes easily to you, regardless."

"No." He shook his head, serious. "Not like when I'm with you."

I looked down at the plush rug, the heat rising from my neck to my cheeks.

"I thought about you a lot these past couple of weeks. I know you said I have to wait until January, but I was invited to the Ford's Theatre Gala next month, and knowing how much you like history, I thought you might enjoy attending with me." He spoke quickly—more like a young, untried schoolboy than a representative in Congress. "It's for a good cause, and it won't be a date. I promise. Just two people who want to support DC's history and performing arts having a lot of fun together."

"I do love Ford's Theatre."

"I thought so. And it's not until June eleventh, so you'd have a lot of time away from me before then."

Laughing, I shook my head. "I don't want to be away from you."

His eyes lit up with hope.

"What I mean," I said quickly, "is that I just don't have the time to date seriously right now."

"I know." He grinned, apparently loving that he made me blush. "Will you come?"

Nibbling my bottom lip, I thought about all the reasons I shouldn't. Nothing had changed. If anything, I was closer to January and my decision. Seth complicated that decision. But I remembered what my mom had said. If he was on the Committee of Military Construction, might he be able to help my dad with funding? If I went with him to the Ford's Theatre Gala, could I find an opportunity to put in a plug for Dad's project?

"I'd be happy to go with you," I said. "As long as it's *not* a date."

He grinned. "It will be whatever you want it to be."

The way he smiled told me I would have to remind him that it wasn't a date several times before the evening was done.

A couple of hours later, Delilah and I arrived home, and I went to my room to change into a pair of pajamas and do a little studying. I had an early morning at the hospital the next day, and I needed to get some research done for a paper.

But after thirty minutes, I realized I wasn't able to focus. It was rare when I couldn't get lost in my work. I leaned back in my chair as I stared at the computer screen. I should have been reading the online article, but my mind was in a dozen different places—and almost all of them had Seth at the center.

The last thing I wanted was regret—for any reason—but I knew that in January, I would have a lot of things to mourn. I wanted to pursue my feelings for Seth, but I had made a promise to myself. Was it a mistake to go to the Ford's Theatre Gala?

Perhaps I should throw all caution to the wind and see where my feelings took me. Maybe it would make my decision easier. Then again, maybe it wouldn't.

I leaned forward and put my chin into my hands, staring at the screen. It was an article about anaphylactic shock and emergency allergic reaction protocol. It made me think of Dr. Philips and my suspicion of celiac disease. The shift in my thoughts was a welcome reprieve from Seth. Was Dr. Philips suffering from something so easy to treat? It was a shame that I knew a way to help him and couldn't.

For the first time in my life, I was tempted to look for an answer from the past. I never looked for history. If God revealed something to me through natural means, that was one thing. But to search for an answer seemed dangerous, even reckless.

Either way, there was nothing I could do to help Dr. Philips. My hands were tied. What would it matter if I knew the truth?

I pulled up a web browser and typed in *Captain Dr. Zechariah Philips* and pressed enter.

Several links appeared, some with nothing to do with Dr. Philips, and others just lists of doctors who served during WWII. Finally, I came to a biography from his alma mater, Yale School of Medicine. With a deep breath, I clicked the link. The article had been written in the 1990s and listed several Yale doctors who had served during WWII.

My heart fell at the first line.

Capt. Dr. Zechariah Philips, class of 1930, died on March 13, 1950, of an unknown digestive disease, though modern speculation suggests he suffered from celiac disease.

I immediately closed the browser without reading anything else and stared blankly at the screen.

Dr. Philips would die within nine years from a preventable cause—one that would be linked to gluten just two years later in 1952. It was not only a shame, it was a travesty. He was a brilliant surgeon and could save countless more lives if his own wasn't cut so short.

Anger started to build within me—not only at Dr. Philips's fate, but at everything.

I pushed away from my desk and walked over to the window to look outside. I hadn't spent much time talking to God lately, and I suddenly realized why. I was angry at Him. Angry that He would make me choose between three equally remarkable lives. Angry that He chose for me to be born this way. Frustrated and scared that if I had a child one day, he or she might be forced to make the same choices. What kind of an existence was this? As a healer, it was especially heart-wrenching to know how to heal someone but not be able to give them what they needed. Just like Grandfather Hollingsworth.

I hated this—hated it with a burning anger that had been building for a long time.

"Why?" I asked God, looking up at the ceiling, wanting Him to answer me. "I don't understand any of this. You have given me a heart to heal, yet You tie my hands. You have given me three amazing lives, yet You tell me I must give up two of them. You bring wonderful men into my life, yet I cannot follow my heart." I shook my head as tears came to my eyes. "And worse, You remain silent when I need you the most."

I sat down on my bed and put my face in my hands. Mama told me that God had a plan, but I didn't see one. All I saw was a lot of confusion and heartache and disappointment. I knew all the reasons I was blessed, but it didn't ease the pain or anger. It seemed to increase it.

With tears flowing down my cheeks, I climbed under the

covers. I had so much to do, but I couldn't focus anymore. I was exhausted in body, soul, and spirit, and I just wanted to sleep.

I doubted that God was going to answer me anytime soon. For whatever reason, He was keeping silent, leaving me mired in doubt and confusion.

10

MAY 24, 1861
WASHINGTON, DC

Almost a month had passed since the 7th New York Regiment had arrived in Washington, and now the city, which housed sixty thousand citizens before the war started, was teeming with twenty thousand volunteer soldiers. New camps popped up every day, and the sound of drumming could be heard almost constantly. Soldiers clogged the streets, the parks, and the public buildings. They bivouacked in the White House, the Capitol, Georgetown College, Columbia College, the Washington Arsenal, churches, and dozens of other buildings the government rented for their use. In addition, the army had set up bakeries in the Capitol basement. Twenty ovens were installed, producing fifty-eight thousand loaves of bread a day.

And now, just days after Virginia's official vote to secede from the Union, troops were moving across the Long Bridge and the Chain Bridge from Washington to overtake Alexandria County, Virginia, and Arlington House, the home of Robert E. Lee, the Confederate General.

Though the war was imminent and there was so much to

do, I still had to go on with my social life as usual, at Papa's request. Luncheons, balls, and soirees. Entertaining and being entertained. There was a part of Washington society that still pretended nothing had changed, though to their credit, they turned many of their events into fundraisers. But not all the events I attended were used for the Union's cause. Some were simply to socialize.

Regardless, at all of them, I petitioned for supplies and watched for spies. So far, I hadn't been able to identify a single spy, though I had my suspicions.

Today I was invited to a luncheon at the home of Rose Green-how. We met Rose and her late husband when they lived in San Francisco in the early 1850s, her husband having been sent there by the State Department. She returned to Washington almost ten years ago after he died.

It took me less than two minutes to walk to Rose's house that afternoon. Spring was in full bloom on Lafayette Square, with summer-like temperatures, the smell of blossoming flowers, and the sound of birds twittering in the trees. The sun was bright as I walked up the front steps and onto the porch of Rose's home. Her butler answered my knock and welcomed me into the foyer. The house wasn't large, but it was decorated well—though the furnishings were showing their age. The carpet was thin and worn, and the draperies looked bleached by the sun. It was a surprise that Rose had not remarried for financial security, though she never seemed to be alone or desperate.

"Margaret," Rose said the moment she saw me. Her parlor was full of people, both men and women, standing with beverages in hand. They were laughing and talking as if a war wasn't looming beyond the front door. I immediately saw abolitionist Senator Henry Wilson from Massachusetts, as well as a gentleman from the State Department, one from the Department of the Treasury, and one from the War Department. It was rumored that Rose dallied with several of them, even though all were married. I had my doubts, though, and assumed none of the rumors were true.

"Good afternoon," I said. "Thank you for inviting me today."

"What are old friends for?" She smiled. "I believe there are several people here you know, my dear."

I was surprised to see one familiar face. He met my gaze at the same moment.

"Mr. Cooper," Rose called, motioning for him to join us.

"I hadn't realized you and Mr. Cooper were so well acquainted," I told Rose, feeling at a loss. Hadn't they just met at Kate Chase's ball a month ago?

"We got along so well at the Chases' home, I knew I needed to include him in my inner circle." She touched my arm and leaned toward me. "Isn't he exquisite? I intend to make him my conquest."

Her words shocked me, though they shouldn't have, given the rumors I'd heard. Perhaps they *were* all true.

"It's nice to see you again, Miss Wakefield," Gray said as he arrived at our side and offered me a bow.

"I'll leave you two to visit." Rose winked at me. "Don't keep Mr. Cooper all to yourself, though. I intend to have him at my side during luncheon." She brushed Gray's arm with her hand before she walked away.

It rankled me—for more than one reason.

Gray smiled at Rose's retreating form, clearly taken with her, and my stomach fell. Was he already one of Rose's conquests? Had I been a fool to think his attention toward me was special?

The room felt overly warm, and I no longer wanted to be there. I had started to think of excuses I could make to leave when Gray asked, "How goes your work with Miss Barton?"

I didn't want Gray to see my disappointment in his relationship with Rose. If the connection I felt with him wasn't special, then I would look the fool. And there was still the matter of his allegiance to the Union. I had not put my suspicions to rest.

113

"It hasn't been easy," I answered, lifting my chin. "Each time I think we have enough supplies to meet the needs, another regiment arrives, and we are woefully unprepared."

He held a glass of punch, though he didn't seem interested in drinking it. "Miss Barton is bringing supplies out to the new camps at Arlington this very afternoon."

"You've spoken to her?"

"She has returned to the War Department several times, and although I cannot get the government to help her, they cannot dictate what I do in my free time. I volunteered to meet her at her boardinghouse today at four and help her bring supplies to Arlington."

"I did too," I said quickly. Though it wasn't true, I would make it true. If Papa knew I was going to a military camp, he would have a fit, but if Clara could go, why couldn't I? Clara would appreciate the company—wouldn't she? And it would give me more time to interrogate Gray.

A new arrival entered the parlor. We looked up to see one of the doormen from the White House. He locked gazes with Gray and strode to his side, breathing heavily.

"What's wrong?" Gray asked, his entire body going rigid.

"Colonel Ellsworth has been killed."

"Killed? When? Where?"

My heart felt like it stopped. Colonel Ellsworth had been so young and so full of life and promise. He'd come to Washington with the Lincolns and had been like a surrogate son to them. This would devastate the Lincolns—the entire Union army.

The others in the room had stopped their conversations to listen. No one said a word as we waited for the doorman to continue.

"He led seven soldiers from his regiment into the Marshall House Inn while taking over Alexandria today," the doorman said. "The inn's owner, Mr. Jackson, had been flying a Confederate flag from the roof. Mr. Lincoln could see it with field glasses from the White House, and Colonel Ellsworth wanted the honor of removing it for his president." The doorman stopped to swallow hard. "After Ellsworth cut it free, he was leading his men back down the stairs when Mr. Jackson stepped out of a dark passage and leveled a shotgun at Colonel Ellsworth's chest. The colonel died instantly, and one of his men, Private Brownell, returned fire on Mr. Jackson, killing him. The colonel is the first officer to die for the Union's cause."

The room remained quiet as the guests absorbed the news.

"I must go," Gray said, turning to me. "Please excuse me." He sought out Rose and made his apologies and then left the house with the doorman.

Several of the men also excused themselves, leaving the party in a somber mood.

"Well," Rose said, letting out a deep breath. "How inconvenient that Colonel Ellsworth has ruined my party." Her forced laughter felt strange and out of place. "I suppose there will be plenty of food to go around now."

Papa would be shocked by the news and would want to console Mr. and Mrs. Lincoln. I wanted to join him to pay my respects.

"I'm afraid I must leave, as well," I said to Rose. "Thank you for your hospitality."

"What a disappointment this day has turned into." Rose sighed. "If you must go, you must go."

"I think I should. Good-bye." I nodded at her and a few others, then lifted the hem of my skirt to make my way across Lafayette Square.

It would be somber at the White House.

The day had worn on in a dark cloud of grief. After leaving the White House, where I stood by awkwardly as Mrs. Lincoln wept over the death of her dear Colonel Ellsworth, I had returned home to change.

Gray had said that Clara was planning to leave her boardinghouse at four that afternoon to drive the supplies over the Long Bridge to Arlington House. She had been storing and distributing the supplies from her personal living quarters and often borrowed a horse and wagon from a friend to transport the cargo. I wanted to be early so I could make it look like I had planned to go all along—that was, if Gray was still planning to go.

It occurred to me that he was probably needed at the War Department after Colonel Ellsworth's death. I tried to ignore my disappointment and focus on helping Clara.

Joseph drove me to Clara's boardinghouse. I had brought food and medical supplies in case anyone needed assistance, and Joseph helped me load them into the waiting wagon. The fighting had not yet begun, but where there were men, there were usually illnesses, accidents, and fisticuffs.

When we were done, I said to Joseph, "I will stay with Miss Barton this afternoon, so you may go home."

He stared at me, his dark brown eyes filled with uncertainty.

"And please do not tell Papa where I am."

"What if he comes home early?"

"He will work late tonight, but if he does come home, tell him I'm with a friend and not to expect me for supper."

I could tell Joseph didn't like the secrecy—I would not admit it was lying—but I told myself I was doing this *for* Papa. I was helping the Union.

"Margaret," Clara said as she stepped out of her boardinghouse, placing a hat upon her head. "This is a pleasant surprise."

I motioned to Joseph that he could leave, noticing him frown at Clara's greeting.

"I hope you won't mind a little company. I've come to help you bring the supplies to Arlington."

"Oh dear." Clara pushed a hatpin into place. "I'm so sorry to tell you this, but I've been called to a meeting of the Ladies' Aid Society. They want me to speak to them about the work we've been doing. They could be helpful in gathering more supplies. It was a last-minute invitation, but I don't want to pass it up."

"You won't be going to Arlington?"

Clara shook her head, obviously in a hurry as she pulled on her gloves. "No, but—"

The door to the boardinghouse opened again, and Clara's smiling landlady held it as Gray exited, carrying a wooden crate full of items wrapped in dishcloths—bread, most likely.

My heart leapt at his unexpected appearance.

"Mr. Cooper has volunteered to take the supplies, since Captain Gains is expecting them," Clara continued. "You could go with him, if you'd like."

In 2001 or 1941, I could get away with being alone with Gray. But in 1861, Papa wouldn't like it—if he found out.

"I wish I had known you were coming," Clara said, and I cringed when Gray looked at me. "I would have asked to speak to the ladies' aid meeting another time."

"It was a last-minute decision," I said quickly, not meeting Gray's gaze.

"I'm happy Mr. Cooper will not be going out alone." Clara smiled. "You can leave the horse and wagon at the livery down the street, and I'll see that they're both returned to my friend. Now, I really must be off." She waved as she hurried away to her meeting.

When she was gone and the landlady was back inside, Gray crossed his arms over the side of the wagon, a knowing grin in place. "Why did you lie to me about your plans to come today?"

I turned from him, making myself busy with the supplies,

checking the ropes that held all the boxes in place. What could I possibly tell him that wouldn't embarrass me?

When I didn't answer, he came around to my side of the wagon and grasped the rope I was testing. His gloved hand brushed against mine, but I still refused to look at him.

"If you wished to spend the afternoon with me, you didn't need to lie." His voice was so close to my ear, it sent a delicious shiver down my back. "After all, I thought we were friends."

I inhaled but couldn't think of a response. He completely unraveled me.

"Are you ready?" I asked, giving the rope one more tug. "Everything looks secure."

He chuckled and offered me his hand to get into the wagon. I took it, trying not to be aware of his touch. I lifted the hem of my skirt to climb aboard as he rubbed his thumb over the top of my hand.

The sensation surprised me, even through our gloves, and I turned to look at him.

He winked.

I scowled. "You're incorrigible."

With another self-satisfied grin, Gray let go of my hand, walked around the horses, and climbed up on the other side.

Suddenly, the next few hours spread out before me with great anticipation.

He slapped the reins against the back of the horses, and the wagon creaked as we pulled into the muddy street.

"I wasn't sure you'd come," I said, growing serious, "after hearing of Colonel Ellsworth's death."

"It's a devastating blow, but there's little I can do." He sat next to me on the tight seat, his leg pushing against my skirts. "I wanted to keep my word to Miss Barton."

"I'm happy you did." The words slipped out before I could hold them back.

He smiled and looked out at the street. "So am I."

We drove in silence as he maneuvered through Washington, eventually coming to the Long Bridge. Dozens of wagons were moving across, bringing supplies and soldiers to the newly occupied Alexandria County. A sentry asked us our business and looked through the wagon before letting us pass. Several other wagons had pulled up behind us as we waited.

The Long Bridge was almost a mile long and spanned the Potomac River, connecting Washington to Arlington, Virginia. I had never been on it and was impressed with its length and stability. The sound of creaking wagon wheels and shouting drivers filled the air.

I couldn't help but feel depressed watching these men prepare for war. I knew what was coming, what they would all face. And though I also knew it was necessary, it would be devastating.

"Don't you think we'll win this thing?" Gray asked.

I glanced at him, surprised. "Why would you ask me that?"

"The look on your face is one of defeat."

"It's not defeat but sadness. I can't help but think of everything we will sacrifice before this is done."

"You don't believe this will be over in a few months? That we'll win without trouble?"

"I hope it will be over soon." I did hope for that, though I knew it wasn't to be. "I think many of these men underestimate the South. Take, for example, Robert E. Lee. He sacrificed his home and property to serve in the Confederacy. If he—and others like him—are willing to sacrifice everything and walk away from life as they know it, then what makes us think they will give up the fight at the first skirmish?"

"I agree," he said quietly. "Passions have been running high for a long, long time and will not be settled easily. But we must hold on to the hope that God has given us, or we will be unable to bear up under this weight."

We were soon over the Long Bridge, approaching the newly acquired Arlington plantation. Overnight, an encampment had been set up, with the beautiful mansion, built by George Washington's step-grandson, on the rise of the hill overlooking Washington, DC. It was a necessary gain, though it made me sad for the Lee family and everyone else who would lose so much in this war—though the ultimate gain of freedom for enslaved men, women, and children was worth the sacrifice. Having lived in this path, I knew there was no other way.

Gray drove the wagon to Arlington House, where Captain Gains was expecting us. Countless soldiers milled about the thousand-acre plantation, cutting down trees, pitching tents, tending fires, butchering animals, and moving in supplies. It was a mind-boggling feat.

An officer in a blue uniform stood on the wide portico giving orders when we pulled up to the white Greek Revival mansion. A half-dozen pillars held up the portico roof. It was a magnificent home, one I was sure Mrs. Lee was mourning at that very moment.

"Miss Barton?" asked the officer on the portico.

"I'm Miss—" I almost said Wakefield, but I couldn't risk my father hearing about my visit here today. "I'm Miss Barton's friend," I said instead. "She was called away and could not come."

"Do you have medical supplies? I have a severely injured man in the house. Could you help?"

Gray had jumped out of the wagon, and he offered me his hand as I stepped down. "I would be happy to," I told the man, who I assumed was Captain Gains. I knew right where Joseph had put the medical supplies, so I pointed at the crate. "Would you haul this one inside?" I asked Gray, my instincts taking over. I was already on my way into the mansion to assess the situation.

The front hall was impressive, but I hadn't come to gawk at the home.

"Where is the soldier?" I asked Captain Gains.

"In here." He motioned to a room to my right. It was a small, comfortable parlor. A soldier lay on an ornate sofa, moaning.

"What happened?" I asked, taking off my gloves and hat. I wore the outfit I'd been donning for this work—a simple, plain blouse and a black skirt with only a few petticoats for propriety's sake.

"He was chopping firewood," Captain Gains said. "Missed and put the ax into his foot. I tried finding the surgeon, but no one knows where he is."

I had seen an ax wound in the ER before and knew how gruesome it could be. Here in 1861, without antibiotics or proper antiseptics, it was likely the soldier would lose his foot.

Though I would try not to let that happen.

Blood was soaking into the cushions of the sofa as I knelt by the soldier's side. "I'm—" I paused again. "I'm Maggie, and I have some nursing experience and would like to help you, if I may."

The man moaned, his eyes closed.

"What's your name?" I asked.

"Private Federgill," he said as he winced. "Will I lose my foot?"

"I'll try hard to ensure you keep it." I looked up at Gray, who was holding the medical supplies, watching. I motioned for him to set the crate beside me and pulled out a bottle of whiskey. Placing it against Private Federgill's lips, I instructed him to take a long drink, and then I set the bottle down and moved to his foot.

The ax had landed between his first and second toe. Thankfully, it hadn't gone far, though it had still done some damage. I found shears and cut off his stocking, then held a cloth under his foot while pouring whiskey directly onto the wound.

Private Federgill moaned even louder.

"Can someone please give him morphine?" I asked as I continued to work on his foot. "It's in the crate."

Slowly, I poured more whiskey onto his foot, cleaning it off with the cloth as someone did as I asked.

There wasn't much I could do without a proper operating room, but I made it work. Within thirty minutes, I had the wound stitched and bandaged. Private Federgill had passed out, which was for the best. I hated working on a patient without anesthesia, but there was nothing to be done about it.

I cleaned up the mess and put all the supplies back into the crate, then stood and faced Captain Gains. "He'll need to stay off his foot for two to four weeks. Have him change the bandage every day, pouring whiskey on the wound three to four times a day for the first week to try to prevent infection. If it starts to look infected or develops a rotten stench, please send for me by contacting Miss Barton, and I'll come immediately."

Captain Gains stared at me, slowly nodding at my instructions, a bit of awe and confusion on his face. I smiled at him and took up another cloth. I needed to find some water to clean my hands.

Gray stood near the door, his brow furrowed into a deep V. His gaze was almost accusatory, as if I had done something wrong.

It was the last thing I wanted to see. I didn't want him to be upset that I was a capable woman—doing something very few other women were doing in 1861.

Trying to hide my disappointment in his reaction, I moved around him and left the parlor in search of water.

He followed me. "What was that?"

I ignored him, walking through the foyer and into a back hall that led outside. Surely there was a pump or well in the yard.

"Maggie," he said. "What was that?"

"I stitched up a wound. It's not much different from sewing a garment." I cringed saying it. There was a vast difference.

"No." He put his hand on my arm to stop me. "Your competence back there indicates you've done that before—many times."

"I helped Miss Barton when the soldiers came in from Baltimore. It's not that difficult, if you can stomach it."

"You're telling me that you gained enough experience helping injured soldiers a mere five weeks ago to perform surgery on that mangled foot? And to do it like an experienced surgeon, with complete confidence and control? Your hands didn't shake, you didn't break a sweat, and you were so focused, you didn't even notice when the room filled up with soldiers watching you."

I glanced back the way we'd come. *Had* the room been full of soldiers? "It isn't that hard."

His brown eyes were filled with incredulity. "I disagree."

My throat was suddenly dry, and my voice didn't feel like it was working properly. I had no way to explain myself, and I had a feeling he wouldn't let this go until he understood what had just happened. "I've always had a knack for healing," I told him, trying to sound innocent. "Something just takes over me, and I don't think—I use my instincts."

It was partially true, and it seemed to ease his disbelief. Just a bit.

"I need to wash my hands," I said. "Please excuse me."

"I can't leave you alone here." He looked around the hall where soldiers were coming and going. "It isn't safe."

I was alone all the time in 2001 and seemed to do just fine. But I wouldn't disagree with him, so he accompanied me to the summer kitchen, where we found fresh water.

As I washed my hands at the pump, I glanced at him and saw that his gaze was still full of unanswered questions—but something more, something even deeper. Perhaps he hadn't been looking at me with accusation after all.

"That was incredible," he said quietly in a sort of hushed wonder. "No matter how you knew what to do, it was amazing."

His praise meant more to me than it should.

11

JUNE 3, 1941
BETHESDA, MARYLAND

Rain slashed against the windows in the cafeteria where I ate spaghetti and garlic bread for lunch. With me were Anna and a couple of other nurses we had befriended since arriving at the Naval Medical Center six weeks before.

"My favorites will always be the Andy Hardy movies with Mickey Rooney," Anna said with a sigh. "I saw *Andy Hardy's Private Secretary* three times when it released in February, and I plan to see *Life Begins for Andy Hardy* in August when it comes out."

"You would choose Mickey Rooney over Clark Gable?" Betty LeGrow lifted an eyebrow at Anna. "Or Humphrey Bogart?"

Anna's green eyes shone in a way they rarely did anymore, and she nodded. "Don't you think Mickey Rooney's cute?"

"Not Clark Gable or Humphrey Bogart cute," Betty said.

I smiled as their conversation continued. Movies were a fun pastime, but I didn't love them like Anna loved them. I knew enough about the actors and actresses to have a decent conversation, but that was all. In 1861, there were no films, and in

2001, I rarely took the time to go to a movie theater or watch television. Once in a while, Delilah could talk me into watching an old film on the Turner Classic Movies channel or seeing a blockbuster like *Titanic* or *Jurassic Park*. But for the most part, my movie-watching happened with Anna in 1941.

Twirling the spaghetti on my fork, I lifted it slowly to keep the noodles in place and tucked it into my mouth.

"Nurse Hollingsworth?" Dr. Philips's voice almost made me choke as I spun to look behind me.

He stood in the doorway, wearing his white operating uniform with a white cap over his dark hair. His blue-eyed gaze slid across the table of ladies before he turned his full attention back to me.

It took me a second to swallow my food. He had never come looking for me before, so I quickly wiped my mouth. The other nurses gave me a quizzical look as I excused myself to see what brought Dr. Philips down to the cafeteria to find me.

"I'm sorry to bother you on your lunch break," he said, "but I would like to speak to you in private."

For reasons I couldn't identify, my heart began to pound a little harder. "Of course."

He walked out of the cafeteria and stopped in the hallway. Lifting his chin, he said, "I have a patient who is presenting with an unusual set of symptoms, and I'd like a second opinion."

"From me?" I could hardly believe it.

"Do you not think you're qualified to give an opinion?"

"No—I mean, yes, I think I could at least examine the patient and see if I'm familiar with his symptoms."

"Are you able to come now?"

I had lost count of how many meals had been interrupted by my work. One more meal meant nothing. "Yes. Give me a moment, please."

Anna and the others were still watching for me when I reentered the cafeteria to pick up my lunch tray. "I'll see you back in the dorm," I said to my sister. "Dr. Philips would like me to examine one of his patients."

A series of knowing and teasing grins lifted the red lips of the other ladies, and Anna said with a sly smile, "One of his patients—or himself?"

I would have rolled my eyes at her comment if it hadn't made me hopeful. She rarely teased me since Richard's death, though she used to be happy and carefree. "I don't think Dr. Philips is capable of flirting or romance, so you have nothing to worry about."

"The famous last words of Maggie Hollingsworth," Betty said with a chuckle.

I shook my head and brought my tray to the scraping station before rejoining Dr. Philips in the hall.

He was standing where I'd left him, his arms crossed. He wasn't scowling, per se, but he wasn't smiling either. I had never seen him smile.

"I'm ready," I told him.

With a quick nod, he led the way to the elevator.

Neither of us spoke as he pressed the button for the third floor and the doors closed. I noticed his hands were no longer covered in dermatitis, and there was a bit of color in his cheeks today.

I usually didn't mind silence, but with him, it felt deafening. Besides, there was so much to say. "Has your patient found any relief from the issues we discussed last month? On the evening you were looking at digestive diseases?"

"The night you went to the Army and Navy Club dance?"

I glanced at him and saw that he was staring straight ahead. "Yes. That evening."

"He actually has found some relief," Dr. Philips said. "It appears that your suggestion to try an elimination diet has helped. He's been subsisting on mostly bananas, rice, and water and has been feeling a lot better. He will start adding other foods back into his diet, one by one, and keep a detailed journal of his symptoms to track his progress."

It took all my self-control not to smile, forcing me to bite my upper lip for a moment. "I'm happy to hear that." I wanted to check the internet in 2001 to see if his biography had changed, but I couldn't. I didn't want to risk changing anything else.

But it puzzled me. If my suggestion *had* changed his prognosis, did that mean he wouldn't die in 1950? And if he didn't die in 1950, did that mean I had changed history? Everything Mama had told me suggested that if I knowingly changed history, I would forfeit this path . . . yet I was still here.

What did that mean?

I tried to think through the series of events that had occurred. When I suggested to Dr. Philips that he try an elimination diet, I hadn't known yet about his death in 1950. I had assumed he had celiac disease, but I didn't know for sure. Was that the difference? I hadn't *knowingly* changed history?

A sense of freedom stole over me. Did that mean I could treat patients in 1861 and 1941 with knowledge I had obtained in 2001 if I didn't *knowingly* change their history? I wasn't about to challenge the theory, but it gave me a lot to think about.

Dr. Philips looked at me as the elevator moved up to the third floor. "Do you have any other suggestions for my patient?"

Quiet calm settled over me, and I decided I wasn't going to pretend with Dr. Philips anymore. He was starting to view me as his equal—at least, that was what it felt like. He was turning to me for my knowledge and advice. Perhaps it was time I treated him as my equal, as well.

"When will you admit to me that you're the patient?"

He studied me, and I could see another piece of his self-defense slip away. "Why does it matter?"

"I want you to trust me."

A question tilted his brow. "Why?"

"So we can be friends."

The elevator stopped on the third floor with a ding, and the doors opened.

Dr. Philips indicated that I should precede him out of the elevator. "This way," he said, motioning me down the hallway.

The smell of floor polish and cleaning products burned my nose as we walked through the maze of linoleum. Several moments passed, and I was convinced he was going to ignore my comment, but then he said, "I don't think it's a good idea for us to be friends."

"Why?" It was my turn to ask this simple question.

Dr. Philips stopped and turned to me. "I don't have friends, Nurse Hollingsworth—especially female friends who are . . . are—"

"Beguiling?" The word slipped out, and I instantly wanted to take it back. My cheeks warmed.

He stared at me, and I wondered if I had embarrassed him. But slowly, ever so slowly, a smile tilted his lips, transforming his entire demeanor.

He was handsome.

"Beguiling?" he repeated.

I wanted the floor to swallow me, but instead I tilted my head and smiled, forcing myself not to feel awkward. "Isn't that what you said? That I should go to the dance and let the others be beguiled by my brilliance?"

"You remember that?"

"It isn't every day that someone suggests I'm beguiling."

He finally looked away, seeming to pull himself back together, and when he returned his gaze to me, he'd hidden his smile away. "I was going to say that I don't have female friends, especially ones who are so headstrong and exasperating."

"I'm exasperating?"

"It's difficult to keep up with you."

"What does that mean?"

He tore off his surgical hat and ran his hand through his hair.

"You're constantly one step ahead of me, and it's exasperating. I'm usually the one in full command of my operating room, and now many of the nurses and orderlies look to you."

I crossed my arms. "I cannot help what I know. Besides, that's not a good reason to keep me at a distance."

The look on his face shifted again, and this time, his gaze slipped to my lips before coming up to meet my eyes with an intensity that I felt all the way to my toes.

"Believe me," he said, his voice a bit gruff, "there are many good reasons to keep you at a distance, Nurse Hollingsworth."

With that, he turned and strode down the hall.

I had to race to catch up to him—trying to catch my breath.

It was an hour before I was able to return to my dorm room. Anna was lying on her bed, looking through a *Life* magazine with a picture of an army nurse on the cover. On her record player, Frank Sinatra was crooning, "Oh! Look at me now."

As soon as I entered our room and closed the door, she sat up and set aside her magazine. "Well?"

"Well, what?" I took off my nursing cap and set it on my desk.

"You know what. Why did Dr. Philips ask for you?"

I sat on my bed and slipped off my heels before unclipping my silk stockings from my garter belt. Slowly, I began rolling them off my legs. "He had a patient presenting with symptoms he had never seen before and wanted my opinion."

Anna turned so her feet were hanging over the side of her bed. "He could have asked for any other nurse to assist him. Why you?"

I shrugged, though I knew the answer.

"Maggie?"

Sighing, I set the stockings next to me on the bed and wiggled my bare toes. "I've been giving him advice, and he's been impressed with my knowledge."

"What kind of advice?"

"Medical advice."

She frowned. "You mean, from the future?"

"Not necessarily—though, sometimes it's knowledge that isn't readily available yet."

Anna stared at me, something akin to panic settling in her features. "You know what Mama and Daddy told you—you're not supposed to change history, Maggie."

My defenses rose. "I'm not *knowingly* changing history, Anna. I don't *know* the outcome of a person's health—whether they'll live or die or what will kill them. I can speculate, but that doesn't mean I know for certain."

"Why even take the chance?"

"I'm not doing it on purpose. Sometimes I can't help it. Like with Dr. Philips. I suspect he has a condition called celiac disease, which means his body does not properly digest a protein found in some grains. But without proper diagnostics, it's only a guess. So when I suggested he do an elimination diet, I wasn't knowingly changing the future. It appears he took my advice and has eliminated everything but bananas and rice from his diet. As he adds foods back in, he'll hopefully realize which ones cause his symptoms."

"You're doing this with other patients?"

"Not all of them. And it's something I just realized I could do today."

"What about Grandfather? Did you tell him what he needs to do for his problems?"

I studied my sister, watching her face to read her emotions. "I'd rather not talk about Grandfather."

"Why?" She frowned, sitting up straighter. "Because I'm too delicate? Too fragile? I'm not a child, Maggie. And I'd appreciate if you stopped treating me like one."

My mouth slipped open. "I'm not treating you like a child—you've been through a traumatic experience. I don't want you to worry about things that you don't need to."

"It's not your job to shelter me. I'm more capable than you realize, and when you treat me like a child, you're telling me that I'm not."

"That's not—"

"I know you want to make things better, but sometimes you can't fix people or situations. And you, of all people, should know that it can be dangerous to try. You're not God, Maggie."

Her words hit me like a blow to the gut. Had I been acting like God? Trying to control and change things that weren't mine to control and change? I didn't want to admit that her words offended me, especially because I had sacrificed so much to help her.

"I'm not trying to play God," I told her, my voice unsteady. "I'm just trying to do the best I can with the tools I've been given. I didn't ask to be born this way, and frankly, it's more than I can handle sometimes." Tears pricked my eyes, and I wiped at them with anger. "You have no idea what it's like, Anna—to know things about the future that I can't tell a living soul, not even Mama and Daddy. My hands are tied in so many ways. So when there is something I *can* do, I want to do it."

Anna was quiet as she looked down at her hands. "I know it's not easy for you," she said, "but please don't treat me like I'm incompetent. I'm trying so hard to be strong again."

I went to her and put my arm around her. "The last thing I want to do is fight with you."

"Because I can't handle it?" She gave me a saucy look, making me smile.

We were both quiet for a moment, and then she said, "Are you falling in love?"

Was I falling in love? And if so, who was I falling for? I immediately thought of Gray when we were at Arlington House, of the way he had admired me after I treated the soldier, and the way he made me feel like the only woman in the world when we were together. We had chemistry and attraction, but was it love?

And what about Seth? I couldn't stop thinking about the Ford's Theatre Gala, which was quickly approaching. It had been weeks since I'd seen him at my parents' house, and I was counting down the days until I saw him again. Was that love brewing?

Or what about Dr. Philips? Just thinking about the way he had looked at my lips, or the way he had smiled at me . . . I had to close my eyes for a moment to focus my thoughts. What did I feel for him? He had a gruff exterior, but I sensed it was only a mask for a tender heart.

"There's something there," Anna said. "I can see it in your face. You're falling in love."

"Is it possible to fall in love with three different men at the same time?"

She lifted her eyebrows. "Are you serious?"

With a deep sigh, I told her about each of the men I had met on April 18. When I was done, all she could do was smile, though it was a sad smile.

"I don't know what you're going to do," she said, "but no matter what, follow your heart, Maggie. I've been in love, and I can assure you that there is nothing worse in life than trying to live without your soulmate."

"Do you believe in soulmates?"

"With all of my heart."

"Even though you lost yours?" I whispered.

"Especially because I lost mine. But I'm coming to realize that we don't each have just one soulmate. I believe that whoever God intends for us is our soulmate. And I think there might be another one out there for me somewhere. I just hope and pray I find him."

"Could Gray, Seth, and Zechariah each be my soulmate?" I asked, hoping she had an answer.

She looked pensive for a moment and then lifted a shoulder. "I don't know. Only you can answer that question. Just make sure that whoever you choose brings out the best version of yourself. Richard brought out the best in me, which is why I feel so lost without him."

"The qualities he loved about you are still there, Anna. You haven't lost them, you've only lost sight of them."

She wrapped me in a tight hug. "No matter who you choose, he will be the luckiest guy in the world."

"I'm not supposed to make my decision based on one person. That's never been the plan."

Anna pulled back. "Then what are you basing it on?"

"Delilah said I should answer the question of who I am. And whichever path is truly me is the path I should choose."

Anna frowned. "Isn't each path you?"

My shoulders fell. "I suppose."

"You are a combination of each path. You can't separate one from the other and say one is you over the others."

I briefly closed my eyes as the truth settled over me. "Then what? How am I supposed to choose?"

She examined me, her green eyes probing. "What is the most important thing in the world to you—besides the people you love?"

"Healing." I didn't even hesitate. "Doing the most I can with the time I've been given."

"Then perhaps that's how you answer the question. Where can you do the most healing, Maggie?"

Was it that easy? But where could I do the most healing? In 2001, I had the benefit of modern technology and ongoing medical discoveries. Did that allow me to do the most healing? In 1861, I had the least technology and information, but with my advanced knowledge, I could do more in that path than most. Did that mean I should eliminate 1941, since it had neither?

That didn't make any sense.

Maybe I needed to answer both questions. Which path was truly me? And where could I do the most healing?

With a sigh, I realized I still had no idea.

It was easier to pretend I wasn't running out of time.

12

JUNE 11, 2001
WASHINGTON, DC

The night of the gala had finally arrived. As I stood in my bedroom, looking at my reflection, I couldn't help but smile into the mirror. My dress was new, a rare splurge for such a special night. Most of Washington's elite would be attending the event, with six hundred invitations accepted by politicians, entertainers, business owners, and patrons of the arts. It was a black-tie affair, which meant I needed a new gown.

I tried to remind myself that I had agreed to this event because I wanted to talk to Seth about my dad's project, but my excitement made it difficult to remember.

Delilah entered my room with a couple of bobby pins to secure the loose curls that had escaped my updo. "You look nervous," she said as she attacked my scalp with a pin.

"Ow." I took the pin from her to do it myself. "I am a little nervous. This is an important event."

"Because President Bush will be there . . . or because Seth will be?"

"Both—but it's excited nerves, mostly." I secured my hair,

happy with the style. My gown was an A-line, scoop-neck ensemble with a white satin skirt and a black lace top. The sleeves went down to my elbows, and the same lace lined the hem. I paired it with black heels.

"You look stunning," Delilah assured me.

The doorbell rang, and I grabbed my black satin clutch. "I'll meet him downstairs."

"I won't get to see him in his tuxedo?" Delilah made a face. "I was looking forward to it all week."

I smiled. "Maybe when we come home. But don't wait up for me. I don't know how late we'll be."

"Have fun."

It was a warm evening, so I didn't grab a wrap. Instead, I pressed the speaker and told Seth I'd be down in a minute. When I finally arrived on the main floor, a little out of breath, I opened the front door and found him waiting on the stoop.

He turned at the sound and simply stared at me.

"Meg." He shook his head. "You're gorgeous."

"Thank you." I closed the door behind me, trying to calm my pulse.

Seth came up to me and paused before leaning forward to place a kiss on my cheek.

My breath stilled. He smelled amazing and looked even better in his tuxedo and bow tie. It was the same thing he had worn the night I met him at the White House, but I hadn't been nearly as interested in him then.

"Ready?" he asked, offering me his elbow.

"I think so."

He drove me to a parking garage near Ford's Theatre while the sun began to set in the west. We walked to the theater talking about some of the mundane events that had filled our life since the last time we'd been together. He told me of his work at the Capitol, and I told him about my rounds. I'd been working in pediatric emergency and loved every minute of it.

As we drew closer to Ford's Theatre, the commotion on Tenth Street increased. A red carpet had been rolled out on the sidewalk, and several reporters were camped out near the doors as guests arrived. I recognized several politicians, many of whom fought publicly but were laughing and slapping each other's backs now.

"This is one of the more popular bipartisan events in Washington," Seth said, following my line of sight. "Or so I've been told."

"Thank you for bringing me."

He looked down at me and smiled. "Thanks for coming. I've been looking forward to this night all month."

I wanted to tell him that I had been too, but I didn't want to encourage him. I was having a hard time not encouraging myself. In this moment, with the warm air, the fancy clothes, and the handsomest man in the crowd by my side, I could almost pretend like this was it—this was my life. The one and only.

"Congressman Wallace," one of the reporters called as we approached the theater. "Who is your date this evening?"

"Don't you know Margaret Clarke?" Seth asked with an incredulous look, though I knew he was teasing. "She's the youngest medical student at Georgetown University's School of Medicine. Daughter of retired General Jonathan Clarke and President Bush's social secretary, Peggy Clarke."

The reporter lifted an eyebrow, clearly impressed. "Can I get your picture?"

"Do you mind?" Seth asked me.

What I minded was that he hadn't asked if it was okay to share so much personal information with the reporter. Though I'd gained a bit of attention a few years ago when I graduated from college with a pre-med degree at the age of seventeen, I liked to lead a quiet, private life. Partially because I didn't like my photo saved in public records. What would happen if someone in 2001 saw a photo of me from 1941 or 1861? I looked exactly the same in all three time periods. People would think it a coincidence, but what if it drew questions I didn't want to answer?

Seth had already told the reporter who I was, though, so what would it matter if he took a picture of us too? "I don't mind," I said quietly.

Grinning, and apparently unaware of my discomfort, Seth wrapped my arm around his elbow as we turned to the reporter. He took a few pictures of us, which caught the interest of some of the other reporters.

"Congressman," they shouted, "who's the lucky lady?"

"Margaret Clarke," Seth said with pride.

"Can we get a picture?"

We smiled for all the cameras, and my excitement about the evening started to wane. I just wanted to get inside, away from the reporters and the attention.

Finally, Seth turned me toward the doors, and we entered the theater lobby. After going through security, he took me to the bar and ordered a glass of red wine for himself and a Sprite for me. I wasn't thirsty, but it gave me something to do with my hands.

The lobby was full of people in tuxedos and evening gowns. A photographer was roaming the room, and each time he got close, I tried to turn my back.

This would be the perfect time to talk to Seth about my dad's project, but I couldn't get him to focus. He seemed to know everyone in the room, and those he didn't know, he introduced himself to. He moved from one person to the next like the good politician he was, shaking hands and making small talk. He soaked it all up with a smile while keeping me close to his side, letting everyone know who I was and dropping my parents' names, too. It was clear he thrived in this environment when all I wanted to do was find a quiet corner and hide.

After thirty minutes of exhausting small talk with strangers, Seth finally led me into the auditorium. I'd been at Ford's Theatre a few times in my 2001 path but had not been there in 1861. The building had been painstakingly renovated through the years to maintain its original integrity. The carpet and chair upholstery were red, while the trim and walls were a creamy white. Yellow doors and accents matched the curtains. Tonight there was red-white-and-blue bunting everywhere, as the theme of the evening was "American Celebration."

Extra bunting and Americana decor adorned the upper right-hand box where Abraham Lincoln had sat on April 14, 1865—the night he was shot by John Wilkes Booth.

Our tickets placed us in the mezzanine. After we found our seats, we watched as the room began to fill.

I realized I might not get another chance all evening to talk about my dad. "Seth."

He turned and smiled at me, giving me his full attention.

I almost faltered—he was so handsome. But I forged ahead. "My dad mentioned you're on the Committee of Military Construction."

"It's one of several committees I'm on."

How did I approach this subject? Did I come right out and say my dad needed his support? Or did I just keep things general and, if Seth liked me, maybe he'd be more likely to work with my dad?

I decided to keep it general. "He's excited to work with you. He has a lot of plans for the Pentagon."

"I like your dad." It was all Seth said before President Bush and Laura Bush arrived, to great fanfare, and took their seats in the front row.

The evening unfolded with several performances by comedians and singers. Seth sat close to me, his shoulder brushed up against mine, and while a country band performed, he reached over and took my hand in his. His touch was gentle, but though he looked at the stage, I knew he was just as aware of my touch as I was of his.

When he finally looked at me, there was a question in his eyes.

Should I let him hold my hand? Did it give him the wrong idea? Was there any harm in giving him the wrong idea? Couldn't I enjoy his company while I was still here? I wasn't committing my life to him.

But what did that mean about my growing feelings for Gray and Zechariah? Was it wrong to enjoy each of them? It wasn't like I was cheating on anyone—was it? I wasn't married or committed to any of them. I didn't even know how Gray or Zechariah truly felt about me—not like Seth, who'd made it known.

In the end, I allowed him to hold my hand, reveling in the feel of his touch and attention and trying to push aside all thoughts of Gray and Zechariah, and all the work I had ahead of me in 2001. Work that could be jeopardized if my mind was not focused on my job.

A very real possibility, with the way Seth distracted me from everything but him.

After President Bush closed out the evening at the theater by quoting President Lincoln on the importance of theater to provide rest, inspiration, and laughter, the party of six hundred moved to the Organization of American States, about a twenty-minute walk from Ford's Theatre, for a sit-down dinner.

"Do you mind if we walk?" Seth asked as we left the theater and stepped into the dark evening. Streetlights illuminated the sidewalks, lighting up the shuttle buses they'd arranged to take people from the theater to the meal.

"I don't mind." I wanted some fresh air to help me collect

my thoughts. The crush of people in the theater had made me feel unsettled—that, and Seth's hand.

"It'll give us a little time to ourselves." He took my hand in his again. "Do you mind?"

"Having a little time to ourselves, or you holding my hand?"

"Both, I guess." He brought my hand up and kissed it. "I like the way you feel, Meg."

My cheeks warmed at his words, and I had to look away, not used to people talking to me that way.

"Have I embarrassed you?" he asked, a smile in his voice.

"A little."

"I'm sorry." We walked down Tenth Street and then took a right onto E Street. It wasn't easy to walk on the uneven sidewalk in my heels, but it was better than being crowded into a tight shuttle bus.

We walked in silence for a few minutes, though all I could think about was the pressure of his hand holding mine. The city was still alive and vibrant at this hour. Businesses, shops, and restaurants lit up the night.

But my thoughts and feelings were so conflicted, I finally had to pull away from him.

"I'm sorry, Seth. I'm not sure we should—"

"What?" he asked, not skipping a beat, though I was sure he was disappointed that I'd pulled away.

"Nothing has changed," I told him. "I enjoy your company, but I don't have time to date. Not yet."

"This isn't a date. We're just friends."

"I don't hold hands with my friends."

"Are they as good-looking as me?" he asked with a charming smile.

I chuckled and shook my head. "No. But you know what I mean. You can't say this isn't a date and then hold my hand. It doesn't work that way."

"Okay." He looked duly chastised. "I won't hold your hand again—unless you ask me to. Which I really hope you do."

We stopped at a streetlight, waiting for it to turn green.

I tried another tactic as we crossed the street. "The next six months of my life are going to be busy and intense. I need to focus all my attention on my work. I can't complicate matters by getting my heart invested in a relationship."

He paused, grabbing my hand so I had to stop. His face was bathed in light from an Italian restaurant. The doors were flung open, allowing the sweet, melodic sound of "Bella Notte" to spill out onto the sidewalk.

"Is your heart in danger of getting invested, Meg?" He was as serious as I'd ever seen him.

My throat suddenly felt dry, and all I could do was stare at him.

He moved closer, taking me into his arms, and started to dance to the music.

I was surprised, but I allowed him to hold me close and closed my eyes as I laid my head against his chest. His heart was beating hard—matching my own. Suddenly I thought of Gray and the dance we had shared. I hadn't seen him in weeks, so why was I thinking of him now?

Confusion warred within me, but I allowed Seth to keep dancing. People walked by us, smiling at the sight of a couple in a gown and a tuxedo slow dancing on the sidewalk.

When Seth finally pulled back, he looked down at me and smiled. "I'll wait for you, Meg. I promise. And if you'll let me, I'd like to keep seeing you. I won't ask anything of you; you have my word. We'll just spend time together whenever you have a spare minute and get to know one another—no romance or strings attached."

"You can't even walk me past an Italian restaurant without dancing with me. Why would I believe you when you say it won't be romantic?"

He let me go and held up his hands. As he stood there in his tuxedo, his boyish good looks and magnetic personality pulling me toward him, I couldn't believe him when he said he could keep me at a distance. I knew better. He wasn't the kind of person who could hold himself back from romance or life. Just as he had a way of pulling people to himself, life had a way of pulling him. It was fun to watch—but it also felt dangerous.

I had agreed to go out with him, hoping to put in a good word for my dad. Now, though, I wanted to see him again, to be near him, and that was a problem. I shouldn't want to see him, but I couldn't imagine going six months without talking to him or spending time with him. I didn't want to make my final decision because of a man, but what if that was the only way I could? What if I was supposed to use the next six months getting to know Seth, Gray, and Zechariah to see if one of them *was* my soulmate?

Maybe I shouldn't be pushing them away. Instead, maybe I should be drawing closer to them. It was, after all, the biggest decision I would ever make. Shouldn't I have all the information?

Though that didn't mean it had to be a free-for-all, either.

"I will have to put boundaries on our time together," I told Seth, almost pleading. "You cannot hold my hand, or dance with me, or kiss me, or say such sweet and romantic things to me. Do you understand?" I was laughing, but I was very serious.

"I promise." He nodded, so grave it made me laugh even harder.

"I won't be able to see you often, but when I get some time, I'll let you know."

"Do *you* promise?"

I nodded. "But if it gets to be too much, I will have to pull away. Okay? I really do need to spend a lot of my time studying. I have responsibilities, and I can't shirk them. I've been working my whole life for this. I really want to stay at GUH."

"I know, Meg." He let out a sigh. "I really do know."

"Good."

We started to walk again, and this time he kept his distance from me.

"Can we put work aside when we're together?" he asked. "Can we just pretend like we're two average adults, ready to have some fun?"

"That sounds nice."

"We'll start tonight. Let's put this conversation behind us and just have fun. Agreed?"

"Agreed."

The problem was that I could agree to almost any suggestion Seth Wallace made.

13

JULY 21, 1861
WASHINGTON, DC

"Are you certain you want to go to Centreville today?" I asked Papa as I pulled on my gloves. Papa and I had been invited out to the battlefield with Senator Henry Wilson of Massachusetts, the gentleman who had been at Kate Chase's ball and Rose Greenhow's luncheon. Goldie was packing a picnic basket, which Papa had instructed her to fill with dozens of sandwiches for the Union soldiers we might meet along the way.

I couldn't understand why he wanted to go—why anyone would want to go.

"It's about time we show these so-called Confederates what we're made of," Papa said with a smile as he slipped his top hat onto his head. He wore his Sunday best, as if we were heading to the park for a leisurely day and not a battlefield. "Our men will have them rushing back to Richmond tonight, and by tomorrow at this time, we'll have overtaken their capital. The Confederate States of America will die, and Jeff Davis will be out of a job. The war will be over."

"What if we don't win this battle?" I asked, knowing very

well that we wouldn't. By the end of the day, we would not have a Union victory but a mortifying defeat. It was something I had been dreading since I learned about it years ago in a history class in my 2001 path. The First Battle of Bull Run—because there would be a second—would end in chaos and confusion today.

The only reason Papa and the others wanted to go was because they truly thought it would be a simple confrontation and the Confederates would turn tail and run. They didn't expect a lot of bloodshed. Since I knew the truth, it made me hesitate. But if Papa wanted to be there, and he was willing to take me, I couldn't let him go alone. If he was hurt, I could help. I had buried my medical supplies in the bottom of a picnic basket in case we needed them.

"What are you saying, Margaret?" He frowned. "Do you doubt our army?"

I needed to keep my mouth shut and silently watch history unfold. There was nothing I could do to change this or stop it from happening, because I *was* aware of the outcome, and if I tried to change something intentionally, I *would* forfeit this path. Of that, I was certain.

"I don't doubt our army, Papa." I smiled, putting my hand on his arm. "The North will be victorious. I believe that with all my heart."

He returned my smile and nodded. "Good. Now, shall we see if Senator Wilson has arrived?"

Joseph opened the front door for us, and we stepped outside.

It was a glorious Sunday morning. A bit warm, but the humidity was low, and a gentle breeze swept the heat away. We were greeted by a waiting carriage and a beaming Senator Wilson.

The carriage top was down, revealing several occupants sitting on the seats facing each other. Mrs. Wilson was there, a congenial woman close to forty, with blond hair and a penchant for ribbons and lace. Their son, Henry Jr., was seated next to her. At the age of fifteen, he was as tall as his father, and if his eager expression was any indication, just as excited to see the battlefield.

Across from the Wilson family sat another gentleman I was surprised and delighted to see.

"Gray," I said just above a whisper, hardly realizing I had said his name.

Papa looked at me. "Gray?" he asked just as quietly.

I put my hand on Papa's arm and squeezed it, not wanting to concern him. "I'm surprised to see Mr. Cooper, that's all."

It had been almost two months since we'd gone out to Arlington House, though I had seen him several times since then. He had been helpful with our supply efforts, but we hadn't had the opportunity to be alone again.

"He's a fascinating man," Papa said, almost to himself. "Seems to be everywhere at all times—just like now."

What was that supposed to mean? And why had Papa said it in such a strange way, as if he was accusing Gray of something?

Both Gray and Henry Jr. rose when we approached the black carriage. Senator Wilson offered his hand to me to step up into the vehicle.

"Good morning, Miss Wakefield," Mrs. Wilson said. "How nice that you could join us. You look lovely, as usual."

"Thank you for inviting us." I greeted Henry Jr. and then turned to Gray.

"It's nice to see you again, Miss Wakefield," he said, taking off his hat. "Won't you have a seat?"

He motioned to the spot next to him. It would be a tight squeeze to Centreville, but I didn't mind.

I sat in the center of the bench, my skirts taking up a great deal of space. I was not wearing a hoop today, but the thick petticoats still turned my skirt into a bell shape. I tried tucking them in around my legs to make room for Gray on my left and my father on my right.

The conversation was strangely pleasant as we rode toward the west in a great exodus of Washingtonians going to see the battle. It made no sense to me, and as I looked around at the crowd, I wondered how it could make sense to them. Would I feel differently if I didn't know the outcome of this battle?

"I made an inquiry about the patient at Arlington House," Gray said for my ears only while Papa and Senator Wilson spoke passionately about the recent investigation into federal employees' loyalty to the government. "I was pleased to hear that he made a full recovery with no complications. I thought you'd like to know."

I turned more fully to look at him.

Gray smiled. "It seems you have a healing touch."

It made me happy that Private Federgill had made a full recovery—and that Gray had been thoughtful enough to inquire for me.

The countryside was beautiful, with rolling hills, streams, and lush green trees. We passed several people as they walked the twenty-five miles to Centreville, while others rode on horseback, and many more were in carriages, buggies, and wagons. Parasols abounded, and laughter could be heard drifting on the wind.

Everyone truly believed this would be a frolic today. A fun way to watch the beginning and end of the American Civil War. Some thirty-six thousand soldiers would face each other on the battlefield around the river Bull Run, and we would watch from the hills at Centerville.

At least, that was what everyone thought. When we arrived at Centreville, it was a different story.

"Why," Mrs. Wilson said, straining to see through her opera glasses, "we can't see a thing. Just smoke from the battlefields."

She was right. The valley beneath Centreville was covered by trees and hills, blocking our view of the actual battle. A beautiful backdrop of the Bull Run Mountains some fifteen miles in the distance made the landscape stunning, but the five hundred people who stood along the hillside—shading their eyes and straining for a glimpse—saw nothing of consequence.

"We must get closer," Senator Wilson said to his driver. "Take us to Blackburn's Ford. It's along the Centreville and Manassas Road. I believe Captain John Tidball will have his battery positioned there."

The driver took us about a mile southeast of Centreville to a ridge where a battery of soldiers was positioned. We were not the first civilians to make our way to the battery, and others had followed us.

But to Senator and Mrs. Wilson's great disappointment, we could see nothing here either. We ate our lunch, sharing the extra sandwiches with the soldiers, and spoke to Captain Tidball, who reassured everyone that the Union was in good position and winning the day.

"This is ridiculous," Mrs. Wilson said several hours later, putting down her opera glasses again. "We've come all this way in the sunshine and heat, and I still see nothing."

It was already close to four in the afternoon. We had all grown tired and weary of the flies, the heat, and the lack of entertainment. The conversation had ebbed and flowed and was now nonexistent. I sat in the carriage with Mrs. Wilson and Henry Jr. while the men talked to Captain Tidball a few yards away.

"Do you mind if I stretch my legs?" I asked Mrs. Wilson, wishing for a bit of reprieve from her whining.

"Of course not, dear. But stay away from the soldiers."

I assured her I would and stepped out of the carriage. The sunshine beat down on my head, though I wore a wide straw bonnet secured with a ribbon beneath my chin. Mrs. Wilson and I were the only women who had ventured to the battery other than a few hucksters who were selling pies and pastries they had brought from Washington.

For a long time, I stood, looking across the valley, watching the rising smoke from the battlefield, thinking of the countless men lying in the heat, suffering. My fingers itched to tend to their wounds and relieve their pain. But I had no way to reach them.

"You have that same look about you," Gray said as he joined me.

There was no one within hearing distance, so I turned to him. "What look?"

"The same one you had when we were crossing the Long Bridge into Arlington." He crossed his arms as he studied me. "While everyone else appears hopeful and optimistic, you look melancholy and defeated." His voice was very serious. "Do you harbor Southern sympathies, Maggie?"

I snapped my head up to meet his gaze, almost insulted at his accusation. "Of course not."

"Then why this melancholy? From all reports, we will win this day. Why aren't you as excited as everyone else?"

Looking out at the smoke again, I wrapped my arms around my waist. "Perhaps we'll win," I said slowly, "but at what cost? There are men on the battlefield literally dying at this very moment—and here we sit, picnicking and gossiping, upset that we cannot see them suffer. Am I truly the only one troubled by that?"

He was quiet for a few seconds, but then he nodded. "I'm sorry. I was wrong to question your loyalty. I don't think anyone is thinking about the possible loss of life today. All they can imagine is a thrilling victory and an end to war."

Papa approached us. "Senator Wilson and I are going to walk to the Stone Bridge to get a better look. Would you like to join us, Mr. Cooper?"

"Please don't go, Papa," I begged him. "It's not safe."

"It's perfectly safe." Papa smiled, as if that would reassure me. "Captain Tidball said the fighting is still several miles away and the Confederates are running toward Richmond. If we want to see action, we need to go now or we'll miss it."

"If you're going," I told him, "then I'm going."

"Don't be ridiculous, Margaret. The battlefield is no place for a woman."

"It's perfectly safe. You just told me so." I didn't usually question or contradict Papa, so he looked a bit surprised.

"Fine," he said. "But we'll be walking over the field."

"I don't mind." I went to the carriage and found the small bag of medical supplies I had tucked into the basket.

The tide would turn soon, and there would be a need for medical help—though when and where, I didn't know.

Within an hour, we arrived at a ridge overlooking Stone Bridge, which crossed Bull Run near the Warrenton Turnpike. About fifty other civilians had already arrived there, though I was the only female in sight. From our vantage point, we could finally see soldiers—but they were not Union men.

No sooner had we arrived than a line of Confederate soldiers appeared from a wooded area about a hundred yards away. Out of nowhere, a bullet grazed the dirt near Papa's foot.

"What the devil?" Senator Wilson asked, his voice panicked as he jumped and scurried backward. "What is this? I thought the Confederates were running back to Richmond."

Spectators began to shout as more bullets hit the ground near us. Gray grabbed my arm and pulled me to the protection of a large tree, while Papa and Senator Wilson took their own cover.

I stood motionless, my breathing shallow as Gray wrapped his arms around me. I was certain my billowing skirts would give us away, but there was nothing I could do about it now. I had put myself here, knowing better.

Gray's chest rose and fell against mine, and despite the

danger around us, we were both very aware of each other. He looked down at me with an intensity that enveloped me.

"What will we do?" I whispered, trying to focus on the danger and not my attraction to him. "We can't stay here forever."

"We'll wait until the line shifts away from us and then head back to the battery." His British accent had deepened significantly, and his hold tightened. "You shouldn't be here, Maggie. I don't know what I'd do if you were hurt."

I swallowed the emotions surging through me and tried to still my breathing. "I have medical supplies in my shoulder bag," I told him, trying in vain to ignore the dip and curve of his body pressed against mine. "If you need anything, look there."

"You brought medical supplies?" he asked quietly, surprise and humor tinting his brown eyes for a moment.

"I rarely leave home without them."

"If I didn't know better, I'd think you were a doctor in a former life."

His words hit far closer to home than he could ever imagine, so I stayed quiet.

Soon the shouts of men drew closer and louder, and we both peeked out from our hiding spot. The sight before us made my blood run cold, even though I had been expecting it.

Hundreds of Union soldiers were clamoring to cross the bridge, heading back toward Washington.

"What's happening?" Gray asked, bewildered.

"It looks like they're retreating—quickly."

Men were discarding their guns, their knapsacks, and in some cases their clothing to get away from the Confederate army in haste.

"Cowards," yelled Senator Wilson from his spot behind a tree. "Fight! Chase after them! Push them back to Richmond!"

Had I not known how it would all end, I would have truly believed we had lost the war that day. I saw panic and cowardice like I'd never seen—and these were the men who had claimed the South would give up without a fight when they saw the North's determination.

"The Confederates will be right behind this line," Gray said, taking my hand. "We must flee now, or we will never get out of here alive."

Not needing any more encouragement, I practically pulled him along as we left the protection of the tree. "Papa," I called, "meet us at the battery."

"Go," Papa yelled, and I wondered if he had heard me in the melee. "Get to the carriage."

Gray and I began to run with the others, though it was difficult to do in my gown. I hiked up my skirts in the most unladylike way imaginable. Confederate soldiers were chasing the Union men, firing shots into the crowd. My heart had never beat so hard in my life as we ran toward the battery and the carriage awaiting us there.

It took us almost thirty minutes, but when we finally arrived at the battery, sweating and out of breath, it was no better than it had been at Stone Bridge. Soldiers were already fleeing their posts, while others had followed us, trying to get back to Washington.

Mrs. Wilson was in her carriage, clutching her son as the driver tried to hold the horses in check. I was so distracted by Mrs. Wilson's wailing, I collided with a soldier, who stepped aside and stretched out a hand to steady me.

A shot fired in the distance, and the soldier yelled in surprise and pain.

Immediately, blood began to spread over his pant leg, and he fell to his knees and then his back.

He couldn't be much older than Henry Jr., and the panic and terror in his eyes was heartbreaking. Without thinking, I stopped to see what I could do to help him.

"Come on, Maggie," Gray said, tugging at my hand. "The Confederates will be here soon. They're within firing distance."

"I can't leave him to die." I bent in the dirt and blood to see where the soldier was injured. His left pant leg was soaked with blood, and it was pumping out with each beat of his heart.

"I've been shot," the boy said in shock. His face was draining of color as the blood poured out of him.

Without even flinching, I put my fingers into the hole in his pant leg and tore the fabric away. His femoral artery had been hit by the bullet, causing him to hemorrhage. If I did nothing, he would be dead in minutes.

This boy was supposed to die. If I had not come upon him now, knowing what I did about hemorrhaging and how to stop it, he would have died. I *knew* he was supposed to die. Did I allow it to happen as it was supposed to happen? Or did I stop it?

I would be changing history, just as Mama had told me never to do.

It was one thing to make a suggestion to Zechariah to go on an elimination diet. Another to stop a man from bleeding to death right before my eyes.

"We can't wait," Gray said to me. "He's dying, Maggie. There's nothing you can do to stop it. We must get Mrs. Wilson to safety."

Even Gray knew this man was destined to die.

But I couldn't walk away. I just couldn't. I knew exactly what to do to keep him alive. At least, I knew it in theory, as I had watched a surgeon fix a ruptured artery during rotations.

I pressed my hand against his inner thigh where the artery ran and applied as much pressure as I could. His leg was wet and slippery, but I had found the artery, and the bleeding began to slow.

"Tear off the hem of my gown," I told Gray. "There are a pair of scissors in my bag. Cut the fabric and tear it."

He stared at me, shocked.

"Do it!" I said loudly. "He'll die if we can't stop the blood flow, and I can't hold on to his thigh forever."

Gray quickly did as I instructed. The sound of tearing fabric was lost in the din of noise and bullets hitting the dirt around us.

"Now wrap it as tightly as you can around his upper thigh."

Doing as I instructed, Gray wrapped the fabric around the soldier's thigh several times, pulling it impossibly tight—tighter than I could have done. Sweat dripped from his brow. Dozens of soldiers and civilians fled past us, heading east without stopping to help.

"We need to get him into the Wilsons' carriage," I told Gray. "I'll need to perform surgery when we get him back to Washington. The artery will need to be bypassed with a graft, or he could still bleed to death."

Gray stared at me. "What?"

I realized too late that I had said something I would have said in 2001 in the ER. But it didn't matter, I needed to perform the surgery to save his life. It would be close to impossible, and he could still die, but I had to try.

"Will you help me get him into the carriage?" I asked, trying to calm my voice.

"Of course." Gray gently scooped the teenager into his arms as if he weighed nothing and carried him to the carriage, where Mrs. Wilson was weeping and wailing in fear.

"Where's my husband?" she cried, clutching her son's hand so hard it had turned white. "Has he been killed?"

"He and Papa are coming," I told her.

"We're here," Senator Wilson said from behind me. "We're all here, and we must return to Washington posthaste. The rebels will follow us and overtake Washington if we don't warn the president and defend the capital."

Papa and Senator Wilson were red-faced and sweating profusely. When Papa saw the soldier and my blood-covered hands and gown, his face paled. "Are you injured?"

"No. It's the soldier. We're taking him home, Papa. He needs help."

"There's no time to argue with her," Senator Wilson said. "Let's hurry home. We'll make do."

The solider was laid on the floor of the carriage, having passed out, as we all piled inside. At any minute, his tourniquet could fail, and he'd bleed to death right there at our feet. But we had to try to save him. Every few minutes, I checked his pulse. It was still beating, though weakly.

We were silent all the way back to Washington except for the random outbursts of Senator Wilson, who called the Union soldiers cowards and weaklings. He was mortified by their behavior and ashamed at their unpreparedness.

When we finally reached Washington, it was late. Others had arrived ahead of us, so the city had already been warned, and chaos had ensued as people ran into the streets to hear the news.

"I'll help you bring him inside," Gray said to me.

"Thank you."

Papa didn't say a word as Gray hauled the soldier up the front steps. The Wilsons pulled away without saying goodbye, just as shaken as the rest of us. Senator Wilson was going straight to the White House.

Goldie, Saphira, and Joseph met us at the door, and I asked for warm water, fresh bandages, as many lamps and lanterns as they could find, and the medical kit I kept in the kitchen.

"What do you plan to do?" Papa asked, his voice grave.

I might be sacrificing everything I held dear in 1861 for this stranger, but I couldn't live with myself if I didn't try to save his life. Papa would never understand, but he deserved some kind of explanation—especially if this was the last day I'd be alive in this path.

"I need to perform a surgery to save his life," I told him while Gray stood by, waiting to be directed.

"Surgery? What are you talking about, Margaret? Have you lost your mind?"

"I cannot explain right now, but perhaps I can later. Just trust me, please."

"I will send for a doctor," he said.

"There won't be any available with all the other injured soldiers. But if you must, you must." I turned to Gray. "Please bring him upstairs to the last room on the right."

"I don't know what you're going to do," Papa said to me, a deep frown on his brow, "but I want a full explanation when you're done."

Nodding, I left him in the foyer and lifted the hem of my soiled gown to join Gray upstairs.

For the next three hours, I performed an incredibly delicate surgery under the most difficult and unpredictable circumstances of my life. I was relying on what I had learned in textbooks and observed just once. I did not have any of the proper tools and only the help of Gray and Saphira, who agreed to stand by my side. I was creating more trouble and questions as they watched me, but there was nothing I could do.

How would I ever explain this to Gray? Or Papa? What could I possibly say that would make any sense? And what would Saphira tell the others? That I was a butcher? A freak?

When the surgery was done and the soldier, who was still nameless, lay comfortably sleeping, I washed my hands in the basin on the stand. Saphira had already left the room with the soiled laundry, and Gray sat on a chair near the patient's bed, watching me.

I was so tired I could barely keep my eyes open, but I couldn't rest yet. It was past midnight, so if I went to sleep, I would wake up in 1941. It would be a full two days before I knew if I was going to wake up in 1861 ever again.

I owed Gray an explanation, but Papa was the only person I could think about right now.

"Will you sit with him?" I asked Gray. "I need to speak to my father."

A myriad of emotions played across Gray's face. "Will you ever tell me?" he asked quietly, gently.

I swallowed hard. "I—I don't know."

Slowly, he stood and came around the bed. The light radiated behind him, casting his face in shadows. He was close—dangerously close—and I was reminded that I had clung to him behind that tree. What might it be like to have those arms around me in a moment that wasn't fraught with fear?

"I know you're hiding something, Maggie," he said. "Something I can't figure out now, but I will. You're a remarkable woman, capable of things I've never seen before—things I don't even think a real surgeon could do. And somehow your father has no idea either. None of it makes sense, but there's always an explanation. Always."

"There is an explanation." My voice was just above a whisper. "But even if I told you, you'd never believe me."

"Try me."

I wanted to, desperately, but I shook my head. "I can't."

"That's what I thought." He was quiet for a heartbeat. "Are you a spy?"

I couldn't help but smile. "No." But then I sobered, wishing I could ask him the same thing.

"I'm a patient man, Maggie Wakefield." He crossed his arms. "I won't rest until I know the truth."

If I died tonight and didn't return to 1861, he would never know, so it didn't matter.

It also wouldn't matter if I kissed him.

So I did, on the cheek, slowly and tenderly, placing my hand on his other cheek.

He covered my hand with his and inhaled deeply.

"Thank you for all your help today," I whispered. "I couldn't have done it without you."

We stared at one another for a heartbeat, and his gaze dropped to my lips. I felt a charge of electricity hum between us. Suddenly the kiss on his cheek was not enough. I ached for more.

Yet there was a soldier lying close to death on the bed—and Papa pacing in the parlor, waiting for an explanation.

I took a step back, swallowing the longing within.

Gray recovered as well. "I'll stay with the soldier tonight. Tomorrow, we can talk."

Nodding, I left the room and went down into the parlor. Papa stood near the cold fireplace. The house was quiet. I had not changed out of my soiled gown, but we needed to have this conversation. I wasn't sure if he'd even believe me.

"Did the soldier die?" he asked.

"I think I saved his life."

Papa sighed. "Are you going to explain?"

"I will try, but I don't know if you'll believe me." I spoke quietly, hoping no one else would hear.

He took a seat on the sofa and patted the spot next to him. "Tell me."

I lowered myself onto the sofa, my arms and legs heavy with exhaustion. "I was born with a gift," I said without preamble. "I do not simply live here in 1861. I also live in the years 1941 and 2001. When I go to sleep here, I wake up in 1941, and when I go to sleep in 1941, I wake up in 2001. As soon as I fall asleep in 2001, I wake up back here, and no time has passed while I've been away. In 1941, I'm a navy nurse, and in 2001, I'm a medical student, working to become a surgeon. My parents in 1941 are marked with this gift, and I inherited it from them."

Papa didn't say anything for a long, long time. He just stared at me with very little emotion on his face.

I held my breath, afraid he'd think I was insane and send me to an asylum.

"This explains a lot," he finally said. "When you were little, you used to talk about the strangest things and about people who seemed so real to you. You told me about horseless carriages, vehicles in the sky, boxes that had moving pictures inside them, and a whole host of things that made no sense. You told me about other parents and siblings and places I had never taken you before. At first I wrote it off as imagination or fancy, but you were so adamant and so convincing that I always wondered. And then one day you stopped talking about those things quite suddenly, and I put it out of my mind."

"That was the day I finally understood that I was different," I told him. "My marked mother warned me to stop talking about those things with you, since you would never understand and it would just complicate my life."

Papa gently placed his hand over mine. "It is truly real, Margaret?"

I nodded. There was so much I wanted to tell him, so much I wanted to explain. Foremost in my mind was the fact that I might never come back to 1861, and now that he knew the truth, I needed to tell him the rest.

"My marked mother told me that if I knowingly change history in one of my paths, then I would forfeit that path." I swallowed, my pulse beating hard. "I saved a man's life today with a procedure that is not yet developed in 1861—a man who would have died had I not helped him."

Papa stared at me. "What does that mean?"

"It means that I might have forfeited this path, Papa. It means I might not wake up here tomorrow. But I had to do it. I couldn't sit back and watch him die if I could stop it from happening. I'm so sorry."

He drew me into his arms, and I began to cry.

After today, I might never see him again. But I had finally told him the truth.

14

JULY 21, 1941
BETHESDA, MARYLAND

The next morning, I lay in my dorm room for a long time after I woke up. Anna was already in the shower down the hall. I needed to get dressed since I was supposed to be on duty in half an hour, but I couldn't make myself get out of bed.

Rain drizzled down the windowpane, making the world look bleak. It had been raining for so many days now that I wondered if the sun would ever shine again.

Memories from the night before, as I'd cried on Papa's shoulder, returned to me, and I felt the heaviness sink deeper into my soul. Would I ever see him again? Would I see Gray? Were they waking up, at this very moment, to discover that I had died? Papa would be inconsolable. And it was all for the life of a soldier I'd never met before. A nameless face who had been destined to bleed to death at the disastrous Battle of Bull Run until I'd come across him.

I closed my eyes tight, my soul searching for answers. "Lord," I prayed quietly, "please don't take 1861 away from me. I know the rules, and I know I broke them, but I didn't intend to change history for my own gain or the gain of a loved one. I was doing what You created me to do—heal. I want to keep healing there, to take care of my father, and . . ."

I let the next part of my prayer trail off, though God knew what I was going to say.

I wanted to spend more time with Gray.

The sound of Anna's slippered feet met my ears a moment before she opened the door, and I realized, belatedly, that I'd been crying.

"I hope you're not getting sick," she said as she hung her wet towel on the hook just behind the door. She wore a kimono and a shower cap over her hair to protect her waves. "Do you feel sick?"

I wiped my tears and pushed back my covers. "I'm okay." I didn't want to talk about yesterday, about the battle or the soldier or Gray. I wanted to forget all of it for now and turn my attention to this day. To this life. To this calling.

"You'll be late if you don't hurry."

Thankfully, I didn't have to worry about what I was supposed to wear. I quickly put on my garter belt, undergarments, and silk stockings, then slipped into my white nurse's uniform. I'd slept with a hairnet the night before to preserve my high curls and had to touch them up a bit to make them look presentable. After going to the bathroom to brush my teeth, splash cold water onto my face, and apply a little rouge and lipstick so I didn't look so pale, I was ready to work.

Anna had already left to start her duties, so I walked to the surgery ward on my own. As hard as I tried, I could not stop thinking about Gray and how much I would miss him if I never saw him again. It wasn't just disappointment I felt, but grief—more than I would have expected. I'd only known him a few months, yet I had felt a connection to him that I didn't feel with anyone else. He was so perceptive, so present in each situation. Even on the battlefield, he'd never lost his cool or panicked. When I barked orders at him, he had followed them and not been angry or insulted by my behavior. He'd helped me during the long surgery and never questioned my abilities. I wished I had thought to apologize to him for my tone on the battlefield . . . but at least I had kissed him.

Just the thought of my lips on his cheek brought heat to my own. I'd never kissed a man, other than my fathers, and though it was a chaste kiss, it had still filled me with an inexplicable feeling. What would it be like to truly kiss him?

I might never know.

My mood was foul as I entered the operating room. I just wanted this day to end so I could wake up in 2001 and then survive that day so I could see if I'd lost 1861 forever. Part of me wanted time to hurry, while the other part was deathly afraid of knowing.

"You're late," Dr. Philips said as he looked up from a clipboard.

I tried not to scowl, though if anyone deserved the blunt end of my bad mood, it was him. He'd been moody almost every day I had known him.

"Our first case was canceled," he said. "Our next surgery is not scheduled for another hour."

"Then why does it matter if I'm late?" My voice was sharper than I intended, surprising us both.

A frown deepened his brow. "What's wrong?"

I tried to calm my mind. He didn't deserve my wrath. No one did. Thankfully, there was no one else in the room. "Nothing."

"You're usually the brightest one in here. I've never seen you like this."

"Perhaps I'm finally giving you a taste of your own medicine."

Dr. Philips was my senior officer and the head surgeon, but at the moment he was just a man—one who confounded me daily.

He set down the clipboard and walked over to me, concern on his face. "What made you decide that today was the day?"

His usual scowl was missing, and he didn't look well. His face was pinched with pain, and the skin on his hands looked red and blotchy again.

My anger fizzled, replaced with concern. "What's wrong with you?"

He looked down at his hands. "I've been adding foods back into my diet. I think I found the culprit—at least, one of them. Yeast."

I frowned. "Yeast?"

"I added bread back into my diet, and I began to have symptoms again."

Shaking my head, I opened my mouth to tell him it wasn't the yeast, it was the wheat causing his problems. But I shut it again. He'd have to figure it out for himself or not at all.

It made me angry all over again.

If I knew, why couldn't I tell him? Why had God given me this gift if I couldn't use it? It was Bull Run and the soldier all over again. Would I be penalized for using my skills and talents?

Turning away, I went to the instrument table and began to look over the tools we'd need for the next surgery, rearranging items with more force than necessary.

Dr. Philips was quiet for a few minutes, and then he slowly walked over to me. "Have I made you upset?"

I turned and found he was a bit closer than I had anticipated. He had never cared if he'd made me upset before.

"No. At least, not recently."

One of his elusive smiles appeared—and then just as quickly disappeared as he went over to the clipboard again and picked it up. "I have some news, actually, and I thought I should tell you before you hear it from someone else."

I was still a little shaken by his behavior and had to work to focus on what he was saying. "News?"

"I've been given new orders. I'll be leaving the Naval Medical Center in less than a week."

His announcement took a moment for me to process. He was leaving? Now, when we were just learning how to work well together? I wasn't prepared to say good-bye to him.

"Where are you going?"

He set the clipboard aside again and hitched up a leg on the corner of a desk, crossing his arms. "For most of my naval career, I've worked on hospital ships. I was only sent here to help get this place up and running. I'm being sent to a new ship, the USS *Solace*. It's being converted from an ocean liner to a hospital ship in New York City as we speak. It will be sailing out of New York on August ninth. At least, that's the plan right now."

"You'll be on a hospital ship?" I felt like my feet were sinking. I didn't want to feel so disappointed that he was leaving, and I didn't want it to show on my face. It didn't make sense. He was difficult, moody, and hard to please. But he was also brilliant, thoughtful, and he'd come to trust me enough to ask for my opinion.

And when he smiled? He lit up the room.

"Where will you be stationed?"

"Our eventual destination is Pearl Harbor, in Honolulu, Hawaii."

The room felt like it tipped on its side, and I had to reach for something to steady me. "Pearl Harbor?" I whispered.

He watched me, nodding slowly as he frowned.

He couldn't go to Pearl Harbor. It would be the site of one of the most devastating moments in American history—and he'd be in the very midst of it.

But what could I say or do to stop him? Nothing. Absolutely nothing.

"I've asked for Nurse Daly to join me," he said, "as my Chief of Nurses. She'll be putting together a team of eleven nurses to join her." He paused. "I've requested that you be one of them."

"Me?" I felt the air leave my lungs. "I can't go to Pearl Harbor."

"If this is about your sister, we can have her transferred there as well. I think you'd like Hawaii. It's a magnificent island in the Pacific Ocean. There's nothing else quite like it."

"Why me?" I asked. "I've only just started—I'm not even twenty-one, as you've pointed out. Surely you'd want someone with more experience."

"You know there's no one else like you."

I stared at him, wondering if he realized what he'd just said. "I thought you said there were many good reasons to keep me at a distance."

He was quiet again. When he finally spoke, his voice was lower than normal. "Perhaps there are a lot more reasons to keep you close."

The look in his eyes was so intense, I had to remember to breathe.

Was it smart to go to Pearl Harbor? Not only because of what I knew would happen, but especially because of what I *didn't* know.

"I'll speak to Anna," I finally said. "When do you need our answer?"

"A few days, at most."

"I'll let you know by Friday."

The door opened, and another nurse entered, her arms full of linens. She didn't seem to notice the tension in the room as she set down the towels and began to separate them.

Dr. Philips met my gaze one last time before he went back to his work. He would not pressure me to come, but just knowing he wanted me there was an honor.

At least this would give me something to focus on today so I didn't have to worry about 1861.

"You told him we would go, right?" Anna held a tray as she walked through the cafeteria. "How many people are sent to Hawaii on the government's tab? It would be like a dream vacation!"

A nightmare was more like it.

"But it's so far away," I reminded her. "And I'll have to make my final decision while we're there. I won't get to say good-bye to Mama and Daddy if I don't choose 1941."

"Then let's ask for leave and go see them now, before we go to New York."

I couldn't deny that I wanted to see Mama and Daddy again. We'd been writing and had called a few times, but there was something special about being back in Williamsburg.

"Teddy is visiting," Anna said. "We could spend the night and then return the next day. I'm sure we could get leave."

I didn't have the heart to tell Anna what would happen at Pearl Harbor, and it was probably for the best. If she knew, she could inadvertently change history, and I would be to blame.

It was already hard enough not knowing if I had forfeited 1861.

Besides, Mama and Daddy didn't even know what was going to happen on December 7. They knew we would have another war, because Mama's marked mother had told her, but they didn't know how it would start or what it would entail. I had never told them. If they knew, would they advise us to go? Or would they tell us to stay in Washington?

"Maybe we should talk to Mama and Daddy about the opportunity," I suggested. "They might have good advice."

"What advice do you need?" Anna asked as she accepted a plate of mashed potatoes and meatloaf from the cook. "We'd be fools not to go. Can you imagine? A big ocean liner docked in Honolulu?"

Her green eyes lit up at the possibility, and it gave me hope. I'd thought about not telling her we'd been asked to go, but that hadn't felt justifiable. Anna had every right to make up her own mind—especially since I couldn't tell her the future. She needed her own freedom to choose, just as I did. But since I had foreknowledge, my options were different.

"I already know what I will choose," Anna said as she took a glass of milk and grabbed a dinner roll. "I want to go."

I accepted my own plate of mashed potatoes and meatloaf and followed her to one of the tables near a window. It was still raining.

"Unless," Anna said, moving her carrot cake off her tray and onto the table, "the offer only stands if you go."

I shrugged. "I think they'd want you either way."

"You know why Dr. Philips asked for you."

I tried to pretend I was oblivious. "No. Why?"

"Maggie, the man is falling in love with you."

"Don't be ridiculous." I couldn't meet her gaze. She'd see right through me.

"Everyone's talking about it. It's so obvious when you're in a room together. You've captivated him, and you're probably the only woman who's ever had that effect on him before. No wonder he wants you in Hawaii with him. Can you imagine being romanced on Waikiki Beach?"

"He didn't ask me to go there to romance me. I know that for certain. He respects my opinions and has come to rely on my help in the operating room. Nothing more."

"You're either lying to yourself or lying to me." She cut into her meatloaf with her fork, shaking her head. "Even though he has a tough exterior, most of the nurses in this hospital would love to have his undivided attention."

"I'm not most nurses."

She kept cutting her meatloaf and muttered, "You're most definitely not."

My meal sat on my tray, unappetizing. Even if I had liked

meatloaf, it wouldn't have appealed to me today. Everything felt off, and my stomach was in knots.

"I think Mama and Daddy will encourage us to go," Anna said after a few bites of her food. "We could both use a change of scenery."

But what we couldn't use was the horrors of Pearl Harbor. She didn't know what was coming, but I did. And I needed to decide whether it was up to me to prevent her from more death and devastation. She'd already had more than her fair share.

Yet I recalled what she'd told me before. It wasn't my job to play God or to fix things for her. She was able to make her own decisions.

Perhaps going home to Williamsburg would help me find the answer.

15

❧

P Street was quiet as I walked toward home from my parking
spot. My shift in the emergency room had been busy, for which
I was thankful. But the thought of 1861 had always been there,
like a splinter under my fingernail, irritating and worrying me.
I was tired and my feet were sore, but I had several hours of
studying ahead of me before I could go to sleep and face my
fate.

It was Saturday evening, so I wasn't sure if Delilah would be
home. She was often out on the weekends. Sometimes, she'd
invite me to go along with her, but since I usually said no, she
didn't always extend the invitation. It didn't matter, since I
would have said no tonight.

Dusk had fallen over DC, bringing cooler temperatures after
the heat of the day. I took out my ponytail, since it was giving
me a headache, and shook my hair. All I wanted to do was
soak in a hot bath, but I needed to get a paper finished before
Monday, and with church tomorrow, that only left tonight to
finish researching before I'd start to write tomorrow afternoon.

My cell phone rang, so I pulled it out of my bag. "Hello?"

"Hey, kiddo. It's Dad."

"Hi, Dad." He didn't call often, but when he did, he usually had a reason. He wasn't much for chatting. "What can I do for you?"

"Well, it's kind of silly, but I thought I'd call and ask how things are going with Seth."

I stopped walking and frowned. Dad never asked about my personal life. Our conversations were mostly business in nature. He hadn't been one for exploring thoughts and feelings when I was growing up, and not much had changed since then. "Why?"

"I was just thinking about you today, wondering." He cleared his throat. "Truth is, we have a big meeting with the Committee of Military Construction early next week, and I know he'll be there. I thought it might be awkward if I ask him about you and find out from him that things aren't going well. Mom said you've been seeing him a bit lately, and she's showed me some of the newspaper articles about you two. But I wanted to hear from you how it's going."

Seeing Seth "a bit" was an understatement. Since the gala in June, I had seen him a lot more than I had imagined. Whenever I had a hint of a moment and he was free, he was there making fun suggestions about what we should do with our time. We went bike riding around the monuments, ate dinner at unique restaurants, toured the Smithsonian American Art Museum, went to comedy night at DC Improv, cruised on the Potomac River, and even took in a flea market. And it seemed that no matter where we went, people were paying attention. Pictures of us showed up in the gossip columns of *The Washington Post*, *The Hill*, and other online papers. We had even been coined the youngest power couple in Washington.

I leaned against a retaining wall near the sidewalk, trying to figure out how to answer my dad's question. "Seth and I aren't a couple, Dad. We're friends, and we're getting along great."

"You're not a couple? But I thought your mom said—"

"Seth and I are together a lot, but we're not dating."

"It sure seems like you are."

The wall was warm against my back. "He'd like to date me, but I told him I need to wait until after med school is over."

"You're still seeing him, though, right?"

"Yes—just not in the way most people think."

"Oh." He paused for a second. "I just want you to be happy, kiddo."

"Thanks, Dad."

"Well, I guess that answers my question. I didn't want to put my foot in my mouth when I see him at the Pentagon next week."

"Speaking of the Pentagon, how are the renovations going?" Anything to change the topic.

"Great, though it's a pain in the butt to work around. It's on schedule to be completed by early September. You should stop by and check it out when you have some time. You haven't been there in years."

It had probably been five or six years since I'd visited my dad at work. The Pentagon was an amazing building, more like a city, complete with its own zip code. I had been in awe of it and very proud my dad worked there.

"I'd like that."

"Come when the project is complete. You'll be impressed with the changes we're making."

"Okay. I should probably go, though. I have a lot of work to do tonight."

"It's Saturday evening, Meg. You should be out on the town like other young women your age. We live in one of the most dynamic cities in the world. Go have some fun."

"I wish I could. After January, I will get busy having fun." Though if I stayed in 2001, I'd be busy with residency after med school.

"Love you, kiddo."

"Love you too, Dad." I hung up and put my phone back in my bag.

I continued walking home. The steps leading up to our building were steep, so I had my head down and didn't see the person sitting there until I almost tripped over him.

"Seth!"

He put up his hands to stop my fall, laughing. "Sorry. I thought you'd see me here."

My heart was beating fast at the unexpected encounter, and I started to laugh too. "What are you doing here?"

"Surprise." He lifted the picnic basket at his side. "I brought supper. We've both been busy this week, and I thought we could use a little break."

I sat on the step next to him, my heart starting to calm down. The sun was setting, but there was still plenty of light in the sky. "How long have you been waiting?"

"About thirty minutes. You told me you worked until eight today, so I canceled a meeting I had this evening."

"I also told you I had a lot of work tonight. You shouldn't have canceled a meeting." Disappointment weighed down my words. I felt bad that he had gone to so much trouble and I wouldn't be able to enjoy it with him—especially because he had ignored what I said. "I have a lot of research to do. I need to be upstairs studying right now."

"My aide got your favorite Chinese takeout from the restaurant you took me to in Chinatown." He leaned into me, and he smelled amazing. "I thought we could go to the Waterfront Park and watch the boats. It would be a great way to unwind and relax after a long week."

I closed my eyes, thinking about how good it sounded.

He opened the picnic basket, and the aroma was enough to make my stomach growl. When was the last time I had eaten today? I had grabbed an apple from the snack cart and had a yogurt and granola parfait at one point. But that was about it.

"We don't have to stay long," he promised. "We can walk down there, eat, and then come back. An hour tops. You can sacrifice an hour for some good food and great company, can't you?"

Sighing, I shrugged. "What's an hour? Sure."

"Great." He stood and offered me his hand. I grabbed it and ended up standing just inches from him. "Your hair's a little crazy." He smiled. "But I like it."

It *was* a little crazy. I gathered it up and secured it into a ponytail again.

"I meant it," he said, his voice lowering. "I like it down."

I didn't say anything for a moment and then slowly took it down again.

He smiled and touched one of the curls. "You're so beautiful, it hurts sometimes."

"Hurts?"

His breath was warm on my face. "Because I can't have you—at least, not yet."

"You promised," I said quietly, though I was having a hard time remembering why I told him we had to wait.

Seth took a step back and lifted his hands in surrender.

We left the house and walked toward the waterfront. Guilt plagued me about the work I was putting off, but I had made my decision, and I was determined to enjoy my time with Seth.

"Why do you work so hard?" he asked as we walked. "Are you trying to prove something to someone? Did you really have to start medical school at the age of seventeen? Or finish it by twenty-one?"

A lot of people had asked me that question over the years, and I had given them lots of different answers. But tonight I paused. Why *was* I working so hard?

The truth hit me hard. I wanted to complete something important to me before it was taken away. I wanted to be done with medical school if I chose to leave 2001 behind.

But was it worth the sacrifices I had made? If I didn't choose 2001, then I'd never see Seth again—and was it worth sacrificing my time with him?

"You know," I said, "I'm not sure why I work so hard."

It wasn't a great answer, but it was an honest one—at least, the best one I could give.

A rim of light hovered just over the western horizon as we sat in the park, facing the Potomac River. It was so much cleaner in 2001 than in 1861, used more for pleasure than necessity.

Seth had brought a blanket, which he spread out on the soft grass. I wondered which of his aides had provided it, since Seth was almost as busy as I was. He also made a lot of sacrifices to be with me.

We sat there, eating our Chinese takeout, and for a few minutes, I *was* able to forget about everything else. About my work, my research paper, whether or not I should go to Pearl Harbor, what life I would ultimately choose, and my fears about not waking up in 1861 tomorrow.

Boats floated by on the river. A large dinner cruise went past, followed by a tour boat and several personal watercrafts. People were walking and jogging along the paths, sitting on blankets, or enjoying the last moments of the day playing catch with their dogs. But what everyone had in common was that they were enjoying life.

"Thank you for bringing me here," I told Seth. "It's easy to get caught up in my responsibilities and forget to have some fun."

We put away the leftovers, and Seth set the picnic basket aside. He took my hand and tugged me down to lie on the blanket and look up at the sky. The first of the stars were starting to twinkle.

I lay with Seth at my side and looked at the vast heavens, feeling very small and insignificant. When I was younger, my gift had always made me feel like I was unique and special to God. But as I grew older, I realized that everyone had a unique and special purpose on earth. It provided a strange sort of comfort. Maybe I wasn't so different after all.

A sigh escaped my lips. Seth turned and propped his head up on his palm, looking down at me. He was close—so very close—and the way he looked at me sent an exciting shiver up my spine.

"What are you thinking about?" he asked, his voice so low I almost didn't hear him.

"How utterly insignificant I am in the scope of things."

Slowly, he placed a hand against my cheek. "You're not insignificant to me."

I held my breath, uncertain if I should push him off again, or if I should let him continue and see what happened.

He ran his thumb over the contour of my cheek, his eyes following the movement lower and lower, until his thumb grazed the corner of my lips. He paused, and his gaze came up to meet mine, as if waiting to see what I would do.

My heart wanted him to continue, to see what it would feel like. Yet my mind told me to put a stop to whatever this was. But I couldn't make my voice work.

Slowly, he ran his thumb over my top lip and then my bottom—and when he let his thumb fall away, he lowered his lips to hover over mine. For a split second he paused, and then he kissed me.

At first, his lips were firm against mine, a foreign sensation that made my pulse skip a beat. I'd never been kissed before—not like this.

When I didn't pull away, he deepened the kiss, and my hands

came up to touch the sides of his face. I kissed him back, though I became more and more aware of what we were doing, of the fact that there was no going back from a kiss. I couldn't say we were simply friends anymore, but what were we?

His touch should have felt amazing. My senses should have been heightened, and I should have been lost in the moment, oblivious to everything around us.

But I wasn't. I was completely aware of the dog barking to our right, the church bell ringing in the distance, the smell of the river floating on the cool air. And the more fervent he became, the more aware I became that this wasn't as magical as I had imagined. Kissing him wasn't what I thought it would be.

I pressed my hands against his chest, putting enough pressure there to let him know I didn't want to continue.

He was breathless and dazed as he pulled back, and a slow smile tilted his lips. "That was everything I hoped it would be, Meg."

I wanted to say the same, but it wasn't true. Instead of feeling dazed and breathless, I felt disappointed. It wasn't horrible—just not enchanting.

His smile faltered, and I think he misread my response.

"I'm sorry—I don't know why I did that. You made me promise, and I broke my promise." He scoffed as he sat up. "A politician through and through."

I also sat up, not wanting him to beat himself up. "I could have stopped you, but I didn't."

"You're right." He turned back to me, his gaze hopeful. "You didn't stop me." He reached for me again, but I put up my hand to stop him this time.

"I don't think it's a good idea, Seth." I shook my head. "I'm not ready."

He frowned. "Why not? It can't just be your work. I don't get it. Am I not good enough for you?"

"What?" It was my turn to frown. "You're wonderful. It has nothing to do with you."

"Of course it does—how could it not?"

I put my hand on Seth's shoulder, not wanting to make a bigger deal of this than necessary. "It's truly me, Seth. I have so much riding on the next five months of my life. When I fall in love, I want no regrets and nothing standing in my way. If I let my heart go now, I'm afraid it would be divided, and that wouldn't be fair to you."

He thought I was talking about my work, but I was really talking about the broader aspects of my three lives. I didn't want to divide my heart right now—though it was happening anyway.

Pulling my legs up, I pressed my forehead against my knees. "I'm so confused."

He put his hand on my back. "I'm sorry, Meg. You've been clear with me from the beginning. I should apologize."

I looked up and tried to smile, but a movement near the bike path caught my attention. A man leaned out from behind a tree, focusing a camera on us.

"Who is that?" I asked, pointing.

The man ducked behind the tree, though I could still see part of his body.

"Where?" Seth asked.

"Right there, behind that tree. He had a camera and was taking pictures of us."

"I doubt it. It's too dark to see anything, anyway."

"It's not that dark yet. How long has he been there?" I felt violated. We were enjoying a quiet moment—a private moment—and the photographer had probably captured every bit of it.

How had he known who we were? Was it some weirdo just photographing people in the park? Or was it a journalist who had been passing by and saw Seth and me? The gossip columns were feasting on our time together. It wasn't until the pictures were published that I even knew we were being watched on our outings—just like now. But this wasn't a major event or destination. It was a park. How had they known to look for us here?

"Who is it?" I asked Seth.

"What does it matter?" He shrugged. "Probably another gossip columnist."

"Doesn't it bother you that they're following us?"

He shrugged again. "It's good publicity."

"I don't need publicity."

"Because your job isn't dependent on public perception or popularity. I need all the publicity I can get."

For the first time, I wondered if Seth was seeing me because of the attention we received. Being part of the youngest power couple in DC was good publicity—for him.

But I didn't want to assume the worst. Seth seemed to genuinely like me. Maybe the publicity was a by-product of our relationship.

"I should get home," I told him, starting to stand.

"Really?" He sounded disappointed. "Want to take a stroll through the park first?"

"No. I need to study tonight. I can't put it off any longer."

He sighed but stood up so I could fold the blanket and tuck it into the picnic basket. As we left the park, he glanced behind us, though I couldn't see what he was looking at.

The closer we came to home, though, the less I worried about whether or not Seth had told a photographer where we would be and when. All I could think about was tomorrow and whether or not I would wake up in 1861.

16

꧁꧂

My mind slowly came to consciousness, but I didn't open my eyes. For a few seconds, I just lay in bed, wondering what I would see when I finally had enough courage to look at the room around me. Would it be my bedroom on Lafayette Square in 1861, or would it be the dorm room at the Naval Medical Center in 1941?

With as much nerve as I could muster, I lifted my eyelids and took in the scene.

A canopy bed stretched overhead, and a feather tick mattress cushioned me.

I was in 1861.

It took all my willpower not to shout for joy, though I did spring from the bed, tossing my covers aside as I raced to the window—just to make sure.

A carriage drove by on Lafayette Square, headed toward St. John's Church. The blue sky spread out over the rooftops and trees, and soft white clouds drifted by.

Slowly, I sank to my knees and clasped my hands together as

I pressed them to my forehead. "Thank you, God," I whispered, never more grateful than I was in this moment. "Thank you for not taking this away from me."

My relief was so profound that I realized how much this path truly meant to me. The thought of losing it forever had weighed heavily upon my heart, but whether it was because I had thought I lost it or because it meant more to me than the other two, I wasn't certain.

The first thing I wanted to do was check on my patient and see if he had lived through the night.

My heart sank at the thought. Perhaps he had died, as fate had planned, and that was why I was still here.

Rushing through my morning toilette with Saphira's help, I dressed as quickly as possible in a simple morning gown, leaving my hair in a braid to rest over my shoulder, and left my room.

Papa stepped out of his own bedchamber with a desperate look on his face and ran into me. He braced me with his hands as pure relief washed over him. Pulling me into a hug, he held me tight. "Margaret, you're alive."

I returned his embrace, tears filling my eyes and spilling onto my cheeks. "I'm still here."

He pulled back, and I saw the moisture in his eyes. "I hardly slept last night. I checked on you several times to make sure you were still breathing. I've never prayed so hard in my life. I don't understand what you told me last night, but I believe you. And I'm so relieved you're still here with me."

I hugged him again, thankful I was back and that he finally knew the truth.

"Where are you going?" he asked.

"To check on my patient."

He shook his head, his expression troubled. "I've instructed Joseph to see to the soldier's needs. You are not to be in his room again."

"I must see him." Desperation stole over me. "I need to check his vital signs and make sure he's not suffering any complications from the surgery. I performed a very delicate procedure, and I need to make sure he's stable. I do this all the time in my other paths, Papa. It's completely acceptable."

"Perhaps in a different time and place," he said quietly, lifting his chin as he removed his hands from my arms. "But not here. I'm still trying to comprehend what you told me last night, but it changes nothing. You are a senator's daughter, my hostess, and a rising figure in Washington society. I cannot have your name muddied with talk of injured soldiers or convalescing patients. I'm already worried about what Mrs. Wilson might tell others."

"Please." I put my hand on his forearm. "This is my calling. I was born to be a healer. I will not go into his room alone. I'll bring Saphira with me at all times. Will that appease you? I must check on him, or he may die from complications I could prevent."

His exhaustion showed as he studied me. Finally, he sighed in resignation. "Fine. But you must take care, Margaret. I cannot abide gossip or slander about you, and if anyone knew what you have done, they would say vile things—perhaps even report you to the authorities."

"I know. I will take utmost care with my reputation. You have my word."

"We have much to discuss, but for now, I should get to the White House. Yesterday was a disaster, and the president will need all the support he can get."

I nodded. "I will make sure everything is taken care of here."

Saphira was still in my room, making my bed, so I asked her to come with me into the soldier's room. My heart pounded hard as I slowly opened the door, not sure what would greet me.

I was completely surprised to find Gray, sitting in one of the chairs near the bed, asleep.

My heart softened as I wiped away the last of my tears. I had forgotten that he said he would stay with the patient overnight.

Papa probably didn't realize he was still in the house either, or he would have never left.

Saphira stood by the door as I slowly walked across the room and leaned over the still body of the soldier. I held my breath, praying that he was alive, and laid two fingers over the radial artery in his wrist to feel for a pulse.

It was there—faint but steady.

Tears of joy filled my eyes as Gray stirred and looked up at me.

"How is he?" Gray asked, his voice husky from sleep.

"Alive, thank God."

"And thanks to you." He stood and rubbed his hands over his face, then stretched.

"Did you get much sleep?" I stayed on the opposite side of the bed, still amazed that I had returned to 1861 and that Gray had held vigil over the soldier throughout the night.

"I dozed off a few times, but I didn't get much sleep." He was still wearing the suit he'd had on the day before, though his stained coat hung over the back of a chair and his shirtsleeves were rolled up to his elbows. In 1861, it was considered a state of undress—but to my twenty-first-century eyes, it was completely acceptable, and Gray didn't seem to notice.

"You should go home to sleep," I said. "Saphira and I can see to the soldier's needs today."

"I must go to work. We have a mess on our hands, and we'll need to strategize and pick up the pieces." He started to roll down his sleeves as he looked around the room. "May I have some water to freshen up?"

"Of course." I turned to Saphira. "Can you please have Joseph bring up fresh water for Mr. Cooper?"

Saphira nodded and left the room—which meant I had already broken my promise to Papa, though there was nothing to be done about it. I owed a debt of gratitude to Gray for all his help last night.

He put on his suit coat and ran his hands through his hair a few times. With a day's growth of beard, he looked dangerously handsome.

"May I come back later?" he asked. "To check on our patient . . . and talk?"

The room was dark, since the shades were still drawn, and even with the patient asleep on the bed, it was a little too intimate. I wanted Gray to come back, but what could I say about what had happened? I was still trying to process it all and wondering how it was possible that I had changed history and not forfeited my path here.

"Of course," I told him. "I'd love to see you again."

He smiled and came around the bed. The door was wide open, allowing in natural light from the hallway windows—and making his beautiful brown eyes seem more bottomless than usual.

"What you did last night was nothing short of a miracle, Maggie." He paused, frowning slightly. "I'm a very perceptive person and can read most people within minutes of meeting them, and I'm usually never wrong. It's been a blessing and a curse. But you?" He shook his head. "As soon as I think I've figured you out, you surprise me again. You've left me completely undone, and it's driving me—" His frown softened, and he looked at me with something akin to wonder. "The war has complicated everything, and nothing is as it should be." He paused, as if he couldn't articulate what he meant. "I'd like to come back—but not just to check on the soldier. I'd like to come back and see you again—call on you—if I may."

It was one of the most inelegant soliloquys I'd ever heard, but it was sweet and candid and earnest.

Yet spending more time with Gray—if his intentions were romantic—presented the same problem I had with Seth. Along with the added predicament of the surgery he had helped me perform. It was a procedure that no one else in 1861 could have performed, especially a young society lady. He would have questions and would need some answers. Whether I let him call on me or not, he'd be looking for the truth.

If I was honest with myself, I wanted him to call on me. I wanted to get some answers of my own, like why he intrigued me the way he did and made my heart skip a beat when he looked at me the way he was right now.

"I would like that," I said quietly.

"So would I."

A moan came from the bed, startling me out of my reverie. We both looked at the soldier, who was starting to move.

"Lie still," I instructed as I approached the bed and gently laid my hand on his arm. He was so thin and young. "You were injured at Centreville yesterday, and you've lost a lot of blood. But you're safe now."

The young man blinked his eyes open. "Are you an angel, ma'am?"

Gray came up behind me, standing closer than necessary. "Yes, she is."

"That's what I thought." The boy smiled and closed his eyes again.

My cheeks warmed as I felt the heat from Gray's body. "What's your name?" I asked the soldier.

"My name's Virgil Earp, ma'am, of the Illinois Volunteer Infantry."

I took a surprised step back, bumping into Gray, who put his hand on the small of my back to steady me.

Virgil Earp? "Do you have a brother named Wyatt?"

Virgil frowned and nodded. "Yes, ma'am, I do. He's a mite younger than me. How do you know him?"

I felt Gray's eyes on me as well, and I realized, too late, that I had no way to explain this knowledge. But I was still reeling from the information. Virgil Earp wasn't supposed to die on the battlefield—he was supposed to end up at the O.K. Corral

185

in the 1880s. I'd watched *Tombstone* as a teenager in my 2001 path and knew at least that much about him and his famous brothers.

I racked my memory. Moments before he had been shot, I had collided with him. He had stepped aside, and that was when he had been hit by the stray bullet. Was I the reason he had stepped out of place in history? Was that why God had allowed me to save him?

Both men were staring at me, waiting. How did I explain my knowledge?

"I was born in Illinois," I said quickly, which was true. "I'm familiar with your family name, though I've never had the pleasure of meeting you, Private Earp, until now."

My explanation seemed to appease Virgil's curiosity, but Gray didn't seem so easily mollified. He lowered his hand from my back and shifted away from me.

"You've been through an ordeal," I said to Virgil. "I want you to lie as still as possible while your leg heals. If you need anything, please let me know."

"I sure will." He smiled from me to Gray. "It's nice of you folks to take me into your home. Your wife is heaven sent, sir."

My cheeks warmed again at Virgil's assumption. I looked up at Gray, waiting for him to correct the young man, but he simply smiled at me.

"Mr. Cooper helped me bring you home," I told Virgil, reveling in his mistake for just a moment. "This is my father's house. He'll be home later to meet you. But Mr. Cooper is just about to leave."

"I'm sorry, miss. I just assumed."

"It's alright," Gray said, putting his hand on Virgil's foot to still his apology. "I could only be so lucky."

The heat in my cheeks increased, and when I glanced up at Gray again, he winked at me.

I couldn't hide my smile.

Rumors and fear had spread through Washington like wildfire, and at any moment we expected the Confederate army to march through our weak defenses. The defeat at Bull Run had made two things alarmingly clear to everyone: the war would not end anytime soon, and we were not as strong as we had thought.

Clara came to visit me early in the day. She had taken a couple of injured soldiers into her home, but there were countless wounded men lying in the streets all throughout Washington. The City Infirmary could not meet all their needs. We went out for the afternoon with medical supplies and did what we could, though it was a daunting task, and we were not prepared for the challenge.

After several hours, I came home to change for supper, hoping Papa had not returned to the house yet, knowing he would not approve of my activities. I didn't know if he would come before Gray, so I waited eagerly for both men.

In the end, Papa walked up to the house first. It was past eight, and his shoulders were stooped like never before.

I met him at the door and took his hat and coat. Though I had a hundred questions, I wanted to let him share in his own time. He had probably spent most of the day talking and was clearly exhausted.

"I've delayed supper for you," I said.

He put his hand on my cheek and offered a sad smile. "It wasn't necessary. I had a bit of supper at the White House. You should eat."

"I'm not hungry."

We walked into the front parlor, and I moved a pillow aside on the sofa so he could sit. He let out a weary sigh as he sat back and pressed a hand to his head.

"Do you have a headache?"

He nodded. "It's been plaguing me all day."

"I will ask Saphira to make you a cup of willow bark tea for the pain." I turned to do just that, wishing I had some Tylenol or Excedrin for him, but he stopped me.

"Please stay, Margaret. I have something I'd like to ask you."

I nodded and sat beside him on the sofa, my pulse thrumming. "Yes?"

He leaned forward, his blue eyes intense. "If it's true that you live in 1941 and 2001, then it occurred to me that you know how this war will end. Please." He gripped my hands in his. "Tell me."

The air left my lungs as I stared at him, slowly shaking my head. "I wish I could, but it's impossible."

"Why?" He frowned, almost angry. "We were beaten yesterday, in a shameful and embarrassing loss. I must know if we will win this war."

"It is not for me to say. No one else in 1861 knows the outcome of this war, and if they did, it could alter the future. Like I told you, if I knowingly change history, I will forfeit the path I change. If I tell you, then I might not wake up here tomorrow. It's as simple as that."

"But you know, don't you?"

"Of course I know."

He stared at me. "When we left yesterday for Centreville, you knew the outcome, didn't you?"

"I did."

"And that's why you looked so defeated."

He was baiting me, though whether he knew it, I wasn't sure. I didn't blame him for wanting to know. But I could not tell him. "I'm sorry, Papa. I truly am. I wish I could tell you."

For a long time, he just looked at me. Then he leaned back on the sofa and ran his hands over his face. "How is our patient?"

"He is doing well." I wanted to tell him that it was Virgil Earp lying in our spare room upstairs, but it would mean nothing to him. "If there are no infections, I believe he will make a full recovery."

"That's very good." He smiled, though his focus seemed far away.

I wanted to tell him my intentions, though I knew he would not be happy. "Everyone is saying the war is here to stay, which means we will need to improve our hospitals and medical capabilities."

"It is here to stay, isn't it?" he asked, searching my face again.

"I will not tell you anything you do not already know."

"How does it work?"

"What?"

"The time-crossing. Do you go on this way indefinitely?"

I could not meet his gaze as I shook my head. "I must choose which path I want to keep on my twenty-first birthday and give up the other two forever."

"Your twenty-first birth—what does that mean?"

"On my twenty-first birthday, I will stay awake past midnight in the life I choose to keep, and my conscious mind will remain there. My physical bodies will die in whichever paths I choose to leave."

He looked incredulous as he sat up straighter. "You'll choose this one, of course."

How could I tell him that I wasn't certain? "I have three lives and dozens of people pulling me in different directions. I do not yet know what I will choose."

The pain in his eyes cut me deeply. "Are you telling me that you might *die* in January? How can that be?"

"I'm so sorry, Papa."

"Were you ever going to tell me?"

I shook my head, feeling guilt press down upon my grief. "I don't believe so. I knew it would be hard."

The confusion and hurt on his face tore at my heart. I wanted to change the subject.

"I want to be helpful," I told him. "Miss Barton plans to speak to President Lincoln as soon as possible about starting more hospitals, and I would like to volunteer and be of assistance to her. I have a lot of medical knowledge, and I believe it could be put to good use."

Papa shook his head. "It isn't seemly, Margaret. You are my daughter—not a doctor or nurse."

"Perhaps not here, but I am in my other paths. And I want to be something similar here, Papa. I have not pressured you about this before, but I want to be useful. I cannot sit back and watch people suffer when I could do something about it."

He looked defeated in every possible way, but there was fire and determination in his gaze. "I cannot abide the idea of you doing such menial work with men you do not know. You are a lady. This war is already changing everything we hold dear. I cannot let it change my hopes and dreams for you as well. One day you will preside over a fine home with an honorable husband at your side. If I allow you to do this, it could put all of that in jeopardy."

"Please do not ask me to sit back and watch while I could be doing something useful." I didn't want to beg, but I could not let this go.

"I will not hear of it, Margaret. You've already told me the most devastating news I've ever received, and you want to ask more of me? It's too much. I cannot bear any more." He stood without looking at me and started to leave the room but then paused near the door and lifted his chin. "I have news of my own. I've been contemplating it for some time, but after yesterday, I became resolved. I am returning to military service. I've asked President Lincoln to petition the Senate to commission me as early as next week, and I plan to start soon after."

I stood, my heart pounding. "What?"

He turned, his eyes shadowed with pain. "You may be a healer, but I am a military man. I cannot ask others to do what I would not do myself. I will fight for my country."

He left the parlor and walked up the stairs, his head held high.

I sank onto the sofa again, pain and confusion piercing my soul. Tears burned my eyes, and I let them fall unchecked.

My father's decision not to let me get involved made me angry, yet I knew he was speaking out of pain and fear. Everything was spiraling out of control, and he was trying to grasp onto something he could command. It just happened to be me. Not only was he dealing with the disappointment of the war, but I had just told him I might die here in five months, and it would be because I had chosen another life over him.

The front bell rang, and I quickly wiped my eyes, afraid Gray had arrived and he would find me crying.

Joseph exited the kitchen and made his way to the front door as I stood to receive my caller. My eyes were probably red, and I was not fit to receive company, but I wanted to see Gray. His very presence seemed to give me strength.

"Can you please give this to your mistress?" someone said at the front door.

"Yes, sir." Joseph closed the door and entered the parlor with a note. "This just came for you."

I accepted it with a quiet thank-you. Joseph excused himself. The note was from Gray, and it was brief.

Dear Maggie,

I deeply regret that I am unable to come to you this evening. My work has called me away, and I do not know how long I will be detained. I was looking forward to seeing you again, but I cannot deny my country at a time like this. Please know I am thinking of you and will call the moment I am able.

Yours respectfully,
Gray

My tears fell in earnest.

17

JULY 23, 1941
WILLIAMSBURG, VIRGINIA

A few days had passed since Dr. Philips asked Anna and me to go to Pearl Harbor. My heart had been so heavy after my conversation with Papa that I was distracted in each of my paths. He was determined to enter the fight, and no matter how much I protested, I could not change his mind. Virgil was healing well, for which I was thankful, but Gray had not come to visit, and I had not received another note from him.

But today was a new day, and I had a whole different set of problems to deal with in 1941.

The sun was setting on the horizon as the train pulled into the depot at Williamsburg. It had been three months since Anna and I had left, but to me, it was much longer, and I missed Mama and Daddy.

"It was nice of Dr. Philips to get us a pass to come home," Anna said as she gathered her belongings. "I think he'd do almost anything for you."

I lowered the netting of my hat over my face and smoothed

out my skirt before I rose to leave the train. "He's eager for us to join the USS *Solace*, that's all."

Anna gave me a knowing look as we walked down the aisle and out onto the busy platform.

"There they are." I waved to Daddy, Mama, and Teddy, who were waiting for us. They all waved back and moved through the crush of people to wrap us in their arms.

After hugging Mama and Daddy, I went into my older brother's embrace. Teddy was five years older than me. His father had died in WWI, and because Teddy was so young when Mama remarried Daddy, Teddy knew no other father. The only thing that really set him apart was that he was the Marquess of Cumberland, the heir of a beautiful manor house in Whitby, England, and divided his time between Whitby and Williamsburg. Though, with the war approaching, I wondered what would become of him. Would he fight? He was only twenty-five years old, with his whole life in front of him. I didn't want to think of him fighting.

"Hello, Maggie," he said, shaking his head as he held me at arm's length. He was so handsome, with Mama's coloring and an aristocratic bearing that had been born into him. "When did you grow up and stop being a kid?"

"Be careful," I said with a facetious smile. "I'm much older than you in time and experience."

"Almost sixty-three years now?" he asked with a laugh. "No matter, you'd be more mature than me even if you occupied only one path."

"Come," Mama said. "I'm eager to get the three of you home where you belong."

It felt good to be crushed into the back of the Studebaker with my siblings again. Soon we were on the Palace Green where our dear, familiar house stood next to the reconstructed Governor's Palace.

As part of the restoration project of Williamsburg, Mama

and Daddy had purchased the house where Daddy lived in 1775 with his parents. They had returned it to its original appearance, but though it looked like a museum, it had always been a warm and comfortable home to grow up in.

I was eager to speak to my parents alone about Pearl Harbor, but Mama had prepared a late supper, and then we all sat around the dining room table to visit. It wasn't until much later that I finally found a moment to talk to my parents without my sister and brother able to overhear.

Anna had gone up to take a bath, and Teddy had retired to his room to write a letter. Daddy and Mama always ended their day in the study, and today was no exception. Daddy was sitting at his desk, looking over essays from the summer class he was teaching, and Mama held a book. The fireplace, which usually blazed in the winter months, was empty. A window was open, allowing in a cool evening breeze, and a few lamps cast a soft glow over the bookshelves, comfortable furniture, and throw rugs.

"Maggie." Mama's face lit up with a smile when she noticed me. She set aside her book and patted the sofa. "Come in."

Daddy looked up from his paper and took off his glasses, his blue eyes sparkling at my arrival. They had always looked at each of us as if we were truly remarkable. Though I had been blessed with three sets of wonderful parents, my marked mother and father were special. I bore their marks and could speak to them openly about time-crossing, so I had always felt a unique bond with them.

"I could tell something was on your mind as soon as I saw you at the depot," Daddy said, swiveling his chair away from his desk and giving me his full attention.

"Your call was a surprise." Mama tucked a wisp of hair back into the roll along the side of my head. A hint of worry filled her green eyes. "Did something happen in one of your other paths?"

"Many things are happening." I looked down at my hands. "We just endured the First Battle of Bull Run in 1861."

Daddy nodded, understanding completely. As an American History professor at the College of William and Mary, he probably knew more than I did about what was happening. "Are you any closer to making a decision?"

I shook my head. "No, although I thought I had lost 1861, and when I returned there, my relief was so profound that it has made me wonder if I am not meant to stay there permanently." I quickly told them about saving Virgil Earp's life. "I don't understand what happened," I admitted. "I thought I was changing history, but he lived, and I was allowed to stay there."

"Why do you think you were so relieved to return?" Mama asked. "Has a special young man caught your eye?"

There was a special young man, but was he the reason I was relieved? "I have met someone, but he is not the reason. I hardly know him." I didn't want to talk about Gray right now. "But that's not why I've come home. I have a problem in this path that I need help navigating."

"What happened?" Mama asked.

My parents could be trusted with future knowledge. Having lived with this gift, they knew, better than anyone else, how to keep information to themselves.

"I have never told you," I began, "but there will be a catastrophic event on December seventh of this year that will lead us into the war."

"I knew there would be another world war," Mama said. "My marked mother told me as much. And with the growing tension, I knew it would be soon."

"Japan will attack America at Pearl Harbor in Honolulu," I told them quietly. "They will destroy most of the Pacific fleet and take thousands of lives."

Mama and Daddy looked at one another, unspoken

communication passing between them. I'd never met two people who understood each other like they did.

"President Roosevelt will call for our entrance into the war," I continued, "and we will fight until 1945."

"We'll win," Mama said as more of a statement than a question.

"We will."

"Why are you telling us this?" Daddy asked. "You know the risks."

"I'm telling you because Dr. Philips has asked if Anna and I would like to be transferred to the USS *Solace*, which will be heading to Pearl Harbor in a couple of weeks. The hospital ship will be there on December seventh."

My parents did not speak as they stared at me.

Finally, Mama asked, "Will the *Solace* be attacked?"

"I don't know. I haven't done much research on Pearl Harbor because I didn't think it would affect me. And now I'm afraid to in case I learn something I could change. It would be hard enough to be there in the days leading up to the attack without that temptation."

"We both understand," Mama assured me. "Your father and I knew of many events in the 1770s that we could not prevent. It's one of the burdens of this gift."

"One of many," I said.

"What do you want to do?" Daddy asked.

I shook my head. "I don't know."

"If you didn't know what was going to happen," Mama said, "would you want to go to Pearl Harbor?"

"Yes—without a doubt. I would love to work on a hospital ship and see Hawaii. Who wouldn't?"

"Then," Daddy said, "perhaps that's your answer. You can try to enjoy the experience before December and see why God is calling you there."

Was it that easy? I had so many decisions facing me, it didn't seem possible that I could come to a conclusion with such simple logic.

"What about Anna?" I asked, looking from Mama to Daddy.

"She seems happier." Mama smiled. "I think going to Washington was a good idea. Does she want to go to Hawaii?"

"Very much."

"Then she should go too." Daddy leaned back in his chair. "Life is a gift and an adventure. We should never let fear hold us back from doing the things God has called us to do. The risk isn't always in going, sometimes the risk is in staying and missing out on the journey."

"Should she know about the attack?"

"No." Mama shook her head adamantly. "There's no purpose in weighing her down with the truth before it's necessary. I know it's hard for you, Maggie, but it would be even harder for her to keep the information to herself."

"But what about her grief?" I asked. "Hasn't she suffered enough?"

"Suffering is not the worst thing in this world," Daddy said. "We all suffer. Letting your grief hold you back from living is the true travesty. It will be hard for her, but it will be hard for everyone who is there. And overcoming tragedy makes you stronger. Maybe she'll realize how very strong she truly is."

"I wish you could help me make my final decision as easily as you helped me make this one."

"You'll be in Hawaii over your birthday," Mama said. "This might be the last time we see you before you make your decision."

I nodded. "I've thought about that."

She took my hands in hers. "Your father and I understand how difficult this decision is for you, and we want you to know something."

Daddy left his chair and joined us on the sofa, sitting on my other side.

"No matter what choice you make," she said, "we will trust that it is the right choice. Don't feel a moment of guilt over leaving us if that is what you decide."

Tears stung my eyes at their selflessness.

"We love you," Daddy said. "And we don't want to make your decision any more difficult than necessary."

"I know." I smiled as I wiped at my cheeks. "You've always eased my burdens."

Mama had tears in her own eyes. "And as much as you want to ease your sister's pain, you are not her keeper. You cannot base your decision on guilt over leaving her, either."

"Or anyone else, in any of your paths," Daddy added. "We know how responsible you feel for your father in 1861, as well."

"And how responsible you feel for your patients in 2001." Mama understood me better than anyone else. "It is not your job to fix all the pain in the world, Maggie Hollingsworth. You have been given a special gift, and it carries with it a lot of responsibility, but perhaps God is trying to teach you how to let go and trust Him. Not only with your life, but with the lives of everyone you love. Don't let anyone else pressure you into choosing a path that isn't right for you."

"That seems impossible."

"It won't be easy," Mama acknowledged. "But in the end, it will be necessary. If you choose a path out of obligation or guilt, then you could become bitter. For example, if you chose this path for Anna, and then she goes on to get married, move away, and leave you without a purpose here, you might grow resentful. If you chose 1861 out of obligation to your father, and something happens to him and you're all alone there, you might feel cheated. Make the choice out of faith, not fear or obligation."

"We know that goes against your character," Daddy added. "You've lived most of your life caring for others. But there will come a day when you will need to do what's best for you and you alone."

I nodded slowly, knowing that what they were saying was true, though it felt impossible. How could I not take the people I loved into consideration as I made my choice?

"You should get some sleep," Mama said. "I have a full day planned for us, and your body here needs some rest."

I gave each of them a kiss and a hug and then returned to my old bedroom.

As I moved through the house, letting my hand trail against the wallpaper, the wainscotting, and up the railing, I wondered if this would be the last time I ever slept in this house.

As promised, Mama had a full day of activities planned for us. While it was in a constant state of improvement, the bulk of Colonial Williamsburg had been either restored or rebuilt by 1941, and it made for a fun day of playing tourist. As a teenager, I had volunteered in several of the buildings and shops, and I enjoyed reconnecting with those who still worked there. Mama especially loved to volunteer. She often helped in the printing shop, dressed in authentic colonial clothing, educating visitors about life in Colonial America. Little did they know she had been the first female public printer in Virginia in 1774.

I told Anna that I had decided to join the crew of the *Solace*, and she spent the day talking about our upcoming adventure. She seemed buoyed by the idea of going to Hawaii and was almost like her old self.

Mama took us shopping for a few things we would need on the island, like new swimming suits and sunglasses, and I reveled in Anna's excitement. If I hadn't known about December 7, I would have been thrilled at the prospect of going to Hawaii as well.

Eventually the day came to an end, and we were back at the train depot, twenty-four short hours after we arrived in Williamsburg.

"I can't believe we're saying good-bye once again," Mama said as she hugged Anna and then took me into her arms. She held me so tight, tears stung my eyes, and I squeezed her in return. "Thank you for spending the day with me," she said as she pulled back, tears in her own eyes. "I will be praying for you every single day, Maggie. And no matter what you choose, Daddy and I will understand."

"I'll write to you," I promised.

"You'd better." She used a fresh handkerchief to wipe at my tears and then at her own.

Daddy stood by, his gentle eyes taking in the two of us. He had always been handsome, but he'd become even more so as he aged. I walked into his embrace next, feeling completely enveloped in his strength and love.

"I'm so proud of you," he said quietly, for my ears alone, though I'm sure he said the same to Anna when he had hugged her. "No matter where you decide to stay, Maggie, you will be a blessing, and that's exactly why you were created."

"Thank you, Daddy." I stood on tiptoe and kissed his cheek. "I love you."

"I love you too."

Steam released from the engine, and the conductor called all aboard.

I gave Teddy a hug and told him to be safe, and then it was time for Anna and me to board the train back to Bethesda and on to our future.

After we were situated on the train and it had left the station, I sat back on the bench and sighed.

"Saying good-bye is so hard," Anna mused as she looked out the window at the passing countryside. "Sometimes you get to the point that you just want it to be over, even if that means heartache and pain. The anticipation and dread of it is exhausting. Sometimes it's even harder than the actual parting."

I couldn't agree more.

Part of me wanted it to be January so I could just get it over with. It was getting harder and harder to pretend like the end wasn't in sight.

I had five months left before my birthday.

Although I was thankful I had control over which path to choose, a small part of me wished God would choose for me. No matter which path I ended up in, there would be pain and heartache, so what did it truly matter?

18

AUGUST 3, 2001
WASHINGTON, DC

The day had been long and difficult in my trauma and emergency surgery rotation. We had lost a cardiac patient that morning, and I had gone in with the surgeon to tell the patient's wife and children he wasn't going home. It was truly the worst part of my job, no matter which path I occupied, and it would take me days to shake off the heaviness.

But it hadn't ended there. Dr. Erdman had called me into his office to tell me I had been given a poor review by one of my professors. She'd said my recent research papers lacked depth of study and I'd been late to several shifts. If things didn't improve, Dr. Erdman would remove me from the running for a position in the surgical residency program.

I left the hospital with a heavy heart, disappointed in myself, though I shouldn't be surprised. Since meeting Seth, I had been falling behind. I couldn't blame him, though. I had said yes to each of his invitations. Why was it so hard to say no to him? Other than the fact that he made me feel young, attractive, and wanted?

I glanced at my watch, realizing how late it was. I had promised Seth I would attend a black-tie fundraiser with him at the Smithsonian's National Air and Space Museum that evening, and he was picking me up at my apartment in less than an hour. I had seen him several times since he kissed me in the park, but neither of us had discussed it or what it meant, and I wanted to keep it that way for now.

Delilah wasn't home when I arrived at our apartment, so I got dressed without her help. I chose the simple black gown I'd worn to the White House the night I met Seth and twisted my hair into a low chignon. My heart wasn't in the event, but again, it wasn't Seth's fault, so I didn't want to blame him.

There was no one to blame but myself.

As I prepared for the evening, all I could think about was what I needed to tell Seth. Even before getting the poor review, I knew things had to change. We needed to slow down. It helped that Seth was returning to South Carolina for the next three weeks. I had toyed with the idea of not telling him we needed to take a serious break, to just let those three weeks settle between us, but the bad review suggested I needed to stand stronger. I needed to tell Seth that we couldn't see each other when he came back to DC in September. It would be better to put more time and distance between us. Then maybe I could finish medical school strong and make a decision about my path without the complication of my feelings for him.

I was more determined than ever when he finally buzzed my apartment. It was hot, so I didn't grab a shawl as I left to meet him in front of our building.

He wore his tuxedo again—and when he turned to greet me, I couldn't deny he was handsome. His all-American good looks never ceased to amaze me. How could one man be so attractive, both in personality and appearance? No wonder it was so hard to say no to him.

"Meg." He grinned and met me on the sidewalk, kissing my

cheek, though the look in his eyes suggested he would have liked to do more. "You are stunning, as usual."

"Thank you. You are, too."

"We're a good-looking couple, aren't we?" He laughed, spinning me around. "No wonder the cameras love us."

I hadn't thought about the gossip columns for a few days—not since the stir from the last set of pictures had died down. Photos of us kissing in the park had been everywhere—just as I suspected. Everyone had seen us lying on that picnic blanket. My parents had both called, elated to hear that we had taken our relationship to the next level, though I told them the pictures were misleading. I had tried to ignore all of the publicity, telling myself it wasn't anyone's business, but it wasn't easy.

Seth hadn't been upset about the pictures—not in the least. He told me it was part of the package deal of being a public servant.

But it was one more reason I needed a break from him. It was all too much, especially because I worried that he had set up the photographer. I didn't have proof and I didn't want to unjustly accuse him, but what were the odds a photographer happened to be there at the right time? Was Seth using me? Or just taking advantage of the situation?

He led me to his car, carefree. I held back, not ready to go. "Can we talk?"

"Yeah." His eyes shone with excitement. "But we're going to be late, and I want to hear the Smithsonian Director speak. Can we talk later? Maybe take a stroll? I have a surprise for you."

With a sigh, I nodded. Maybe it was a good idea to talk about it later. I didn't know how Seth would take the news, and I didn't want to ruin our evening before it got started.

The National Air and Space Museum was housed in an impressive two-story building on the south side of the National Mall. When we entered the museum, my eyes immediately rose to the high ceiling, where several important airplanes were suspended in the air. It was hard not to feel awed by the vast space of the building and the majestic aircraft that had advanced humankind's quest to understand the world and universe around us.

The museum was closed to the public for the fundraiser, and we had a front-row seat to each of the exhibits. No lines, no crowds, and no school groups to contend with.

"I've changed my mind," Seth said as we walked around the Wright Flyer, marveling at the thin struts and wires and canvas that launched man into the air. "If I lived in a different time period, I wouldn't want to live during the Civil War. I think I'd like to be alive at the birth of aviation. I think I would have been an airplane fanatic."

I could easily see Seth walking on wings, racing experimental aircraft across the ocean, and doing barrel rolls in a rickety airplane. He had that exciting, charismatic personality so many of those early aviators possessed.

After we enjoyed refreshments and listened to the Smithsonian Director talk about the past, present, and future of the institution, I was getting anxious to have my talk with Seth. I was about to suggest we take that walk he had promised when he said, "Want to get out of here? There's an Italian restaurant close by that I'd like to take you to."

I wasn't very hungry, but maybe it would be easier to talk over a meal, so I nodded.

We left the museum, and Seth took my hand to lead me across the street and down the block. He was excited, his fingers entwined with mine, looking back at me with a grin. I frowned, wondering what he was up to. Then I remembered he had promised me a surprise. Was it waiting for us at the restaurant? Whatever it was, I hoped it wouldn't make our conversation more awkward.

"We're a little late," he said, "but I don't think they'll mind."

I pulled on his hand to stop him, but he was impatient and tugged me to keep going. "Who won't mind?"

"You'll see." He winked at me and nodded to a restaurant down the block. "There it is. Come on."

The restaurant looked really upscale—the kind that needed reservations weeks in advance. At least we wouldn't be too out of place in our formal attire.

A delicious garlic and basil aroma met me the moment we entered the lobby. The restaurant was dimly lit with candles on the tables and the sound of tinkling laughter and conversation.

"There they are." Seth nodded toward the dining area.

I looked in that direction but didn't recognize anyone.

"It looks like our party has already arrived," Seth said to the hostess. "Howard and Maribeth Wallace."

Howard and Maribeth Wallace? Who—?

My breath froze as I realized who was sitting in the dining room.

Seth's parents.

He still held my hand, so I pulled him back. "Seth, why are your parents here?"

"They wanted to meet you." He grinned and kissed my cheek. "They flew all the way up from Charleston for this evening."

"Why?" I choked on the word.

"What do you mean, why?" He frowned. "I told them how important you are to me, and they wanted to meet you."

The hostess watched us with wide eyes but made no move to take us to our table.

I was still shaking my head, trying to grasp what he was doing, when the door opened behind us, and my parents walked in.

"Surprise!" Dad said as he came close to hug me. "Seth invited us to join you for supper tonight."

"Isn't that sweet?" Mom asked as she also hugged me. "He said his parents were visiting and thought the four of us should meet."

I turned back to Seth, feeling completely upended and alarmed—and angry. This was the opposite of what I wanted tonight. I was planning to put things on hold, and Seth had brought our two families together!

"Shall we go in to eat?" Seth asked. "It looks like my parents are already here."

"No." I shook my head, anger making me breathe heavily. I couldn't meet his parents, not like this.

"No?" Seth laughed, looking, for the first time, a little uncomfortable as he glanced at my mom and dad. "What do you mean *no?*"

My parents were both frowning and confused. They had no idea what Seth had done. They thought I wanted this.

"My parents came all the way from Charleston," Seth said under his breath as he tried to remain cool.

My jaw was locked together, and I spoke through my teeth. "You should have asked me first."

"Meg?" Mom put her hand on my back. "Is everything okay?"

It wasn't okay, but I couldn't make a scene here in the restaurant. My parents—and Seth's—didn't deserve that.

I swallowed all the things I wanted to say to Seth and forced myself to calm down enough to be rational. "I'm okay."

The hostess seemed relieved when Seth finally told her we were ready. She led us to a table where an older couple sat. It was easy to see where Seth got his good looks. Both his mother and father were attractive individuals. His father looked like an older version of Seth.

"Seth!" Mrs. Wallace said, her eyes glowing. "There you are."

Seth turned to me and put his arm possessively around my waist, all traces of the uncomfortable moment in the lobby gone. "This is Meg."

"It's so nice to meet you," Mrs. Wallace said as Mr. Wallace rose and extended his hand to me.

"It's a pleasure to finally meet you, Meg," Mr. Wallace said. "Seth has told us so much about you."

All I could do was force a smile and shake their hands. I was afraid if I spoke, I'd regret everything I said.

Mom and Dad still looked uneasy, but they quickly plastered smiles on their faces.

"These are Meg's parents," Seth continued, "Jonathan and Peggy Clarke."

"I'm Howard, and this is my wife, Maribeth," Mr. Wallace said as they all shook hands, and my parents took a seat.

"Howard Wallace, the quarterback for the Carolina Panthers?" Dad asked, clearly impressed.

Mr. Wallace smiled and nodded. "Not anymore, but at one time."

Of course Seth's father had been a professional football player. And soon we learned his mom had been Miss America at one point too. No wonder Seth had been elected to Congress at the age of twenty-five. His parents were famous, and just as charismatic and charming as he was.

From all appearances, the evening went off without a hitch. Except that it hadn't. I played nice, even commenting from time to time on conversation topics. But the entire time I was raging internally, preparing the things I wanted to say to Seth the second we were alone.

Thankfully, our parents kept the conversation going without much effort and were soon the best of friends. It was clear they had a lot in common. They were all overachievers, to begin with, but my dad and Mr. Wallace were avid golfers, Mrs. Wallace and my mom were both excellent cooks, and they were mutually impressed with each other's chosen professions.

Of course, Mr. and Mrs. Wallace had a lot of questions for me, and I was polite and conversational, though I was growing more and more upset with Seth as the night progressed. Our parents were under the impression that Seth and I were a serious couple, and they all appeared excited at the prospect. I hated disappointing four innocent bystanders.

As we were wrapping up the evening, my parents and Seth's were chatting about how they all needed to get together sometime soon in South Carolina. Mr. Wallace would take Dad golfing, and Mrs. Wallace would take Mom on a foodie tour of Charleston.

After I said good-bye to the Wallaces, Seth walked them outside, leaving me in the restaurant lobby with my parents.

"What an incredible family," Dad said, shaking his head in admiration. "You lucked out with Seth, kiddo."

"I'm just happy that you're happy." Mom hugged me, looking at me closely. "You are happy, aren't you?"

Now was not the time or place to get into the state of my mental health, so I simply smiled. "Seth and I have a lot to talk about."

"You couldn't ask for a nicer family to be connected to," Dad said.

Seth returned to the restaurant and said good-bye to my parents, then turned to me as they walked out.

"Surprised?" he asked, looking pleased with himself.

The facade I had worn all night finally slipped away, and my eyes burned with angry tears. "Why didn't you ask me first?"

Seth glanced at the poor hostess, who seemed to be watching our every move, and gently put his hand on the small of my back to guide me outside.

"Are you angry, Meg?"

"Angry?" I just stared at him. Was he truly that clueless, or was he purposely trying not to understand me? "Angry does not begin to describe how I'm feeling."

"Why?"

A group of people were leaving the restaurant, so he led me to the side of the building where we'd have more privacy. Was this all an act? Was he seriously surprised that I was angry?

"People do not introduce each other to their parents until they are serious, and never without consent. I don't know how to be clearer with you. I am not ready for a serious relationship."

"I don't get you." He finally looked angry, too. "We're so good together. Everyone thinks so."

"Who is everyone?"

"The newspapers, to begin with."

That was his first response? "That's another thing. How are they getting such intimate pictures of us? How did the photographer know we were going to be at the park?" I looked around the dark street. "Is there someone here now? Hoping to get a picture of us meeting each other's families? Will I see photos tomorrow morning of all of us sitting at the table?"

The look on Seth's face revealed everything. He briefly glanced toward a building on the opposite side of the street.

My mouth fell open, and my voice rose. "There is a photographer here, isn't there?"

"It's not what you think, Meg." He put up his hands to shush me. "Pictures don't hurt anyone. If you care about me, then you care about my career. I'm always campaigning."

"Are you admitting that you've been hiring the photographers? Staging events to benefit your political career?" I looked across the road, my jaw tight with fury. "What will they do when they see us fighting? Will they publish those pictures, too?"

"They only publish the ones I approve." His answer was so weak, so pathetic, and I took a step away from him.

"Meg." He tried to take my hand in his, but I pulled away.

210

"I'm leaving in the morning, and I won't be back for almost a month. I have a lot of meetings and events to attend in South Carolina while I'm gone. I don't want to leave on a bad note."

"This is over, Seth." I shook my head. "If I can't trust you, and you can't take no for an answer, then there's nothing left to say."

"You can't be serious." He stared at me, anger and confusion written all over his face. "This isn't supposed to end this way."

I lifted my eyebrows, incredulous. "Did you have that all planned out, too? How was it supposed to end, Seth? In an epic break-up that would somehow make me look bad and strengthen your approval rating?"

"No." His anger receded, and he just looked sad. "It wasn't ever supposed to end. I know I did some foolish things, Meg, but I'm in love with you. Surely you have to see that."

In some strange way, I did know he was in love with me. But it didn't matter.

"Your trip to South Carolina is coming at a good time. We both need some distance. Maybe you'll realize that what you've done isn't acceptable." I shook my head. "Good-bye, Seth."

And with that, I walked away from Seth Wallace.

19

AUGUST 8, 1861
WASHINGTON, DC

It had been five days since I'd said good-bye to Seth, and each day I felt better about my decision. He'd tried to call and email me, but I refused to respond. There had been so many red flags along the way that I should have ended it sooner. Now it was time to focus on other things.

As more and more soldiers arrived in Washington, Clara and I could not keep up with distributing all the supplies being sent to her from friends in the North. After checking on Virgil each morning, I joined Clara at her home, and we visited the new hospitals popping up throughout the city. President Lincoln had listened to Clara's plea and instructed the army to begin acquiring buildings throughout the city to use as military hospitals.

Papa was busy at the White House night and day and had said very little to me since our conversation on the evening he asked me how the war would end. He was usually gone before I woke up and didn't return until after I was in bed at night. This allowed me to continue volunteering with Clara—though if he found out, he would be very disappointed in me. Thankfully, Joseph, Saphira, and Goldie kept my secret and even helped when they were able.

It had been two and a half weeks since Virgil had come home with us, and he was healing well. He kept asking when he could return to his regiment, but I wanted him to stay off his leg for another week, if I could restrain him. I didn't visit with him often, since I tried to honor my father in that regard and only entered his room when necessary.

But it wasn't just the war effort, Papa, or even Virgil Earp that occupied my thoughts throughout the day. It was Gray—or rather, his absence in my life. He hadn't come to call or sent a note of explanation since the day after the Battle of Bull Run.

There was talk that the battle had been lost because a spy sent information to the enemies ahead of the fight. With Gray's absence, I couldn't help but wonder if he had something to do with the espionage. Had he sent information to Richmond? Was he responsible for the Union loss? Had he gone into hiding or even left to join the South?

I went about my work, day after day, trying not to think about the possibilities.

As I walked home from the C Street Hospital on a sultry August day, it was Gray who was on my mind. The irony of the situation didn't escape me. In 2001, I could not keep Seth away, and in 1861, I had no idea where Gray had gone.

I took in a breath of humid air and tried not to think about Seth, or the fact that I was just a few days from arriving at the USS *Solace* in 1941. I chose instead to focus on the here and now. It was the only way I knew not to be overwhelmed and to give each path its own attention.

Lafayette Square appeared ahead of me, the spire of St. John's Church pointing to the blue sky, and I let out a sigh. I had been invited to Rose Greenhow's house for a dinner party that evening, and while I appreciated the invitation, I didn't feel like socializing.

Papa had left a note with Joseph that morning telling me he wasn't sure if he could attend the party, but he would try. It might give us the opportunity to talk again, though what we would say to each other, I wasn't sure. He refused to give up the idea of serving in the military, and I was willfully disobeying him by helping Clara.

All I wanted was a cool bath before changing for the evening festivities. I had been working in the hospital for hours, and the tight, unkempt rooms had left me feeling grimy.

Joseph was at the front door even before I placed my hand on the doorknob. "Good afternoon, Miss Margaret." His gaze flittered between me and something in the front parlor, anxiety evident in the way he held his shoulders.

I stepped over the threshold, wondering what could make him so anxious—and soon found out.

"Margaret?" It was Papa.

I forced myself to smile as I entered the front parlor, removing my gloves, trying not to look guilty or worried. "You're home early."

Joseph closed the front door and scurried out of the foyer, disappearing into the back of the house.

"I wanted to get home in time to prepare for Mrs. Greenhow's party." Papa sat on the sofa, his arms crossed. "Imagine my surprise to find you gone."

"I'm often out during the day," I told him.

"Were you at the market?"

I untied my bonnet and took it off my head, then focused on straightening out the ribbons. "No."

"Where were you, Margaret?" He uncrossed his arms and stood. He looked as if he had aged a decade in the past month, with extra lines creasing his mouth and eyes and more gray hair at his temples.

I could not lie to him, nor could I continue to hide the truth. I hated living this way. "I was delivering supplies to the C Street Hospital with Miss Barton." I didn't tell him that I had assisted in the care of several soldiers, helping the surgeon on staff there to identify typhoid fever, which was spreading through the wards.

Papa stared at me for a long time, disappointment and pain evident in his gaze. Slowly, he shook his head as if he didn't know me, and that shattered me.

"Papa, don't look at me that way."

"I don't know how else to look at you."

"I'm not doing anything wrong. God created me to heal. This is my purpose."

"Disobeying your father isn't wrong?"

I took a deep breath. "I am an adult woman. Perhaps that doesn't matter as much in 1861, but in my other paths, I am independent and able to make my own choices. How long must I obey my earthly father when my heavenly One is calling me to action?"

I was presenting ideas to him that were foreign—and perhaps unwanted. But they were no less true.

Finally, his shoulders stooped, and he said, "I do not want to be in discord with you, Margaret."

"I don't either."

"I know that." He sighed heavily. "I've relied so much upon you since losing your mother, but that's not fair to you. You're an intelligent, accomplished young woman, and now that I know you have even more to deal with, my own needs and wants seem ridiculous in comparison."

"They're not ridiculous. I want to honor you, Papa, and take care of you."

"You do, Margaret. Every day. Your entire life has been devoted to me." He walked over to the empty fireplace and looked down at the grate. "I've decided not to stand in your way any longer."

"What does that mean?"

"If you want to continue helping Miss Barton, or if you want to volunteer in the hospitals, you have my blessing."

I opened my mouth to thank him, but he continued.

"With one condition." He looked back at me. "I would still like you to be my hostess, and to be available for events like the one Mrs. Greenhow is hosting tonight."

"Of course."

"And do not discuss what you are doing in polite society. I know things are changing quickly, but there are still those who do not condone a young woman working in such conditions."

"I won't."

"Good." His gaze grew tender. "I'm very proud of you, Margaret. Even though I don't understand what you told me about your other paths, I would really like to try—if you'll let me. I know you have a big decision to make, and I don't want to hinder you in any way."

I entered his embrace, tears gathering in my eyes. "Thank you, Papa. You don't know how much that means to me."

With his blessing, I was already starting to plan how I might be of more service to the military hospitals in the city. I had heard that the United States Sanitary Commission was taking on capable nurses to fill the new hospitals. In the morning, I would seek the letters of recommendation they required and see if I could find work.

Papa pulled back. "Now, I believe we have a dinner party to attend."

I smiled at him and nodded, and then decided to ask him one more question, since he appeared to be in a better mood. "Have you heard anything about Mr. Cooper? I haven't seen him since the day after the Battle of Bull Run."

"Were you expecting to see him?"

I wasn't sure how Papa would feel about Gray's intentions, but I didn't want any more secrets between us. "He asked if he could call on me but then sent a note telling me he had been called away for work and would come when he had the opportunity. But it's been over two weeks, and I haven't heard another word from him."

"Unfortunately, I haven't either. It seemed he was everywhere all the time before the battle, and now I haven't seen him even once since then."

I swallowed my dread at Papa's words. He was at the White House every day, working with members of the War Department—shouldn't he have crossed paths with Gray at least once? Did I dare voice my worries that Gray was a Southern spy? Wouldn't Papa have heard something about it if he was?

Papa watched me closely. "I am not sure if I trust Mr. Cooper, Margaret."

Apprehension tightened my stomach. "What do you mean?"

"There is something about him, something I haven't quite placed."

"Do you not like him?"

"It isn't a matter of like or dislike." He lifted his palms and shrugged. "I don't know much about him."

In truth, I didn't either, but that was why I had given him permission to call on me, wasn't it?

"Perhaps," Papa continued, "my distrust of this young man is not a character flaw of his. Perhaps I simply mistrust him because I saw that he was interested in my little girl."

"I'm not so little anymore."

"Indeed, you are not." He shook his head. "I just want you to be happy."

It was the same sentiment Mom and Dad had uttered in 2001 and my marked parents had said in 1941. They all wanted my happiness, but how could I be happy when I would be devastating several of them in just five short months?

Papa and I walked across the corner of Lafayette Square to Rose Greenhow's house later that evening. The heat of the day still bore down on us with oppressive humidity, and my skin was slick.

"One day," I said, my arm secure in the crook of Papa's elbow, "someone will invent something called air conditioning. It cools the air in your home and takes away the humidity."

"Truly?" He shook his head in wonder. "What else?"

I smiled as I pressed a little closer to him. "There's too much to share, and I will probably say something I shouldn't."

"I understand, Margaret. I'm still trying to believe what you've told me, but if I've learned anything in life, it's that there is a lot out there we can't explain."

He led me up the steps to the front door, and it was opened by Rose's butler, who bowed to us and welcomed us into the home. Laughter and conversation filled the air as Papa handed his top hat to the butler and then led me into the front parlor.

Rose's voice could be heard above all the others, though I couldn't see her. If her voice was any indication, she seemed to be in high spirits—something that wasn't witnessed often in the city since the Battle of Bull Run.

There were eight individuals in the parlor, including Senator Wilson, who had been with us at Centreville. Mr. Seward, Lincoln's Secretary of State, was also in attendance with his wife. They lived across the street from Rose, so I was not surprised to see him there. Papa and I joined the others, accepting their greetings. I could still hear Rose laughing in the dining room. Excusing myself, I left the parlor and walked across the worn rug toward the dining room to let her know we'd arrived.

Rose stood near the sideboard, a drink in her hand, as a gentleman stood next to her—closer than was necessary—saying something in her ear that made her laugh again. He looked in my direction, and his smile disappeared.

"Maggie." Gray took a step back from Rose, his face revealing his surprise at seeing me.

Rose didn't seem to notice Gray's shock, or my dismay, and smiled as she glided across the room to greet me with a kiss on each cheek. "Good evening, dear Margaret. Did your father come with you tonight?"

I was still looking at Gray as I accepted her kisses and nodded absently. "He's in the parlor."

"How nice." She went to greet my father, leaving me alone with Gray.

He didn't say anything for a moment, and I didn't know if I should be angry or hurt or just disappointed. Gray owed me nothing, yet he had said he'd call and hadn't. I had assumed he was too busy, but apparently he wasn't too busy tonight.

I was about to leave, ready to feign a headache and go home, when he moved toward me.

"Don't go."

Pausing, half turned away, I didn't meet his gaze. "I didn't mean to interrupt you and Mrs. Greenhow."

"You didn't interrupt us." He moved in front of me, his voice low. "I'm sorry I haven't been able to call on you, Maggie. I've thought about you every day we've been apart."

His apology sounded so much like something Seth would say that it made me sick to my stomach. Had I been ignoring red flags with Gray too?

"I've wanted to get away from work," he said, "but things have been happening so fast that I've been needed both night and day since Bull Run."

"That's strange," I said, frowning. "Papa hasn't seen you since the battle."

"My work has kept me away from the White House." He

reached out to me but then paused and lowered his hand. "I really am sorry. I hope to come soon, if you'll still have me."

Would I? Shaking my head, I took another step back. My relationship with Seth had left me raw and bruised. I had trusted him, but he had betrayed me by using our relationship to further his own cause. Was it the same with Gray? His loyalty had been in question from the day I'd met him—and now this? With Rose?

"I'm confused," I said, finally meeting his gaze, accusation in my own. "If you're so busy, how could you find time for Mrs. Greenhow's dinner party?"

Gray looked toward the parlor as if searching for an answer and sighed. "I'm sorry, Maggie." His British accent had deepened. "I wish I could explain. I wish I had a plausible excuse, but I do not. I'm asking you to trust me."

Trust him? Why? I had spent every day thinking about him, wondering why he hadn't come—only to find him here, whispering in Rose Greenhow's ear. I was not only disappointed but embarrassed. Why had I allowed myself to care so much in such a short amount of time?

I began to turn again, but he put his hand on my arm. Surprised, I glanced down at his hand.

The look on my face made him pull back, but he said, "May I walk you home later? I promise there is a reason I have not had the opportunity to call. Believe me when I say I have thought of little else but you these past two weeks."

I wanted to say yes, but I also needed to protect my heart. More than anything, I wanted answers. Besides, we lived so close that he would have just a few minutes of my time before we reached my home.

Looking up at him, I was struck again by the depth of awareness in his eyes. He seemed to see me—truly see me—something Seth had never been capable of.

"You may walk me home," I finally said.

Relief and joy filled his gaze.

"But I do not want to be trifled with, Mr. Cooper."

"Which is one of the reasons I have such admiration for you, Miss Wakefield."

Despite my disappointment in him, I smiled.

Gray sat across the table from me during supper, and all throughout the meal, our gazes caught on each other's.

He truly seemed concerned about me. There was an anxiousness in his behavior I had never witnessed before, and it all seemed directed at me. Not Rose. Not the other members of the dinner party.

Me.

When the conversation lulled, Gray would ask for my thoughts or observations, and he would listen as if what I had to say mattered. Even if he had been unable to call on me, it was clear he was still interested, perhaps even more so than before.

But was it authentic? What would he have to gain from a relationship with me? Seth had gained publicity being linked with me in 2001, but I couldn't think of anything I had to offer Gray except myself. If he was a spy, I was useless to him since Papa never confided in me or anyone else outside the president's office.

When it was time to leave, Gray was at my side.

"Senator Wakefield," he said to my father, who was putting on his top hat, "may I walk Miss Margaret home?"

Papa looked at me, a question in his eyes. "Would you like that, Margaret?"

I nodded.

"Then I shall leave her in your care, Mr. Cooper." Papa said his good-byes and left Rose's house.

Gray and I also said good-bye to our hostess and to Senator

Wilson, who was lingering behind, and then stepped out into the sultry night.

Darkness had fallen, and a blanket of clouds covered the sky, making it a moonless and starless night. The heat was still oppressive and promised a miserable night of sleep.

"May I walk you through the square?" Gray offered me his arm.

My mind was still swirling with questions and uncertainty, but I nodded.

His arm was strong and steady as I wrapped my hand around his bicep. He drew me close as we walked south toward the White House on the opposite side of the square.

"I'm sorry," he said again. "I wish I could explain my absence, but much of it has to do with my work, and I cannot reveal what I am doing for the War Department."

His words sounded sincere, and he was right. He couldn't tell me what he was doing for the War Department. I tried to think what Mama or Daddy would say in this instance, and it came to me. They would tell me to trust Gray unless he proved untrustworthy, as Seth had. Other than a bit of suspicion on my part, he had done nothing wrong that I knew of. And the truth was, I was suspicious of almost everyone in Washington.

He stopped when we came to a bench and motioned for me to sit. Bushes rose up around it, offering a bit of privacy.

My gown spread out as I took a seat. He sat beside me, crushing my skirt against his leg. He sat forward on the bench so he could turn toward me as he spoke.

"How is Mr. Earp?"

"He is recovering better than I could have hoped. I expect he will be able to return to his regiment within the next two weeks."

"That's truly amazing." He seemed pensive. "I have thought a lot about that day, Maggie."

My eyes had adjusted to the dark, and I was able to see him

clearly. "I've thought a lot about it, too," I admitted. That day and all the others I'd spent with him.

"I have so many questions for you," he said. "So much I am trying to understand."

In all my uncertainty of Gray, I'd forgotten he would be suspicious of me, too. I'd done things he couldn't begin to understand.

"How did you know what to do for Mr. Earp?" he asked.

"I wish I could answer you, but you wouldn't understand even if I did."

"Try me. I might surprise you." His face was so serious, so intense, that for a moment, I believed he just might.

I shrugged. "I'm sorry."

He leaned back, his shoulder pressing against mine. "So we both have secrets, is that it?"

"I think we both suspected that from the beginning."

"What I don't understand is how your father could be so surprised by your skills. You're twenty years old and have lived under his roof your entire life. When could you have possibly learned such medical expertise without his knowledge?" He spoke almost as if he was talking to himself, working out a great puzzle in his mind. "And then there was the strange conversation with Mr. Earp."

I looked at him, and he turned to meet my gaze. We were so close—so very close.

"When he said his name," Gray continued quietly, "the strangest look came over your face." He touched the curve of my cheek with his gloved hand—for only a heartbeat, but the sensation lingered. "You were surprised to hear his name, and a bit in awe, as if he was someone really important. Yet he's just a boy from Illinois with a little brother named Wyatt—a name you also knew and said with reverence in your voice. But he didn't know who you were."

He had once told me he was perceptive, but until now, I had no idea how perceptive.

"Add to all of that," he continued, watching me, "your melancholy as we waited for news of the battle—a battle we lost with such embarrassment and shame—as if you knew the outcome even before it started."

I lifted my chin, almost in defiance, realizing I wasn't doing as good a job of hiding my thoughts and emotions as I had hoped. I would have to do better. "Well? Have you figured me out?"

"If I didn't know better, I would think you're living a double life. Perhaps your father is in on it? He appeared surprised at your medical abilities, but maybe he was acting. Is he truly a Republican Senator from Oregon? Maybe he's a spy with Southern sympathies who moved to Oregon to run as a Republican and insert himself in the White House. Perhaps you both knew something about the Battle of Bull Run because you had fed information to the South beforehand."

I stiffened. "You questioned my loyalties one other time. I can forgive you for such an error, but I'm not so forgiving when someone accuses my father of being disloyal to his nation and president."

Yet the words pricked at my conscience. Wasn't I questioning Gray's loyalties? Perhaps not out loud, but wasn't that almost the same thing? It colored my thoughts and attitude toward him.

"You're right." He sat up straighter. "I am sorry, once again. But it's driving me mad not knowing the truth about you."

"I could say the same about you."

He looked at me. Gone was the teasing gleam he often had. "I haven't lied to you, Maggie."

"Neither have I lied to you."

We were both quiet for a moment, and though it was still hot, I didn't want to leave the bench or his side.

He looked down at my gloved hands lying clasped in my lap

and slowly reached for one. I allowed him to take it and watched as he gently turned it over. "Your hands are so small but so capable and strong. How is it possible at such a young age?"

My stomach filled with butterflies as I found myself leaning into him, my breathing shallow.

Slowly, he lifted my hand to his lips and pressed a kiss to its back. Though I was wearing a glove, I could feel the lines of his lips and the added heat against the fabric, and I held my breath.

"I like you, Maggie."

"I like you, too." I was very aware of the rise and fall of my chest against my corset as I tried to breathe.

"I don't know when I will be free, but I would very much like to call on you."

"Even though I have secrets?" I tried to tease, but my voice sounded more serious than I intended.

"Perhaps because of your secrets." He lowered my hand but did not let it go. "You are the most remarkable woman I've ever met. Kind, thoughtful, intelligent, compassionate, fearless, bold—not to mention beautiful." He smiled. "I was beguiled by your dimples the first time we met, and I've never seen eyes such a stunning shade of blue in my life. They captivate me. You captivate me."

It was hard to concentrate, to keep my wits about me—though the word *beguiled* made me think briefly of Dr. Philips. "My feelings have not changed, Gray. If you would like to come, I will not turn you away. Though if you intend to stand me up again, I will not be as understanding the next time."

"I understand." He smiled. "I would be at your house every day if this war did not require so much from me."

"It is requiring a lot from all of us."

He brought my hand back up to his lips, kissing it again. It was nothing like the kiss Seth had given me. It felt vulnerable, authentic . . . dangerous. When he kissed my hand, it was all I could think about, all I could feel or see in that moment.

Everything else faded away.

"I hate to bring this evening to an end," he finally said, "but your father will wonder what keeps us."

I nodded, not wanting to break the spell that surrounded us but knowing that we must.

He stood and then drew me up, tucking my hand into the crook of his arm again.

As he slowly walked me home, I decided to put aside my misgivings about Gray. I hated that we were both keeping secrets from one another, but I wanted to believe the best in him, and I wanted him to believe the best in me.

20

AUGUST 9, 1941
NEW YORK, NY

The USS *Solace* was anchored like a majestic beacon of hope in the New York Harbor as we walked up the gangplank. That very morning, it had been commissioned into the United States Navy and would be leaving within hours to make its way to Pearl Harbor via the Panama Canal and Long Beach, California.

"I feel like Rose on *Titanic*," I whispered to Anna as I looked at the impressive ship, the seagulls circling overhead, and the bright blue sky. The vessel had been painted white with a green stripe around the hull and a red cross in the center. At the top, the smokestack had also been painted white with a red cross. There was no mistaking the purpose of this ship.

"What does that mean?" Anna asked. "I know what the *Titanic* is, and I would thank you not to mention it as we board a huge ocean liner, but who is Rose?"

I laughed, feeling a bit lighthearted, though the future looked bleak for the almost five hundred officers, enlisted men, and nurses boarding the ship. My evening with Gray had left me feeling hopeful in a way that surprised me, even if we couldn't share our secrets. I had to trust that he had a good reason for not sharing his, just as I did. "It's a movie that came out a few years ago in my 2001 path. Rose is the protagonist. You would love it."

"I'm sure I would." She smiled, her face shaded by the brim of her hat. "Maybe I'll live long enough to see it."

"I hope you do." I gave her a side hug and readjusted the grip on my valise. Maybe she already had. It was strange to think that Anna might be living as an older woman in my other path. Mama had warned both of us not to look for each other, so I never had. If our paths crossed unexpectedly, that was one thing, but nothing good could come of seeking each other out.

There were only twelve nurses in all, led by our fearless Nurse Daly. We wore our blue uniforms, and despite our relative rank as lieutenants, a few of the enlisted men whistled at us from the dock as we entered the ship.

Before the USS *Solace* was a hospital ship, it had been a luxury ocean liner, and it still bore the markings of elegance. Beautiful dark wood covered the walls and ceilings with thick, ornate trim. Crystal chandeliers hung overhead, and plush carpet padded our heels.

"We will have our own quarters," Helen Daly said to the group of nurses. "Our own dining room, staterooms, and recreational area. The only time we will interact with the other members of this crew are when we are on duty." She smiled. "And during the occasional social gathering, such as tonight."

The nurses looked at each other excitedly.

"Captain Benjamin Perlman is holding a dance for the officers in the ballroom. There are over three hundred officers on board, including eleven medical officers, whom you will be working with directly. With only twelve women, I can guarantee you will have a dance partner, if you so choose."

Eager exclamations erupted from several of the ladies.

Anna and I hadn't been to a dance since that night at the Army and Navy Club, and I knew my sister was anxious to put her dancing shoes back on. I hadn't seen a trace of her former melancholy since we'd left Washington.

"There are over a hundred enlisted hospital corpsmen, but though you will get to know many of them, they will not be at the dance this evening." Helen looked at each of us, one by one. Anna and I were the only nurses who had come from the Naval Medical Center with her. The other nurses came from all over the United States. "I believe this goes without saying," she said, her voice grave, "but beyond the occasional dance, there will be no fraternizing with the crew. Do I make myself clear?"

Eleven heads bobbed in unison.

"Very good." She smiled. "Now, I will show you to our quarters, and you can get settled in your rooms. The dance will be held after supper, when we're out to sea. After you get unpacked, we will take a tour of the ship and meet the medical officers, whom we will dine with this evening in the captain's quarters."

More pleased murmurs rose from the group.

Despite everything, it was exciting to be on board the *Solace*. Anna and I found our stateroom, which was at the head of the hall, closest to the captain's quarters. We had two beds, a desk, a closet with a mirror, and a private bathroom. The rugs on the floor matched the draperies at the window and the coverlets on the beds. It wasn't a fancy room, but it was comfortable and clean.

"Can you believe we're on our way to Hawaii?" Anna asked as she set her suitcase on one of the beds. "Hawaii!"

I allowed myself to bask in her happiness, though I couldn't laugh with her.

Soon we were on that promised tour and learned that the ship was equipped to handle four hundred thirty-two patients, as well as the four hundred sixty-six crew members. There were five decks on the ship, which housed operating rooms, recovery rooms, ward rooms, a laboratory, a pharmacy, and a sick call clinic, among other things. The medical officers, including the nurses, were housed at the front of the ship—the bow—with the other officers and enlisted men in the middle.

After our tour, and after we watched the ship depart from the docks, we returned to our staterooms and freshened up for supper with the other medical officers in the captain's quarters.

I hadn't seen Dr. Philips since he told me that Anna and I were being requested for service on the *Solace*. After we returned from Williamsburg, I discovered he had already been sent to New York to help outfit the ship. If I had not agreed to come, I would have never seen him again. Knowing he was somewhere on this massive ship sent a strange shiver up my spine. Did he know I was here? Was he pleased? Or would he go on treating me with indifference?

We walked to the captain's quarters with the rest of the nurses. My navy-blue uniform was freshly pressed, and I had touched up my hair. I tried not to feel nervous, but I couldn't quell the anxiety I felt in the pit of my stomach.

"You look lovely," Anna said as she winked. "Do you think he's nervous to see you too?"

"Who said I'm nervous?"

She gave me a look. "You're one of the easiest people to read, Maggie. You always have been."

Was that why Gray had been able to perceive my thoughts and emotions so well? I would have to work harder at hiding them.

"Welcome," Captain Perlman said as we entered his opulent parlor.

Almost a dozen men stood in small groups throughout the room, their uniforms making each of them look dashing as they visited with drinks in their hands. At our arrival, they all turned to greet us—and my gaze connected with Dr. Philips's immediately.

It was as if a string was pulled taut between us, vibrating with the intensity of our gazes. Why did he have such an effect on me? He did not smile or even acknowledge me, but I saw something flash in his eyes—a hint of relief? Approval? Pleasure? It was gone as soon as I noticed it, and my attention was pulled away as introductions were made and beverages were handed out.

There were twelve men and twelve women, and we were placed every other around the table, which meant I was sandwiched between two medical officers I had never met before. Both were attentive table companions, eager to get to know me better. Dr. Philips was across the table and down several chairs, near Captain Perlman and Nurse Daly. It meant my gaze did not land on him unless it was on purpose, and vice versa. Several times throughout the meal, I glanced in his direction and found that the only person he spoke to was Helen, who was on his left. He did not look at me once, which disappointed me more than it should have.

He was pale, and his eyes could not hide his exhaustion. I paid attention to the food we were served. He did not eat the bread or the pasta, but he did eat the beef and barley soup. I wanted to call out to him not to eat the soup, since barley contained gluten, but I could not. At least he had seemed to isolate the wheat as a culprit, but he would also need to learn to avoid rye and barley, as well. I prayed he would figure it out soon.

When the meal had come to an end and we had risen from the table, I tried to find him, but he was gone.

"Is everything alright, Lieutenant Hollingsworth?" Lieutenant Daniel Shepherd, one of the medical officers who had sat next to me, asked. "You look disappointed. I hope my company was not tiresome."

So much for hiding my emotions. I smiled and lifted my chin, not willing to let Dr. Philips ruin a pleasant evening. "You were a wonderful table companion."

"Good." He grinned. "May I ask you to save me a dance this evening?"

"I would be honored."

And I would be. Dr. Philips wasn't the only gentleman on board the *Solace*.

And perhaps *gentleman* was too kind a word for him.

Within hours, the ship was out to sea, and the brilliant stars shone like little drops of shimmering mercury in the inky black sky. As the *Solace* made its way south, we danced our hearts out as the military band played rumbas, mambos, sambas, fox-trots, and swing music. All other thoughts, fears, and worries vanished as I danced to one song after another, always in the arms of a different officer.

Laughter flowed freely as I did a foxtrot with Lieutenant Shepherd, who proved to be a talented dancer. "I can't keep up with you, Lieutenant," I said as we jumped and trotted. I was breathless and happy.

"I have not danced the last six dances in a row," he said with a boyish grin, "so I have all the energy in the world. You, on the other hand, have been a busy young woman." He paused and then said, "And call me Danny when we're not on duty."

I smiled and nodded. "I'm Maggie."

"The prettiest Maggie I've ever met." He winked, and I could tell he had a lot of experience sweeping young women off their feet.

By the time the song ended, I was in desperate need of a break. I had to refuse seven gentlemen who approached me for the next dance, claiming that my feet were going to fall off if I didn't rest.

With promises to dance with them later, I left the ballroom and stepped out onto the promenade deck to get a breath of fresh air. The wind was exactly what my hot face needed, and I closed my eyes, inhaling the salty smell of the ocean.

"You need to report to the operating room at first light. Should you be out dancing so late?"

I opened my eyes and spun on my heels.

Dr. Philips was sitting on a deck chair, his hat perched on his knee. His voice did not hold censure—and his gaze was full of something else entirely.

"You didn't say hello to me." It was the first thing that came to mind.

He slowly rose to his feet and joined me near the railing. We were the only ones on the promenade deck. It was just us, the sound of "Hands Across the Sea" played by the band, and the Atlantic Ocean spread out before us.

I faced him, the wind blowing against my face, carrying with it a soft cologne he wore.

"Hello, Nurse Hollingsworth," he said, his voice quiet.

"My name is Maggie," I said just as quietly.

"I know your name."

The same tension reverberated between us. It was an indefinable feeling, and I wasn't sure if I enjoyed it or not. It felt as if it could either pull us together or snap suddenly, sending me reeling through time and space.

"Did you know I was joining the crew?" I couldn't tear my gaze away from his.

"I saw your name on the roster this morning." His eyes moved to my hair, as if caressing it in the moonlight, though he kept his hands to himself.

I tried to remember to breathe. "I wasn't sure if it was a good idea to come."

He didn't respond right away but inhaled and let out a breath before turning to lean on the railing. The moon cut a swath across the sparkling water, trailing to the edges of the ship. "I wasn't sure either. You're a brilliant nurse, but you're a distraction I've never had to deal with before."

Surprised—and a little riled—I leaned on the railing next to him. Was that an insult or a compliment? "You've never worked with a brilliant nurse before?"

He turned to me, his gaze intense. "I've worked with several brilliant nurses, but none who try to pull down my defenses and demand my vulnerability."

I stared at him. *I* did that? "I have never thought of you as vulnerable."

"I fight it every time I'm with you." He looked back at the water, scoffing. "I fight every feeling you elicit in me."

I was stunned—not only at his admission, but because he was opening up to me. He *was* making himself vulnerable, and it put me in a position of power. Zechariah Philips didn't open up with just anyone, and if he revealed parts of himself to me, the parts he kept hidden behind his defenses, I could wound him easily.

I wasn't sure if I wanted that power.

"What are you trying to protect?" I asked.

When he looked at me, the tenderness in his eyes slayed me. "My heart."

"Hands Across the Sea" came to an end and was followed by "Moonlight Serenade," a gentle, haunting song from the Glenn Miller Orchestra.

Dr. Philips looked toward the ballroom. "You should probably go back to the dance. You seem popular with the officers."

"You were watching?"

"How could I not?"

I swallowed the rush of nerves at his words, needing to return to solid ground. "I'm only popular because I'm one of twelve women on a ship of four hundred men."

"That's not why you're popular, Maggie."

I caught my breath at my name on his lips. Gone was the cross voice and demanding mood, and in its place was a gentleness I had only witnessed when I saw him with his patients.

"You could be one in a crowd of a thousand women, and you'd still draw every eye in the room."

"You flatter me, Dr. Philips."

"My name is Zechariah."

"I know your name," I said, just above a whisper, my heart pounding so loudly I could hardly hear myself speak.

We stood that way for several moments. He did not smile, and I could tell he was battling a war within his own heart. He was revealing a great deal to me, and it cost him. I wanted to reassure him that I was a safe harbor—but even as I formed the words, I realized that I wasn't safe. I was an unknown port. Would I be here after January? If he opened his heart to me, would I be here to hold it safe? Did I *want* to hold it?

Perhaps, for the time being, I could be a safe place for him.

"Tell me something about yourself," I said, hoping I wasn't pushing him further than he was willing to go.

He stiffened, but he didn't deny my request. Instead, he appeared to be gathering his thoughts. "I remember the exact moment I wanted to be a doctor. I was ten years old, and I watched as my mother, a doctor herself, tried to save my father's life. He died of a heart attack, and there was nothing we could do. I felt so helpless, and even though my mother *and* father were doctors, and neither could save him, I knew that one day God would allow someone, somewhere, to find a way. I determined then and there to dedicate my life to alleviating as much pain and suffering as I could in the world."

"I remember the exact moment I wanted to be a doc—" I paused and amended, "a nurse."

It was much the same for me when my mother died, though I was only five years old in my 1800s path. I had been living for fifteen years and had a great deal of self-awareness. She had died in childbirth, and I knew that had cesarean sections been developed by then, she would still be alive. It would have prevented so much pain, heartache, and suffering. I decided then and there that I would be a doctor in one of my paths—or all of them, if I could be. But I could not tell Zechariah that story, so I altered it.

"I lost someone very special to me when I was five, and that was when I knew I wanted to serve in the medical field."

"You and I are much the same," he said. "Though perhaps you are a bit gentler than me."

I smiled. "You *do* know how to tease."

He also smiled, revealing that handsome man I had glimpsed a few times before.

"Why are you so stern and foreboding?" I asked, feeling emboldened by his openness. "At first I thought it was because you didn't feel well. But now, as you seem to be healing, you're still cross."

The silence stretched on for a long time before he finally said, "My parents were missionaries to China, and I grew up as an only child, spending much of my formative years in strict boarding schools. When I was finally allowed to come home, my father passed away, and my mother became driven, almost obsessed. It was not easy for her to remain in China, though she was determined to complete the work she and my father had started. She was a passionate, emotional person, and in the end it destroyed her. She was always outspoken against the Chinese for their treatment of women, and when the National-ist Party rose to power in 1927, she was one of forty foreigners who lost their lives."

He paused and lifted his chin. "I learned from a very early age that emotion means weakness, and weakness means destruc-tion. I was eighteen when she died, and it prompted me to join the navy. They fostered and encouraged me to keep my emo-tions in check, and it has served me well these fourteen years."

His story moved me, and I stepped closer to him, unsure if he would welcome my touch but wanting to alleviate the suffering he was feeling. I slowly laid my hand on his forearm.

He stiffened but did not pull away.

"Protecting your emotions might serve you well in some areas of life," I said, "but in others, they are one of God's greatest gifts."

"When are they a gift?" he asked, his voice low.

"When we are excited, hopeful, and full of joy. And sometimes negative emotions can be a gift. When I feel jealous or bitter, I know I am in the wrong, and my emotions act as warning signals and redirect me." I paused, unsure if I should continue. "But perhaps the greatest gift emotion gives us is the feeling of love."

"Have you ever been in love, Maggie?"

His question made me hesitate. Was I in love with Gray? Was I falling in love with Zechariah? My heart pounded harder as I realized I couldn't answer honestly.

"I don't know," I said. "Have you?"

Zechariah turned to me, slowly, cautiously putting his hand over mine. His touch was as gentle as I imagined it would be as I watched him perform surgeries. "I didn't think I was capable of falling in love until recently."

It was my turn to stiffen as my pulse thrummed wildly in my veins. An image of Gray flashed before my eyes, of the moment we sat on the bench together in Lafayette Square, of him kissing my hand and how I hadn't wanted it to end.

Was it possible to fall in love with more than one man at the same time? More importantly, was it wrong to let each of them pursue me? Granted, they were in different time periods, but I possessed only one heart and could give it to only one man.

I gently pulled my hand from Zechariah's and tried to smile to lighten the mood, to do anything that would break this spell that had been cast around us.

"Do you dance?" I asked as the band began to play "In the Mood."

A slight frown tilted his brow, and I could see his defenses rising again. "No."

I licked my lips, trying to look unaffected by our encounter, hoping I was not hurting him. "That's too bad. I don't know when we'll have another opportunity to dance."

"If you'd like to go back to the dance, I won't stop you."

"Perhaps I should. I'm surprised no one has come looking for me yet."

If I stayed, I was afraid he'd say something we might both regret. I couldn't allow Zechariah Philips to fall in love with me—at least, not yet. Despite his tough facade, he possessed a defenseless heart underneath, one that could be easily destroyed. I could not be the one to hurt him.

"I wish you danced." I offered a hopeful smile.

He turned away again, looking out at the water. He was a smart man, and he knew I had pulled away on purpose. How could he not?

"Go on," he said. "I'll see you in the morning."

I hesitated, vacillating between staying or going, but in the end, I knew it was best to leave.

21

SEPTEMBER 11, 2001
WASHINGTON, DC

A brilliant blue sky domed over Washington, DC, as I got dressed. There wasn't a cloud in sight, and the temperature was perfect. I had a rare day off, since I had finished my latest paper the night before, and I was in the kitchen making an omelet when Delilah rolled out of bed.

"You're awake early," I said with a smile, glancing at the clock. It was a quarter to eight.

"Your food smells amazing." She yawned and went to the coffeepot to pour a cup.

"Would you like an omelet?" She usually ate sugared cereal in the morning, despite my lectures about starting her day with something healthy.

"Sure. I'll try one."

"This is nice," I said to her a few minutes later as I set a plate on the counter. She sat on a stool, her purple hair in disarray as she hugged her coffee. "When was the last time we had breakfast together?"

"I can't remember." Delilah lifted the plate and took a long whiff. "Mmm. You're going to make a lucky man very happy one day."

"For more reasons than my omelets, I hope." I smiled as I said a silent prayer of thanks for my food and then dug in, hoping she'd like her breakfast.

"For more than your omelets," she assured me. She took a bite, and her eyes widened in surprise. "This is actually good."

I smiled to myself. "Thanks."

"By the way, how *is* your love life going?"

I groaned and slouched on my stool. Did she want to know about Gray, Zechariah, or Seth? I was so confused about the first two and still angry about the last one.

"I saw that Seth sent you flowers." She nodded toward the red roses sitting in a vase on the counter and batted her eyes playfully. "I thought maybe you two made up."

"He wants to, but I honestly don't think I can trust him again." I toyed with the red bell peppers that had fallen out of my omelet. It had been over a month since I ate supper with Seth's parents, a month since I sat with Gray on the bench in Lafayette Square, and a month since I talked with Zechariah near the railing on the USS *Solace*.

It had given me time to reflect on each of my paths. Gray had only visited me once, though he often sent notes, quickly scrawled. Zechariah had put up his defenses again, keeping me at a distance, though once in a while I saw his facade falter. Helen kept a watchful eye on all the nurses, even when we had shore leave, as we slowly made our way toward the Panama Canal, so there were no more stolen moments.

But it was Seth, who had returned from Charleston a week ago, who was on my mind today. The moment he came back to the city, he had showed up on my front steps with a dozen red roses and plans to take me to my favorite restaurant in Georgetown. Though my anger had started to dissipate, I had refused and told him I wasn't ready to rekindle our relationship. He'd left dejected.

Last night he had showed up again with another bouquet of roses, and it had been too much. I was writing a paper, and he tried to cajole me into putting it off so we could take a bike ride. The weather had been perfect, and though I didn't want to be cooped up in my apartment, I couldn't go with him.

"Seth and I had an argument last night," I told Delilah, losing my appetite. "He left here upset with me. I think it's officially over."

"What kind of a fight? I didn't hear a thing."

"We didn't yell, but I told him I needed more space, and he accused me of leading him on."

"You? Leading him on? How?" She frowned and put down her fork. "You have a right to pull back, Meg. If he's the right guy, he'll understand."

"That's what I keep telling myself." I tried to take another bite, but it didn't taste as good as it should. "I need to tell my dad what happened. He and Seth have a meeting tomorrow, and Dad will assume things are going well between us, especially because of the dinner last month."

"Your parents were pretty excited about you two, weren't they?" Delilah asked.

"More than I was."

"You don't like Seth?"

"I do like him—did like him, but it was all too much."

"And there's Gray and Zechariah to think about."

"What am I going to do, Dee?"

She offered a sad smile. "I wish I could tell you."

"What would you do, if you were me?"

"That's impossible to say. I love 2001, but I'm sure if I lived in 1861 and 1941, I'd love those time periods too."

"Sometimes I wish God would just choose for me."

"You wouldn't really want that, would you?"

I shrugged. "I don't know. It would be easier." I had continued putting off my conversations with God about the issue, since He remained silent. I'd accepted that if He didn't make it clear to me which path to take, then I would have to draw straws or resort to some other method of unbiased decision-making.

"Maybe it would, maybe it wouldn't." She finished her omelet, licked her fork, and pushed her plate aside. "Sometimes we need to take a step of faith. If God isn't clear about a decision, then we do what we think is best and hope that it's the right choice. I truly believe He honors our choices when we make them out of faith and not fear. You'll know what to do when the time is right."

I hoped and prayed she was right.

She smiled. "Thanks for the yummy omelet. I should probably get dressed. I have a lunch date today."

"A lunch date?"

"Yeah. I met him in my sculpting class. He's pretty cute." Her cheeks blossomed with color. "His name is Solomon, and he's an art history major."

"You like him! And you haven't said a word to me?"

She lifted a shoulder. "I was waiting to see if he liked me, too. Apparently he does. Who would have guessed?"

"Me, that's who. I'm so happy for you."

Delilah held up her hands. "Don't go planning the wedding yet."

I laughed and shook my head. "You'll have to tell me all about it tonight."

"I will." She pushed away from the counter. "What will you do with your day off?"

Sighing, I cut the last two bites of my omelet with my fork. "I should talk to my dad about Seth. I was going to call him, but he's been bugging me to visit him at work, so I think I'll surprise him this morning. The remodeling project is supposed to be done soon, and I know he's proud of what they've accomplished."

"Sounds like a fun way to spend your morning." She rinsed off her plate and set it in the dishwasher. "Say hi to him for me."

"I will."

She left the kitchen, calling over her shoulder, "I'm jumping in the shower. Lock the door when you leave."

"Have fun on your date with Solomon."

"Will do!" Her voice trailed down the hallway.

After setting my plate in the dishwasher, I grabbed my purse and keys and left the apartment.

I thought about calling Dad to tell him I was coming, but a surprise visit was probably a better idea. He would be disappointed about Seth, and it would be better to tell him face to face. If I called, he might ask why I was coming, and I would be forced to tell him over the phone.

As I stepped outside, I took in a deep breath, marveling at the blue sky, trying not to feel nervous about the upcoming conversation. It was silly to be nervous. Dad would understand. I just needed to get it over with, and then I could focus on finishing med school and getting a position at GUH.

I glanced at my watch as I walked along the first floor of the D Ring in the Navy Department at the Pentagon. It was quarter after nine. The smell of fresh paint and new carpet stung my nose, and I admired the changes that had been made since the last time I had been there. Dad worked in the Navy's main office, near corridor four, and had recently relocated to the remodeled space. He'd told us all about it at dinner with Seth's parents. He was proud of their work, and rightfully so.

Ironically, initial construction on the Pentagon had just begun on September 11 in my 1941 path, so the building was seventy years old and had no doubt needed many improvements. They had begun renovations in the 1990s, but Wedge One, where Dad worked, had finally been completed over the past year.

"Meg!" Dad's administrative assistant, Dorothy, greeted me as I walked into his office. She sat at her desk, a grin on her face as she turned down a radio. "What a nice surprise."

"Hello, Dorothy." I smiled. "Is my dad here?"

"Oh, he's not here, honey." She looked just as disappointed as I felt. "He had to run to a meeting at the Navy Yard. He should be back in about half an hour, if you'd like to wait."

"You don't mind?"

"Of course not."

The Navy Yard was on the other side of the Potomac River, about five miles away from the Pentagon. Maybe I should have called first after all, but now that I was here, I didn't mind waiting a bit.

Dorothy's face grew serious. "Have you been listening to the news?"

I shook my head. "No. What's happening?"

"It's so sad." She turned up her radio again, and I heard a man talking in a grave voice. "The Twin Towers have been hit by commercial airplanes in New York City."

"What?" I shook my head, feeling like I hadn't heard her correctly. "How could that happen?"

Her brown eyes were hooded with concern. "They thought the first one was an accident about thirty minutes ago, but then the second tower was hit about ten minutes ago, and now they think it's a terrorist attack."

"A terrorist attack? Are you serious?"

"I'm afraid so."

A man stuck his head through the door and looked at Dorothy. "Did you hear what's happening?"

"I'm listening to my radio now," she said.

"We have a television, if you want to see the towers."

"Come on, honey." Dorothy stood and motioned for me to follow. "Let's go see what's happening."

I followed her through a door and into a large office space with several gray cubicles. About a dozen people were standing and sitting around a small television on one of the desks. Morning sunshine poured in through the windows, lighting the recently remodeled space. Dorothy and I joined the group, and they moved over to let us get a good look at the screen.

Thick, black smoke billowed out of the Twin Towers of the World Trade Center, highlighted by the magnificent blue sky over the city. I put my hand to my mouth.

As we watched, all I could think about were the people trapped inside those buildings and those who had already died. It was horrifying beyond anything I had ever lived through, and I had survived the Battle of Bull Run. But at least there we had known our enemies. Who would want to bring terror upon New York City in 2001?

"Do they know who did this?" I asked.

There was silence as several people shook their heads, shock on all of their faces.

"They're saying the airplanes were full of passengers when they were hijacked," said a man in a hushed voice. "So it wasn't just the people in the towers who were killed. This could mean thousands of deaths."

"The last time America was attacked like this," a woman said in quiet dread, "was Pearl Harbor."

Pearl Harbor. I had tried to push that reality to the back of my consciousness, but it was there again. I couldn't imagine the horror I would have to endure right before my eyes. At least here, watching the Twin Towers burn, I was safely sheltered over two hundred miles away.

In Hawaii, I would be in the midst of the attack.

My cell phone rang, and I pulled it out of my purse. Mom's phone number appeared on the screen. "Hello?"

245

"Meg, are you watching the news?"

"I am. I can't believe what's happening."

"I've been trying to get ahold of your dad, but no one is answering the phones in his office. Do you think he's okay? Have you heard anything about other planes?"

"I'm actually at the Pentagon," I told her. "I came to surprise Dad. He's in a meeting at the Navy Yard. Dorothy said he'll be back in his office in about thirty minutes."

"Oh, thank God." Mom let out a shaky breath. "I've been so worried about him."

"He's okay, Mom." I'd never heard her so worked up. "I'll have him call you when he gets back."

"Thank you."

"It looks like President Bush is addressing the nation," I said as the news broadcast was interrupted by an emergency message. "I'm going to listen to what he has to say."

"Okay. I love you."

"Love you, too, Mom. I'll talk to you later."

"Bye."

I hung up and clutched my phone as I watched the president's address. A split screen showed President Bush at an elementary school in Sarasota, Florida, as well as the smoking Twin Towers in New York City. He briefly shared that the towers had been hit, that he had spoken to the vice president, the governor of New York, and the FBI, and had ordered the full resources of the federal government to assist the victims and their families. He promised to hunt down those responsible for this apparent act of terrorism, and then asked for a moment of silence.

When he was done, a newscaster started to recap what the president had just said, but all we could do was stare at the television screen, watching in horror as the towers continued to billow out black smoke.

"We should probably get back to work," Dorothy finally said. "We'll know more as the day unfolds, and we'll likely be needed."

"Go call your loved ones," said a woman near the television. "No one in those towers knew today was their last morning at work."

A few people murmured in agreement, and several left the cubicle to go back to their own desks.

I followed Dorothy to my dad's office, wishing he would hurry. I had been looking forward to a quiet, restful day, but now all I wanted to do was get back to my apartment and turn on the news. Heaviness weighed on my chest as I thought about all those who were suffering in New York City. The fear and uncertainty must be horrifying.

The phone rang, and Dorothy answered. I was so caught up in my own thoughts, I didn't realize she was talking to me until she said my name.

"Meg?"

I turned to her. "Sorry?"

"It's your dad. He'd like to talk to you."

I took the phone and smiled my thanks. "Hey, Dad."

"Hey, kiddo. I didn't know you were stopping by today."

"I thought I'd surprise you."

"You succeeded. I was calling to tell Dorothy to cancel my morning appointments. My meeting was interrupted by the news from New York, and we're running longer than I expected. I'll be here for another hour or two, at least."

"Oh." I was disappointed that I'd come all that way, but it didn't matter. I could talk to him later.

"Did you have anything in particular to talk to me about?"

I thought of Seth, but I didn't want to tell him this way. "It can wait. Maybe I'll stop by for supper tonight—oh, Mom said to call her when you get a chance."

"I'd love if you came by for supper. I'll tell Mom to expect you."

"Okay. I should let you go."

"Thanks for coming." He chuckled. "Sorry I couldn't be there."

"It's okay. I knew I was taking a risk in surprising you. I'll come back another time, and you can show me the remodeling yourself."

"Okay. I'll see you later."

"Bye." I remembered what the lady had just said a few minutes ago. "I love you."

"Love you too, kiddo."

Dad hung up, and I handed the receiver back to Dorothy. "I guess I'll take off," I said. "Next time I'll call before I come."

She smiled at me. "It was nice seeing you. Bye, honey."

"Bye."

I walked across the room and opened the door.

A loud, thunderous sound erupted. I turned, confused, not knowing where it came from. For a brief moment, I met Dorothy's shocked expression, and then a blast, so loud and intense that it shook the very foundation of the Pentagon, threw me to the ground and made the walls around me explode. Then the most intense heat I'd ever felt—which seemed to be everywhere, choking the very air I breathed—rushed through me, swallowing me whole.

And then my world went black.

22

SEPTEMBER 12, 1861
WASHINGTON, DC

I slowly opened my eyes, blinking several times as the sunshine poured in my window, blinding me.

The day beckoned with a stunning blue sky, and the leaves on the trees outside my bedroom window on Lafayette Square fluttered in the breeze. I turned on my side, my thoughts a little fuzzy. I had a full day spread out before me. My father had asked me to host a dinner party for several close friends that evening. I had extended an invitation to Gray, and he had responded that he would come.

A slow smile spread over my face. But thoughts of Gray led to thoughts of Zechariah and Seth—

Seth.

I frowned and sat up, trying to remember what had happened yesterday in 2001. Why couldn't I remember leaving the Pentagon and going home? Wasn't I supposed to go to my parents' house for supper? I couldn't remember doing that either.

I couldn't recall anything after saying good-bye to Dorothy.

Pressing my hands to my head, I tried to recall what had happened. I'd been at Dad's office. We'd watched the Twin Towers burning on television. Mom had called, and then President Bush had addressed the nation. After that, I had spoken to Dad on the phone and then said good-bye to Dorothy.

And then, nothing.

Except—there *was* something else. A deafening noise and intense heat.

I slowly lifted my gaze to stare at the wall directly in front of my canopied bed.

What happened after I said good-bye to Dorothy? It didn't make sense. I never had trouble remembering one day after the next.

I racked my brain, trying to understand. I could recall people sitting around the television, talking about the airplanes being an act of terrorism, comparing it to Pearl Harbor.

The air fled my lungs as I put it all together. Were there more hijacked airplanes? Had one of them crashed into the Pentagon? My father worked near the Department of Defense—could the terrorists have targeted the building? And if so, how many other planes had been hijacked? How many other attacks had occurred?

I placed both of my hands over my mouth, trying hard to put the pieces together.

Had the Pentagon been hit?

Had I died?

There was no way of knowing until I went through the cycle of days again, just like I had done after the Battle of Bull Run. If I didn't wake up in 2001, then I would know.

It seemed inconceivable. It couldn't possibly be true. Maybe I'd just been knocked unconscious. Yet the searing pain and heat . . . it had felt like it went right through me before everything went black.

A light knock sounded at my door before Saphira entered.

The soft smile on her face faltered, and she frowned. "Is something wrong?"

Slowly, I lowered my hands and shook my head. I could not let my fear and uncertainty taint today. I had so much to do, and I didn't want to worry Papa or hinder our dinner party plans. There had to be an explanation for what happened in 2001.

"Everything is fine," I told Saphira, forcing myself to smile.

But as I went about my day, the heaviness refused to lift. I'd never felt like this before, like something was terribly wrong. I was unsettled. Whenever I thought about the sudden end to my day yesterday and what it could mean, panic squeezed my heart. I had to remind myself that nothing was lost—not yet—and that I wouldn't know what had happened for two more days. I had to get through today and tomorrow before my questions could be answered, so it didn't pay to worry about it now.

When Papa finally returned home to dress for the dinner party, I had been able to distract myself enough to set my concerns aside.

"Good evening, Margaret," he said as he found me in the dining room, making sure the table was set to my specifications. I loved the order and precision of a well-set table, just like the order and precision of an operating room. "You look lovely." He kissed my cheek.

I was wearing the dark-green silk gown he favored, with wide hoops. The neckline dropped off the shoulders, and small sleeves complemented my thin arms. Saphira had styled my hair parted down the middle in a low chignon. She'd tucked one of my mother's emerald-studded hair combs in the back, matching my long emerald earrings, and I wore a pair of black lace gloves.

"Good evening, Papa," I said as I accepted his kiss. "How was your day?"

His eyes sparkled with interest. "Rose Greenhow was arrested!"

"What?" I straightened, frowning. "What do you mean?"

251

"It has become increasingly evident that we lost the Battle of Bull Run because our enemies knew of our plans."

"Yes, I know."

"President Lincoln hired Allan Pinkerton and his men to watch for spies when he first came to Washington. Mr. Pinkerton confirmed that the Southern spy was sending information to the Confederates in Richmond, so he put his men on the case. They have been working night and day to locate the spy, and they've found her!"

"Rose Greenhow is a spy?"

"Pinkerton's agents traced leaked information to her house. And while searching her home, they found evidence that she tried to burn, including scraps of coded messages and reports she was preparing for her handler. She also had maps of Washington's fortifications and military movements."

My eyes grew wider with each bit of evidence.

"The worst part," he said, dropping his voice, "is that Pinkerton's men found numerous love letters from Henry Wilson among Mrs. Greenhow's personal papers."

"Senator Wilson?" I blinked several times. "He was really having an affair with Rose?"

"That's how it appears. He probably inadvertently gave her information about Bull Run, which she leaked to Richmond. It sounds like she might have been having liaisons with several men throughout the government, possibly even someone in the War Department."

My heart felt like it stopped beating. I had suspected as much, but it still shocked me. "The War Department?"

Was Rose having an affair with Gray? Was that why he'd been whispering in her ear the night of her dinner party? Had he also given her information about Bull Run?

"Rose and her youngest daughter are on house arrest," Papa continued, unaware of my swirling thoughts. "Pinkerton will supervise visitors to Mrs. Greenhow's house and has moved at least one other Confederate operative into her home, a Miss Lily Mackall, who is a suspected courier."

I was speechless and overwhelmed at this news. All I could think about was Gray. Had he been feeding information to Rose? Could my suspicions of him be true?

"Washingtonians will sleep better tonight," Papa said as he started to leave the dining room. "With Mrs. Greenhow's arrest, I believe more will follow. There are spies all around us, I'm afraid. We cannot be too careful. Please send Joseph up to help me change."

He left the room, and I could hear his footsteps up the stairs. I stood where he had left me, staring down at the china and silverware, wondering if Gray would come to our dinner party after all. If Rose had been arrested and Senator Wilson had been linked to her, would her other conquests soon be named? Would Gray be one of them?

"Was that the senator?" Joseph asked, coming into the dining room.

"Yes." I swallowed the lump in my throat. "He asked for you to help him dress."

Joseph nodded and left to attend my father.

I was still reeling thirty minutes later when Papa received our first guests, Mr. and Mrs. Seward, our neighbors. We had invited the Lincolns, but they sent their regrets, as I'd suspected they would, though other cabinet members had accepted our invitation, including Mr. Cameron, the Secretary of War. We would host twelve guests in all, and Gray was supposed to be one of them.

But as the night progressed and he did not show, my heart grew heavier and heavier. It took all of my willpower and skill as a hostess to hold my emotions in check. One of my responsibilities was to keep the conversation flowing at the table, which I did, trying to find topics that did *not* involve war.

I was so sick of war and destruction that I wanted to scream.

It was all around me. Why couldn't God have placed me in an era of peace? I had thought 2001 was such a time, but the attack on the World Trade Towers—and possibly the Pentagon—suggested otherwise. It struck me hard that if my dad had been in the Pentagon with me, he might possibly be dead as well. And what about Dorothy and the others? I'd been so preoccupied trying *not* to think about it, I hadn't contemplated all the ramifications.

Tears threatened. Was there no such thing as peace? Why did humans have such anger and hatred toward one another? I understood why we were fighting the Civil War and why we would eventually enter WWII, but why had some unknown terrorist group hijacked airplanes to kill innocent people? It was unfathomable and senseless.

Add those concerns to my disappointment at Gray's absence and his lies, and I was ready to be done with our guests so I could climb into bed and have a good cry.

The wind picked up outside, rattling our windows. Lightning filled the sky, promising a storm. Good. The weather matched my mood.

It felt like dinner lasted a decade, but eventually all the courses were served and the after-dinner entertainment came to an end. Our guests gathered their hats and gloves and started to depart, commenting on the foreboding weather.

Finally, it was just Papa and Mr. Cameron who stood in the foyer while I made small talk with Mrs. Cameron in the parlor. I kept one ear on Papa's conversation, waiting for the telltale signs that Mr. Cameron was ready to leave and I could send Mrs. Cameron on her way.

"I'm afraid Mrs. Greenhow's contacts reach all the way to Jefferson's desk," Mr. Cameron said. "It's fair to say the Battle of Bull Run was tipped in the South's favor because of her intelligence gathering."

"What a shame," Papa said. "So many of our men lost and

such an embarrassment because of one woman's machinations."

"She's not the only one to blame, but hopefully we will soon have more answers. Pinkerton has his men guarding the house around the clock. He's detaining anyone who visits her, and I'm surprised at the number of people in and out of her home in one day—and such high-ranking government officials, to boot. Cooper was one of the first men to arrive."

I wished I hadn't been listening, but it was inevitable that I would learn of Gray's involvement. At this very moment, he was across the square at Rose's house, under arrest.

Anger boiled, replacing the desire to cry, and all I wanted to do was confront him—point fingers at *him*. I couldn't believe I had been tempted to tell him the truth about myself.

"Come, Mrs. Cameron," Mr. Cameron called. "If we are lucky, we will get home before the rain starts."

"It was so nice of you to have us this evening," Mrs. Cameron said to me. "Such a lovely diversion from the difficult days and nights we've all been enduring. We will be sure to reciprocate as soon as possible."

"Thank you." I forced a smile for her benefit and then walked her out to the foyer where Papa was saying good-bye to Mr. Cameron.

When the door was finally shut behind them, I let out a weary sigh, and Papa smiled at me.

"You did an admirable job tonight, Margaret. I'm so proud of you."

"Thank you."

He stifled a yawn behind his hand.

"It's been a long day for you," I said. "Why don't you head up to bed? I'll see to turning out the lights and making sure everything is set to rights in the dining room."

"Do you mind?"

I shook my head. "Good night."

He kissed my forehead. "Good night, my dear."

As he walked up the stairs, I moved into the parlor to look through the front window. I had a perfect view of Rose Greenhow's house, and almost every room was aglow with lights.

Anger and resentment burned in my gut. If Gray had not intended to come to my dinner party, then why had he made promises? For over a month now, he'd been making such promises, sending notes, convincing me he cared, when he was simply keeping me on a leash in case he needed me for his work.

I had told him I wasn't to be trifled with, and I had meant it.

With determination born of disappointment, I walked into the hall and grabbed a shawl off the coat rack. I didn't know how I would get an audience with him, but I would tell him what I thought of his game.

He'd played with my heart, but I would not let him win.

The first drops of rain began to fall as I walked alongside St. John's Church, directly across the street from Rose's house. Lightning flashed overhead, filling the sky with a brilliant burst of light, followed by a clap of thunder. I looked up at the sky, questioning my decision to venture out, though I was more determined than ever to tell Graydon Cooper what I thought of him.

A gust of wind whipped at my skirts, tugging them this way and that as I climbed the steps to Rose's front door. The porch was empty, but I could see the silhouettes of people through the front window. What would I find? Would Rose's butler answer, or would it be one of Pinkerton's men? Mr. Cameron had said he was surprised how many people had visited Rose today, and all of them were probably questioned. Would they question me? Would I be linked to Rose's spying?

It was too late to care as I knocked on the front door.

There was some shuffling inside, and then the door opened and a middle-aged man with a dark beard and hooded eyes stared at me. "May I help you?"

If I asked for Gray and he was being detained, would they even allow me to speak to him?

"Is Mr. Cooper here?" I was breathing heavily.

The man's eyebrows lifted at my request, but then Gray was behind him, looking surprised at my arrival.

"Maggie, what are you doing here?"

"Do you know this woman?" the man asked Gray.

"Yes. This is Miss Margaret Wakefield, Senator Wakefield's daughter. She lives just across the square."

"Is she one of Mrs. Greenhow's couriers?"

Gray shook his head, frowning, and then looked at me, a question in his gaze. "Are you?"

"No," I said through a clenched jaw. I was so tired of being questioned by him. *He* was the one who should be answering *my* questions.

"What are you doing here?" he asked.

"I should be asking you the same—" I paused, not wanting to reveal the truth in front of this strange man, though I didn't think I'd have a choice. "You said you were coming tonight."

Gray briefly closed his eyes as regret played across his face. "I'm sorry, Maggie. So much has happened today. I—"

"Would you like to speak to Miss Wakefield in private?" the man asked, turning to Gray.

"I would, yes." Gray stepped around him. "Call me if you need me, Pinkerton."

"Will do." The man—Mr. Pinkerton, apparently—moved farther into the house and out of sight.

Gray stepped through the open door and joined me on the porch. If he was on house arrest, why would Mr. Pinkerton allow him this freedom?

He closed the door behind him, and I had to back up to

allow him space. The rain was coming down at a steady pace, blowing a cool mist on us as we stood under the covering of the porch. It hit my hot cheeks but did nothing to calm my anger. It was dark, though the light from the parlor window offered enough glow for me to see him clearly.

"I'm sorry, Maggie. I meant to send you a note of apology, but things happened so quickly today that I had no opportunity."

I stared at him, confusion and anger warring with hurt. "How could you lie to me?"

"Lie? When did I lie?"

"You accused me of being a Southern sympathizer, when this whole time you were working with Rose Greenhow to assist the Confederacy." Saying the words out loud intensified my anger.

He just stared at me, dumbfounded. "What are you talking about?"

"This." I motioned to the house. "I heard you were one of the first to visit Mrs. Greenhow today, taken into custody." I had to swallow the revulsion that raced up my throat as the next question formed on my lips. "Are you in love with her?"

A slow smile spread across Gray's face. "Are you jealous, Maggie?"

His question—and attitude—infuriated me. I hated myself for the truth, especially because he was the enemy, so I refused to answer. Instead, I crossed my arms and lifted my chin.

"I am not in love with Rose Greenhow," he said quietly. "My heart is otherwise engaged."

My bluster started to fade, though I tried desperately to hold on to my anger. "Then why would you help her?"

"I didn't help Rose. I helped uncover her spy ring." He took a step closer to me.

I backed up.

"I'm a Pinkerton agent, Maggie. I came to Washington as one of Lincoln's guards, and I was placed in the War Department, undercover, to help identify rebels in the government. I was working the day you saw me at the Capitol Building." He took another step closer, and this time there was nowhere for me to go. My back was against the wall of Rose's house. "I've been working day and night since Bull Run to find the spy who revealed our plans to the Confederate army. Pinkerton was put in charge of a secret service by President Lincoln, and he asked me to lead this investigation. I couldn't tell you the truth, since I was undercover, but now that we've arrested Mrs. Greenhow, I can share this information with you. I was the first agent here today. I caught her trying to burn her papers."

I blinked several times, unsure if I had heard him correctly.

"The night of Mrs. Greenhow's dinner party," he continued, "when you came across us in the dining room, I was attempting to uncover her lies. I knew I had hurt you, but I couldn't risk telling you the truth—not yet."

I swallowed, trying to make sense of everything he was saying. "Y-You weren't dallying with Rose?"

This time, he was serious as he answered me. "No."

My pulse had been pounding, but it suddenly started to beat a different rhythm. Gray wasn't in love with Rose. His heart was otherwise engaged.

Did that mean . . . ?

"I know you must have a hundred questions," he said. "And believe me, I have wanted to tell you everything since Bull Run." He stepped back and ran his hand over the back of his neck. "I worked my way from England to New York to Illinois, where I met Allan Pinkerton. He recognized in me an ability that I had always thought was a curse—to correctly read people and their intentions. He trained me to be one of his agents. I've been working for him for over a year now, and I can see why he recruited me. I was born for this work. I have a keen sense of perception, and I can recognize a person's motives within minutes, just as I told you. It's how I knew Rose was involved in the spy ring very early on." He crossed his arms and leaned back against the porch railing. "You are the only person who puzzles me, and it's left me completely defenseless. For the life of me, I cannot figure out what you're hiding. You wear your emotions on your sleeve, yet I'm baffled as to what they mean."

"You're a Pinkerton agent?"

He smiled. "That's all you can say after I just admitted to you that I'm defenseless where you're concerned?" He became serious, his voice low. "I've never been defenseless, Maggie. Never."

I blinked a few times and put my hand to my throat. Gray wasn't dallying with Rose, and he hadn't been intentionally leading me on or standing me up. He'd been searching for a rebel spy.

He moved away from the railing and drew close to me, blocking me from the mist and the wind. He was much taller than me, and his shoulders were broad and confident.

My pulse thrummed at his nearness.

"I'm sorry you were disappointed in me," he said, touching a tendril of hair that had fallen loose from my chignon. "But I loved seeing the fire in your eyes tonight when you thought I was a villain." His hand gently grazed my cheek, sending a delicious chill down my spine. "I'm happy I am not the villain, however, because I would not want to be on the receiving end of your anger."

I smiled, my fervor beginning to fade. "I told you I was not to be trifled with, Mr. Cooper."

"I did not doubt you for a moment, Miss Wakefield." He traced the curve of my jaw with his thumb, causing my lips to part in surprise.

He paused, studying me, his gaze intense.

"Thank you for telling me the truth," I finally said, feeling breathless.

Gray lowered his hand, much to my disappointment. "I will

always tell you the truth, Maggie. No matter what it costs me—and that's not a promise I make lightly."

I wanted to promise him the same, but I could not. It was too dangerous.

He waited for me to reciprocate. When I didn't, he finally said, "I became a Pinkerton agent because I like a challenge. I love the thrill of finding clues and putting pieces together. And when the whole picture is complete and I've unearthed the hidden secrets, there is nothing more fulfilling or satisfying. Unfortunately, most of the time, the truth is ugly and damaging, revealing the selfishness in a person's soul. But you are different," he said in a gentle, tender voice. "When I learn the truth about you, Maggie Wakefield, I know it will reveal something remarkable."

"What if the truth is too difficult to believe?"

He shook his head, the smile returning to his handsome face. "I don't think that's possible. Pure selflessness drives your passion. I don't know where it comes from or how you possess the knowledge you do, but I will discover the truth. I promise."

Somehow, I believed if anyone could, it would be Gray.

23

SEPTEMBER 12, 1941
PANAMA CITY, PANAMA

The heat was oppressive as I stood on the quarterdeck of the USS *Solace*. Stevedores loaded and unloaded cargo from several ships that were docked at the US Naval Station Rodman on the west bank of the Panama Canal. Sunshine streamed down on my neck and shoulders, tanning my skin. Several of the nurses had been given shore leave, including myself. Anna had begged me to go into Panama City with her and the others, but I had chosen not to go. My heart was unsettled, and I wouldn't be a good companion.

I was torn between the fears and worries about my life in 2001 and the excitement that filled me whenever I thought about standing on Rose's porch with Gray in 1861. That he was a Pinkerton agent made my estimation of him rise considerably. So many things made sense now, and so many questions were answered. I loved that he had trusted me with the truth.

And when he had stood so close to me on Rose's porch—my heart sped up just thinking about it. I closed my eyes to the naval station so I could imagine being near him again. Hearing his voice. Looking into his beautiful brown eyes. Feeling him—

"I hope I'm not interrupting."

Zechariah's voice tore me out of my reverie, and I opened my eyes to find him standing near the railing, several feet away from me. He wore street clothes today, which surprised me, since I'd never seen him without a uniform or surgical attire. His dark trousers were clean and freshly pressed, and the top button of his short-sleeve shirt was undone. He wore a black fedora low on his forehead. The look changed so much about him, making him appear less formidable and more relaxed. Even younger.

Heat climbed up my neck and into my cheeks. Though he didn't know what I was thinking about, it was still embarrassing for him to find me reveling in the memory of Gray's attention.

"You're not interrupting me," I said as I looked back at the dock. "I was just enjoying the sunshine." It was partially true.

He leaned on the railing to look out at the landscape. Low-lying hills encircled the bays and peninsulas surrounding Panama City. Beyond the station, the city was a burgeoning metropolis, made more so by the increased presence of US military as President Roosevelt pressured Congress to ramp up operations in the Pacific.

"Aren't you going into the city today?" Zechariah asked me. "I thought you had shore leave."

"I do, but I didn't feel like spending the day with the others."

He was quiet, and instead of asking me why, he seemed to understand my need for solitude—perhaps because he often needed it himself.

We stood on the quarterdeck for several minutes, not saying a word to one another, as we watched the activity below the ship. I could not think of Gray when Zechariah was near, but my mind still slipped to 2001. It was almost impossible not to think about the Twin Towers, or why I could not remember what happened after I said good-bye to Dorothy.

Panic tried to settle into my heart at the possibilities, so I straightened, needing to do something to stop it from turning into a full-blown attack. It would be a long day if I did not find a way to distract my mind. Perhaps it hadn't been such a good idea to stay on the ship.

"Have you been to Panama City before?" I asked Zechariah.

"Several times. Most recently when I was sent back to Washington, DC, from California. Have you?"

"I haven't been many places," I confessed. I rarely traveled in my 2001 path, since the majority of my time was spent on schooling and my parents' schedules had always been so busy. In 1941, my marked parents had been content to stay in Williamsburg much of the time, with an occasional visit to New York or Washington, DC. I had been to Whitby, England, once, when Teddy came of age and took over Cumberland Hall, his family estate. Ironically, I had traveled the most in my 1861 path, as Papa had moved us to California, then Oregon, and back to Washington, DC. We had gone around the horn of South America to California and back by ship. That journey would have been half the distance if the Panama Canal had been built at the time.

"Casco Viejo is one of my favorite places in Panama City," Zechariah said. "It's a charming neighborhood in the oldest part of the city. There is a cathedral there and a beautiful plaza with some of the most charming architecture you will see in the Pacific."

"It sounds delightful."

"It's also very peaceful. I often go there when I am visiting Panama City."

"Do you plan to go there today?"

He studied me, as if trying to read my thoughts. "I was on my way there when I saw you standing here, alone."

We had not spoken outside of the operating room since the night of the dance. My actions that evening had sent him a message that he had read loud and clear. Zechariah didn't appear to be the kind of man who would risk rejection, and until now, I wasn't sure if he'd ever speak to me again. I didn't want to reject him, yet I couldn't lead him on either. I cared too much about him to hurt him.

His gaze was hooded and hard to read, so when he spoke, he surprised me. "Would you like to join me?"

"Helen wouldn't approve of us fraternizing."

"Helen trusts me."

I did want to see the city, especially the plaza he had just told me about. He would be a good companion, unlike the nurses, who would be chatty and draw unwanted attention. The prospect of spending the day with them had seemed draining and exhausting, but the idea of spending it with Zechariah felt refreshing—if we didn't fight.

"If you don't think Helen would mind," I said.

The barest hint of a smile warmed his blue eyes. If I had not spent the past six months familiar with his scowl, I might have missed his smile. But it was enough to know he was pleased that I had agreed.

It took me a few minutes to retrieve a bag with things I might need that day. I was wearing a black-and-white polka dot summer dress with a red belt and a wide-brimmed hat. I didn't wear makeup often, but I put on a little red lipstick to match my belt. It felt fun to dress up a bit, and when I joined Zechariah on the quarterdeck again, I could see that he liked it too. The admiration in his eyes surprised me, since he rarely let his emotions show.

"Ready?" he asked.

I nodded, and we left the ship to head into the city.

Zechariah hired a cab, and it took us directly to the Casco Viejo neighborhood. Red tiled roofs and ornate wrought-iron railings dominated the pastel-colored buildings on the small peninsula. There was a distinct Spanish Colonial influence to the buildings and the narrow alleys. Palm trees dotted the red-brick streets, and the smell of the ocean on the breeze lifted my spirits.

"Casco Viejo is part of the original walled city," Zechariah said next to me in the tight cab. "It was built after pirate Henry Morgan looted and pillaged the first city in the late 1600s."

"It's beautiful," I said. "As charming as you promised."

His face softened as he met my gaze, and I smiled.

The cab driver let us off at the Plaza de la Catedral. I stepped out of the vehicle and immediately took in the old Metropolitan Cathedral with its stone facade and white towers. There were not a lot of people, but it was still busy enough, with street vendors selling food and other wares. In the center of the plaza was a white pavilion, green grass, and palm trees.

After we toured the cathedral, Zechariah led me along the narrow streets, pointing out various buildings and commenting on the history of Panama City and the canal that had made it so famous.

"How do you know so much?" I asked, amazed at his ability to share facts so effortlessly.

He shrugged. "I read a lot."

"I read a lot too, but I can't retain information like you."

"That's not true. You're one of the smartest people I've ever met."

His compliment surprised me.

It was fun to see him in an environment outside the operating room. He was relaxed and almost like a different person—we didn't fight once.

He took me to the tip of the peninsula to El Conjunto Monumental de las Bóvedas, the walls that had originally protected the city. All around were the ocean and the shoreline of Panama City.

Zechariah found a small restaurant with rooftop dining, and we sat with a view of the sparkling water, under a large umbrella. After we ordered fresh yellowfin tuna and shrimp, he leaned back in his chair, and I had the opportunity to study him as he admired the ocean. He was not a man I would consider classically handsome, though he was definitely distinguished and attractive. His brilliance was one of the qualities I most admired, that and his compassion for his patients. I had never once heard him say an unkind thing to a patient, and when he spoke with them, a gentleness came over him that sometimes took my breath away. Why couldn't he be that way with his coworkers?

"How are you feeling?" I ventured to ask, noting that he was still thin and the dermatitis had not healed on his hands. "Have you had any luck with your elimination diet?"

He lifted his water glass and took a sip. Condensation coated the outside of the glass, dripping from his hand. "As soon as I think I know what it is, I'm baffled all over again."

"Have you narrowed it down to a set of culprits?" I needed to be careful, but I wanted to know if he was even close.

"I think it may be related to grains." He sighed as he set his glass on the table. "But I would rather not talk about it today."

I nodded, relieved that he was on the right track.

The waitress brought us two bowls of broth soup with roasted chicken, a variety of herbs and seasonings, onions, and a root vegetable I didn't recognize.

"This stew is called *sancocho*," Zechariah told me. "It's a traditional recipe here in Panama."

It looked a lot like chicken soup to me, but when I tasted it, I realized it was much richer than any chicken soup I had ever eaten.

We enjoyed our food in companionable silence, but when the soup was finished and we were waiting for our fish, Zechariah leaned back, catching my eye.

"Why did you pull away from me the night of the dance?"

His question surprised me. I didn't think he'd bring up such a sensitive topic, especially that one. But his candor gave me permission to be just as frank.

"I was scared."

"Scared of what?" he asked.

"The future."

"Why does the future scare you?"

"I'm afraid I'll make the wrong choices and live with regret the rest of my life." I had dealt with that fear since I was a child, and it was only growing with intensity as January drew near. I didn't know if it was causing my faith in God to strengthen or wane, and that scared me even more.

"Am I the wrong choice, Maggie?" His straightforward questions were startling—yet refreshing.

"I'm not sure. That's what scares me." It was my turn to lean forward in my chair and be blunt with him. "Are you an option, Zechariah?"

He looked at me for a long time, emotions warring within his gaze. "I think I would like to be."

A breeze blew across the rooftop, offering a bit of respite from the heat and ruffling the hem of my dress. "Would you?"

That same tension became taut between us as he hesitated and then looked down at the napkin in his lap. "To be honest, I don't know if I should be an option. You're young and vibrant, full of passion and intelligence. I know what I am, and I could never pretend to be anything else. You deserve so much more."

"What are you?" I asked, truly curious how he saw himself.

He scoffed and shook his head. "I'm cantankerous, old, and stuck in my ways." His gaze found mine as he added, "And terrified that I've found the most incredible woman I will ever meet, and she sees me for what I truly am."

"I do see you for what you truly are," I said, my voice soft and gentle. "I see a man who hides behind his irritable moods so he doesn't have to get close to people, for fear he will lose them, especially when those people come and go so quickly in his profession. I have a feeling those tendencies started when he was a child, moving to a foreign land, attending boarding schools." I smiled. "I also see an incredibly brilliant man who is strong, compassionate, and fearless in the face of the human condition. He has a great capacity to love if he would only learn how to trust his own emotions. But more importantly, I see a man capable of changing, though he's convinced himself otherwise."

Zechariah's expression relaxed and he smiled. It touched his eyes first and then his lips. "Do you truly see me that way?"

"I truly see you that way."

"Then you may be the first."

"And *you* may be surprised. Your facade isn't foolproof, Dr. Philips. Helen Daly has a pretty good handle on you, and I'm sure there are others."

"As long as you see me," he said.

The waitress arrived with our seafood, interrupting the conversation, for which I was thankful. It had become too serious. Was Zechariah falling in love with me? The possibility was both thrilling and alarming.

After the waitress left, I said a silent prayer and then took a bite of tuna. It was local and fresh and practically melted in my mouth. "My mother loves tuna," I said, trying to change the subject so he would not ask something of me that I could not offer. "I will need to tell her to come to Panama City for the best tuna in the world." I was speaking of my mom, Peggy Clarke, from 2001, but it still applied.

Talking about her reminded me that I didn't know if I would ever see her again. Tomorrow was fast approaching, and with it, answers to a question I wasn't sure I wanted to know.

24

SEPTEMBER 13, 1861
WASHINGTON, DC

Thunder shook the windows, tearing me from my sleep. Though it was morning, the sky was as dark and foreboding as night. Lightning rent the sky, followed immediately by another clap of thunder so powerful, it felt as if the very earth tore apart around me. Wind rushed at the house, howling like a wild beast.

I was in 1861 again, and the truth shook me deeper than any storm, ravaging my heart and soul with a reality I had tried to ignore for the past two days.

My body had died in 2001, and I would never return there again.

Pain and grief wrapped around my heart, squeezing so hard that I could not breathe. My body began to shiver violently, and I tried to pull the covers around me, but it was no use. I was in shock—and though I had some awareness of it, I could not seem to calm down. Great sobs racked my body, and I became so nauseated, I had to leave my bed to vomit into a wastebasket.

I sat on the cold floor, hugging the wastebasket as tears streamed down my cheeks.

For a split second, I tried to convince myself that perhaps I had been knocked unconscious and was lying in a hospital in 2001, but I knew it couldn't be true. I could not have possibly survived whatever happened to my body in 2001. The searing heat and explosion had blasted through me.

I rocked back and forth, shaking my head. I couldn't believe that I would never see Mom and Dad again, or Delilah, or my coworkers at GUH. There had been a possibility that I would have to say good-bye someday, but I wasn't ready. If I had known—if I had been able to say good-bye properly—would it hurt so much? I thought I had at least four months left, but it had been torn from me without consultation.

"Why?" I called out to God, who felt more like an angry storm than a gentle breeze in this moment. "Why didn't you let me choose?"

I remembered the last conversation I'd had with Delilah. I had told her I wished God would choose for me. Now that He had, it hurt far worse than I had realized it would. Why was I so flippant that last day? Surely God hadn't taken 2001 from me because of a glib comment.

My only consolation was that Delilah knew I was still alive—somewhere. She knew the truth, even if my parents did not. Would she try to tell them, to relieve them of some of their pain? Or would she keep the secret forever?

I set the wastebasket aside and hugged my knees to my chest, my long nightgown covering my legs. I couldn't imagine the pain my loved ones were feeling in 2001. Had the attacks stopped with the Pentagon? Or had they continued, taking out other government buildings? What was the fate of America?

And what about my father? Had the Navy Yard been attacked? I doubted it, though I feared for the US Capitol and the White House.

I suddenly understood how Papa felt when I refused to tell him how the Civil War would play out. I wanted to know the fate of my loved ones and my country. Was it wrong of Papa to want the same?

My heart broke there on my bedroom floor as the tears continued to flow. For me, for those I loved, for the thousands who were mourning after the attacks, and for the loss of my hopes and dreams in 2001. I cried for America too, as I thought of all she had sacrificed for freedom, and would continue to sacrifice as history unfolded.

I didn't know how long I sat on the floor with the storm raging outside. But eventually I climbed back into my bed on shaky legs and pulled the covers up to my chin.

"Lord," I prayed quietly, my eyes burning from all the tears, "I knew I would eventually lose two of my paths, and I knew it would be difficult, but why does it have to hurt so much? Is this punishment for my lack of faith? For my anger toward You for giving me this gift?"

Even as I asked, I knew it wasn't true. No matter how angry or faithless I was, God was good and He loved me. He understood what it was to be human, to be uncertain and angry. For my lack of understanding, He would not punish me—and I would not allow myself to see Him as mean and uncaring. I had asked Him to tell me what path I should choose, and He had given me an answer. At least, a partial answer. I was not supposed to choose 2001. It was as simple as that. I hadn't wanted Him to rip it from me, but perhaps that was the only way I would have let it go.

"I don't want my other paths torn from me," I whispered to God as thunder rumbled through my room. "I'm sorry I've been angry about making my final decision. My life *is* a gift— a unique and rare gift. And I will use the next four months to truly seek Your will for my future. I will choose to believe You have a plan and that You will fulfill that plan in my life."

I still had two lives to live. Granted, I had lost a great deal, and I would mourn the loss for the rest of my life, but my story had not ended. One chapter had simply been closed. And I still had time to discern which path He wanted me to take.

I hadn't found the answers I'd been searching for, so perhaps I had been looking in the wrong places. I was comparing my lives based on my career, my purpose, and the people who populated each path. What I hadn't done was turn inward and ask myself what my heart was longing after. Wasn't that what Daddy and Mama had been trying to tell me in Williamsburg? That I needed to make the best choice for me and not anyone else?

But today wasn't the day to ponder that question. My heart had just been broken, and I couldn't trust it to be honest.

As the storm slowly abated, so too did my tears. I could almost hear Mama's gentle voice telling me it would be okay. My life would go on, and I would ultimately make the right choice. And no matter what, God would be sovereign, and He would show me the way. I just needed to trust myself and Him.

A knock sounded at my door a moment before Saphira entered. Her black hair was caught up in a handkerchief, and she wore a fresh, crisp apron over her colorful dress. She saw me and immediately came to my side.

"Are you feeling poorly?" she asked, her eyebrows tilted in concern.

"Yes." My head pounded, and my eyes felt like sandpaper. "I do not feel well at all."

"Would you like for me to send for Dr. Ayers?"

"No." My malady was a condition of the heart, and no amount of doctoring could fix it.

I stayed in bed for most of the morning, tending to my heart. When I finally got up, my limbs felt heavy, as if I were treading through a pool of mud. Everything exhausted me, from my toilette to walking down the stairs, to sitting at the dining room table and forcing myself to drink a cup of tea. Goldie tried to get me to eat some toast, but I couldn't stomach anything.

The intensity of the storm had moved on, but it was still raining, filling the streets with mud. I had planned to go to the Sanitary Commission to apply to work as a nurse, but I wasn't fit to do anything today. Besides, it would be difficult to go out in this weather, and I didn't want to ask Joseph to hitch up the carriage. Since Papa wouldn't be home until evening, I contemplated going back to bed, but I didn't want to alarm Saphira, who was already concerned.

I was still at the table with my tea, debating what to do, when there was a knock at the front door.

As Joseph came through the dining room to answer it, I said, "Whoever it is, please tell them I'm not receiving visitors today."

"Yes, Miss Margaret." He smiled, his face filled with compassion, and I was certain Saphira or Goldie had told him I was not feeling well.

I stayed in the dining room, planning to hide there until the caller left, and heard Joseph say, "Good morning, Mr. Cooper."

"Good morning," Gray responded. "Is Miss Wakefield receiving callers?"

Gray had come out in the rain to see me? To him, it was less than twenty-four hours since we stood on Rose's porch. Had he come to call on me so soon? It was odd to come early in the morning. Perhaps something was wrong.

I left the dining room, running a hand over my hair, conscious that I probably looked frightful. My face was still puffy and my eyes were red, but I couldn't risk Gray leaving.

Joseph's back was toward me as I entered the foyer. "Miss Margaret isn't recei—"

"I'm here, Joseph," I said, walking up behind him.

Gray stood on our front stoop, looking handsome in his tailored suitcoat, his hat in his hand. His dark eyes glowed with pleasure at the sight of me, but within a heartbeat, I could tell he knew something was wrong.

"Good morning," he said, his brows dipping. "May I come in?"

"Yes, please." I tried to smile, but it was almost impossible. "Thank you, Joseph. That will be all."

Joseph nodded and left the foyer as Gray entered.

I closed the door behind him, thankful that Joseph had set a fire in the hearth earlier that morning. The air was cool and wet. "Come into the parlor and warm yourself."

Gray did not move from the foyer, concern darkening his eyes. "What's wrong, Maggie?"

"I'm not feeling well this morning."

"Has your father been home to tell you the news? Is that it?"

"News? What news?"

Gray frowned. "He hasn't told you yet?"

"I haven't spoken to Papa since last night. Is something wrong?"

"I'm sorry for speaking. It's not my news to tell. I just thought, with the way you look, that you'd heard something upsetting. I assumed—" He paused, clearly disappointed with himself. "Again, I'm sorry."

"You cannot leave me in suspense. What hasn't Papa told me?" I didn't think I could bear more bad news, but I also couldn't live in a state of not knowing.

Gray set his hat and gloves on the hall table and then came closer to me. He laid gentle hands on my arms. "If your father has not spoken to you, then what has you so upset? And don't tell me it's nothing. It's clear something has devastated you."

The tears started again, and I leaned into his embrace. Gray wrapped his arms around me, cradling me. It was the first time he had held me since Bull Run. He was warm and strong, and he smelled of soap. He didn't ask any more questions or hurry me, but allowed me to weep. I knew I could not explain myself, but I also knew that I needed someone else's strength and comfort—his comfort.

Slowly, my tears subsided, and he gently handed me a clean handkerchief, then led me into the parlor and drew me onto the sofa with him. His touch anchored me to the moment—to him—offering immeasurable reassurance.

"Can you tell me what's happened?" he asked quietly.

I shook my head. "I'm afraid I cannot."

He was silent for a moment. "Does this have something to do with your double life?"

I looked up at him sharply to see if he was goading or teasing me, but he was not. Apparently, he had concluded that I *was* leading a double life, but did he have any idea the extent of it?

"My d-double life?" I asked.

"I know that things are not as they seem, Maggie. It's my job to look for signs and clues, and it's evident you are leading two very different lives. You are your father's daughter and hostess, but you must also be working as a doctor or, at the very least, a nurse somewhere else. Am I wrong?"

I swallowed hard and shook my head, wanting so desperately for him to know, to understand, at least in part. "You are not wrong."

"You don't need to tell me anything else," he said cautiously, "but if you'd like to tell me, I can assure you that your secrets are safe with me."

"I wish I could tell you," I whispered and clung to the handkerchief he had given me as his arm settled around my waist, holding me steady.

"Perhaps one day you will." He hesitated and then said, "Does this have something to do with your medical work?"

I took several long, deep breaths. I was heartbroken that I would not complete my medical schooling in 2001, but it was so much more than that. "Yes," I finally said. "Something devastating has happened, though there is nothing I can do to change it."

"I'm very sorry, Maggie. I wish I could make it better for you." He removed his arm from my waist and took my hand in his.

I offered him my first smile since I woke up and nodded through my heartbreak. "I know you do."

"Then I will pray for you, because I know nothing is impossible with God."

His words sounded like Mama and Daddy's, and it was the second indication he'd given that he was a man of faith. It bolstered me, and my breathing began to settle. "Why have you come?"

Gray's smile was the most beautiful thing I'd ever seen. No wonder Mr. Pinkerton had hired him and put him in charge of uncovering Rose Greenhow's espionage. He was handsome, charming, and intelligent. A perfect combination for an agent.

"I know it's not customary to pay calls during the day," he said, "but I didn't want to wait until evening to see you again. I hope you're not upset that I'm here."

"How could I be?" My affection for Gray grew exponentially in that moment, but then I recalled what he had said when he first arrived. "What did you think my father had told me?"

He frowned. "It's not my place to tell you, but I can't leave you wondering." He let out a breath. "Your father was given his orders this morning. He's been commissioned as a colonel and placed in command of a brigade in Stone's division, guarding fords along the Potomac River north of Washington."

I closed my eyes, trying not to give in to despair at the news.

"It is the safest place he can be," Gray assured me, squeezing my hand and drawing my eyes open again. "We have not seen any action near Washington, and I don't think the rebels will try to attack the city with all the soldiers we have here. The war will most likely take place on battlefields outside of Washington."

"Do you truly believe that?"

"I do." He smiled again, his gaze filling with reassurance. "Every man I know wants to fight for his country, and God calls each of us to different battlefields. I've been called to Pinkerton's agency, Mr. Lincoln has been called to the White House, and your father has been called to military service. Each of us must answer that call, or we will feel we have failed. I know you understand this, since you have been called to the medical field, and you would feel that you have no purpose if you weren't allowed to heal. It's the same with your father."

Gray did understand me—more, perhaps, than I realized.

He set his hand over mine, affection filling his eyes with something that warmed me from the inside out. "I know how desperately he wants to do this. You have to believe in him." He was offering me his strength for whatever I would face, and I realized I loved him for it, and for so many other reasons. Losing my path in 2001 had shown me that life was precious. What if I lost Gray? Or Papa? Or the purpose God had given me in 1861? Life was too short to hold back, and I didn't want to any longer. I wanted to throw myself headlong into nursing, into supporting Papa's dreams—and into loving Gray.

Here, perhaps, was the key to unlocking what my heart wanted.

Yet the same was true for 1941. Yesterday Zechariah had told me he wanted to be an option in my life. His feelings for me were growing, and mine for him. Would it be wrong to court both men at the same time, even if I was the only person who knew? I could try to sort out my feelings for them, but would it be fair to tell them how I felt until I had chosen between them?

"Papa has a good friend in you, and so do I."

"A friend?" Gray asked, his gaze teasing.

"Aren't all the best relationships based upon the foundation of friendship?"

"Perhaps," he said, his voice low as he ran his thumb over the back of my hand, "but I was hoping for something more enduring than friendship."

"What is more enduring than friendship?" I whispered.

"Love."

My pulse began to thrum, but my attention shifted when I noticed someone approaching our house. It was Papa.

Gray stood and walked to the fireplace, setting another log onto the flames while I sat on the sofa, trying to collect my emotions.

Papa entered the front door and came into the parlor, smiling in surprise at seeing Gray.

"Good morning, Senator Wakefield." Gray's voice sounded a bit strange, making me realize how strongly our conversation had affected him, as well.

"It's nice to see you here, Mr. Cooper," Papa said, but then he looked at me and frowned, probably mistaking my puffy face and red eyes for an argument between Gray and me. "Is something wrong, Margaret?"

"No." I forced myself to smile. "I'm not feeling myself this morning, but Mr. Cooper's visit has brightened my day considerably."

That seemed to mollify Papa's concerns.

"What are you doing home so early?" I asked.

Papa looked from me to Gray and then back again.

"Perhaps I should go," Gray said, moving toward the foyer.

"No, please." Papa put up a hand to stop Gray. "I think you already know what I'm going to tell Margaret. I'd like you to stay."

Gray nodded and then looked at me. I straightened my back, ready to accept and support Papa's decision. Though it made me worry, I would not let him see the truth.

"President Lincoln has recommended me for colonel, and the Senate has commissioned me as such. I am to command a brigade to guard the fords along the Potomac River. I will begin training immediately."

I was thankful Gray had already told me the news so I could offer Papa a smile, which I did. I rose to give him a hug. "Oh, Papa. I'm so proud of you."

"You're not angry?"

I held him tight, thankful I still had him and my marked parents in 1941. "No," I said. "I could never be angry at you. I know you are doing what God has called you to do. How could I be angry about that?"

As he embraced me, I could see Gray behind him, offering me an encouraging smile.

25

OCTOBER 19, 1941
LONG BEACH, CALIFORNIA

It had been over a month since I'd lost 2001, and I still woke
up each day after 1941 expecting to be in my apartment in
Georgetown, listening to Delilah's eclectic music and rushing
to work at GUH.

Instead, I found myself in 1861.

The first couple of weeks were the hardest, but slowly, as I
devoted my time and attention to my work in 1941 and 1861,
I was coming to terms with reality. I still longed to know what
had happened after I was killed at the Pentagon, but I was
content to know that I had said my good-byes. I had no regrets
from my life there, though I would miss my loved ones and my
studies. I prayed Delilah would find happiness and that my
parents would take solace in knowing I had accomplished so
much in my short time with them.

But today was a new day. The USS *Solace* was docked at
the Long Beach Naval Station in Long Beach, California, and
we were slated to leave for Pearl Harbor in the morning. Tonight was another dance, the first we'd had since we left New

York. Influenza had been ravaging our ship, and we'd all been given extra shifts to meet the needs. Many of the nurses were excited about the prospects of an evening off duty to have a bit of fun.

Anna, especially. She'd taken a liking to one of the medical officers, Dr. Timothy Church, an orthopedic surgeon who was not only handsome but also very kind. It appeared to be a mutual attraction, though they were doing their best to stay professional and aboveboard. But almost everyone saw the growing interest between Anna and Dr. Church and knew it would only be a matter of time before one or the other made the first move. No matter how much Helen cautioned us, it was impossible to keep love from growing.

I stood inside the mail room that evening. I hadn't had time to pick up my mail in a few days, so I was pleased to see several envelopes. One had come from Teddy in England, another thick envelope had come from Mama and Daddy, and there was one from Grandfather Hollingsworth.

Leaving the mail room, I went out onto the promenade deck and found a chair. The naval station was loud and busy, and the *Solace* was docked between two piers, so I was forced to look at another ship on the next pier, but I didn't care. All I wanted was a bit of news from home.

I opened Grandfather's letter first. He'd been seeing a doctor for his high blood pressure and had taken my advice to try the rice diet. He was pleased to report that he'd lost almost fifty pounds and was feeling better than ever, walking and exercising more frequently. I missed him but was happy to hear he was well.

Next, I tore open the envelope from Mama and Daddy, postmarked October 9. With our ship moving so often, it took time for the letters to find us and vice versa. I had written to my parents immediately after learning about my death in 2001 and wasn't surprised to see Mama's letter addressing my grief and concerns. But it was the last part that gave me the greatest sense of relief I'd felt since September 11.

There is nothing I can say or do to ease the pain you are feeling, Maggie. I remember my own grief when I lost 1775. I could not imagine how God could bring anything good from my circumstances, but He did. He was faithful to me, and He will be faithful to you. It's hard to see the end from the beginning, but please know that you will have happiness again. I am certain.

After we received your letter, Daddy and I discussed the little bit we know about the future. I am only sharing this with you to ease your burden and worry. We both agreed a long time ago to tell you only what you need to know, and we have decided that this is something you need to know.

I never met my marked grandmother who lived in my 1700s path, but my mother spoke of her a few times, and one of the stories was about her path in 2022. She lived in Maryland in the 1720s and in the 2020s. Before she chose to stay in the 1720s to raise my mother, she was a student, studying journalism at Washington and Lee University in Lexington, Virginia. The summer before she turned twenty-one, she had an internship with a major newspaper in Washington, DC, and spent time on Capitol Hill and in the White House.

I'm telling you this to say that though the United States might have been attacked in 2001, it was not overcome. It continued on, at least until the 2020s. I hope you can take comfort in knowing that. It makes me sad that there was an attack in 2001, but if I know anything about the heart and soul of America, it's that no matter what she faces, she has courage and resolve to get back up and keep fighting.

I hope and pray that you are finding comfort and joy in

*your paths, and that you are taking pleasure in pursuing
God's purposes for your life.*

You are such a blessing, Maggie. I love you.

Mama

Her words encouraged me, and for the first time in over a
month, I felt hopeful for my loved ones in 2001. I missed them
and would always miss them, but at least not all was lost for
them.

Daddy's letter was much like Mama's, though he didn't re-
iterate the news she had shared, just mentioned it. They both
assured me that they were praying for us as we neared Pearl
Harbor and told me again that no matter what I chose in January, they gave me their full blessing.

I finished reading my letters and went to my stateroom to
destroy the two from Mama and Daddy. Anytime a letter contained information about the future, I had no choice.

As I was changing into a dress for dinner and the dance, Anna
entered the room. She was smiling in that quiet, secret way of
hers since meeting Dr. Church. I was sitting at the desk, putting
on a pearl necklace, and caught a glimpse of her reflection in
the mirror. Her cheeks were glowing, and she didn't seem to
notice I was even there.

"How are your patients today?" I asked her.

She blinked a few times and then smiled. "Everyone seems
to be on the mend. I hope the influenza outbreak is subsiding."

"I think it is." I applied a bit of lipstick and pressed my lips
together. "And how is Dr. Church?"

Anna's cheeks blossomed to a deeper shade of red, and she
ducked her head. "You're not supposed to know about that."

I laughed and turned to face her. This was the first time she
had shown interest in another man since Richard. "Is it getting
serious?"

She put her hands to her face, trying to cool her cheeks. "I don't know."

"Has he said anything to you?"

"He doesn't have to." She sat on the edge of her bed. "But there is so much tension and . . . and awareness when we're together. Words are unnecessary."

I thought of the tension and awareness I felt with both Zechariah and Gray. I had been giving myself a bit of time to heal after September 11, but I had lost another month and was no closer to knowing what my heart wanted.

"Perhaps he doesn't have to speak for now." I smiled at her happiness. "But eventually you'll want to say something to each other."

"I think he'll say something tonight, at the dance. I plan to make myself available for a little chat, maybe on the promenade deck under the moon."

Thoughts of my own conversation with Zechariah on the promenade deck made my cheeks warm. The *awareness* between us had intensified since we'd spent the day in Panama City, but I'd been so overcome with grief that I hadn't pursued conversations or time alone with him. He continued on as before, though perhaps not as gruff with me as he'd once been. Would we talk again tonight? Would he even attend the dance?

For the first time in a month, I was excited about the prospect.

After dinner, the nurses made their way to the ballroom. It was hot and stuffy, but all the doors and windows were open, allowing a cross breeze to filter through the room. The military band was already playing popular songs, and it didn't take long before every nurse, including Helen, was swept away to dance with an officer.

It was while I was dancing to "Alexander's Ragtime Band" that I noticed a new arrival to the ballroom. Zechariah had come, looking handsome in his uniform.

He stood near the door and did not speak to anyone else as his gaze scanned the room. I focused on my dancing partner, a lieutenant who had just been promoted, and decided to let Zechariah come to me, if he so chose.

I danced for two more songs, purposely not looking in Zechariah's direction. Finally I saw him approach. He arrived at my side the same moment as an ensign did. When Zechariah looked down at the ensign without saying a word, the junior officer turned on his heels and left.

"Do you dance, Dr. Philips?" I asked, a bit surprised.

"As a rule, no." He stood before me, looking more out of place than I'd ever seen him. Every muscle in his back was tense. It was taking a huge amount of effort for him to be part of the crowd. "But I know you enjoy it, so I've learned."

"You didn't know how to dance before?" The band began playing "It's All Yours," a foxtrot by Tommy Dorsey.

"I never learned to dance at boarding school," he said as he looked at the band, apprehension in his gaze. "But I've recently read all about it."

A grin broke out on my face as I thought of him studying a book, trying to memorize the dance steps from diagrams and pictures—for me.

"Will you dance with me, Maggie?" he asked.

"Yes." I approached him, put up my arms as if we were going to waltz, and waited for him to join me.

He took a cautious step, wrapping one arm around my waist while clasping my hand. We were closer than we'd ever been before, and I was very aware of how tall and broad he was, of how his large, gentle hand lay against my waist, his fingers tightening just a bit.

He seemed very aware of me too.

"Is this correct?" he asked, a bit breathless.

"Yes," I whispered. "Just follow me."

I wasn't used to leading, but it was obvious Zechariah had no experience on the dance floor. He was stiff, unnatural, and awkward, but he was doing it for me. I didn't care if it wasn't smooth. I just cared that he knew I appreciated his efforts.

He was so focused on our feet that he didn't say a word to me, and after a few minutes, before the song was even done, I said, "Would you like to take me outside to get some fresh air?"

"Yes." His relief was so palpable, I began to giggle.

"What?" he asked as he pulled out of our embrace.

"I've never heard someone sound so relieved in my life."

One of his rare smiles came out to play. "It was a bit painful, wasn't it?"

"It was marvelous."

"It was awful."

"You have a lot of room for improvement."

"That's a nice way of saying it was awful." He put his hand under my elbow and led me out to the promenade deck.

This time we weren't the only people on deck, so he walked me to the stern, which faced the ocean and was tucked out of sight from the ballroom. Thankfully, there was a refreshing breeze on this side of the ship. I briefly closed my eyes and took a deep breath.

"Do you think we're headed toward war?" Zechariah asked, surprising me again.

Would I think so if I didn't have foreknowledge? Most people suspected that we would soon be in Europe's war, so I nodded. "I wouldn't be surprised."

He looked toward the ocean, his gaze hard to read in the darkness. "Neither would I. That's why we've seen a stronger military presence in Panama and California, and why so many of us are being sent to Pearl Harbor."

"Are you afraid of war?"

He turned to face me. His back was toward the deck, giving us even more privacy. "I have never been afraid of it before."

"But you are now?"

"I'm afraid of what it might mean." He moved closer to me and took my hand in his, reminding me of the gentleness he had for his patients. His hands were those of a healer, sensitive yet confident. I could smell his shaving soap and cologne. It was subtle but enticing. "After my mother died," he continued, looking at our hands, "I promised myself I would never care about someone so much again. I was afraid for her safety, and I prayed for her constantly, but God didn't hear me. My worst fears were realized, and I lost her. It almost destroyed me—and I knew that the only way to survive in this world was never to love again."

I looked up at him, hearing the pain in his voice, and could see how it ravaged his features. He came across to the world as a hard, unfeeling man, when the opposite was true. His heart was unbelievably tender, and that was why he guarded it so faithfully.

"You have unraveled my resolve, Maggie. I find myself thinking about you all the time, hoping to get a glimpse of you or to work alongside you just to be near you. I've found myself begging God to protect you—yet, I'm afraid He won't hear me again."

He moved even closer, taking me into his arms, and I felt him trembling—or was it me?

"I've faced the threat of war before," he said, his voice low, "but I've never faced it with someone I love beside me."

"You love me?"

In answer to my question, Zechariah kissed me.

It wasn't anything like the kiss Seth had given me. Seth's had seemed planned and practiced. Zechariah's was unexpected and fervent, as if he was afraid I would slip through his fingers if he didn't hold me tight enough. He pressed me to his body, heightening all my senses. His lips were gentle, yet his kiss was intense, and I could feel his heart pounding through the fabric of his uniform.

I responded to his kiss, wrapping my arms around his neck, feeling the need to anchor myself to him, to this moment, to this path. I'd lost so much recently that it felt good to find something new.

When he finally pulled back, his chest heaved, and his breath was ragged. I was struggling to find my own breath, and I was surprised when he pulled away completely, putting space between us.

He turned his back to me.

All I could do was stare at him, wondering how he would handle the emotions sure to be cascading through him.

When he finally faced me again, he didn't move closer but stayed several feet away. "I can't do this, Maggie."

"Do what?"

"I can't be in love with someone I might lose."

"Why—"

My question ended abruptly as he strode away and disappeared around the corner of the ship.

I stood there for several seconds, my mouth open, as I stared at the empty place where he had just stood. In a matter of minutes, he'd kissed me with more passion than I'd ever experienced, then told me he couldn't be in love with me.

Anna appeared, her face wild with worry. "What happened? I saw you and Dr. Philips come this way, and then a few minutes later, he strode past Timothy and me in the opposite direction, looking like he was about to kill someone."

She was alone, which meant she'd probably left Dr. Church to find me.

I was heartsore and tired, so I went into her arms and allowed her to hug me. It was strange, after all these years, that Anna was the one comforting me. For the first time in a long time, as I told her what had happened, I needed her to be strong.

And she was.

26

OCTOBER 20, 1861
WASHINGTON, DC

The next morning, when I woke up in 1861, all I could think about was Zechariah and his kiss. After I went back to the ballroom, I had continued to dance, but Zechariah had not returned. His strange behavior after our kiss troubled me throughout the night, and I had finally fallen asleep sometime after midnight. What would happen tomorrow when we had to work together? Would he pretend like nothing had happened? Would he explain himself?

Saphira entered my room, and I pushed aside the covers—realizing, with a start, that it was the first time I had woken up in 1861 and not been jolted by surprise that it wasn't 2001. Did that mean I was getting used to my new normal?

I thought about this as Saphira helped me dress in a simple outfit, since I was going to work at Judiciary Square Hospital, one of the newest military hospitals commissioned by the government. It was housed in the old schoolhouse near Judiciary Square and was just as unsuitable as all the others. I had been trying to suggest ways to better meet the needs of the soldiers and the staff, but my recommendations were falling on deaf, nineteenth-century ears.

Today I chose to wear a white blouse with a black skirt over several layers of petticoats. It had served as my unofficial uniform since I'd become a military nurse, and though it wasn't as serviceable as a pair of scrubs, it worked well.

After my hair was secured in a snood, I went downstairs for breakfast and was surprised to find Papa at the dining room table.

He stood when I arrived. "Good morning, Margaret."

"Good morning, Papa." I received his kiss on my cheek and then took the seat to his right. "I didn't know you'd be home today."

He'd been training with his men in Arlington, going on missions along the Potomac, and sleeping in a field tent, only coming home sporadically this past month. He wore his uniform at all times, and though it was hard to get used to seeing him dressed in the dark blue wool coat, with its gold buttons and the shoulder boards with gold eagles, he looked handsome and important.

He smiled as he lifted his coffee and took a sip. "I am only here for a few hours, I'm afraid. I've had orders to take my brigade north to do a little reconnaissance work in Loudoun County. We will leave this afternoon, and I will be gone for a few days."

I nodded, thankful that he kept me abreast of his whereabouts.

Joseph entered the dining room with an envelope on a tray. He stopped by my chair and lowered the tray for me. "A letter came for you this morning, Miss Margaret."

"Thank you, Joseph." I took the envelope and immediately recognized the handwriting.

Papa watched me as he took a bite of his toast. "Mr. Cooper?"

I couldn't hide my smile. He had called on me several times over the past month. Since Papa was gone so much, Saphira usually sat in the room as a chaperone, or Gray escorted me to dinner parties and soirees.

"Yes. It's from Mr. Cooper." I opened the envelope and pulled out the card, reading it to myself.

I have tickets to see a play at Ford's Athenaeum tonight. Might I escort you to the theater? —Gray

It had been several months since I'd seen a show—not since I'd been at Ford's Theatre with Seth. Ford's Athenaeum was the same theater, though under a different name. It would be strange to be back there, but I wanted to go. Not only would I enjoy being in his company, but a play would take my mind off Papa's next mission.

"You're smiling," Papa said as he set his toast on his plate. "It must be good news."

"Mr. Cooper would like to take me to a play this evening. I hope you don't mind."

"How could I?" He smiled and placed his hand over mine. "I am pleased with Mr. Cooper's attention, Margaret. He is a good man."

"I think so too."

Papa was quiet for a few seconds, and then he asked, without looking up from his plate, "Are you in love with him?"

For some reason, his question embarrassed me, and heat warmed my neck and cheeks. Instead of answering, I asked my own question. "How did you know you were in love with Mother?"

He stared off into the past—a tender smile lifting his mouth. When he finally looked at me, he said, "I knew I loved her because she was all I could think about. No matter where I went or who I was with, she was on my mind."

"Is that all there is to it, then?"

"No, I suppose not." He laughed. "One day, when I was paying a call on her, she asked me a question that I couldn't answer immediately. But when I realized what my answer was, I knew I wanted to spend the rest of my life with her."

I leaned forward. "What did she ask you?"

"She simply said, 'Am I enough, Edward?'" He paused as he clasped his hands on the table. "I didn't know what she meant at first, but then it dawned on me. Was she enough for me, even if I had no money, no possessions, no friends, no family, no future, no prospects—if all I had was her—was she enough for me to be happy?"

Neither of us spoke for a moment, and then I whispered, "And you realized that she was enough."

He met my gaze, a sheen of unshed tears covering his eyes, and he nodded. "She was more than enough. Losing her was the most devastating thing that has ever happened to me. I still weep for her when I am alone, though I would not change a single day we had together."

I touched his hands, tears stinging my own eyes. "I miss her too."

After he composed himself, he was able to offer me a wobbly smile. "So that, my dear, is how I knew I loved her and I wanted to spend the rest of my life with her. I was able to say, 'Yes, you are enough, Constance.' Perhaps that is the question you must ask yourself about Mr. Cooper. Is he enough for you? No matter what obstacles you face, what disappointments you encounter, or what troubles might come your way? If you lose all else, would he be enough for your happiness?"

It was the most important question he had ever asked me, and I wasn't sure. I wanted to be honest with Papa, though he wouldn't understand. "Gray is not the only man who has captured my heart."

He looked at me sharply, as if I had been seeing someone else behind his back.

"In 1941," I said quickly but quietly, hoping it would not carry to the kitchen.

The look Papa gave me was so strange, I couldn't read it.

"It is odd for me," he said, "as your father, to hear you speak of another man I have not met. To know that you do not seek my approval or blessing where he is concerned."

I laid my hand over his and smiled. "He is a doctor and a captain in the navy. He is a good man."

"Is he enough for you?" Papa asked. "If you lost all else, would either man be enough for your happiness? I think that once you know the answer to that question, you will know the answer to your future."

He made it sound so simple.

I only wished it were.

The play Gray took me to was called *Jeanie Deans*. It was a serious play, based on Sir Walter Scott's 1818 novel *The Heart of Midlothian*. The play was done well, and it felt good to be in the same space I had occupied in a later time, though it looked much different. My eyes wandered up to the balcony where Lincoln would be shot in less than four years. When I felt Gray watching me, a question in his eyes, I looked away and tried not to think about the assassination.

After the play came to an end, Gray asked, "May I escort you to Willard's Hotel for supper?"

Willard's Hotel was one of the most fashionable in Washington and the place to see and be seen. I hadn't been there since Papa and I had come to the city last October.

"I would love to." I smiled at Gray, taking his arm as we left the theater.

It was a cool evening, but I wore a full gown with wide pagoda sleeves and a heavy shawl. Clouds moved across the sky, sliding over the full moon and casting shadows over the buildings and streets as we walked to the hotel less than half a mile away.

"You're quieter than usual tonight," I said to Gray.

"I apologize." He touched my hand, which lay over his forearm, causing me to step closer to him. He made me feel safe and protected as we walked along the dark streets. "I received a letter from home today, telling me that my mother is ill."

"I'm sorry."

He had not spoken much about his family, though I recalled he was raised at his mother's ancestral home with his cousins and had been in line to inherit his uncle's title until his aunt produced a son.

"My uncle wrote to me," Gray continued, "which surprised me, since he said he never wanted to speak to me again."

I frowned. "Whyever not?"

He was quiet for a moment, then let out a sigh. "I've told you that my gift of uncovering the truth is both a blessing and a curse, and that when I uncover the truth, it often reveals unpleasant secrets."

I nodded.

"One of the first discoveries I made was soon after my cousin James was born—my uncle's heir." He paused as if collecting his thoughts. "All my life, I noticed things about my female cousins. Their unique green eyes, though both my aunt and uncle had brown eyes. Their red hair, though no one else in our family had red hair. There were other things—subtle things—so when James was also born with green eyes and red hair, I started to investigate. What I discovered is that my aunt had been having a longstanding liaison with the gardener. When I brought it to my uncle's attention, thinking he would praise me for discovering the truth and reinstate me as his heir, he turned his wrath on me instead, banishing me from his home. I realized he had known of the affair for years, but as long as she could provide a male heir, he overlooked her indiscretions."

I didn't know what to say.

"I was sent to America," he continued, "without connections or money, and was left to my own devices. My mother did not stop him. I decided to head west and took any job I could find to get from one city to the next, until I reached Chicago and met Allan Pinkerton."

"And now your mother is ill," I said. "Will you return to England to see her?"

He shook his head. "I knew when I left that I would never see her again, and I made peace with that. I wrote to her, and I pray the letter will arrive in time."

"I'm sorry, Gray. Nothing can prepare us for the heartache, no matter how long it's been since we've seen them."

He drew me closer as we continued to walk, each of us in our own thoughts. Lights glowed from several buildings around us, and soon the Willard Hotel was just ahead. People came and went, but where we stood on E Street, we were alone, cast in shadows.

Gray stopped walking and looked down at me, studying my face in the dim light, slowly putting space between us. "Maggie, this gift I have—I notice things and then put all the pieces together until they fit and make sense."

I waited, unsure if he was still speaking of his uncle or something else.

"If a piece doesn't fit," he continued, "I rearrange it, thinking of all the possibilities. Sometimes one piece doesn't fit until another locks into place first." He stood in front of me, his hands at his side. "I have been collecting the pieces of your puzzle for months, trying to make sense of the things I've seen you do, the knowledge you have, the lack of knowledge your father has, the devastation you experienced a month ago, the little things you've said when you haven't been paying close attention. Your behaviors and turn of phrase."

My heart started to pound.

"I know you're living a double life," he said, studying me closely, gauging my reaction. "You admitted it yourself. But I don't think it's the kind of double life most people lead."

"Gray—"

"I don't believe you leave your father's house to lead this second life. I don't think you go anywhere."

I couldn't breathe and reached out to touch his arm, to somehow stop him.

But he wasn't finished. "You might think I've lost my mind for saying this, you might laugh, but I've tried to think of every option, imagine every possibility, and I can come to only one conclusion."

My chest rose and fell on long, shallow breaths, and I pulled my hand back.

"I can't even believe I'm saying this." He ran his hand through his hair. "I don't know how it's possible, but do you—or have you ever—"

He paused, and I held my breath.

"Have you ever lived in another time, Maggie? A future time?"

My lips parted, and I could only stare at him. How had he guessed? Not even my parents in 2001 or my papa in 1861 had uncovered the truth. How had Gray?

His face went from uncertainty to shock. He took a step back, staring at me as if I were a ghost or unearthly being. "I can see I'm right. It's written all over your face."

I took a step toward him, not wanting him to think I was a monster. I had to swallow my astonishment and try to breathe. "No one has ever guessed the truth."

We stared at each other, and then he finally came to me, putting his hands on my arms, as if anchoring himself to me to make sure I was real. "How is it possible, Maggie? How does it work?"

I swallowed hard, surprised he had figured it out—and even more surprised that he believed me when I said it was true. Would he believe me when I told him the details? "I was born with this gift. My parents in 1941 have the same gift—"

"1941?" He put his hands to his head and lowered his voice. "You live in 1941?"

"I also lived in 2001, until a month ago."

"2001?" Gray kept his hands at the back of his neck, staring at me in complete and utter amazement. "That's a hundred and forty years from now. You know what's going to happen in a hundred and forty years?"

I nodded, knowing what his next question would be.

"You know how this war will end?"

"I do, but I cannot tell you anything about the future. Please don't ask."

He turned from me, his hands still on his neck, and paced. Suddenly, he looked back and said, "What do you mean you lived in 2001 until a month ago?"

We had come this far, and I knew he'd never let me rest until he knew it all. "Let me start from the beginning."

My legs felt weak, so I sat on a pile of crates in the nearby alley. I told him about Mama and Daddy and how they each bore a mark that sent them through time and space—the ones I had inherited. I told him all about each of my families and each of the paths I had occupied.

The entire time, he paced, asking questions, making comments, and staring at me whenever it was too much to believe.

When I was done, he didn't say anything for a long time. I wanted to know what he was thinking, but I didn't want to push him. I'd just given him the surprise of his life, and it was a miracle that he even believed me.

Finally, he stopped pacing and sat next to me on another pile of crates. We looked at each other for a long time before he took my hand in his. "I knew the truth would be remarkable. I just had no idea how remarkable."

I threw my arms around him and pressed close to him in a hug. "Thank you for believing me. I didn't realize until now how much I wanted you to know."

He hugged me back, holding me with the same tenderness that he had in my parlor.

"Maggie, I admire you for sacrificing your dream to be a doctor in 1941 for your sister."

I smiled as I pulled away from his embrace. Out of everything I'd told him, that was what he had focused on? "I would do anything for Anna."

"Just as you'd do anything for your father here." He shook his head. "You are living an amazing existence." He frowned, as if a new thought had struck him. "You said your marked parents only live in 1941 now, and they no longer live in the 1700s. Did they die there too, like you did in 2001?"

"Yes. My father was hanged as a spy in the American Revolution, and my mother forfeited her life there trying to save his."

"Forfeited?" His frown deepened.

I swallowed and looked down at my hands, wishing I didn't have to tell him the next part. "I am only given until my twenty-first birthday to choose which path I want to keep and which path I want to forfeit forever."

He sat up straighter. "You have to give up one of your lives on your twenty-first birthday?"

I nodded. "On January first, I must decide. If I choose my life in 1941, my body here will die—and vice versa."

Gray shook his head, almost in denial. I could already see him putting the pieces together. "Your marked parents and your sister and your work with the navy are in 1941."

"But I have Papa in this path, and my work with the military hospital, and my desire to help the Union." I paused, my heart pounding harder. "And you."

Gray studied me in the dim light, astonishment in his eyes. "You would list me among your reasons for choosing 1861?"

"May I?"

He touched my cheek, his hand gentle. "I hope I would be a reason for you to stay, Maggie."

I put my hand over his, my smile pressing against the warmth of his palm.

"You've surprised me yet again," he said with a smile of his own, removing his hand. "I'm so used to uncovering selfishness and betrayal. I almost don't know what to do with sacrifice and hope."

"You can hold it close," I told him, "just as I am trying to do."

He looked at me with such longing, I was certain he would kiss me. I wanted to know what it felt like to be held in his passionate embrace. Would it be practiced and polished, like Seth's? Wild and uncertain, like Zechariah's? Or something altogether different?

I waited for him to kiss me, but instead he stood and offered me his arm. When I rose, he tucked my hand into the crook of his elbow and then led me away from the alley toward the lights of Willard's Hotel.

And though he was affectionate, holding me close at his side, he made no attempt to take the kiss I would have freely given him.

27

OCTOBER 20, 1941
PACIFIC OCEAN

A storm raged around the ship as we made our way toward Honolulu. I lay in bed, feeling the dip and sway of the vessel, watching the rainwater slash against my stateroom window, and thinking of Gray.

Warmth infused my limbs, and for the first time in a long time, I was completely relaxed. I could still see the look in his eyes as he listened to me tell him about my paths. It was as if I could see all the gears in his remarkable mind moving, adjusting, clicking together as he put the pieces in place. He was captivated by the miracle of my life—perhaps captivated by me, too—yet he hadn't tried to kiss me.

A disappointed sigh escaped my lips because I knew it was probably for the best. I would have to face Zechariah in less than an hour, and his kiss—or rather, the way he'd reacted afterward—still had me reeling in confusion.

Perhaps it was best if I didn't kiss anyone again until I knew what my fickle heart wanted.

I finally got out of bed, wondering what I'd face when I saw Zechariah today, and started to get dressed.

Anna was in the bathroom, singing in the shower, when I felt a shudder pass through our stateroom. Everything shook—just for a second—but it was strong enough that I slapped my hand on the desktop to stop a glass bottle of perfume from falling to the floor.

The shudder was followed by silence as Anna stopped singing in the bathroom.

Wind and rain still lashed the side of the ship. Had the storm caused the shuddering? Or was it something else entirely?

As I rushed to get dressed, Anna stepped out of the bathroom in a terry-cloth robe. "Did you feel that?"

I nodded. "I'm trying to hurry so I can see what happened."

A knock sounded at our door a second later. "All hands in the emergency ward," Helen called. "There's been an explosion, and several crew members were injured."

"Coming!" I quickly secured my hair with a ribbon. Had the explosion come from another ship? An enemy ship? Two US destroyers had been attacked in the past month by Germany, and eleven sailors had been killed.

I hadn't been afraid to be in the middle of the ocean until now.

Anna frantically dressed as I pulled on my shoes. "Go on without me," she said. "I'll be there as soon as possible."

I raced out of the stateroom and ran to the emergency ward. A dozen men had already been brought in, and two nurses were doing triage while a couple of surgeons prepared for surgery.

Zechariah was there in his white surgical attire. He was focused and serious as he scrubbed his hands, glancing up at me when I went to the washbasin beside him. "Our first patient has a piece of metal protruding from his abdomen." He rinsed the soap off his hands and forearms and walked toward the operating room without another word.

After I washed my hands, I followed, pulling on a surgical gown. I grabbed one from the wall and hurried to help Zechariah into it. He accepted my help, barely acknowledging me as he looked at the patient who lay on the operating table.

We worked side by side for hours, removing shrapnel from those who had been close to the blast, stitching up deep wounds, and treating third- and fourth-degree burns. As we worked, I learned it hadn't been enemy fire but a boiler explosion. Miraculously, no one was killed, though a few of the patients would need to be monitored closely to make sure infection or bleeding did not threaten their lives.

It was a long day, with the storm causing the ship to list, bringing on seasickness in several of the nurses. Thankfully, I didn't suffer the malady, though by the end of the day, my head was pounding and my eyes felt like sandpaper.

I was sitting in the breakroom, drinking a cup of coffee by myself, when Zechariah walked in. Night had fallen, and dinner was waiting for me in the nurse's dining room, but I was too tired to walk down the stairs and cross the ship. I needed a strong cup of coffee to give me a bit of energy first.

Though I had worked alongside Zechariah for the past eight hours, we had said nothing significant to one another. He'd given no hint or indication that he had anything to say to me, or that he was even going to acknowledge the kiss.

After he filled his cup of coffee, he turned and paused, apparently surprised to see me sitting there. I met his gaze, knowing that I had questions in my own. I had nothing to explain to him. I hadn't been the one to kiss him and then storm off.

For several heartbeats, he just stared at me, and then he left the breakroom without his coffee.

My mouth slipped open in surprise, but I would not let him ignore me.

I left my coffee on the table and discovered a newfound surge of energy as I exited the breakroom and looked down the hallway to see which way he'd gone. He was walking toward the bow of the ship, which housed the officer's quarters, no doubt going to his stateroom. I followed, trying to keep my balance as the ship swayed left and then right.

He was almost to his room when I finally caught up to him.

"You're not going to explain yourself?" I asked.

Zechariah didn't turn, but he paused, his hand on the door-knob of his stateroom. No one else was in the hall, and the wind and rain drowned out our words, offering a semblance of privacy.

He finally turned to face me.

"Were you going to ignore me?" I asked, a little hurt. "After last night?"

"I don't want to talk about it, Nurse Hollingsworth."

"Nurse Holling—?" I frowned. "You can't kiss me and then pretend like it never happened."

He tore off his white surgical cap, clutching it in his hand. His hair was disheveled and wild. His gaze was just as storm-tossed as the Pacific, just as unpredictable. "I should never have kissed you. It was a mistake."

I stared at him, confused. "A mistake?"

His gaze was hard—impenetrable. "I should not fraternize with a nurse."

"That's not why you're upset, Zechariah." I crossed my arms, unwilling to let him hide behind his facade any longer. "You're scared—just like I'm scared—but I have never run away from you. I would never ignore you. Especially after such a powerful kiss."

A hint of longing flitted through his gaze, softening it for a moment, but then he seemed to steel himself as he lifted his chin. "You have no idea what it feels like to lose someone you love and not be able to protect them."

"You have no idea what I've lost." My heart squeezed for Mom, Dad, and Delilah. I'd told Gray about them at the Willard Hotel, and he had understood. Could I ever tell Zechariah about them? Would he understand or even believe me?

I took a step back, realizing Zechariah couldn't possibly understand. He wasn't even searching for the truth. He was so consumed by his own loss, by his own fear, that he hadn't thought about mine.

Remorse filled his face. "You're right. I don't know what you've lost, and I've never asked. But don't you understand? I lost everything when I was a boy. After my father died, I was afraid of losing my mother. I prayed to God every night that He would spare her life and keep her safe. I knew her life was in danger, and I was powerless to do anything to save her."

I swallowed my grief, thinking about his.

"I promised myself that I would never allow myself to love again," he continued, coming closer to me, anguish giving way to the strongest emotions I'd ever seen in his gaze. "The pain of loss is so intense, Maggie. I don't think I could survive it again." He reached for me, putting his hands on my arms. "I'm so in love with you that the thought of losing you keeps me awake at night. I can't live like that again."

My back was against the wall as I stared at him.

"I've tried not to fall in love with you," he said, "and even admitting it now, I know I am risking everything. But it's impossible to pretend any longer. God may take you from me, but I cannot deny what my heart wants."

I was speechless as I stared at him. Every facade was torn away, and he stood there, vulnerable and exposed. I could see it in his eyes—that childlike uncertainty, both hope and fear mingled together.

"Don't you see?" he asked, moving a little closer. "If I acknowledge that I love you, then I have to acknowledge that losing you would destroy me, and that's the most terrifying feeling in the world. So when I pulled away last night, it wasn't because I was angry or because the kiss didn't matter to me. It was because I knew the truth." He shook his head. "Nothing scares me, Maggie, except the fear of losing someone I love again—of losing you."

"I do see," I told him, my own emotions shaking my voice. "I'm just as afraid and uncertain as you. But it doesn't give me the right to turn my back on you."

"I'm sorry," he said, quietly, almost reverently, and I wondered when he had last said those words. "You're right. You should not be punished for my own shortcomings. It's been so long since I've opened my heart to anyone that I've almost forgotten how it's done. I've spent a lifetime turning people away without thought or feeling. I didn't even think as I turned my back on you last night."

The corridor was dim, and it felt smaller as Zechariah stood in front of me. Part of me wanted to promise that he had nothing to fear, that I wasn't going anywhere. But the other part of me knew he had every right to be afraid. Not only because of my decision, but because of the looming war. I was afraid too. I had no guarantee that we would survive WWII.

"I forgive you," I finally said.

A noise down the hall made both of us look up. One of the lieutenants paused as he saw us. Zechariah straightened and took a step away from me so his back was against the other wall. The lieutenant passed between us, neither looking left or right, and disappeared into one of the staterooms.

I met Zechariah's gaze, and though the hallway was narrow, it felt a little safer having him farther away.

"I don't want to get you in trouble," he said, "so I will try to keep my distance. But remember what I've told you, Maggie."

"That you're scared to lose me?"

"That I love you." His gaze was so intense, so powerful, it made my pulse gallop.

"I will remember," I promised, but I couldn't tell him I loved him in return. Not because it wasn't true—a part of me loved him a great deal—but because it wasn't fair. Not yet.

I left him to return to my room to freshen up for supper. I was weak from the encounter, my emotions running amok. If I knew anything about Zechariah Philips, it was that spending my life with him would be an incredible, passionate adventure.

What I didn't know was if we'd destroy each other in the process.

28

OCTOBER 21, 1861
WASHINGTON, DC

"You have to eat your supper, Private Aleckson," I said to the young man sitting up in his bed at the Judiciary Square Hospital the next evening. "You want to get strong again so you can rejoin your regiment, don't you?"

"I refuse to eat until you agree to marry me, Miss Wakefield." He grinned, revealing his tender youth. Though he said he was eighteen, I wouldn't guess him a day over sixteen.

I readjusted the pillow behind his back. "What would your mama say if you brought home an old maid?"

"You're hardly an old maid." Private Aleckson scoffed. "And you're about the prettiest lady I've ever met, with those blue eyes and dimples. Mama would be proud of me."

My cheeks warmed, though I had grown used to such talk here at the hospital. My work helped keep my mind off Zechariah and his confession the day before. I had known for a long time that his feelings were growing, but I hadn't realized the depth of them until yesterday. Even though I'd always worried about the grief I would cause my marked parents and my siblings if I left 1941, it paled in comparison to the pain I would cause Zechariah, especially with his past.

I didn't like to think about it—so I didn't. At least, not today.

Darkness hovered outside the tall windows in the classroom-turned-hospital ward. Twenty beds had been crammed into the room with less than two feet to walk between each one, and they were all full of men recuperating from camp illnesses and accidents. It was cool, as all the windows were open, since the prevailing belief among physicians was that foul airs, or miasmas, carried poisonous emanations that caused diseases. I knew this not to be true, but the fresh air helped remove some of the stench and staleness.

"I'll eat," Private Aleckson said, favoring his left arm, which he'd broken after falling out of a wagon bed, "but only because I want to be nice and strong for our wedding day."

Laughing, I shook my head and handed him a bowl of ham and cabbage soup.

As he took it, he nodded at the door and said, "Looks like someone's here to see you, Miss Wakefield."

Turning, I was surprised to see Gray standing just inside the room, his hat in his hand. Butterflies filled my stomach, and I couldn't hide the smile that lit my face. It was the first time I'd seen him since he'd guessed my true identity. The bond and rush of affection I felt for him astonished me.

He returned my smile, though his was sad.

"Will you excuse me?" I asked my patient.

"Who is he?" Private Aleckson demanded, half-teasing. "Should I be concerned that he's here to steal my girl?"

I ruffled his hair like I would my brother Teddy's and said, "Eat your soup."

He did as I told him, and I joined Gray at the door.

"This is a pleasant surprise," I said. "What brings you here?"

Gray touched my arm. "Can we talk privately?"

My smile fell as I nodded. "Of course."

I led him out of the room and down the lantern-lit hall. The door at the end exited onto a courtyard where there would be a little privacy, though the kitchen building wasn't too far away, and it was dark out. The air was cool, but not unpleasantly so, and I was too concerned about the gravity of Gray's mood to worry about not having a shawl with me.

"What's wrong?"

The moon cast enough light for me to see him clearly. His brown eyes were filled with such sadness that my heart began to sputter, and I could feel the weight of my fear settle on my face. I grabbed his arm, needing him to tell me why he had come.

Gray swallowed before he spoke, putting his hands under my elbows, as if to hold me up. I could tell it took him a great deal of effort. "It's your father. There's been an ambush at Ball's Bluff on the Potomac. . . . He was killed, Maggie."

For several heartbreaking moments, I stared at him, trying to make sense of what he'd just said, hoping and praying I had misheard him. But the look on his face told me that I had heard correctly. Papa was dead.

My knees buckled, and Gray tightened his hold, capturing me in his arms. He drew me close as the tears began.

"It can't be true," I said over and over again. "Not Papa."

"I'm so sorry, Maggie." There were tears in Gray's voice as he soothed me. "I wish it were not true."

I clung to the lapels of his coat as he held me up, his voice soothing, though I didn't know what he was saying. He didn't rush me, nor did he try to make light of the news. Instead, he allowed me to grieve and tenderly handed me a fresh handkerchief to dry my face.

"I wish I didn't have to tell you, but I couldn't imagine you hearing it from anyone else. As soon as I learned the news, I went to President Lincoln and told him I would relay the information." He shook his head, his gaze heavy. "The president is heartbroken, Maggie. I left him in tears. Your father was one of his closest friends."

I nodded, trying to find my voice, though it was useless.

"Would you like me to take you home?" he asked. "I have a carriage waiting out front."

"Yes, please." My voice was small and hoarse.

"Is there anything I can get for you?"

"My shawl and handbag." I started toward the door, but my legs were still weak.

He rushed to my side and put his arm around my waist. "Let me take you to the carriage, and I'll go inside for your things."

It felt like I was in a dream as he walked me around the building and helped me into the hired carriage. He'd thought ahead, knowing I would need a way home. His thoughtfulness and care bolstered my broken heart.

As I waited for him, I'd never felt so alone in my life. What would I do without Papa? He had been my sole purpose in this path since I was five years old. It had been just him and me against the world, and we were happy. I was proud to serve as his hostess and proud to be his daughter. What would life look like without him?

I began to weep again. I put my face in my hands, allowing the sorrow and grief to roll over me like tidal waves. This loss, combined with my death in 2001, was too much. All I wanted right now was Mama and Daddy, but I couldn't even have them. They were in Williamsburg, and I was heading to Honolulu. They were my only remaining parents, and they were unreachable.

The carriage door opened, and Gray stepped in. He came to my side and pressed close to me, wrapping his arm around me, allowing me to lay my head on his shoulder. He gave a quick tap to the ceiling, and the carriage began to move toward home.

Gray held me tight, and I took comfort in knowing that he understood. He had lost his parents, his home, his country, and his hopes and dreams when he was just fifteen years old. If anyone understood losing everything, it was him—yet he did not speak of his own loss. Instead, he allowed me to mourn mine. More importantly, he had not become bitter, though everything had been torn from him without cause or justification. He'd used his loss to fuel the passion and purpose he had for his work. Even in my sorrow and brokenness, he inspired me.

When we arrived at Lafayette Square, Gray paid the cab driver and then walked me inside. Joseph, Saphira, and Goldie had already heard the news and were mourning together in the kitchen when we entered the house. The moment they heard us, they came out to the parlor to offer their condolences, and I took more comfort in their love and respect for my father. They'd only known him for a year, but they had been honored to work for him and promised to stay as long as I needed them.

But I didn't want to think about the future, or how I would pay for this house and our servants. Not yet. My only concern was staying afloat on the waves of grief threatening to pull me under.

Gray stayed with me throughout the evening, close at my side, until I fell into an exhausted sleep.

OCTOBER 24, 1861

The day of Papa's funeral should have been cold and dreary. Instead, the sun shone, and it was unusually warm for the end of October. I had to shade my eyes as I stepped out of St. John's Church with President and Mrs. Lincoln. It had been three unending days since Papa died, and whether I was in 1861 or 1941, I was still in shock. Thankfully, Anna was there to comfort me in 1941, and I had Gray in 1861.

Word of Papa's death had shaken the entire Union. President

Lincoln came to our home to pay his respects the morning after Papa died, telling me that he felt the loss like a brother and had walked the floor of his room through the night, grieving his old friend. I had received dozens of telegrams from as far away as California and almost every state in between.

But on that Thursday afternoon, as I walked slowly behind the hearse carrying Papa in a glass-front coffin on our way to the Congressional Cemetery, it didn't matter how many people were grieving with me.

I felt utterly alone.

Mourners lined Pennsylvania Avenue as we walked past the White House and toward the Capitol Building. President Lincoln and Mrs. Lincoln walked on my left side and Gray was to my right. Just behind us were members of the president's cabinet, as well as members of Congress.

Gray's hand briefly found mine in the folds of my black gown, reminding me I wasn't truly alone. He had been beside me every waking minute for the past three days, always ready to help in any way he could. Not once had he asked for anything in return, nor had he waited for me to seek his help. He'd arranged many of the funeral plans and had overseen the abundance of correspondence that had come my way, allowing me to accept the condolences of all my callers.

It took over an hour to walk to the Congressional Cemetery, where they would inter Papa. Gray stood next to me as we gathered around the coffin.

I stared at Papa through the glass window, too heartsore to cry again. My body hummed with grief, so deep and so piercing, it felt like it would never end.

Papa had been embalmed, as was the growing custom, and he looked as if he were simply asleep. He was handsome in his uniform, and despite the pain of his death, I knew he would have been proud to know he had sacrificed his life for a cause he believed in with all his heart.

And he was with my mother again. I could almost imagine the reunion they'd enjoyed at the gates of heaven. I would miss him dearly, but he'd never been the same without her, and knowing they were together again was consolation in my grief.

I tried to listen to the minister, to take comfort in his words and in God's promises for eternal life. I wanted to be fully present in this moment, but when they lowered Papa into the ground, I had to turn away. I wanted to think of him as he'd always been—alive, passionate, and selfless as he gave his life to serve his fellow man. I didn't want to think of him in his grave.

Gray was waiting for me, ready to carry my grief. I pressed my face into his shoulder, and he led me away.

Finally, after the funeral was done and I had accepted the condolences of hundreds of people and tried to eat supper with the Lincolns at the White House, Gray saw me home.

Joseph was the only one awake when we arrived back at the house. After we entered, he excused himself and left us alone. Gray was crouched near the hearth, stoking the fire, when I entered the parlor after removing my hat and gloves. My feet and back ached from all the standing and walking we had done that day.

I watched him. When he finally stood, wiping his hands, he turned and offered me a tender smile. "Tired?"

Every bit of love and affection I had for him rushed to the surface, and I crossed the parlor, wrapping my arms around him in a tight embrace.

"Thank you," I said, surprised that I had any tears left within me. "Thank you for everything. I truly don't know what I would have done without you."

He returned my hug, holding me close. When he pulled back and looked down at me, I saw a longing in his face that matched my own. Yet he looked away and put a little space between us. He moved some of the logs with the fire poker and said, "If there is anything you need, Maggie—anything at all—please let me know."

Disappointment washed over me. Why wouldn't he draw me close? Comfort me in a way that only he could?

"I have made an inquiry into your father's financial situation," he continued, "and I'm pleased that he's left you secure. With your nursing income, I believe you will be able to stay in this house and keep your servants for as long as you'd like. But if there is anything else you need, I will see to it."

It was a great relief, and I was thankful that Papa had had the foresight to leave me with a means of survival.

Gray stared into the flames. "I've been thinking a lot about your other path, the one you lost in 2001. I can't imagine how much more grief this adds to your bruised heart."

"It was good to have a funeral for him, to get a chance to say good-bye and have closure. I didn't get that in 2001."

He nodded. "I've also been thinking about the decision you need to make in January, and how your loss must affect your plans. Without your father here—" His voice quieted to a hush. "Is there reason enough for you to stay?"

I lifted my head to look at him and saw the pain in his features. Did he think I would forfeit this path because I'd lost Papa? Though part of my purpose here was gone, I still loved 1861 with all of my heart. And I loved Gray.

I could see he was trying to be strong for me, but he wasn't able to hide the depth of his own grief.

"I love you, Maggie," he said quietly, gently, and when he met my gaze, I saw that longing in his eyes again. "But I won't pressure you to choose me. I won't pressure you to do anything. Even if you didn't have such an enormous decision to make, the loss of your father would be enough for me to give you time and space. But while you are healing and weighing all your options, please know that I will be here for you, no matter what you choose."

I reentered his embrace, and he laid his cheek on top of my head. I could feel his heart pounding. I closed my eyes, wanting to please him and make him happy, to give him everything his heart desired. He was the kindest soul I'd ever known, and I did not deserve him.

When I looked up at him again, his gaze went to my lips. Slowly, he placed his hands on either side of my face, and I closed my eyes—but his kiss touched my forehead. His lips remained there for a long time, as if he was trying hard to force himself to stop there.

He'd said he loved me, and his actions proved it more than his words. He'd been my rock this past week—so why did he not kiss me? Was he holding back because he'd promised he would give me time and space? He knew I had a big decision to make, but he didn't realize it involved another man. What would he think if he knew Zechariah had kissed me?

I had made no promise to either man, but it suddenly felt as if I was being unfaithful to both. I was trying to listen to my heart, but it was filled with grief again, growing more confused every day.

The weight of my decision hung precariously in the balance, threatening to topple one way or the other, hurting the two men I cared about more than any other.

When Gray pulled away and left me that evening, I knew it was for the best.

29

OCTOBER 27, 1941
HONOLULU, HAWAII

It seemed fortuitous that the *Solace* would arrive in Pearl Harbor on Navy Day. As I stood on the quarterdeck, looking out at the famous harbor, goosebumps ran up and down the back of my arms. A rainbow sliced through the sky and seemed to dive into the bay directly in front of us. All around, the green hills and mountains of Oahu formed a horseshoe, almost like a hug, giving the illusion that nothing bad could happen here.

A small pocket of clouds hovered over the highest mountain peak, raining up in the hills, though sunshine glistened in the harbor. That cloud reminded me of my grief. It was always there, hovering, raining on parts of my life, though sunshine still shimmered around it. I had much to occupy my mind and heart, both here and in 1861. My work, my friends, and my joy in serving could not be diminished by my grief. Losing 2001 *and* Papa in just six weeks was devastating, but I'd learned that grief was a strange thing. It never left me, though it dulled over time.

Thoughts of Gray softened the edges of my pain. He had been forced to return to his work, but he came often to keep me company. We read together, ate dinner together, and spoke of our pasts. Saphira acted as a chaperone, and though we still had moments alone, when he said good night to me on the porch, he didn't tell me he loved me or pressure me to return his affection.

And he did not kiss me.

I sighed, wishing he could be here with me now to see the magnificence of Hawaii.

"They call that Battleship Row, don't they?" Anna asked as she came up beside me, pointing at the seven ships docked near Ford Island. The battleships were massive, each named after a state. It was a powerful sight, but I also knew what it meant. The position of the ships would make them easy targets for the Japanese on December 7.

"I believe it is," I told Anna. "Pretty impressive, isn't it?"

"It's a show of strength and power to the Japanese," one of the other nurses said. "Nobody will mess with us."

There were nods of agreement all around, and I had to close my eyes to their unwavering optimism and confidence.

"President Roosevelt is speaking," Helen said as she came onto the quarterdeck. "It's about the German U-boat that torpedoed the USS *Kearney* near Iceland last week."

Many hailed the attack as the beginning of war, though FDR was slow to call it as much.

Everyone left the railings to gather around the radio, reminding me of the last day I'd been in 2001, huddled around the television, watching the Twin Towers burn.

A handful of officers arrived on deck, Zechariah among them. They were wearing shorts and short-sleeved shirts, with fedoras on their heads. I'd heard that several people were getting shore leave in celebration of Navy Day and that there was going to be a dance at the Royal Hawaiian Hotel, but I hadn't realized Zechariah was planning to go along with them.

He smiled at me—a strange new occurrence that had started since the evening in the hallway, though I hadn't seen him often.

As I'd been mourning Papa's death for the past week, I had kept mostly to myself, knowing I couldn't explain my grief. Anna allowed me to talk about Papa whenever I needed to. She understood grief better than most people and helped me through my toughest moments. When I was working, I had purposely distanced myself from Zechariah, not knowing how I could possibly explain my mood, or reconcile my feelings for him and Gray.

But now, as we docked in Pearl Harbor, with the sunshine and the waves beckoning and a soft, soothing breeze ruffling the wayward curls around my face, I felt a renewed energy. It was partially due to Gray's continued care and attention in 1861, and partially due to Anna's steadfast love in 1941. Along with Mama and Daddy, she and Teddy were the only family I had left.

"Anyone interested in joining us on Waikiki Beach?" one of the medical officers asked.

"Shh," a nurse responded. "We're listening to the president."

The officers joined us as the president wrapped up his speech. When he finished, the radio was turned to a local station playing Hawaiian music, the nurses and officers began to mingle, and Zechariah came to my side.

"Some of us are going to the beach," he said. "Would you like to join us?"

"Oh, say you will," Anna said to me with Dr. Church at her side. "It wouldn't be the same without you, Maggie. Besides, we won't have another day off until next week."

"I've always wanted to see Waikiki Beach," I admitted. It did sound like fun—something I sorely needed.

An hour later, we were sitting on the soft sand of Waikiki Beach with waves lapping at our toes. To the left was Diamond Head, the iconic mountain that framed the beach on one end, and behind us were impressive hotels, some of them six to eight stories high. The famous Royal Hawaiian, known for its impeccable luxury and pink stucco finish, was one of the finest on the beach. Tiki torches were being set out for the dance later, though it was still hours away, after the sun set.

Zechariah had rented a large grass umbrella and stuck it into the sand, providing a bit of shade. Palm trees swayed in the soothing wind, and beachgoers were walking along the boardwalk, making sandcastles, or swimming in the ocean.

I wore a pink-and-white striped bathing suit, and Zechariah lay on his back beside me, a hand flung over his eyes, wearing a pair of red swimming shorts. It was the first time I'd seen him without a shirt, and I was surprised at the muscles he'd been hiding under his uniform. Though he was thin from celiac disease, he had an incredible physique, and it was hard not to admire him.

The others had rented surf boards and were so far out in the water that I couldn't hear their conversation, though everyone appeared to be having a good time. Dr. Church had been very attentive to Anna, helping her try to master the skill, though he didn't look adept at it either. They laughed as they went farther out to try to catch some of the bigger waves.

"Are you mad at me?" Zechariah asked.

He hadn't said anything for so long, I thought he was asleep. His voice startled me.

"Mad?"

He removed his arm from his eyes and turned over onto his stomach so he could look at me. Sand clung to his back. "You've hardly spoken to me since the night in the hall."

I looked out at the ocean, trying to decide how to explain, and realized I couldn't.

But I could be honest with him.

"I'm not mad. I just don't feel like myself this week."

He was leaning on his elbows, causing his biceps to ripple. I had to look away.

"I've had a bit of time to do some self-reflecting," he said, "which isn't something I like to do often, since I usually find myself lacking."

"Oh?" I smiled—one of the first smiles I'd had all week. "What did you discover, Zechariah?"

"If I want you to love me, I have to first learn how to love myself—or, at the very least, like myself. I realized a long time ago that I'm not a likable fellow."

I started to laugh—I couldn't help it—and he looked up, a little hurt.

"You think this is funny?" He sat up to face me, his back to the ocean.

I pressed my lips together, though it was difficult to suppress my smile. "I think it's sweet. I've always known that beneath the bark and bite, there was a kind-hearted soul. You could be likable if you allowed yourself to be."

"It's one of the reasons I joined the group today," he said. "If I want you to like me, I should probably try to get the others to like me too."

"You're off to a marvelous start, though I've always liked you. I didn't need the others to approve."

He grinned—truly grinned—and he looked magnificent. "I don't know what you're doing to me, Maggie Hollingsworth, but I feel like a new man. I *want* to be a new man."

I reached out and touched his cheek, smiling. "I'm happy to hear it, but I don't want you to do it for me. I want you to do it for yourself. When we make a change for ourselves, it tends to stick. If we change for other people, we go back to our old habits the second they're gone."

He put his hand over mine. "I hope you don't have any plans on leaving soon."

I shook my head. "Not anytime soon."

"Good." He let go of my hand and moved to sit closer to me, facing the ocean. When our bare legs brushed each other, I suddenly wondered what Gray would think if he saw Zechariah and me like this together, in swimming suits with so much skin showing. His nineteenth-century sensibilities would be appalled, I was sure.

"I haven't felt this healthy in years," Zechariah said, smelling like suntanning oil and salty sea air. "It was your suggestion that I go on an elimination diet that caused me to take it seriously. I think I've finally found the culprit. It is grain, like I said, but not just one grain, several of them. When I leave them out of my diet, I feel amazing. It's been so long since I've felt this good, and it's thanks to you." He leaned closer. "How did you get so smart, Maggie?"

Unlike Gray, I knew that Zechariah's pragmatic mind would never accept the truth. He was a man of science. He understood how things worked by observation and tests. He relied on the things he could see or measure. If I told him I was a time-crosser who had lived in 2001, he'd think I was insane. There was no way for him to observe or test the evidence.

So I shrugged. "I read a lot." It was the same answer I'd given him before, and he accepted it as fact, just like he always had.

We were both quiet for several moments, and then he said, "Maggie, I'd like to show you that I'm changing. I want you to trust me. And maybe one day you could learn to love me the way I love you."

I wanted to tell him I already loved him, but it wasn't wise or kind, not if I still didn't know if I loved him enough to forsake all others. If I told him I loved him and then I died, he'd be even more heartbroken. I cared too much about him to let that happen.

Besides, there was Gray. I could not tell Zechariah I loved him when I also loved Gray. It wouldn't be fair to either man. Just thinking about it now made me feel guilty and ashamed.

Zechariah leaned forward, and I knew he was going to kiss me again. If this was my only path, I would have let him, but I couldn't stop thinking about Gray.

Instead of turning away from him, I put my hand on Zechariah's bare shoulder and kept him where he was.

"Perhaps," I said gently, "we should take it a little slower. We have all the time in the world, after all."

It wasn't necessarily true, but part of me wanted to believe it.

I was trying hard to know what my heart wanted, but I realized, with dismay, that it wanted two very different men equally.

30

DECEMBER 7, 1861
WASHINGTON, DC

I had been dreading December 7 for months, ever since I agreed to go to Pearl Harbor. All I could think about was waking up tomorrow in 1941 to face the bombing in the early morning hours. Everyone else would wake up thinking they would have a nice, leisurely Sunday off, but it would turn into the most horrific day any of us would ever experience and would linger with us for the rest of our lives.

Those of us who lived.

But today I was in Washington, DC, and I tried to focus on the work God had put in front of me. Thankfully, there had been no other major battles since both the Union and the Confederacy had gone into their winter camps, though the need for supplies hadn't ended. I kept busy helping Clara collect and distribute those supplies when I wasn't working at the hospital.

"It will be a dreary Christmas for our troops," Clara lamented as I put on my wrap to leave her apartment.

"Perhaps we can offer a special program," I said as I buttoned up my thick jacket. "Music, dancing, and treats. We can solicit Washington to rally around her soldiers and give them a Christmas they won't soon forget."

Clara's eyes filled with excitement, and she nodded. "I know just who to ask. The Ladies Aid Society will get behind this idea without hesitation."

"Good." I picked up my muffler and glanced out Clara's front window. It was raining again. I had told Joseph I would walk home, but now I wasn't sure it was a good idea.

A carriage pulled up while I was assessing the weather, putting a smile on my face.

"Mr. Cooper?" Clara asked, looking out the window.

"I mentioned I was going to be here this afternoon," I said. "I'm surprised he remembered."

"He must have realized you'd need a ride home." Clara smiled. "Has he asked you to marry him yet?"

If the question had come from anyone else, I might have told them it wasn't their business. But Clara had become one of my dearest friends over the past eight months. "No, he hasn't."

"Oh, he will." She said it with such certainty, I tore my gaze from the window, where Gray was just getting out of the carriage. "A man doesn't look at a woman the way he looks at you and *not* propose marriage." She chuckled. "Well, not if he's a decent sort of fellow, anyway. And Gray is the most decent man I've ever met."

I couldn't deny her claim since I felt the same way. "I'll see you tomorrow," I said to Clara, not wanting to make Gray walk up all the steps to her apartment, and afraid I'd be embarrassed if he suspected what we'd been discussing.

"Good-bye, Maggie," Clara said, a smile in her voice. "Say hello to Mr. Cooper for me."

I left her apartment and almost bumped into Gray on the stairway. My heart did a little somersault, and the cares I had shouldered throughout the day seemed to melt away. Though

I could not shake the heaviness of tomorrow, seeing Gray gave me something else to think about.

"Good afternoon, Miss Wakefield," he said, looking at me the way Clara had just mentioned.

"Good afternoon, Mr. Cooper," I responded with a smile. "I didn't expect to see you today."

"When I saw the rain, I decided to pick you up. I hope you don't mind."

"Of course not."

He looked a little sheepish. "I also sent a note to your house to tell Goldie and Saphira that I'm taking you to supper at the Willard Hotel."

I smiled again. "Thank you. They could use an evening off, and I could use the distraction."

Gray led the way down the stairs and then opened the front door for me. He popped up his black umbrella to hold over my head and followed me to his waiting carriage. The mud was so thick, it sucked my feet down into the mire and lined my hem.

He helped me into the carriage and then climbed in behind me, closing his umbrella. After he shut the door, the carriage pulled away from Clara's apartment building.

When he turned to me, he said, "What's bothering you?"

Could he so easily see the burdens I carried? No one else had noticed.

I let out a long exhale and looked down at my gloved hands. I had told Gray a lot about my other paths, but I hadn't told him everything. He didn't know about Zechariah or about WWII. I hadn't wanted to bother him with the knowledge of either. Just like Papa, I didn't want to tell Gray too much about America beyond 1861.

But it would be difficult to spend the entire evening with him and not mention Pearl Harbor.

"Tomorrow is going to be one of the most difficult days of

my life—and one of the most detrimental days in American history."

The carriage was cold and bounced uncomfortably along the muddy road as Gray took one of my hands in his. "Tell me about it."

Against my better judgment, I had to relieve this burden. I trusted Gray, not only because he had proven to be trustworthy, but because he was a Pinkerton agent and knew the importance of keeping sensitive information safe. "America is on the verge of a world war in 1941," I said slowly, trying to decide how much to tell him. "It will start in earnest tomorrow when Japan bombs Pearl Harbor, an American military base in Hawaii where I'm serving."

"Hawaii? America claims Hawaii?"

"It's an American Territory in 1941. Tomorrow there will be a surprise attack early in the morning, and thousands of soldiers and civilians will be killed in the course of a few hours."

"And you know this because you lived in 2001?"

I nodded. "I'm the only one who knows the attack is coming, and there's nothing I can do to stop it. If I knowingly change the course of history, I forfeit my path in 1941."

"And you'd be stuck here forever."

The way he said it made my heart ache. "I wouldn't consider staying in 1861 as 'stuck,' but yes, it would leave me with no other path. Besides, Pearl Harbor, as horrific as it will be, is one of the most important events in the history of the world. If I tried to warn someone and Japan doesn't succeed, and America doesn't enter the war, who's to say what would happen?" If Hitler conquered Europe, the world would look far different, affecting my parents and loved ones in 1941 and 2001. "There's just no way I could be responsible for such a thing."

"Maggie, I cannot fathom the burden you're under. I admire you more than you know."

"There's nothing to admire." I lifted a shoulder. "I didn't choose this gift. It was thrust upon me. I have no choice."

"None of us chooses the life we've been born into. It's how you decide to deal with it that matters. I imagine others like you have become angry and bitter, but you remain resilient and hopeful, despite all the heartache and loss. You know who you are and why God placed you on this earth. You've said it yourself—you are a healer, and regardless of your circumstances, you find ways to help those in need, never thinking of yourself alone. I think that makes you remarkable."

"But I have been angry at God," I said, "and sometimes I do think only of myself. I've spent much of my life trying to fix people and control the outcomes of their lives, thinking I knew what was best for them. Anna even accused me of trying to play God."

"I think we're all guilty of that from time to time."

"My life is remarkable, but I'm not, Gray. I'm just a woman trying to make sense of it all."

He smiled. "We're all trying to make sense of life. God has given each of us a unique path, one that draws us closer to Him because of the uncertainties and challenges. You're no different. We all make mistakes and have regrets, but I admire you because you are seeking God's will. You could have told Him a long time ago what you wanted, but you didn't. You desire to know what *He* wants."

I was uncomfortable with his praise, though I couldn't deny what he said. I *did* want to know God's will for my life. It was the reason I had struggled so much this past year. "If there's anyone who should be admired, it's my marked parents. They taught me to keep my faith and seek God's will. I wish you could know them, but I'm happy you knew Papa. He also taught me lessons about resilience and purpose. And my parents in 2001 taught me to do what I love, no matter what."

"It sounds like each of your lives prepared you for the plans

God has for you. You learned your loyalty and patriotism from your papa, your sacrificial love and faith from your mama and daddy, and your hard work and sense of purpose from your mom and dad, among many other important qualities from your siblings, your grandfather, and your friends."

An incredulous smile lifted my lips. "You realized that from the little I've told you?"

"When you speak about them, you make them come alive, and I feel like I know each one of them personally. It's not hard to recognize the bits and pieces that have contributed to make you the woman I love."

Tears filled my eyes. His words reminded me of Anna. She had also helped me realize that I was a combination of each of my paths. "You're right. There isn't one true version of me. I'm all of my paths."

"You're simply Maggie," he said with a tender smile. "The result of all of the times you've occupied, all of the people you've loved, and all of the things you've learned. You're you, regardless of time or place. You are not one of your paths, you are all of them."

The longing in his eyes intensified as he put his arm around me, and I wondered if he would finally kiss me.

But the carriage arrived at the Willard Hotel, coming to a stop just outside the front awning. A footman opened the door for us, and I knew the opportunity had passed.

Yet it was a moment I would not soon forget. Gray had helped me solidify a truth I had wondered about all of my life.

Who was I?

I was Maggie, regardless.

A few hours later, after the rain had stopped, Gray walked me to my door.

My stomach was full and my heart was happy, though tomorrow still loomed like an ominous storm on the horizon. I couldn't avoid it. All I could do was try to prepare myself for the inevitable destruction it would bring, praying that God would sustain me.

Joseph opened the front door for us, and as soon as we were inside, he went to the kitchen, where I could hear Goldie and Saphira laughing.

A lamp had been lit on the hall table, casting a gentle glow in the room. Gray helped me with my cape, hanging it on one of the hooks near the door. I slipped off my hat and gloves and then turned to him. He was still wearing his coat and hat.

"Won't you stay?" I asked.

He slowly removed his hat, holding it. "I don't think I should."

My disappointment was keen, but I tried not to show it.

"I'm sorry, Maggie. I—" He set down his hat and removed his gloves, then crossed the hall to stand in front of me. "It's just—you only have three weeks before your birthday. And despite what I said, despite my resolve and my love for you—I'm realizing that I'm not a saint."

I frowned, trying to understand what he was saying.

"I've tried to be a gentleman," he continued. "I've tried to keep you close while holding you at a distance because I didn't want to pressure you or manipulate you into choosing me." He rubbed the back of his neck and looked away. "You don't know how many times I've wanted to pull you into my arms and kiss you—to ask you to marry me, to stay with me forever. And even now, I know this is wrong. I shouldn't—"

I placed my hand on his arm to still his words. "I've wondered why you haven't kissed me."

He turned back to me, yearning in his gaze. "It's not because I haven't wanted to. Maggie, I've never desired a woman as much as I desire you. But I made a promise to myself that I wouldn't have you choose me out of obligation or guilt. I know your heart. You have a natural bent to sacrificial love, which is one of the reasons I admire you." He rested his hands on either side of my face, his thumbs caressing my cheeks. "But I do not want you to sacrifice anything or anyone for me. If you choose me, I want you to choose me because it's what you want, not what I want."

Warmth filled my chest at his words, and I placed my hands over his. He knew me better than anyone else, and I loved him more and more because of it. I wanted him to know how I felt, but I too had made a promise. I wouldn't tell him I loved him if he didn't know about Zechariah.

My pulse sped at the thought. Could I tell Gray that I loved him if I also told him about Zechariah? Would it be fair to Gray? But how could I not tell him? I wanted him to know me fully.

Slowly, I removed his hands from my cheeks and lowered them, until they were clasped between us.

"I want to tell you something," I began, swallowing the fear and misgivings that crawled up my throat. I prayed, with every beat of my heart, that this was the right thing to do. "But I don't know where to begin."

He watched me closely. I'd realized a long time ago that his way of making me feel like the only person in the world was due, in part, to his gift. He saw things in me that others didn't see. It was how he'd uncovered the truth. "Just say what you need to say, Maggie."

"I love you, Gray."

His emotions were difficult to read as he drew me close. Happiness, pain, joy, uncertainty, hope, and fear all mixed together in his beautiful eyes. "I love you, too." He looked at my lips, and I saw the restrained desire there, but now I knew why he waited. My heart longed for that kiss, but my head told me that Gray was wiser than me.

"I need to tell you the rest—the hardest part." I could no

longer look into his eyes, knowing he would be hurt. "There's another man," I said, just above a whisper. "His name is Dr. Zechariah Philips. He's on the *Solace* with me in Pearl Harbor. He's a captain in the United States Navy. I met him the same day I met you."

Gray's hands slowly relaxed, and he eventually let go of me, taking a step back as he inhaled a deep breath.

"I'm sorry, Gray. I didn't mean to fall in love with both of you—"

"You love him?" His voice was strained.

"I—I think so." I swallowed again, my heart breaking. "I wanted you to know so there were no secrets between us."

"Why didn't you tell me sooner?" His voice revealed more than hurt—anger, perhaps, though he was trying hard to hold it in.

"I couldn't tell you when you didn't know about my time-crossing gift. And then Papa died and—"

Gray took a few seconds before he looked at me again. "I can't be another cause of heartbreak for you, Maggie. I knew that falling in love with you, after learning about your gift, was a fool's errand. I've been holding on to hope, trying to believe you would choose 1861, even after you lost your father. But the odds are stacked against me. You have your parents, your siblings, your work—and now I learn you have a man you love there, too." He no longer seemed angry, just sad. "I don't blame you, Maggie. Truly, I don't."

"Don't blame me for what?"

He took his hat and gloves off the side table and moved to the door.

"Gray!" I hurried across the room to stop him from leaving.

"Perhaps," he said, sorrow radiating from every line of his body, "someone should offer you sacrificial love." He leaned forward and placed a lingering kiss on my cheek. When he straightened, he met my gaze. "I won't stand in your way. I know what you have to endure in three short weeks, and I want you to know that while I will miss you every waking moment, I will not ask you to stay. You have a wonderful life awaiting you in 1941, and I wish you every happiness possible."

"Gray, don't—"

"Good-bye, Maggie." He slipped his hat on his head. "If you need anything before your birthday, you know where to reach me. I will always be here for you."

And with that, he was gone. Leaving me more bereft than I had ever felt before.

I wanted to call him back, to beg him to stay, but to what end? Could I promise him I would choose 1861? That I would marry him and we would live a long and happy life together? If I could not, then it would be cruel to ask him to return.

He had done what no one else had done, other than my marked parents. He had laid the decision solely at my feet, not begging or cajoling me with guilt or obligation. Gray loved me and desired me—that was not in question. But his love for me allowed me to leave him behind without blame.

His, truly, was the most sacrificial love, and if I had to make my decision today, it would be Gray. I loved him with my whole heart and soul. He knew me better than anyone else, and he understood me.

Papa's question stirred to life in me. If I lost everything else, would Gray be enough?

In that moment, I realized that, yes, he would be enough. I could lose everything and everyone in 1941, and Graydon Cooper would be enough for me.

But there were still three weeks ahead of me, including the attack on Pearl Harbor tomorrow and the aftermath. I could not pledge my commitment to Gray until I knew for certain what 1941 would bring.

As I laid my head on my pillow that night, with tears in my eyes, it was Gray who was on my mind at the very last.

For the first time in my life, I knew what I wanted. What I truly wanted.

I wanted Graydon Cooper.

31

DECEMBER 7, 1941
PEARL HARBOR, HONOLULU, HAWAII

Even before I opened my eyes, my pillow was wet with tears.
Whether from Gray's departure the night before or from what
I was about to face, I wasn't sure.

I sat up in bed and looked out the porthole toward Pearl
Harbor. The day was brilliant. Perfect. Everything was as it
should be. Hawaii truly was paradise.

My gaze traveled to my clock. It was 7:02, and the bombing
would begin at 7:55. That much I knew. I should get up and
start preparing, but my heart was so heavy, I hugged my knees
and laid my forehead down to allow the tears to flow. I needed
to pull myself together, but I couldn't. Memories from September 11 hit me hard. I recalled the woman in the Pentagon
who compared the attack on the Twin Towers to the attack on
Pearl Harbor—and I was going to live through both of them.

At least I prayed I would live through this one, because I
hadn't survived the one on September 11.

"Maggie?" Anna's sweet, sleepy voice held concern. She

climbed out of bed, her hair in rollers, and put her hand on my back. "What's wrong, sweetheart?"

I quickly wiped my tears. She had no idea what was about to happen, and I couldn't tell her yet because she might rush to warn someone in her fear.

"It's nothing." I offered a wobbly smile.

"Did something happen in 1861?"

Yes. I could blame the tears on 1861. My heart was breaking at Gray's departure. I hated to think he was suffering because of me and I couldn't fix it. It wasn't fair. I didn't want anyone to hurt because of me.

"Gray left," I said, trying not to cry all over again. "He learned about Zechariah—"

"You told him?" Her eyes were huge. "Why would you do that?"

"I had to. I couldn't keep it a secret, not from Gray."

She smiled and sat beside me on the bed. "I can tell you love him a great deal."

"I do." The tears did start then, but the clock was ticking and the attack would start in less than forty-five minutes. We needed to be dressed and prepared.

"Are you going to choose him?" Anna asked, looking down at her nightgown, grief in the lines of her forehead. "Are you going to leave me too?"

"Anna." Guilt weighed heavily upon me as I threw my arms around her, not wanting her to feel sad. "Let's talk about this later. I'd like to get dressed and see what this beautiful day—" I couldn't finish. I tried to be strong, to sound pleasant, but I couldn't do it. "To try to make the most of today."

She seemed to realize my need to stop talking about Gray. She nodded and patted my back. "It's okay, Maggie. If anyone understands the grief of losing someone, it's me. I know how you feel."

It was too complicated to discuss now. Instead, I got out

of bed and started to get dressed. We both had the day off, and Anna thought we were going to church, as we had done every Sunday since coming to Honolulu. I wanted to put on my nursing uniform, since it was the most practical clothing I owned, but if I did, Anna would ask questions. So I decided on the most serviceable dress I could find, since I didn't want to be wearing something impractical when the victims were brought to the *Solace*.

"You're wearing that?" Anna asked about twenty minutes later as she came out of the bathroom. I was completely dressed and ready, my hair tucked firmly into place so it wouldn't be a hindrance. Her hair was still in curlers, and she was in her bathrobe, taking her sweet time.

I looked down at my green dress. It really wasn't appropriate for church, but we weren't going to church. Instead of making excuses, I simply shrugged and said, "Yes."

Anna lifted an eyebrow and then went to the desk, humming.

"Can you hurry?" I asked, looking outside. Which way would the planes come from? The northwest? Probably, since Japan was northwest of Hawaii. Even now they were in the air, on their way to Pearl Harbor.

My heart was pumping so hard, I was afraid I might have a panic attack. Knowing what would happen was pure insanity. I never wanted to know the future again. I prayed that God would spare Pearl Harbor, though I knew it was futile. It had to happen so the war would start and Hitler would be defeated.

What a horrible waste of humanity.

"Why should I hurry?" Anna glanced at the clock as she applied powder to her nose and cheeks. "We don't need to be at church until nine."

It was now 7:44.

"Please hurry, Anna. I want to grab something to eat before we go."

"Go ahead. I'll come to the dining room when I'm ready."

I didn't want to leave her—not today. "I'll wait, but hurry."

She must have heard the urgency in my voice because she started to take out her curlers. I walked over to the desk to assist her.

I couldn't help but glance at the clock and the porthole—waiting, breathless, thinking of the thousands who were unaware of the great suffering they were about to endure. These were their last few minutes on earth. Tears stung the back of my eyes again.

Anna's hand paused on a curler, and a sickly expression came over her face. "You know something, don't you?"

My gaze snapped back to her in the mirror, and there was no use pretending anymore.

"You've always known." Her voice and hands shook as she set the curler on the desk and turned to me. "Ever since we were asked to come to Pearl Harbor, you've known something big was going to happen, didn't you?"

"Anna, you need to get dressed. Now. We only have minutes."

Panic filled her face. "What do you mean, 'minutes'?"

I finished taking out her curlers and ran to her closet to pull out the first dress I found. "Hurry, Anna. Please."

She ran her brush through her hair and then tied a ribbon around it, watching me. "Tell me."

I threw her dress on the desk and grabbed a pair of her stockings and her garter belt, tossing them onto the dress, then went for her shoes. "We're about to watch the most horrific event in American history unfold in the next few hours," I said just above a whisper. The clock said 7:50. "Japan will attack Pearl Harbor, and thousands will die and many more will be severely injured."

She stood, but she had to grasp the back of her chair.

"We have only five minutes before the first strike. Over a

thousand men will die on the *Arizona* alone. Our sailors will need us."

"What about the *Solace*?" she asked, her face turning pale. "What about Timothy?"

"I don't know. I tried not to learn too much."

She looked like she might throw up, and I didn't blame her. I was afraid I might too.

What if someone else I loved died today? What if *I* died?

Anna was dressed in a flash and was just putting her feet into her shoes when we heard the airplanes approach Pearl Harbor, flying low. I ran to the porthole and saw the first Japanese airplane with the telltale red sun under the wing.

The plane was so close, the pilot turned to look at me, and I could make out his features around the goggles he wore.

He waved.

⁂

By the time we arrived on the promenade deck to see what was happening in the harbor, the sky was full of Japanese bombers dropping torpedoes like rain.

Air raid alarms blared from every direction. It looked like almost two hundred airplanes were descending upon Pearl Harbor. Smoke billowed into the sky from Ford Island, just across the channel from where the *Solace* was anchored and to the right of Battleship Row. We were less than a hundred and seventy-five yards from the USS *Arizona*.

Torpedoes dropped from the Japanese bombers, one after the other, in a dizzying pattern against the brilliant blue sky, hitting countless targets. The sound was deafening. Sailors were running on the decks of all the ships around us, looking to the sky in shock and horror. They began to scramble to their stations, trying to return fire, but it would be too late for most of them. The Japanese had achieved complete and utter surprise.

Anna held my hand tight as we watched the carnage unfold before our eyes. We were all speechless. Fires had begun on several ships and buildings on Ford Island, soon turning the sky to dusk, blotting out the glorious sun.

Though there was destruction and chaos all around, the Japanese pilots appeared to be avoiding the *Solace*, for which I was thankful. I watched the *Arizona*, praying fervently for the souls upon that particular ship. Several torpedoes were dropped into the harbor by planes flying low overhead, striking the *Arizona*—and then the air rent with a cataclysmic blast unlike any other. The *Arizona* exploded, shaking the *Solace* and raining debris into the water and onto Ford Island. Within seconds, the forward turrets and conning tower of the *Arizona* collapsed downward, and the foremast and funnel collapsed forward, tearing the ship in half. The explosion was so powerful, it put out fires on the repair ship moored alongside it.

Within minutes, the *Arizona* was beneath the water.

Oil spilled from the assaulted battleships, floating to the top of the water, and fire burned everywhere. Men swam through fire, both drowning and burning to death, screaming for help.

After just moments of shock, the crew of the *Solace* went into action. Two stretcher parties were launched to evacuate men from the *Arizona* while the rest of us rushed to prepare for maximum service.

Zechariah appeared, his stern countenance bringing me hope and anchoring me. If anyone knew what to do, it would be him. He immediately began ordering the hospital corpsmen to prepare the emergency ward, which included an additional fifty beds. He sent other corpsmen to the patients already on board with orders to return as many convalescing sailors as possible to active duty.

"What should I do?" I asked him.

"Start preparing for triage."

Nodding, I found a corpsman and asked him to bring me

all the morphine he could find, and then I grabbed tags and pencils and brought them to a handful of corpsmen standing near the gangplank. "As the victims are brought on board, we'll need to examine them and determine which wards they need to be brought to. You'll write the wards on these tags and attach them to the men for the stretcher-bearers."

"Yes, ma'am." They took the supplies.

I immediately grabbed two deckhands. "I'll need all the stretcher-bearers you can find. Bring them here."

They nodded and went to work.

Even before our rescue boats returned, other evacuation boats began arriving with victims. I stood alongside Zechariah as he quickly assessed each patient, and then I told the corpsmen what to write on the tags. The deck crew began taking them away as fast as they arrived. It was my job to administer morphine to each patient in need—and they were all in need.

It was hard to know how much time had passed, but at one point, the *Solace* was moved to a safer docking station as a second wave of Japanese planes barreled into the harbor.

The entire time, stretcher parties and rescue boats delivered victims and then went back out to find more. I heard that they climbed aboard the burning *Arizona* to save lives, got into the burning water, and put themselves in constant danger of being hit by enemy fire.

I had never seen such wide-scale suffering in my life—not even at Bull Run. I kept thinking of the Twin Towers burning on September 11 and the massive battles that would steal the lives of hundreds of thousands of men at Gettysburg, Fredericksburg, Chancellorsville, Antietam, and more—not to mention all the battles ahead of America in WWII. War was merciless, and I hated it with every fiber of my being. I wanted to weep, but there was no time for emotions. As soon as I was done with one patient, there was another, and then another.

Zechariah's confident voice and presence steadied me

throughout the endless horror. Hundreds of men arrived on the ship, some with minor injuries, and some who did not survive.

"Doc," a corpsman called out to Zechariah as he ran up the gangplank of the *Solace*. "There's a man pinned, and we're afraid to move him in case he bleeds to death. We need a doctor to see if there's any chance of him living."

"I'll go." Zechariah turned to me. "Get someone else to administer the morphine, and you can continue my job."

There was no time to question him or debate the wisdom of leaving the *Solace*. He followed the corpsman off the ship and got into one of the rescue boats without saying good-bye. They pulled away, toward the burning water and smoke, and I lost sight of Zechariah in the melee.

I worked for what felt like hours, watching for him to return. The bombing eventually stopped, but the carnage did not.

As the sun was falling in the west, I was asked to leave my station and help Dr. O'Neal in the operating room. It was strange not to work alongside Zechariah. I assisted Dr. O'Neal as patient after patient was brought to us.

Acrid smoke filled the air, and the smell of death was all around us. I was sweating and covered with blood, but so was everyone else. At some point, the corpsmen began to bring coffee and sandwiches around to the medical staff, but none of us could pause for more than a minute. Exhaustion was a constant companion, exhaustion and fear.

I was just returning to the operating room when a stretcher was brought in—holding Zechariah. His face was pale, and his eyes were closed. Blood soaked his right pant leg, but the rest of his body appeared unharmed.

"Zechariah!" I ran to the stretcher as they positioned him on the operating table. He bore a tag that simply said OR.

He opened his eyes, which were glassy with pain and morphine.

"What happened?" I asked.

"Shrapnel—above my knee." He was breathing hard.

All of the surgeons were busy, but I called out to Dr. O'Neal. I didn't want Zechariah to wait. Every minute mattered.

Dr. O'Neal quickly finished his procedure and then came to us. "Dr. Philips!"

"You'll need to remove the shrapnel," Zechariah said to Dr. O'Neal, his face grave. "But I want to walk again. Make sure I can use my leg."

Dr. O'Neal placed his shaking hand on Zechariah's shoulder. "I'll do my best."

He cut away the bloody pant leg and swallowed hard. When he looked back at Zechariah, concern and uncertainty clouded his gaze. I knew he wasn't convinced he could save the leg. Dread filled me, but I couldn't let Zechariah see it on my face.

As the doctor began to prepare for the surgery, I clung to Zechariah's hand.

"Don't leave me," Zechariah said, his eyes pleading. I'd never seen him so defenseless before.

"I won't," I promised, though I wasn't sure if I had it in me to watch Dr. O'Neal operate on him.

"You're the best nurse I've ever worked with," Zechariah said to me. "Don't let him take off my leg."

Tears filled my eyes, and I realized it was the first time I had cried all day. There simply hadn't been time to respond emotionally to everything we'd endured. "I won't," I promised again. I would try my best, advising when and where I saw fit.

Zechariah tugged me down, and I lowered my ear close to his lips.

"I love you," he whispered hoarsely. "Please don't leave me."

I placed a kiss on his forehead, though Dr. O'Neal was watching, and said, "I won't leave you. I promise. And I'll be praying for you."

"Maybe God will listen to you."

"God has always listened to you, Zechariah. But that doesn't mean we always get what we want. Sometimes, in His infinite wisdom, He gives us what we need instead." I was speaking to myself just as much as I was speaking to him.

"I need my leg, Maggie."

I nodded as I wiped away my tears.

Moments later, Zechariah was given anesthesia, and Dr. O'Neal began the surgery. I was able to assist, though it was horrible. Zechariah's leg was so mangled, I had to accept that he would never be able to use it as he had before.

After fifteen minutes, Dr. O'Neal looked up at me with an apology in his eyes. "I don't think I can do it."

"Please," I begged him, holding Zechariah's hand, though he was unconscious. "He cannot lose his leg. It would destroy him."

Dr. O'Neal sighed and shook his head. "I'll do what I can, but he'll be lucky if he keeps it. The next few weeks will determine the future course of his life."

No truer words had ever been spoken.

The next few weeks would be difficult for all of us—and somehow, somewhere, in the midst of it all, I would have to choose which path to take for the rest of my life.

I could no longer pretend the decision was not upon me.

32

DECEMBER 25, 1861
WASHINGTON, DC

It had been two weeks since the attack on Pearl Harbor—two weeks since I'd last seen Gray. Though I was physically exhausted in 1941, the fatigue poured over as mental and emotional weariness in 1861. It was all I could manage just to work at the Judiciary Square Hospital during the day and then come home and fall into a deep sleep in the evenings. But that meant I was soon awake in 1941 and the work would begin all over again. We had almost three hundred patients aboard the *Solace* after the attack, and many of them were still recovering.

As the days passed, we learned of the catastrophic losses we had endured on December 7, 1941. The attack lasted one hour and fifteen minutes, though it had felt like an eternity. One hundred fifty-nine US aircrafts were damaged, one hundred sixty-nine were destroyed, sixteen ships were damaged, and three were destroyed. Eventually, all would be recovered, though the USS *Arizona* would stay beneath the water and become a memorial to all those who had died onboard that day.

One of the hardest things facing me in 1941 was Zechariah's

345

recovery. He might never be able to use his right leg as before since the knee was likely never to bend properly again. For a man who prided himself on his work and who had done nothing but serve as a navy surgeon for most of his adult life, the news was a crushing blow. If he could not use his leg, could he perform surgeries again? He had gone into a depression and had put up all his old defenses, becoming impossible to talk to.

Besides the unknown future, the wound also gave him intense pain, but he refused to accept morphine, concerned he'd get addicted. Worse, he'd been eating wheat again, aggravating his celiac disease, and he didn't appear to care.

How could I leave 1941 when he needed me? Almost every day, when I went to see him, he asked me to stay. I cared for Zechariah, but as my birthday drew closer and closer, I doubted that Zechariah was enough for me.

Snow fell on Lafayette Square as I accepted Saphira's help in the foyer. She lifted a cape up to my shoulders and smiled with admiration.

"You've never looked prettier, Miss Margaret. That black gown suits you."

I smiled at her compliment, though I knew the black mourning gown was stark against my complexion. I was wearing it in honor of Papa, and I didn't mind. "Thank you."

"Will you be out late?" She handed me one long black glove after the other.

"No. I'm tired." I couldn't remember when I hadn't been tired in the past two weeks. "I don't think I'll stay long."

"Would you like me to send Joseph for you later?"

"I'll be fine to walk home on my own." I lifted the hood over my intricately styled hair. Saphira had outdone herself preparing me for the Christmas ball at the White House. The teardrop onyx earrings I wore had been a present from Papa last Christmas.

"If you change your mind," she said, "send a runner over here to get him."

"I will." I took the gift I'd wrapped for the Lincolns and tucked it into my reticule as Saphira opened the door for me.

"Good night," she said. "And Merry Christmas."

"Merry Christmas. I hope you enjoy your evening festivities."

"The same to you, Miss Margaret."

I stepped out into the chilly air and took a deep breath. Large snowflakes fell from the dark sky, resting along the frozen street in front of the house.

As I walked toward the White House, I thought of the night Gray had walked me home from the dinner party at Rose's house and we'd sat on the bench. It was the first time I realized I was falling in love with him.

My heart ached at the memory, causing me to miss him more than ever. But I lifted my chin, soldiering on as Papa had taught me to do.

I arrived at the White House front door, and a doorkeeper allowed me in. After taking my wrap, he directed me to the East Room, where the Lincolns were entertaining. I'd heard rumors that many of their relatives from Kentucky and Illinois had arrived for the holidays and that they'd also invited the cabinet, members of Congress, and other military officials and staff. I was there because the Lincolns still thought of Papa and me as family. And this year, more than any other, I needed that family bond.

As I walked into the East Room, I wondered if Gray would be there. After two weeks apart, I understood the deep longing and desire he spoke of. It was a constant companion, like a hollow echo in my chest that would not stop aching unless he was near. My life was not the same without him. I had started several letters, begging him to ask me to stay, but I didn't send them. It wasn't fair to put the burden of my decision on him.

I had just one more week to choose. One week to know, for all time, what path I was meant to take. I longed to see Gray at least once more, to know for certain what my heart truly wanted. Did I have the courage to make the best choice for me?

Did he still want me? What if he had already moved on? Or left Washington? The very thought made my spirits sink lower than they'd ever been.

Yet—was I meant to stay in 1941 and care for Zechariah? To stand by his side and help him heal? After all, that was my highest calling, wasn't it? His depression was severe, but I was familiar enough with trauma to know that he could recover, given the right therapy. Was I supposed to be the one to administer that therapy? The thought of leaving him brought on such guilt, especially now, given his injury. Would it eat me alive forever if I didn't stay to help him?

The East Room opened up before me, filled with laughter, conversation, and the delicious scent of fresh pine garland, apple cider, cinnamon, and oranges. It should have made me feel joyful, but it didn't.

"Margaret," Mrs. Lincoln said when she spotted me from the receiving line. "Do come here."

I approached the Lincolns as Mr. Lincoln nodded farewell to two other guests. He turned and smiled, and I noted a marked difference in the lines on his face. He looked as if he'd aged a decade since the war started. It broke my heart to think he would give everything to keep the Union together and emancipate the slaves—and then die just days after victory. It was senseless, and just like Pearl Harbor, I hated that I knew the future and could do nothing to stop it.

Mrs. Lincoln accepted my hand and lowered her chin as she looked me over. She wore a stunning silk gown with beautifully crafted satin roses along the neckline and matching roses in her upturned hair. "Merry Christmas, my dear. I'm so happy you chose to join us this evening."

"Thank you for inviting me."

Mr. Lincoln took my gloved hand next, clasping it within both of his. "I wish you a Merry Christmas, Margaret, though I know it will be a difficult season without your father. We miss him every day."

"Thank you." I handed him the present I'd brought. "I hope you'll accept this gift."

"You needn't have done that," he said, though he smiled and untied the brown string.

"It's very thoughtful of you," Mrs. Lincoln said, her drawl a little more marked tonight, no doubt from being surrounded by her Kentucky family.

When the paper fell away, revealing a gilt-framed photo of Papa, Mr. Lincoln inhaled a deep breath and lifted his chest. "Edward."

"He had his likeness taken the day he was commissioned as a colonel," I said. "It was the proudest day of his life. He died doing what he loved, for the country and president he loved."

Mr. Lincoln's eyes misted over as he smiled from the picture to me. "I hope you haven't given me the only copy."

"I have another," I reassured him. "Now we both have one."

"I'll treasure this, as I did his friendship."

I accepted Mr. Lincoln's handshake again, and then Mrs. Lincoln said, "Please enjoy yourself this evening, Margaret, and try to forget the weight of your grief, if even for a moment."

"Thank you." I turned from them and faced the room. Many people were strangers, but there were a few I knew well—and one I knew best of all.

Gray stood alone near the hearth, staring into the fire, a punch glass in his gloved hand.

My heart began to sing at the sight of him. Two weeks was too long.

How would I go a lifetime?

I approached Gray slowly, feeling the rustle of my gown against the rug, wondering why my legs felt like lead. Until now, I hadn't realized how much I dreaded this encounter. My greatest fear was that he wouldn't look at me the way he had before—or worse, that he would turn from me. I had lived through Pearl Harbor, yet the thought of facing Gray and seeing his loveless eyes put terror in my heart.

I stopped a few feet from him, causing him to look up, and the moment our gazes locked, I knew all I needed to know.

Gray loved me.

It was written all over his face, in the depth of his sad brown eyes, and in the way he looked at me, as if seeing water in a dry land. He would always love me.

"Maggie."

"Merry Christmas, Gray."

"Merry Christmas."

I clasped my hands, not knowing what else to do with them. "I hoped you'd be here. I've missed you."

He set his punch on the mantel and came to me, taking my hands into his, as old friends would do with a room full of curious onlookers.

"I've missed you too." He looked at me in that way I had come to love, as if no one else were in the East Room with us. As if President Abraham Lincoln were not thirty feet away. Slowly, he lowered my hands. "I've been thinking about you a lot—praying for you, wondering how things went in . . ." He let the sentence trail away, and I knew he meant Pearl Harbor.

The depth of concern in his gaze almost made me choke up. He really did care how I was faring in 1941. He was the only person, outside of Mama and Daddy, who could understand.

Gray and I had been through so many difficulties. Now, more than ever, I wanted to experience the good times with him too. Surely, there had to be good times on the horizon.

"It's been—" I paused, trying to contain my emotions. They were so close to the surface that I was afraid I might weep. "Horrifying," I finished. "It's been horrifying."

"I'm so sorry, Maggie."

I tried to smile, though the effort was wobbly at best. "Things are getting a little better. It has been two weeks . . ."

He broke our eye contact and looked toward the fire. "I've been aware of every minute."

I wanted desperately to tell him how much I missed him, but there was no privacy here, and it would be unseemly to say something so intimate in front of all these people.

Mrs. Lincoln soon announced that dinner was ready, and we were paired off to enter the State Dining Room. I was coupled with one of Mrs. Lincoln's gregarious Kentucky nephews, while Gray was paired with a beautiful and charming niece. We were placed at opposite ends of the table, on the same side, so I couldn't even catch his eye throughout the meal.

I tried to enjoy myself, to engage Mrs. Lincoln's nephew in interesting conversation, but my heart was not in the festivities. I had no energy or will to be charming and witty. Tomorrow, I would be celebrating Christmas on the *Solace* in a war-torn harbor, trying to keep everyone's spirits up. It was exhausting, and I allowed myself to wallow in self-pity. I had always been the strong one. For Papa, for Anna, for my patients. But I didn't have the strength left. This was my first Christmas without Papa, without Mama and Daddy, and without Mom and Dad. *Bereft* wasn't a strong enough word for how I felt.

After dinner there were to be games, but I had no capacity to engage. I longed to be a part of the fun, but I couldn't imagine trying to keep up a brave face for one second longer. Especially when I saw Gray offer his arm to Mrs. Lincoln's niece and escort her from the dining room.

Tears pricked the back of my eyes. What did I expect? I had made no promise to him, had not even given him hope that there was a future for us. If I left 1861, as he thought I would, it was only natural that he would move on with his life. Perhaps marry, have a family—

I couldn't continue the heartbreaking thought and had to swallow several times to keep the tears at bay long enough to give my excuses to the Lincolns.

"Thank you for the lovely evening," I said to Mrs. Lincoln when I finally had a chance to speak to her.

"You're not leaving, are you? The fun has just begun."

"I'm afraid my grief is getting the better of me tonight. I'm sorry."

Her expressive eyes filled with a deep sadness I knew all too well. "I understand completely, my dear. More than I should. But remember you are never truly alone. Your father's love is still with you, even if he is gone. Everything he did for you, everything he taught you, is a part of you, and nothing can take that away."

My tears finally overflowed, and I had to wipe them away. "Thank you. And I hope you'll forgive me."

"Of course. Good night, Margaret."

"Good night and Merry Christmas. Please extend my well-wishes to President Lincoln."

"I will." She squeezed my hand and then turned back to her retinue of relatives.

I left the dining room, glancing toward the East Room where Gray was just entering with the others, and then walked in the opposite direction to retrieve my cape. It took a few minutes for the doorman to find it, but once it was settled upon my shoulders and I stepped through the front door of the White House to face Lafayette Square, the tears began to fall again.

At first, I tried wiping them away, hoping and praying I could gather myself together before I returned home, but as I walked off the portico, across the large lawn, and then crossed Pennsylvania Avenue, I realized it was hopeless.

I stopped as soon as I entered Lafayette Square and bowed my head. Behind me, the White House stood tall and almost ominous. Snowflakes fell in a slow cadence to the ground. Everything was so still and silent. Nothing moved on the square, though almost all of the houses were lit from within, indicating that life moved beyond those panes of yellow light.

But here, in this moment, I was alone. Again.

Or was I? Mrs. Lincoln's words returned to me, and I thought of everyone I loved. They'd each become a part of me and would be with me forever. They had been the hands and feet of God when I needed them most. God's presence hadn't always been obvious, but I had never been truly alone. He had brought people into my life, like Gray and Anna, to act as my strength and comfort. Zechariah to challenge me. Mama and Daddy to offer wisdom and advice. Papa to protect me. Delilah to listen and bring fresh perspectives. And Mom and Dad to cheer me along.

My heart began to fill with the knowledge that God had not been far away after all. He had been as close as each of my loved ones, working through their lives to minister to mine.

I'd been standing at a crossroads for so long, not sure which way to go, because I didn't think He was guiding me. But He had been there. He was simply walking beside me. And He was here now. Even if I couldn't see Him. He hadn't made either path clear and was waiting for me to choose. Did that mean He would bless either one?

And if that was so, then could I truly choose which one I wanted?

Maybe, just maybe, what He'd been requiring of me all along was to take a step of faith, as Delilah had said, and believe He'd walk alongside me, no matter what I chose.

"Maggie?"

My heart leapt at the sound of Gray's voice. He was pulling on his overcoat as he walked toward me, a silhouette against the White House. He'd forgotten his hat. "Are you unwell?"

I wiped at my face, embarrassed by my tears. I wanted to rush into his arms, but it was a purely selfish desire. I couldn't continue to cling to him if I was going to leave here.

But *was* I going to leave? I loved Gray more than life itself, and I wanted to be with him forever—forsaking all others.

The realization was so powerful and so stunning, it felt as if a lightning bolt had passed through me. I just stared at him, speechless. Perhaps his absence from my life is what I had been mourning most of all.

I wanted Gray and nothing else.

"What's wrong?" His concern deepened.

"I love you," I whispered, unable to breathe from the weight of it all. "I miss you. I hate seeing you with another woman on your arm. I hate thinking of you going on with your life without me."

He stared at me, his hands at his side, his shoulders sagging. "I'm powerless, Maggie."

"I know." I had always felt powerless too, but I was realizing that I wasn't powerless, not really. I had always had control of my destiny, at least as much as the next person. God, in His infinite grace, was allowing me to choose, and there was no right or wrong decision to make. He was telling me to follow my heart and He would still be with me.

And my heart was yearning for Gray.

He moved closer to me and clasped my arms. "I would do anything—anything in the world—to keep you here with me. But I won't force you or cajole you or guilt you. I love you too much to have you stay because you feel obligated."

"You've never made me feel obligated." I swallowed my emotions, choking on them. "The truth is, I feel guilted into staying in 1941."

There. I'd said it. I didn't love Zechariah, not in the way that I should, not in the forsaking-all-others, till-death-do-us-part way. Yes, he challenged me and there was chemistry between us. But could I make a life with him? Could we be happy? In a way, I supposed. But did he see me like Gray saw me? Did he understand me? Could I ever be real with him, sharing every facet of myself?

No.

"Why would you feel guilted into staying in 1941?" Gray asked.

"There's been an accident. The man I told you about, Zechariah—"

Gray's shoulders became stiff at the name, and he lowered his hands.

"He was injured in Pearl Harbor," I continued. "I don't know if he'll ever have complete use of his leg again. He'll need all the help he can get."

"Help from you." It wasn't a question, but a statement.

I nodded as I looked at the buttons on Gray's coat. "He wants it to be me."

"I can't blame him." Gray studied me before saying, "Are you going to stay with him in 1941, Maggie?"

"I won't stay for Zechariah. But—"

"But you have Anna and your parents to consider."

I nodded. "Mama and Daddy are the only parents I have left. And Anna . . ." I couldn't meet his gaze. "She still needs me. She's doing better, but if I left her now, I don't know how she'd survive her grief. I don't know what to do."

"There's something I need to tell you." His voice was grave as he stood before me, the snow falling onto his shoulders. "I wasn't going to say anything. I didn't want it to affect your decision, but Mr. Pinkerton has given me no choice."

"What is it?"

"A few weeks ago, the War Department asked Mr. Pinkerton to send some of his agents undercover into the South. He's assembling a few teams—men and women—who will pose as

355

married couples and infiltrate Southern society. He's asked me to be one of the teams going into Richmond, to try to get as close to Jefferson Davis as possible."

My lips parted. "If you're caught—" I couldn't finish the sentence. "Must you go?"

He shook his head slowly. "There is plenty of work to do here. I'm not being ordered to go, but he asked me personally." He paused. "Maggie, the truth is, if you're not here, then there's no reason for me to stay. I've spent my entire adult life moving from one place to the next. You're the first and only reason I've ever wanted to stop. When you're in my arms, I don't want to be anywhere else on earth. I wasn't going to say anything until I knew what you planned to do, but Pinkerton needs his teams to leave as soon as possible. He wants my answer tomorrow."

"Tomorrow?" I still needed another week to decide. I loved Gray, but I also loved my parents and my sister.

If I waited until my birthday to decide and chose to stay in 1861, Gray would already be gone, posing as a married man behind enemy lines. The very thought of him putting himself in such danger, pretending to be married to another woman, gripped my heart with alarm.

"Do you want to go?" I asked.

"If you are here, no. But if you're not, then I have nothing to lose."

If I asked him not to go south and then chose 1941 next week, he'd be missing an opportunity to serve Mr. Pinkerton and his nation. I couldn't do that to him either.

"This is why I didn't want to tell you," he said quietly. "I know how difficult this is for you already. But it's your choice, Maggie. If you choose to stay in 1861—if you choose me—" He moved closer again, drawing me into his arms. "I want to marry you and spend the rest of our lives together. I want to have a family and make a home with you. I want to see what this crazy and maddening world has to offer us. And when we come to the end, whenever that may be, I want to know that we lived well."

Affection warmed my soul. I placed my gloved hands on his cheeks, wanting desperately to feel his lips upon mine. I'd been kissed by Seth and Zechariah, but I knew, with every beat of my heart, that Gray's kisses would be different.

"Will you give me one more day?" I asked.

"I would give you an eternity, if I had it to give."

"Tomorrow," I told him, lowering my hands. "Meet me here in the morning. I'll tell you then what I will choose."

"I'll be here," he said, his gaze falling to my lips.

My mouth tingled with the desire to be kissed by him, and I held my breath.

But he lifted his eyes to mine and gave me a sad—yet hopeful—smile. Then he took my right hand into his, gently pulling off my satin glove one finger at a time. The soft fabric slid over my wrist, like the wing of a butterfly, until my hand was free. The cold touched my burning skin as snowflakes landed and melted upon it.

Slowly, he lifted my hand to his lips. He cradled it in both of his, as if it was the most precious possession he'd ever held, and softly laid his warm lips upon my skin. He kissed the top of my hand several times, and then turned my hand over and laid a kiss upon my tender palm.

Closing my eyes, I savored the sensations dancing up my arm, making my heart pound so hard that I was certain he could hear it in the stillness.

Snowflakes landed on my cheeks and clung to my eyelashes. When I opened my eyes, Gray was watching me with a yearning I knew too well.

He set my palm against his cheek. "May I walk you to your door?"

I nodded, unable to use my voice.

Just as slowly, and with great care, Gray put my glove back on my hand, tugging it over my fingertips, up my wrist, and to my elbow, running his hand along the bare skin of my upper arm. A delicious shiver ran along my spine, making me want so much more than his kisses upon my hand. I found myself leaning into him, just as breathless as before, but he did not kiss me again. Instead, he tenderly wrapped my arm around his elbow, drawing me close to his side.

A few minutes later, when he dropped me off at my front door, I wished I could reassure him, tell him that the only reason I needed one more day was to be sure of Anna—and to tell Zechariah I wasn't in love with him.

I didn't know how I would possibly tell Zechariah, knowing how much he had come to love me and how devastated he would be to lose me. But I couldn't let my guilt sway my decision. I was meant to stay with Gray. I knew it like I knew I was a healer. It was an innate knowledge, something that was hard to articulate but that made me feel whole. Complete.

"I'll see you in the morning," I said as I stood on tiptoe and placed a kiss on his cheek, my lips lingering.

His arms came around my waist, tightening, as if it took all of his willpower not to keep me there, to kiss me like I longed to be kissed.

I wrapped my arms around his neck, returning his embrace. He held me so close I could feel his heart thudding against my chest. "I love you," I whispered near his ear.

"I love you too, Maggie."

We held each other for a long time, and I could sense that he was trying to find the courage to let go—just as I was.

Finally, we eased away.

"Good night," I said as I turned the knob and opened my front door.

"Good night." He put his hand over mine to still me. "No matter what you choose, I will love you for the rest of my life."

Tears threatened again, but I forced myself not to cry. "Merry Christmas, Gray."

"Merry Christmas, Maggie."

He left my porch, and I watched him for a few minutes as he walked away, the snow continuing to fall all around him, turning Lafayette Square into a winter wonderland. Right before he took a left down Pennsylvania Avenue, he stopped and turned. I smiled—though he couldn't see it from so far away in the dark—and I hoped he was smiling, too.

As soon as he disappeared, the tears began to cascade down my cheeks.

"Miss Margaret?" Joseph asked from the foyer. "Do you need help?"

I didn't try to hide my tears as I entered the house. "There's nothing you can do," I told him. "But thank you for offering."

I bypassed a confused and worried Joseph and climbed the stairs to my bedroom. There, I knelt by the window to look out at the quickly transforming landscape and prayed with everything I had within me.

I wanted to choose Gray, but I still had a lot of good-byes to say before I was free to give him my whole heart.

33

DECEMBER 25, 1941
PEARL HARBOR, HONOLULU, HAWAII

Even before I was out of bed on Christmas morning, Anna had left our stateroom. A note said she was meeting Dr. Church on the quarterdeck to watch the sunrise. There was so much to do that I forced myself to focus on the tasks ahead, pushing thoughts of Gray—and the difficult conversations I would need to have with Anna and Zechariah—out of mind until later. I hated that I had to talk to them on Christmas, but I didn't want to make Gray wait one more day. Mr. Pinkerton needed an answer, and so did Gray.

Helen had decided, with unanimous agreement from the nurses, to host a Christmas party for the sailors onboard the *Solace*. For days, we'd been working tirelessly to gather decorations, gifts, and candy to serve to the over three hundred patients. We'd solicited a few corpsmen to go ashore and find Christmas trees, holly, and all the tinsel they could gather. They'd brought back four scraggy cedars, several bushels of holly, and more tinsel than we'd expected. Today we were going to decorate the wards and try to bring some Christmas cheer to our ship.

We'd also spent several days gathering all the gifts we could find from among the crews' belongings. Everyone on board the *Solace* had happily donated what they could, including trinkets, toys, and knickknacks. We'd also found a yeoman to play Santa Claus and had asked the sailmaker to create the iconic red costume for him to wear.

By Christmas afternoon, I hadn't found a good time to talk to Anna or Zechariah, but I was allowing the festivities to brighten my mood, even though my heart was still heavy. The sailors had lived through a traumatic event, and they deserved all the good cheer I could muster—especially on Christmas, while they were all away from their loved ones.

"Are we ready?" Helen asked just after supper as all the nurses gathered in the dining room with the bags of gifts and candy.

Everyone nodded, and I was excited for the moment the men realized we were having a party. They had seen the trees and decorations, but they didn't know there would be gifts, candy, and music.

"Are you ready?" Helen asked the corpsman who played accordion. He, in turn, had found six more sailors to sing Christmas carols.

"Yes, ma'am." He saluted Helen.

"Very good. Let's bring some cheer to our comrades."

The bag I was carrying was heavy, biting into my shoulder, but I didn't mind. Inside were gifts that would bring a bit of happiness, and I wouldn't bemoan a little discomfort.

"Timothy proposed," Anna whispered, her cheeks bright pink, as the others filed out, leaving us alone. "I know it's soon, but when you know, you know."

I paused, my mouth slipping open. "Anna!"

"This morning," she said with a girlish laugh. "At sunrise

361

on Christmas Day. I couldn't keep it in any longer! Could he be more romantic, Maggie? I've already written Mama and Daddy. I'll call them the next time I get shore leave. They're going to love Timothy." She sighed. "*I* love Timothy, so really, that's all that matters, I suppose."

I set down the bag of gifts and wrapped my sister in a hug. "I'm so happy for you."

She hugged me back. "Just think, if we hadn't agreed to come to Pearl Harbor, I would never have met him. And had I not joined you at nursing school, I wouldn't have joined the navy, and I wouldn't have come to Pearl Harbor. Isn't it amazing how God can take a hard situation and turn it into something good? Something beautiful?"

"It is amazing," I agreed as I pulled back. Hadn't my life been a series of events that proved the same thing?

I noticed Anna's ring for the first time. It wasn't a large diamond, but it was sparkling and lovely.

She looked at it, too. "He said he had a Christmas gift for me. Imagine my surprise! He bought it in Honolulu. Can you picture me telling our future children how their father proposed? It's so . . . so . . . perfect."

I smiled and nodded.

"He wants to get married as soon as possible, since the war is starting. Later, we'll live in Virginia, close to Mama and Daddy," she continued. "His parents live in Philadelphia, so we'll only be a short car ride from them. And he wants to have a big family, Maggie, just like I do. He's so . . . so . . ."

"Perfect?" I teased her.

She gazed at her ring and sighed. "I won't deny it."

Though my heart was heavy at what I needed to tell her, it gave me courage to know that Anna had found her own happiness. She would have Timothy at her side to help her through the inevitable grief she'd feel at losing me.

"I wanted to talk to you too," I said quickly, wishing I didn't have to say this after she had shared her good news, but realizing there would never be a good time. "My birthday is next week—"

"Oh, Maggie." Her eyes filled with remorse. "I'm sorry I forgot. Here I am, going on and on, and—"

"No." I shook my head. "I'm happy you're happy, more than you'll ever know." I pressed my lips together briefly. "It actually helps with what I have to say—"

"You're staying in 1861." It wasn't a question.

I swallowed, afraid of what she was going to say or do, knowing it would be almost impossible to say good-bye if she was angry or melancholy.

She took my hands in hers and held them tight, her green eyes, so like Mama's, reaching into the very depths of my soul. "Don't be afraid."

"Anna—I love Gray. He's—"

"Perfect?" She smiled.

"He's so much more than that." I'd already told her how he'd rightly guessed about my time-crossing. "He's selfless and thoughtful, and he loves me with a sacrificial love that I've never understood until now. He believes in my dream to be a doctor, and he admires my work—"

"Maggie, when you know, you know."

I stopped rambling and stared at her.

"You've always known," she said. "In our innermost parts, we know what we really want. It's the outside stuff that interferes with our true desires. It's the people, the responsibilities, the obligations around us that hinder our true self. I know—I've been there. It was my grief that hindered what I truly wanted in life. For a long time, I was too afraid to go out into the world and grasp at what I wanted. You were God's hands and feet, pulling me out of that grief and leading me by the hand until I found it."

While she had been God's hands and feet in my life, I had

been doing the same in her life. It was a mystery of God's love that would never cease to amaze me.

She wiped at the tear that fell from her eye. "And now I want you to hold on tight to Gray's hand and grasp what you want. Reach for it until you have it and then never, ever let it go."

"You're not mad at me?"

She pulled me into her arms and held me tight. "How could I be mad at you when you've sacrificed so much for me? I love you desperately, baby sister, and have from the moment I met you. But I've always known that this day might come, and I tried to prepare for it as best as I could. I'll miss you—fiercely—but I also know that you won't truly be gone, because you'll always be as close as my own heart." She pulled back and placed her hand over her heart, her diamond ring sparkling in the sunshine from the porthole. "You're a part of me, Maggie, the best part—just like I'm a part of you. None of us are independent of the ones we love. We're woven together like a big tapestry, with each color unique and vibrant, but making a larger picture possible. You're woven right here for eternity."

Her words echoed Mrs. Lincoln's. I put my hand over my heart and nodded. "And you're woven here, alongside everyone that I love. Even if I can't be with you any longer, you'll always be a part of me."

She lowered her hand and gave me a sad smile. "Have you spoken to Dr. Philips?"

I shook my head. "Not yet."

"It's not going to be easy, but if he truly loves you, he'll let you go."

I thought of Gray, moments before he'd left me at my door, telling me that even if I didn't choose him, he'd love me for the rest of his life. Would Zechariah be as selfless?

"I don't know how to make him understand. I can't tell him the truth."

"Then make him understand as well as you can and pray that God takes care of the rest. It's all you can do."

"What's taking you so long?" one of the nurses asked as she popped her head back into the dining room. "Helen wants all of us together."

"Coming." I lifted my bag back onto my shoulder.

Anna and I left the dining room arm in arm, and I thanked God for the Christmas miracle that had just unfolded. Anna was ready to move on with her life and she'd given me her blessing to move on with mine.

I hoped and prayed Zechariah would do the same, but in my heart of hearts, I knew it wouldn't be so easy.

I didn't realize, until that day, that a heart could break and rejoice at the same time. As I watched Anna hand out gifts, her face radiating with joy and hope amid the devastation of war, I knew she would be okay. She had learned a lot about grief and loss after Richard's death, and though they could crush her again, they wouldn't destroy her. She was made of harder stuff than I had given her credit for.

> Hark! The herald angels sing,
> "Glory to the newborn King;
> Peace on earth, and mercy mild,
> God and sinners reconciled!"

As we walked from patient to patient, handing out our gifts and singing carols, we received smiles from even the melancholiest patients. Helen's admonition that we find gifts as fitting as possible was rewarded when she gave a sailor who had lost his vision the gift of a soft teddy bear to hold. Another sailor, who had written to his wife to give their daughter a music box with a spinning ballerina on top, was given one almost identical. Santa Claus was also a hit, and we were surprised when Captain Perlman joined in the festivities, singing louder than the rest of us.

Eventually, we came to the ward where Zechariah was recovering. As an officer, he'd been given a bed in the corner, and we'd rigged up a cloth partition so he had a little privacy. It was pulled back as we entered the long ward, and I could see him sitting up in bed. He'd either heard the commotion coming or someone had passed along the news, because he looked happier than he'd been in the two weeks since the attack.

> Hail the heav'nly Prince of Peace!
> Hail the Sun of Righteousness!
> Light and life to all He brings,
> Ris'n with healing in His wings.

I met Zechariah's gaze, and he smiled—the first smile he'd offered since December 7. I returned the smile and took out the gift the nurses had chosen for him. It was a toy monkey clutching a banana, since he ate so many of them.

As the other nurses spread out into the ward to deliver their gifts, and the corpsmen went from bed to bed, singing carols, I walked over to Zechariah. I held up the monkey, and he frowned—but when I pointed to the banana, he nodded.

"Merry Christmas," I said as I handed the toy to him. "From all of the nurses to you."

He accepted the gift and shook his head. "I don't know whether I should be honored that they appear to know me so well or insulted to be compared to a monkey."

"Honored," I assured him.

He set the monkey on the table at his bedside and then turned to me. "I was wondering when I might see you today."

"We've been busy preparing the festivities."

He glanced out at the room and then back to me. "Can you close the curtain? I'd like a little privacy, if you don't mind."

I nodded and pulled the curtain around his bed on the rails that had been set up for that purpose. My nursing uniform had been freshly pressed for the day, and as I reached up to move the curtain, I saw Zechariah admiring my form. When I was done, he patted the spot on the bed next to him.

My heart was pounding so hard it drowned out all the other noises in the room. The caroling faded, the laughter dimmed, and the sounds of surprise from the other sailors died away as I sat on the bed and faced Zechariah in the shadows.

I was careful not to disturb his leg, but he still winced at the movement.

"Any better?" I asked.

He sighed and shook his head.

"You need to get out of bed as often as possible," I said, knowing what I did about orthopedic care in the twenty-first century. "Movement will help you recover faster." I'd been encouraging him every day to get up with assistance, but he'd been hesitant, thinking he needed to rest it. "It will help keep up your spirits as well."

"I don't want to talk about my leg." He reached for my hands. "It's Christmas, and I want to talk about us today."

My stomach rolled, knowing what I needed to say to him. I could have simply allowed myself to die here and not had this hard conversation, but that would have been the coward's way out. To Zechariah, I would die in this path, and he would mourn—but at least I would know that I had been honest with him.

It was the right thing to do, even if it hurt.

All I needed to think about was Gray in Lafayette Square tomorrow morning, waiting for my answer, and I had the courage I needed to start.

I looked down at our hands and tried to smile, though my

heart was breaking at what I had to say. "I also think we should talk about us," I began. "But I don't think what I have to say will be what you want to hear."

His hands tightened ever so slightly, but I felt it.

"What's wrong?" he asked.

I looked up into his blue eyes, wishing I didn't have to hurt him. "I care for you very much, but I think you should know that I'm in love with someone else."

For several heartbeats he just stared at me, not saying a thing, and I could see the old shields rising up around him. He was going into defense mode, but I desperately needed him to stay open with me.

"He lives in Washington, DC," I said, wanting to make Gray as real as possible for both Zechariah and me, though I couldn't tell him everything. "I met him around the same time I met you, and I didn't know for a long time which way my heart was leading. I came to care for both of you, but in the last few weeks, I've had a lot of time to reflect on the future and the life I want to live. And in my reflection, I realized that my heart belongs to Gray."

"Gray?" He said his name in a lifeless tone.

"Graydon Cooper. He's—he works in the War Department." I shook my head, knowing it didn't really matter where Gray worked. "Zechariah, I never meant to hurt you—"

"But you have." He pulled his hands away, his mouth set, his eyes hard. "Why didn't you tell me sooner? Before I made a fool of myself?"

"You didn't make a fool—and I didn't know." I shrugged, helplessly. "It wasn't until—"

"I lost the use of my leg?"

"No." I frowned, hating that he would assume something so vile. "That has nothing to do with my decision. If you know me at all, if you love me as you claim, how could you possibly think that?"

His face fell, and with it, all his defenses. "I'm sorry, Maggie." He was silent again as he looked down at the bed. Finally, he sighed. "I'm heartbroken, but I think I've known for a long time. As I pushed my feelings on you, I could see that you weren't ready to receive them. I hoped I could convince you, but I know love can't be forced on anyone."

I took his hands again, thankful that he let me. "I'm sorry too, Zechariah. I never meant to lead you on or—"

"You didn't." His face was still grim but not shuttered. "You were just brutally honest with me. Maybe that's why I've been so enamored with you. No one but you and Helen is willing to tell me what I need to know, to stand up to me regardless of how loud I bark."

I smiled, thinking of how far he had come since I'd met him.

"I don't know how I'll continue to work alongside you," he said, "knowing you belong to someone else." He almost growled. "He's a lucky man."

I didn't have the heart to tell him that he wouldn't have to worry about working beside me for much longer.

"Does he know about me?" he asked.

"He does. I don't have any secrets from Gray." Unlike Zechariah, who didn't know the most important thing about me.

Zechariah looked down at our hands. "This wasn't how I hoped our conversation would go."

"I know. But thank you for making it easy on me."

"I don't want to, believe me. But you were the one who told me that God doesn't always give us what we want, though He will always give us what we need. I'll probably be miserable for a few weeks, but I'll manage to be happy for you—one day."

"Thank you."

"Knock, knock," came a soft voice from the other side of the curtain. It was Helen.

I stood and pulled back the curtain so she could enter Zechariah's space. She smiled at him, her eyes lighting up in a way I had noticed a few times before. She tried to hide it, but I suspected Helen had been in love with Zechariah for a long time.

"Merry Christmas, Zech."

He returned the smile—and something caught in his gaze, as if he'd just realized that the very thing he liked about me was also something that Helen possessed. "Merry Christmas, Helen."

"I see you received the gift the nurses chose for you." She nodded at the little monkey. "I hope we can get you back to eating your grain-free diet again. I think you were having good success before the attack."

"I think you're right." He continued to study her as if he was seeing something he'd never seen before.

She noticed him staring, a question in the tilt of her brow, but offered him a smile. "I also hope you'll feel up to dancing next Christmas."

"I think my dancing days are behind me."

"You'll have the use of your leg again," she assured him.

"That's not why I'm giving up dancing. I was never good at it, and I didn't enjoy it."

Helen laughed. "Your honesty is your best quality." She shook her head, still smiling. "I'll see that you get your candy, Dr. Philips. Merry Christmas."

"Merry Christmas," he said again, and I echoed the sentiment as Helen slipped away.

Had I just witnessed the beginning of something new? I hoped and prayed, for both their sakes, that I had.

"I should leave," I said to Zechariah. "I have a few more gifts to deliver. I hope you have a Merry Christmas as well."

"Good-bye, Maggie." He reached for my hand.

I paused, allowing him to take it. He kissed it and then let me go.

Though I would have one more week to say my final good-byes in 1941, and I would make a call from the island to Mama and Daddy to let them know what I had decided, this felt like a final good-bye to Zechariah. I had said what I needed to say, and I was at peace.

As I walked away from him, I knew, without a doubt in my mind or heart, that I had made the right decision, and I couldn't wait to wake up tomorrow and tell Gray.

I just hoped and prayed he would be in Lafayette Square as he'd promised.

34

DECEMBER 26, 1861
WASHINGTON, DC

My heart started pounding the moment I opened my eyes to the bright sunshine pouring into my bedroom. Snow lined the tree branches just outside my window, set against the brilliant backdrop of a bright blue sky.

The room was chilly as I tossed aside my quilt and put my feet onto the rug next to my bed. I ran to the window to see if Gray was waiting. Through the wavy panes of glass, I searched the square but could not see anyone.

Deep disappointment weighed down my heart. Where was he?

"Miss Margaret?"

I hadn't heard the door open behind me, but Saphira was standing there, a question in her gaze.

"I haven't laid your fire yet." She bustled into the room with a bundle of kindling in her hands. "You'll catch your death in that nightgown without a fire in the hearth. You should get back in bed."

"Can you help me dress?" I didn't care how cold it was in my room. I needed to find Gray.

"Yes, of course." She laid the kindling by the hearth. "Just let me get this fire star—"

"It's not necessary." I went to my wardrobe and pulled it open. "I want to get dressed as quickly as possible."

She frowned but joined me at the wardrobe, wiping her hands on her apron. I wanted to hurry her, to tell her I didn't need all the accoutrements today, but it was cold, and I would want them—especially if I had to wait outside for Gray. I would wait all day, if necessary.

My pulse thrummed as Saphira helped me into my petticoats and gown. I glanced out the window again, but from where I stood, I could not see much of the square. What if Gray didn't come? What if he'd accepted Pinkerton's offer and chosen not to wait for me?

"How would you like me to style your hair?" Saphira asked when she had finished helping me dress.

"Let's leave it in the braid," I said, as I tossed the braid over my shoulder. It was still secure, though several tendrils had escaped, but that didn't matter to me.

"Leave it?" she asked, holding up the horsehair brush.

"For now." I grabbed a shawl from the end of my bed. "I'm going out. I don't know when I'll be back."

"You're going out—with your hair down?" Her dark eyes were filled with shock and uncertainty.

"I'll tuck it up into my bonnet," I said as I walked out of my room. "Thank you."

My mouth felt dry, and my palms were sweating as I lifted the hem of my gown and rushed down the stairs and to the front door. It was still early, but I could not wait inside. I wanted to see Gray the moment he entered the square—if he came.

Opening the door, I paused as I stepped over the threshold. Gray sat on the steps of our front porch.

He stood and turned to face me. Our gazes caught, and I could see all the love, all the devotion—and all the fear—in his brown eyes.

"Gray." I said his name almost like a prayer as I rushed across the porch and down the steps into his arms.

He wrapped me in his embrace, holding me tight, pressing me against him. My cheek rested against his, and all I could do was revel in his nearness, inhaling the scent of bergamot and soap. He'd come. Gray had come, and I was now free to tell him that I had chosen him. Forever.

"I can't be too sure," he said on a happy chuckle, "but I think this is good news."

I laughed and pulled back to look at his beautiful face. I was smiling through my tears as I nodded. "It's very good news."

His face filled with the most tender expression I'd ever seen. "Do you choose me, Maggie?"

"I do. I choose you today and every day. I'm finally ready— ready to begin the rest of our lives together."

Gray lifted his hands and gently ran his thumbs along the edges of my cheekbones, removing my tears. "There's no need to cry anymore. I'm here."

I smiled, though the tears would not stop so easily.

"Will you marry me?" he asked.

There was not a shred of uncertainty in my mind or heart when I said, "Yes."

His face grew serious as he took out his handkerchief and gently wiped the rest of my tears away. It was cold and the snow crunched beneath our feet, but I didn't care. Gray made me feel warm.

When my face was dry and my tears had finally stopped, Gray put the handkerchief back into his pocket and then put his hands on either side of my face, slipping his fingers into the loose strands of my hair.

"I love you, Maggie Wakefield," he whispered as he kissed my forehead, my cheeks, my nose. "And I've been waiting for this day, I think, my entire life."

He pulled back and looked me in the eyes. Even though it was early morning and anyone could see us standing there on the steps, Gray did not seem to mind—and neither did I. I was ready to proclaim to the world that this was the man I chose, that he was the one I wanted for the rest of my life.

That he was enough. More than enough.

"Once I kiss you," he said, with that look in his eyes that told me he knew a secret I didn't, "I will want to keep kissing you forever."

"I know." I nodded solemnly, though I could not contain my delight. "And you may. Whenever you'd like."

"Promise?" he asked, touching my nose with his.

"I promise."

Slowly, with the greatest care, Gray kissed me.

Every sound, every sensation, everything around us vanished, and all I knew was Gray. His lips, his hands, his arms wrapped around me. His kisses were tender and then fervent, taking my breath away. He kissed me deeply, passionately, and possessively. I was his and he was mine, and it was the most glorious feeling in the world.

I wrapped my arms around his neck, and he lifted me off my feet. I pulled him as close as I could, wanting more of him, all of him. I didn't want it to stop, but eventually he pulled away, and we were both breathless.

A smile spread across my lips, matching his in brilliance.

His eyes were alight with longing. "When can we be married?"

"As soon as possible."

"New Year's Day? Your birthday?"

I nodded. "I couldn't ask for a better day to start our married lives together."

"How will I wait six days?" he asked, nuzzling my neck, pulling me close again.

Laughing, I kissed his cheek. "It will give us time to practice kissing so that on our wedding day, we get it just right."

"I do believe we're naturals already."

I had lost so much in my other paths—friends, family, careers—but what I had gained in Gray's arms had become far more precious. He loved me, he understood me, and he had sacrificially allowed me to choose what was best for me—and it just so happened that it was him. There was no one else like him, and in God's amazing grace, He had brought us together to revel in one another's love.

The wedding vows we would soon share were already ringing in my mind, and I didn't want to wait a week to promise Gray that he had my heart, my love, and my devotion for all time.

So on that cold December day, with the past behind me and the future beckoning, I took his warm hands in mine and promised to love him for the rest of my life.

Epilogue

At the first pang of labor, I lifted my gaze from the medical research paper I was writing and met Gray's brown eyes.

He didn't even ask me if it was time. He simply rose from the chair near the fireplace, set his newspaper aside, and came to me. With gentleness and urgency, he helped me to my feet, conscious of the weight I carried in my womb.

The fireplace was lit, warding off the chill that had descended upon our house on Lafayette Square with the rain and wind. The household had been on alert for the past few days, so it didn't surprise me when Joseph appeared at the door.

"Shall I send for Dr. Austin?" he asked.

Another contraction tightened my abdomen, and all I could do was nod.

When the pain subsided, Gray helped me up the stairs, his voice low as he said, "Can you believe that after twenty-five years of prayer, our first child is almost here?"

Despite the discomfort I'd been feeling for weeks, I smiled.

We were married on New Year's Day, 1862, in a small ceremony at St. John's Church. President Lincoln offered to take my father's place and give me away. An intimate reception was held in the Red Room afterward, and then Gray and I settled into married life.

One of the greatest surprises of my life came the next day when I woke up in 1941 again. I had thought I only had twenty-one years to choose which path I wanted to take, but I was wrong. After talking with Mama and Daddy, we realized that the mark I bore on my chest, the one like Mama's, had sent me forward to 2001, where I only had twenty-one years, like she had. But the mark I bore on the back of my head, like Daddy's, sent me back to 1861 and gave me twenty-five years, just like he'd had.

For the next four years, I continued to move back and forth, helping in both the Civil War and WWII. I was thankful when Zechariah made a full recovery and was transferred to serve on a different hospital ship with Helen at his side. She wrote to me often and spoke of their growing relationship, giving me hope for their happiness. I was also able to watch Anna marry Timothy and celebrate the end of the war in September of 1945.

The best part was returning to Williamsburg to spend my last few months with my parents. And it was there, on New Year's Day, 1946, that I finally said good-bye forever.

Through it all, Gray was my constant source of strength. As part of our honeymoon, we traveled to Syracuse, New York, where I met with the dean of students, Dr. Charles Lee, at Geneva Medical College. They were responsible for giving Dr. Elizabeth Blackwell the first medical degree awarded to a woman in the United States in 1849. Upon meeting the dean, I explained that I was self-educated, though it wasn't entirely true, and had years of clinical experience. He agreed to a series of intensive tests and hands-on clinical trials to gauge my aptitude. At the end of several weeks, he was quite pleased with my results and recommended to their board of education that I be awarded a medical degree. It was highly unusual, but Dr. Lee was a man ahead of his time.

I was awarded the degree, and we returned to Washington, DC, where President Lincoln recommended me to serve on the United States Sanitary Commission. Through my contacts with the USSC, I was employed as an army doctor and worked in the hospitals in Washington. In 1864, when the fighting was at its worst, I became a field surgeon, serving at the Battle of the Wilderness, Spotsylvania Courthouse, Fort Stedman, the Battle of Cold Harbor, and Appomattox Courthouse, where the bloody war finally ended in April 1865. Clara Barton nursed alongside me at several of the battles, and our friendship grew.

Through it all, I did not question why I was not getting pregnant. Both Gray and I stayed busy, and I pushed the concern to the back of my mind.

Gray continued his work for Allan Pinkerton throughout the war, serving in various capacities, sometimes undercover, often as a guard to President Lincoln, though he was not with Mr. Lincoln the horrible night he was killed at Ford's Theatre at the hands of John Wilkes Booth.

After the war, we settled into domestic life—as much as our busy schedules would allow. We kept the house on Lafayette Square, which was where we still lived, and after a decade of marriage, we accepted the fact that we were not going to have a family by natural means. I started a medical practice, and Gray became the first Chief of Secret Service in 1865. We were happy and content, though we both longed for a family. We decided to open our home to children who were orphaned during the war, and over the years, we had dozens of children come and go. We loved every single one of them as if they were our own. Through our connections, we were able to place each one into a loving home, though there was always an empty place in our hearts.

But we didn't lose hope, and I trusted that if God wanted me to bear a child, I would.

Gray led me into our bedroom and helped me get as comfortable as I could. I was no longer a young woman at the age of forty-six, and the possibility of complications was high. But I knew that women older than me had successfully brought children into the world. This pregnancy felt different than I expected from the start, but I had accepted that it wouldn't be a textbook case because of my age.

Another contraction overtook my body, and I grasped the bedpost. Gray rubbed my lower back, and when the pain subsided, he helped me into bed.

"I know you're worried," he said.

I should have known I couldn't hide anything from him. Leaning back against the pillows, I met his concerned gaze. "My age complicates things."

"God knows what He's doing, Maggie. This child isn't a surprise to Him."

"I'm afraid—" I paused.

"That the baby will have your markings?"

"I don't know how my mama managed when she knew I had two marks. It's all I've been thinking about lately."

"She trusted God, just as we will do." He smiled. "I think it's exciting. Just imagine the possibilities. If our child lives in the future, we'll get to learn things we can only dream about."

"I should have known you'd be intrigued by a time-crossing child." I returned his smile, thinking of all the times he had eased my pain and worries. We'd been married for twenty-five years, and the time had flown by now that I only occupied one path.

Another contraction bore down on my body, and I tried to let it do its job without resistance, though it was hard.

Dr. Austin finally appeared, and he and Saphira sat with me through the long hours of labor. Gray paced the hallway, for though I longed to have him in the room with me, it wasn't common practice in 1887.

I had never wished for the conveniences of a twenty-first-century hospital more than I did that evening. If I needed a cesarean section, I knew my chance of survival was very slim. I could advise the doctor with the knowledge I had and increase the odds, but I was still concerned about changing history.

When it was time to deliver my baby, it looked as if everything would proceed as planned. Twenty minutes after I began pushing, the doctor held up a beautiful, healthy baby girl. She was small, but her lungs were strong as she cried.

In the dim candlelight I looked at her chest and saw that there was no mark. My relief was palpable, and I lay back against the pillow, exhausted beyond reason, and smiled.

But when the doctor handed the baby off to Saphira to clean her, I noticed she had a mark on the back of her head. My heart fell.

She would have one other path—in a time before this one—and she would have twenty-five years to choose.

Another contraction tightened my stomach, surprising me.

Dr. Austin looked at me, his face serious. "It appears there is another baby, Mrs. Cooper."

"Another?" I frowned, confused.

He smiled. "Twins. You'll need to push again on the next contraction."

Twins? I could hardly believe it, but it made sense with so many of the symptoms I'd experienced in this pregnancy.

After another five minutes of pushing, my second child was born, another beautiful baby girl.

"Does she—" I couldn't bear to ask, but I had to know. "Does she have the same birthmark on her head?"

The doctor turned her around, and a smile lit his face. "She does. They're identical twins."

I stared at him, a dozen questions filling my mind. I had never heard of identical twins with the time-crossing mark. I had no idea what it meant.

When Gray was finally allowed back into the room, I held a baby in each arm. I was tired yet elated. Excited yet deeply concerned.

The doctor and Saphira blended into the background as Gray entered our bedroom. His gaze was upon me first, and I knew he was trying to see if I was okay. I smiled for him, but I couldn't hide my apprehension. He frowned slightly until he lowered his gaze and saw our daughters for the first time.

"Twins?" He looked back up at me, his face filled with wonder.

"Identical girls," I told him, emotions taking control as tears came to my eyes.

Dr. Austin and Saphira left the room, gently closing the door as Gray came to our bed. He sat on the edge and looked at each baby in turn.

"May I?" he asked as he reached for the first.

I handed her to him, and then gave him the second baby. They were both sleeping peacefully, their perfect little faces poking out of their blankets.

I was not prepared for the rush of love I felt at seeing him with our newborn children.

He stared down at the babies and then looked up at me, and even before he asked, I knew what he wanted to know.

"Yes," I nodded, sounding braver than I felt. "They carry one of my marks on the backs of their heads, which means they will have two paths. This one and one in the past."

Awe filled his gaze, and he shook his head. "Will they go together?"

I lifted my shoulders. "I don't know. I've never heard of identical time-crossers. I don't know what it means."

"And we don't know what other times they might occupy?"

"We won't know until they're old enough to tell us."

He sat on the bed next to me, handing me one of the babies again, while he kept the other. He did not seem alarmed or even worried that they would occupy two lives. It filled my heart with hope and contentment, knowing that the three of us had him.

"Do you have names chosen for them?" he asked, his voice still soft with wonder.

"What do you think of Grace and Hope?"

He smiled up at me and nodded. "I think they are perfect."

"Because it was hope that caused us to believe this day would come," I told him. "And grace that sustained us as we waited."

"They were worth the wait." Gray leaned forward and placed a kiss on my lips. "You have done a remarkable job, Maggie. I'm so proud of you. I think all of your mothers would be proud today."

As I looked down at the babies—Grace and Hope—I thought about the incredible women who had proceeded us, and I wondered what amazing things my daughters would do with the paths they were given.

I took comfort in the hope that God's grace would guide them every step of the way, just as He had guided me.

Historical Note

It was so much fun to mash up three unique time periods for *In this Moment*. When I first had the idea, I immediately knew which three I would choose. Ever since I was a little girl, I marveled that the American Civil War and WWII fell on similar-ending years, 1861–1865 and 1941–1945. On September 11, 2001, as I watched events unfold on television, worrying we were entering another war, it occurred to me that the year ended with a one, as well. Since each path my heroine takes must end with the same number, it made perfect sense to choose these three time periods.

I wanted Maggie to live through the beginning of each war. She does this during the First Battle of Bull Run, at Pearl Harbor, and at the Pentagon on 9/11. There were many similarities to explore in each event, especially Pearl Harbor and 9/11. Though these were surprise attacks by foreign enemies, in a lot of ways the Battle of Bull Run was also a surprise—at least for the North, who thought it would be an easy victory.

One of the reasons I chose for Maggie to live in Washington, DC, in each path was to show the contrasts and similarities there as well. I loved having her walk the streets, noting what had changed and what had stayed the same. The biggest difference was probably the security at the White House! Can you imagine walking through the front doors of the Executive Mansion in 1861, without an invitation or appointment, and seeing the Lincoln boys running wild? As I researched this story, I was a little worried that Homeland Security was going to show up at my house as I scoured the internet, typing in the search engine "How to get past security in the White House" and "White House floorplan."

Like the first book in the TIMELESS series, I chose to add real historical characters to my story. Some may be obvious, like President Lincoln, Clara Barton, and Allen Pinkerton, but others might not be as well known. Rose Greenhow was a real woman credited with providing information to Jefferson Davis that enabled the South to win the First Battle of Bull Run. She lived on Lafayette Square, across from the White House, and moved within the inner circle of high-ranking senators like Henry Wilson of Massachusetts. One of the changes I made to history is that she was arrested on August 23, 1861, instead of September 12.

Other characters, like Chief Nurse Helen Daly and even Edward Wakefield, Maggie's papa in 1861, are closely inspired by real people. Helen Daly is modeled after Lieutenant Grace Lally, who served as the Chief Nurse on the USS *Solace* at Pearl Harbor. Nurse Lally organized a Christmas celebration for the patients onboard the *Solace*, much like Helen does, even finding personal gifts for each man. Edward Wakefield was inspired by Senator Edward Baker of Oregon, who was a close friend of Abraham Lincoln. Abraham and Mary's son, Edward Baker Lincoln, was named in honor of him. Senator Baker has the distinction of being the only sitting US Senator to die during active duty. He was killed at the Battle of Ball's Bluff on October 21, 1861, just like Maggie's papa. History tells us Lincoln wept.

I like to add real people to my stories whenever possible to make them feel authentic. When I have a real character, like President Lincoln, I make sure they only say and do things that would be true to their personality. If I'm going to change something about them or use them extensively, like Edward Baker, I make sure to change their name. I never want to dishonor someone by misrepresenting them in history. The one exception I made during *In this Moment* is having Virgil Earp at the First Battle of Bull Run. In truth, Virgil didn't enlist until two years after the Civil War started. I wanted to include him, though, since he would have been a name Maggie instantly recognized *and* because he was from Illinois, the same as her.

One other piece of history I had to change was the date that Ford's Atheneum (later Ford's Theatre) opened. I wanted Maggie to be there with Seth in 2001 and Gray in 1861. In real life, the theater didn't open until March 1862, just six months after Maggie and Gray went to see *Jeanie Deans*.

Like Maggie's character, Gray, Zechariah, and Seth are completely fictional, though Gray's character was created using a compilation of Pinkerton agents who worked in Washington, DC, during the Civil War. It was fascinating to learn about Pinkerton's men (and women!) as they uncovered a spy ring in the heart of the nation's capital and provided security for President Lincoln (who insisted he didn't need it). Several Pinkerton agents even infiltrated the Confederate capital at Richmond, posing as married couples. One couple, Timothy Webster and Hattie Lawton, were caught. Hattie spent time in prison, while Timothy was executed by the Confederacy on April 29, 1862.

I also wanted to make sure the medical history in this story was as accurate as possible. I loved learning about early medicine and how doctors treated diseases before modern inventions and discoveries. I'm so happy I live in a world with antibiotics, antiseptics, and skilled surgeons who can work with microscopic technology. Can you imagine what it would have been like for Maggie to have twenty-first-century medical knowledge and be unable to use it in 1861 or 1941?

There are so many other little historical tidbits tucked into the pages of this story. Real people, places, and events. Too many to name here. Some interact with Maggie, while others are only mentioned, like aviator Charles A. Lindbergh and actress Lillian Gish, who headed the America First Committee in 1941. As a writer and a historian, it is my hope that this story has piqued your interest and encourages you to do your own research. If you do, be sure to drop me a note on my website and let me know what you've discovered. I could talk about history all day.

Author's Note

Writing *In This Moment* was a highlight of 2022. Not only because I love the historical time periods I chose, but because it was fun to step back into the shoes of a time-crosser. For those who have read *When the Day Comes*, you'll note that Maggie's story is very different from Libby's. I wanted to make sure their journeys were unique, while deepening the layers of time-crossing rules and experiences and giving the reader a satisfying adventure.

Just like many things in life, it takes a whole team of talented people to produce a book. I'm honored and blessed to work with one of the best teams in the business at Bethany House Publishers. I love that my editor, Jessica Sharpe, had complete confidence in me when I told her Maggie would have *three* lives to navigate, and that the art department was on board to produce a cover that reflected this unique story. Many thanks to my project editor, Christine Stevens, for fact-checking the hundreds of details in this story. I know how many there are, and I can't imagine her daunting task! I'm so thankful for Raela Schoenherr, Rachael Betz, Anne Van Solkema, and all the others on the marketing and publicity team who champion my books.

It truly is an honor and a privilege to work with you—not to mention a lifelong dream come true.

Thanks also go out to my agent, Wendy Lawton, and the whole team at Books & Such Literary Agency. I love being part of the Bookie family. I want to give a special shout-out to my friends at the MN NICE ACFW writing group, as well. Thank you for your encouragement and support each step of the way. And to my launch teams for *When the Day Comes* and *In This Moment*, you truly make me feel like releasing a book is a team effort!

Research is one of the best parts of writing a novel, and I did a *lot* for *In This Moment*, through books, articles, and in person. Thank you to our neighbors, Nick, Maxine, and Natalie Potter, for going to Washington, DC, and Virginia with our family. I know I ran you all ragged, and I know it was a lot to take in, but I can't tell you how much I appreciate your enthusiasm and excitement (and your long-suffering patience as we trekked through ALL the museums and historic sites). You made the trip fun and memorable.

And to my husband, David, and our children, Ellis, Maryn, Judah, and Asher. I could not have written *In This Moment* without you. Thank you for walking alongside me for miles as we traversed Washington, DC; Richmond, Virginia; and Colonial Williamsburg; and Pearl Harbor (though I know that being in Hawaii wasn't much of a sacrifice). Thank you for standing through endless tours, listening to hours of research audiobooks, driving around battlefields, exploring museums, and listening to me ramble on and on about real and make-believe people. Your thoughts, ideas, and insights challenge me. Your sacrifice inspires me. Your unconditional love strengthens me. You are all my favorites.

Gabrielle Meyer grew up above a carriage house on a historic estate near the banks of the Mississippi River, imagining real and made-up stories about the occupants who had lived there. She went on to work for state and local historical societies and loves writing fiction inspired by real people, places, and events. She currently resides in central Minnesota on the banks of the Mississippi River, not far from where she grew up, with her husband and four children. By day, she's a busy homeschool mom, and by night, she pens fiction and nonfiction filled with hope. Learn more about Gabrielle and her writing by visiting gabriellemeyer.com.

Sign Up for Gabrielle's Newsletter

Keep up to date with
Gabrielle's latest news on book releases
and events by signing up for her email
list at gabriellemeyer.com.

FOLLOW GABRIELLE ON SOCIAL MEDIA!

Gabrielle Meyer, Author @gabrielle_meyer @MeyerGabrielle

More from Gabrielle Meyer

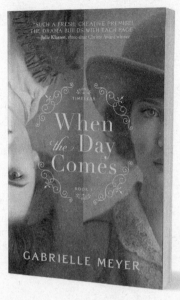

Libby has been given a powerful gift: to live one life in 1774 Colonial Williamsburg and the other in 1914 Gilded Age New York City. When she falls asleep in one life, she wakes up in the other without any time passing. On her twenty-first birthday, Libby must choose one path and forfeit the other—but how can she possibly decide when she has so much to lose?

When the Day Comes
Timeless #1
gabriellemeyer.com